WOLF
GONE
WILD

JULIETTE CROSS

**UNION
SQUARE
& CO.**

NEW YORK

**UNION
SQUARE
& CO.**

NEW YORK

UNION SQUARE & CO. and the distinctive Union Square & Co. logo are trademarks of Sterling Publishing Co., Inc.

Union Square & Co., LLC, is a subsidiary of Sterling Publishing Co., Inc.

ISBN 978-1-4549-5362-3 (paperback)

For information about custom editions, special sales, and premium purchases, please contact specialsales@unionsquareandco.com.

Printed in Canada

2 4 6 8 10 9 7 5 3 1

unionsquareandco.com

Edited by Corinne DeMaagd
Cover design by Jenny Zemanek
Cover images by Shutterstock.com: javarman (ombre); LAVRENTEVA (cat); Kate Macate (ribbon, herbs); Mr. Rashad (paws); Nadeya_V (wolf); Gorbash Varvara (vials); Anastasiia Veretennikova (stars, moon)

For Jessen.
This book wouldn't exist without you,
and you know it. All my love, girl.

CHAPTER 1

~MATEO~

"WOULD YOU LIKE ANOTHER BEER?"

If I thought it would do any damn good, I'd have a hundred more. But it was no use. Nothing helped. It was only getting worse.

That meathead at the bar is staring at us again.

Please just be quiet for five minutes. I need to think.

Yeah, keep lookin', asshole. I'm going to bloody your face good.

Christ. He wouldn't shut up tonight. The intensity of his urges were worse than ever. At least he leaned more toward violence than sex. His push for a fight was somehow easier to tolerate than his constant commands for me to get laid. Small blessings.

Look! He's standing. He's coming to challenge us. Good. Prepare for combat.

He's leaving. Settle down.

Follow him.

"Sir?" The young waitress stared at me, wide-eyed with concern. I didn't blame her.

"No." My eye twitched. "Thank you." I pulled out a twenty and set it on the table, then headed for the door.

That's right. Time to wipe that sneer off that asshole's face.

He wasn't sneering. You're imagining things. As always.

I've been imagining my fist knocking out his teeth. Now I want action.

Once outside, I took two seconds to scan the block, just in case Alpha was right and that guy was looking for a fight. He made me paranoid. Jittery.

My wolf might need to break someone's bones, but I didn't. I needed help. I couldn't put it off any longer. The offending sneerer was talking to some chick and paying us zero attention, so I headed quickly up Magazine Street in the opposite direction.

You're going the wrong damn way!

No, I'm not. We've got more important things to do than brawl on the street.

A growling snort sounded in my head. **Oh yeah? Like what?**

We're going to meet a witch.

You may be a coward, but you're no fool. A woman is exactly what we need to take the edge off.

Aaaaand, here we go again.

Preferably a curvy one. Need something to hold on to when I'm—

A horn honked as I crossed Magazine, the nightlife still kicking even as some bars were closing down.

All supernaturals in New Orleans knew about the Savoie sisters, though I'd never met them. They had individual talents to help supernaturals in need. And sometimes humans. Those who actually knew about our existence, that is. I'd pay anything right about now for their help. I'd take out a mortgage on my gallery and home if necessary. But I also had heard they were fair. One of them was a hex-breaker. She's the one I was looking for.

Coming up on Ruben's Rare Books & Brew, I slowed my stride. The bookstore was closed this time of night, of course, but patrons of another variety veered around the corner and down the alley. Beautiful human women hung on the arms of inhumanly perfect men who escorted them to the back entrance of the Green Light. A throaty laugh belted from a pin-up–gorgeous blonde in a pink latex dress. Vampire. She tugged her handsome catch for the night down the gas-lit alley to the back entrance.

Leaning against the corner of the building, seemingly disinterested in the comings and goings, was a tall, black-haired guy smoking a cigarette. He wasn't just hanging on the corner. He was working for Ruben, the lord of the New Orleans vampire coven. I knew what he was within twenty yards of him. A wave of darker urges tugged on my psyche and my body.

Alpha rumbled a purring growl at the heady sensation the grim reaper stirred. We called them grims. Not because they escorted souls into the afterlife, but because they carried an aura of darkness, pulling on impulses and cravings that people liked to suppress, to keep in check.

Of the four supernatural creatures, grims and their powers were the most mysterious. My cousin Nico told me once that he'd seen six of them show up at an apartment complex fire when he lived in Houston. They slipped into the burning building without the firefighters seeing them. Knowing lives had been lost, Nico thought maybe they did have something to do with transporting souls after death. Who knows? They never gave out information about themselves, but for some strange reason, they always seemed to know a hell of a lot about everyone else.

A grim was the perfect employee to hang on the corner of a vampire den. The supernatural law was that blood-hosts must go willingly to feed a vampire for the night. A grim standing near the entrance—arousing a human's suppressed cravings for danger, lust, and vanity—would definitely tempt them into the vampire underworld.

Most humans were oblivious to the supernaturals living among them. Until they weren't. Those in some inner circles knew about us. But they kept our secrets—out of fear or respect or both.

Though I didn't like standing in the personal space of a grim, I figured if anyone had the information I needed, it would be him. I wasn't sure who the hex-breaker was, but I bet this guy did.

"Hey. You know the Savoie sisters?"

The grim—his features sharp and his intelligence sharper by the looks of his all-seeing brown-black eyes—sucked a deep drag of his cigarette before responding.

"No. I don't know the Savoie sisters." He measured me from head to toe, flicking a tip of ash onto the sidewalk. "But I know about them."

Smart-ass. Break his nose.

Shut up.

4

"Do you know anything about the hex-breaker?"

He regarded me with a nonchalance that rang false. This guy observed, calculated, and stored away everything with those dark eyes. He probably knew more about the people in the bohemian, trendy district of Magazine Street than anyone else.

"The second sister, Eveleen. Redhead. Spunky personality. Expert-level curse breaker. One hundred percent success rate according to the Witch's Coven Guild database. Works four to five nights a week at the Cauldron, which the sisters co-own. Including tonight." He glanced up and narrowed his eyes as if trying to recall something. "I don't think she's closing tonight."

Whoa. "How do you have access to their database?"

He shrugged, refusing to answer as he scanned the street, watching passersby with that hooded gaze. He was done feeding me information.

"Quite a gig you've got here." I nodded to the alleyway.

He blew out a stream of smoke and stubbed his cigarette against the brick wall behind him. "Better than some other jobs grims are hired for." His voice had dropped to a low, threatening level.

Alpha growled a warning.

"Is that so," I said as a statement more than a question. I could believe it. And I sure as hell didn't want to know what jobs he referred to.

"Standing on a street corner, smoking cigarettes, and people-watching for $150 an hour? Yeah. It's a good gig."

Damn. Ruben paid well. I'd never met him, but everyone knew of him. Good to know he appreciated his employees. I was fairly sure Ruben had access to the information database in this dude's head for that kind of hourly rate.

"I guess I owe you a tip for the information." I reached for my wallet in my back pocket.

"Nah." He grinned, his wide mouth quirking up more on one side. "Knowing a wolf is about to walk into the Cauldron is payment enough." Shaking his head and grinning, he looked down and pulled out his pack of cigarettes from his back jeans pocket.

"Why's that?"

He lit a cigarette, squinting as he inhaled. The tip turned orange, his brows creasing in sympathy. Suddenly, I had the urge to punch that look of pity off his face.

Go with this feeling.

His gaze sharpened on my own. He must've caught a flare of the wolf in my eyes. The longer I stood here, the more my insides fizzled with urgent agitation and the need to do violence. Hot blood hummed in my veins, pushing me harder. Shifting from one foot to the other, I kept my hands in my pockets so I wouldn't reach for him.

The grim stood straighter, but not to buck up on me. That would be stupid. He might be near my height, but he had no idea who he was really dealing with. Actually, he probably did. Perhaps he was preparing to run, which told me he was far wiser than I'd suspected.

Bring it on, grim.

He spoke, his tone even and low and full of warning. "They don't deal with wolves. Never have."

I nodded, narrowing my gaze on the witch's place down the street, needing to shift my attention to the goal at hand.

Mmmm. A redhead. I like.

If she's going to help us, you've got to keep your mouth shut.

A dark chuckle rumbled in my mind.

Fine. I had no choice, one way or the other. With a parting nod to the grim, I strode with purpose toward the Cauldron.

CHAPTER 2

~EVIE~

THIS IS THE LAST THING I NEEDED. AFTER A TEN-HOUR SHIFT, A FRAT BOY puking on my boots, and a drunk-ass chick singing an off-tune, super slutty rendition of "Pour Some Sugar On Me" on our bar top, I now had a werewolf begging me to break a hex.

A fine werewolf at that. And, okay, maybe he wasn't begging. I wasn't sure a man like him knew how, but the thought sent a primal shiver from the top of my spine down to where it zinged between my legs.

"You're Eveleen, right?"

While the never-break rule of *No Werewolves* kept pinging around in my head, his smoky baritone told my lady parts it was a silly, silly rule.

"It's Evie. And yes. But I seriously doubt yours is a hex."

"It is."

Did he just growl at me?

"Look, Wolfman."

"Mateo."

"Whatever." I hopped up on the bar top, spun my legs over to the other side, and landed beside him. "I wish I could help. But we've got rules. No werewolves. Sorry."

It didn't matter how beautiful he was with those broody, soulful eyes and that unruly dark hair falling past his chiseled jaw. Jules would kill me. I tried to ignore the pained look hardening his expression as I passed behind him. Jules hadn't laid down the laws for no reason. She was smart and cautious. All in an effort to keep us safe. Ever since our mom relinquished reign of New Orleans to Jules and hightailed it to the Alps with my dad for a well-deserved retirement, Jules had taken her job very seriously. That's why I ignored the torturous tightening of his mouth and furrowed brow and kept on walking.

"I'll pay you whatever you want."

He followed me as I upturned the stools onto the bar top so the cleaning crew could do their job once we locked up. Behind the counter, JJ dried the tumbler glasses, glancing between us and eyeing the Wolfman appreciatively. He arched a perfect brow with a smirk. His smirks could mean a number of things. This one could have said either "Don't let that fine ass out of your sight" or "Danger, don't touch that." I needed to get better at reading JJ's hidden messages.

"Look. It's not about money." After I hefted the third stool upside down onto the bar, a giant hand wrapped entirely around my forearm.

"*Please.*"

Turning to him, my ponytail swished over my shoulder. I looked where he held me until he dropped my arm.

"Sorry," he grumbled. "I'm just . . . I need help."

Okay, maybe he wasn't beyond begging. In the intensity of his eyes flaring hazel-gold then cool brown, I could see he definitely had some kind of supernatural twitch. It bothered me, I admit it. But rules were rules.

I propped a hand on my hip and stared out at the street, still buzzing with nightlife. We closed the Cauldron at midnight, but other bars and clubs on Magazine Street stayed open much longer. Biting my lip, I swiveled back to him. "Have you talked to your people?"

"My people?"

"Yeah, your werewolf club. Lycans. Your *familia*."

His expression blanked. "I have none."

"None?"

"No one."

"No one?"

"Am I making myself unclear somehow?" His scowl deepened, and his voice dropped a few decibels into a super growly range. I didn't point out his dark mood swing was exactly why Jules enforced her no-werewolves rule.

I chewed on my bottom lip and debated. He had that preternatural stillness I'd seen vampires get when they were hyper-aware of every move of every living thing in the room. It made me uneasy. I was about to tell him one more time that I couldn't help him and he should seek out his own kind when the dude in the corner who'd had one too many of our Blood Orange Old Fashioneds stumbled into him from behind.

Wolfman had him by the throat and pinned to a tabletop with wicked-fast speed. The warning rumble building inside the werewolf's chest raised the little hairs on my arms. Then I realized it wasn't a warning. He was squeezing the life out of the drunk guy.

"Whoa, whoa, whoa." I eased closer with slow movements, wrapping my hand around his forearm. A well-muscled and nicely veined forearm, I might add.

JJ leaped over the bar and strode toward us, coming way too fast. The werewolf's growl deepened, but his eyes remained on the dude he was choking. I shook my head at JJ. He stopped mid-stride, keeping his distance but his eyes on the threat.

"Easy . . . easy," I crooned to the dangerous man about to commit murder in our bar.

I maneuvered my body between him and the tabletop and put both my palms on his chest. I sucked in a breath at the furious vibration of his body. He was hot. And I don't mean just fine-as-hell hot. I mean volcano-rumbling-with-lava hot. Hissing between my teeth, I pumped a gentle surge of magic into him, like I would to move an object telekinetically. The pulse didn't budge him, but it jarred his death stare from the drunk to me.

"Mateo," I whispered gently. "Let him go. You don't want to hurt him."

With a flash of his fire-gold eyes and a sudden jolt, he jerked away and released the guy. Spinning around, he planted his hands against the wall behind him and sucked in great gulps of air, his head hanging low, his dark hair covering his face.

In the few seconds I made physical contact, I'd sensed a number of things. The hardest to swallow was the overwhelming wave of painful desperation ripping through the core of this man. I didn't have the gift of reading emotions like my sister Clara, but there was no doubt this man was hurting. Badly. And what kind of witch was I to turn my back on him? When I might be the only one who could help him?

"JJ," I said calmly, nodding toward the drunk guy. "Go help this guy into an Uber and get him home."

"Whuz that 'bout?" slurred the drunk, rubbing his neck and trying to stand. He obviously didn't realize he almost died a second ago.

"Are you sure I should leave you here?" asked JJ, fisting his hands, reminding me why he doubled as a bouncer.

"Yeah." I stared at Mateo's wide back as he heaved air in and out of his lungs, his six-and-a-half-foot frame bowed with what I could only describe as anguish. Regret. "We're good now."

JJ stalled for a few seconds while he got drunky on his wobbly feet and shuffled him out the door. Violet had taken off early, leaving me and JJ to close up, so I was now alone with the werewolf. I should've been scared as hell, but strangely, I wasn't. Though he acted on his violent impulses, it all stemmed from a deep-seated pain. Exhaling a sigh, I knew what I had to do.

"Mateo?"

Slowly, he rolled his muscular shoulders back, the only sign he heard me. He shoved off the wall and cleared his throat before turning to face me, his arms loose at his sides, his eyes downcast.

"I'm sorry. That was . . . unacceptable."

"Yeah," I agreed in a soft voice. "That was a serious lapse in control."

He nodded, finally lifting his gaze off the floor. Semi-calm brown eyes met mine. Though I expected to see the rage still riding him, I found sadness. It reflected what I'd sensed when I touched him.

"Does this happen often?" I asked with a sympathetic lilt.

"This never happens. That has *never* happened before. I need . . . *help*." It seemed to pain him to admit how badly.

Something pinched in my chest. "Right."

I offered a soft smile, but he didn't return it, agony still tight in the set of his mouth and eyes. If I did this, it would likely get my ass chewed out, but I didn't care. A memory of Mom popped into my head.

"A good witch sees the truth, absorbs its goodness, and honors her gift."

"But how do I honor it?" I asked her.

She cupped my chin and gave me her all-knowing Mom smile. "By sharing it with those in need."

I stared at the werewolf, my mind made up. "Okay. Come with me."

I wound through the tables and behind the bar toward the exit to the alley. I didn't need to look to see if he was following. I could *feel* him. This wolf carried a heavy aura. No, not heavy exactly. Potent was more accurate. Whatever it was that made him what he was, it felt like a lick of flame at my back. I led him through the now empty and darkened kitchen, past the storage room to the alley entrance. I unclipped the keys dangling from the short chain that stretched across my belt loops and opened the door.

Holding it open, I gestured for him to walk through. He did, his hands now in his front jeans pockets. Figuring he was trying to look less threatening, I snickered and locked the door behind us. He couldn't look harmless if he tried. Not after that display of crazy in the bar and not since there was an electric charge simmering around his body like a lightning rod that had just been zapped twenty times.

"Is something funny?" he asked. Scowly face was back.

"Yep."

"Care to share?"

He fell in step beside me as we followed the alleyway that separated the Cauldron from our corner shop next door, Mystic Maybelle's. Our house was a short walk down the side street criss-crossing the intersection. The night was still hot but less humid as we crept into late October. Let me clarify. It felt less like swimming in soup and more like bathing in dogs' breath. Any day now, we'd have our first cool front that would slowly shift the tide toward cooler weather, but that please-come-before-we-melt-in-Mordor moment hadn't happened yet.

"Hmm. Let's see." The sidewalk buzzed with a few late-night partiers, the streetlights giving off a sense of security. A false one for anybody who rubbed the anxiety-riddled guy next to me wrong. His shifty gaze roamed the pedestrians talking and laughing among friends. "I had a rather shitty night at work, then a werewolf pops in right at closing time, claims he's got a hex put on him—"

"I do."

"Begs me to help him, but I politely tell him no, so then he nearly strangles one of our regulars to death."

"I wouldn't have killed him."

"Are you sure about that?" I wasn't being snarky. I was asking him seriously.

Silence. He looked away, his dark locks blocking my view of his eyes. Shame, that. When I stopped in front of the wrought-iron gate that opened to the walkway to our front door, he then finally faced me. Measuring me from head to toe, his gaze snagged on my chest. I wasn't sure if he was staring at my perky boobs or my T-shirt with a black cat holding an arm bone that read *I found this humerus.*

I thought he might actually crack a smile, but then he looked at me like I was crazy—not an unusual occurrence—and did that shivery thing he'd done back in the bar, as if shaking off a bad dream. Not exactly the look a girl wanted when a hot guy checked out her goods.

"Are you okay?"

He clamped his mouth shut, his jaw tightening with a hard grind before he said, "You don't understand what not being able to change is doing to me."

I thought about him bending that guy over the table and choking him with one hand. "I think I have an idea."

"I *need* to release the wolf."

That agonizing expression was back. That pleading look. Though I didn't tell him, he didn't have to convince me of anything else. It was clear to me he wasn't lying or exaggerating. He needed my help, and I planned to follow my instincts first. Not Jules's rules.

With a stiff nod, I opened the gate and led a werewolf up the porch and into our house. I must be out of my damn mind.

As expected, soft music played from the back of the house where Jules was doing her nightly wind-down routine. He followed me down the entrance hall, past a small den and an arch leading to the left toward the large living room and our open kitchen. We continued down the hall toward the music. It appeared only Jules was in the main house.

Clara and Violet must be settled in bed in the carriage house over the garage since I didn't hear either poking around in the kitchen. Isadora and Livvy were still out of town. So that left Jules alone in the study. Good. I didn't want an audience to the shitstorm I was about to start.

Before we reached the open doorway, I stopped abruptly. The rhythmic tune of her favorite pagan folk band with its bagpipes, flutes, drums, and Celtic harp floated into the hall. A good sign. If it was that Mongolian metal band with their throat-singing about crushing their enemies, then I'd have pushed him back out of the house and tried this tomorrow.

With a deep breath, I glanced over my shoulder at the man standing a head taller and awfully close. "Don't speak until I tell you to. Or she does."

He ground that perfect jaw again. "Why not?"

"Because my sister is the one who doesn't like to work with your kind. And she's a Siphon."

He flinched at that. Yeah. Siphons, also called Enforcers, were more powerful than Nulls, witches who could freeze a supernatural's powers. Jules could do far more than freeze powers. She could take them all away. Permanently. A Siphon was also the one kind of witch who was more powerful than a centuries-old vampire. Hence, the reason our witch coven reigned in New Orleans and not Ruben Dubois, the overlord of the vampires in this district.

Visibly shaking, Mateo glanced toward the open doorway. A werewolf was cursed in a way that he couldn't lose the beast roaming inside his blood no matter what. But he could lose the magic that comes with the werewolf curse. The added strength and speed, the longer life, and the creative gift that every werewolf was born with alongside their wolfish beastly needs.

I walked into my oldest sister's sanctuary with a bright smile on my face, faking my lighthearted mood as best I could. She was tucked into her love seat by the window, her knees bent, a book open on her upturned lap, a glass of red wine on the side table. Her gaze swiveled to the door, skimming right past me to the werewolf at my back.

I raised my hands in surrender. "Okay. Before you say anything, there's a very good explanation for this."

She didn't move at first. Her steel-blue gaze dragged from Mateo to me then back to him. With forced indifference, she closed and set her book aside, then stood and crossed her arms. Of the six of us sisters, she was the shortest and the tiniest in stature. Her short, blunt bob softened the sharper edges of her high cheekbones and pointed chin. But it did nothing to tamp down the *you're dead* glare she was giving me.

"Jules, this is Mateo. He's a—"

"I know what he is. Why is he in our house?"

She'd dialed her maternal tone up to DEFCON 3. But at least she hadn't reached screechy levels.

"He claims there's a hex put on him keeping him from shifting." I turned to him, his attention fixed on my sister. "How long has it been since you last shifted?"

"This will be the third month." Some of the anguish was gone from his voice, though I wasn't sure what was putting him more at ease. It certainly wasn't my sister's bitch queen impersonation.

Jules just stared and said not a damn thing, but I could see her hamster wheel working hard. She was debating whether to show him the door or hear him out. By some miracle, she chose the latter.

"Why do you believe this is a hex? And not a normal dormancy?"

He chuffed out a sound between a cough and a laugh. "I've heard of wolves going dormant, but in those cases, their beast became distant and quiet. Mine most definitely is *not*."

His eyes flared that fiery gold again, but he kept his posture nonthreatening.

"How so?" she asked coolly.

"I have . . . primitive urges."

I barely contained another shiver at his heated admission. And yes, he'd growled every word. He also seemed to be holding something back.

"Jules," I started, turning serious. "He struggled to control his violence just now in the bar with a customer who bumped into him. More so than I'd say is normal for werewolves. Though I admittedly know none."

"I don't want to hurt anyone," he protested. "This feels like, I don't know, like I have a block. Like my wolf wants to come out, but something is keeping him inside. It's not natural. A hex is the only explanation."

"He's a danger to the public," I added. "And if we don't at least try to help him, then we're as much at fault as he is. *If* something should happen."

I let Jules infer whatever that something could be. He was totally staring at me, but I refused to look at him.

"And what do you sense?" she asked me.

This was where it got tricky. "I don't know for sure." When he grabbed me in the bar, I felt *something*, though I couldn't place what it was.

"You probed him then?"

"Not very deep," I answered softly, hardly able to admit that I'd actually been afraid of him in the bar. There was no way I was about to ask him to gaze into my eyes and let me step inside his mind while he was trying to strangle one of our patrons. Telling Jules the truth wouldn't help me sway her to our side at the moment.

"Try again," she commanded, nodding toward Mateo. "Here."

Alrighty then. I stepped up to face Mateo and blew out a deep breath. Bending my arms at the elbows, I reached out. "Hold your arms like this and grip mine."

He didn't question why, but obeyed quickly. Smart werewolf. When we locked arms, the surge of heat emanating from his body rippled through my fingertips and palms.

Locking on his brown eyes, which flickered fiery gold, I pressed my magic forward. Gently. Very gently. Even so, a rumble stirred in his chest, a rough growl tingling along my senses. And while I knew it was a warning to be careful, I couldn't prevent the delicious sensation it piqued on every nerve ending in my body. Like a lightning zap, it electrified my insides, spreading goose bumps along my skin.

"Easy," I whispered like I would to an injured or scared animal. "I just want to take a look."

That's essentially what I did when I probed for hexes. With finger-light brushes, I slid my magic inside him, seeking out the foreign magic. Usually, I could identify what kind of hex and from what kind of witch a spell had been cast on another person.

Sometimes, it wasn't even cast on the person who was hexed, but had ricocheted off someone near them. That was rare, but it did happen. In those instances, I couldn't always pinpoint the spell, but I could still pull it out and evaporate the magic.

As I swept deeper inside him, I felt . . . resistance. It wasn't just a block, a walled-up spell from another witch, but more like a push. I didn't sense the telltale signs of a hex—the electric spray of foreign magic that didn't belong. I sensed the presence of a powerful being—his wolf—and an invisible fence around him, but also another aura pushing me away.

It was so weird. Hexes didn't typically work that way. They weren't usually aggressive in nature. Just there. Like an object set on a table. Whoever had put this object on Mateo's table had added something extra to the spell. I didn't like the feel of it.

When Mateo's growl rumbled deeper, I let go and took a step back. Not because I was afraid, but because I didn't want to anger the beast.

For a second, all I could do was stare at Mateo. His gaze shimmering with gold slowly melted back to that cocoa brown. His chest rose and fell more quickly, but there was no sign of violence or anger. Just a look of wonder, actually.

"Well?" asked Jules.

Dragging my attention back to her, I said, "There's definitely something there. But I can't pinpoint what kind of hex it is or what kind of witch put it there, if even on purpose. It's very . . . unusual." I glanced from her to Mateo. "To be honest, I think it may be that I'm just not familiar with werewolves and their magic. It's easy for me to do this with humans, other witches, and even vampires. I think maybe your inner . . . wolf is pushing me out for some reason."

Mateo huffed out a laugh with zero humor attached to it. "I don't think my wolf is pushing you out." His intense gaze pierced me with what I could only surmise was the hard truth. That meant we were dealing with a hex I'd never encountered before.

Jules looked over at her bookshelves, filled with just about every damn book ever written on supernaturals—from historical origins, to the Spanish Inquisition witch hunts, to craft, spells, and talismans. She didn't walk over and pluck one off the shelf like I knew she wanted to, but stared hard for a full three minutes. Then she swiveled back to Mateo, and I knew she'd made her decision.

"Do you know of anyone who means you harm? Holding a grudge against you?"

He combed a hand through his hair in frustration, disheveling it even further. "No."

"It's not our custom to work with werewolves," she said in her usual, matter-of-fact tone.

He flinched. Still calm, he sucked in a deep breath, then said, "Yes. Evie said as much." He shifted his weight from one foot to the other, his hands curled at his sides. "But I'm only a danger if this hex isn't broken."

"I see that." Her admission shocked me. Jules was a stick-to-your-guns kind of gal. She stepped closer, arms still crossed but loosened and hanging lower at her waist. "I don't know that we can help you, but I trust my sister. If she says you're a safety hazard, then I believe her. I'd like to do some research and get back to you." She angled her head at me. "Evie will have to do some of her own research as well."

"Thank you." He exhaled a ragged breath, then turned to me, his expression gutting in its intensity. "Thank you."

The *thank you* he gave me was deeper and more passionate. More personal. It came from both the man and the wolf, I was sure of it.

Shaking off a shiver before it became visible, I said, "I'll see you out." I spun for the door before Jules changed her mind, then guided him back down the hall, through the front door, and to the gate.

Tucking my hands into the back pockets of my jeans, I rocked back on the balls of my feet. "Well, you're lucky. She was in a good mood tonight."

He blew out a half-laugh. "That was a good mood?"

"Don't go insulting my sister," I teased. "Only I can do that."

"Does she make all your decisions?"

"Nope. Just the ones that could get me killed if I don't think it through." I tilted my head to the right, my ponytail shifting over the front of my shoulder. "It's not easy, or always safe, being a witch these days. And I tend to—"

I pressed my lips tightly together. For some strange reason, I was pouring out too much information to this man I'd just met.

He leaned closer, his head lowering to capture my gaze. "You tend to what?"

I let out an embarrassed laugh on a shrug. "To trust too easily. To want to help too much sometimes."

His wide mouth slid into a brilliant smile, forcing me to admire his perfectly straight, white teeth. Strange that a werewolf should have such a beautiful smile. No yellow fangs or remnants of his killings anywhere to be seen. I was beginning to wonder if he really was a werewolf. He wasn't scary or intimidating at all.

"I don't see how that's a problem. To be trustful and kind isn't a defect, Evie. It's rather wonderful really."

Oh my. His voice dropped deep and gruff and harsh on my name. He'd framed it with an emphasis that rumbled and tumbled down my spine.

I blew out a nervous breath. "Thank you." Because what else do you say to something like that? I tried not to think about how my tendency to help others had gotten my heart stomped on a time or two. Really just the once, but we won't think about that right now.

Mateo nodded, taking me in again with a leisurely perusal. "I owe you."

"Pretty much."

He chuckled. I wanted to lighten the weighty tension between us. Beyond breaking his hex, this guy needed to laugh. And he needed a friend. I had a feeling he didn't do much of the first and didn't have enough of the second.

"Thank you. And good night, Evie."

Again, his voice dipped into that deep, rumbly register on my name, then he shied away like he'd done something wrong. So strange. Were all werewolves a bit odd?

"Night." With a flick of my hand goodbye, I headed back up the walk, yet again feeling his heavy stare follow me to the door. When I reached the porch and glanced over my shoulder, he was gone.

I knew I wouldn't get to bed without an ass-chewing, so I headed into the kitchen where I heard Jules moving around. Sure enough, she was pouring another full glass of merlot.

I took a seat at the island and popped my butt up on the butcher-block top. "Go ahead and get it over with."

Leaning back against the sink, she said, "You did the right thing."

Wait, what?

"Come again?"

"If what you say is true, then he's a threat to society. That means it's our responsibility to help if we can."

It was the role of the Savoie sisters to keep the peace among supernaturals in New Orleans. Our family had ruled as the head coven here for three generations, therefore it was our role to enforce the laws.

In most regions, it was an old vampire who was most powerful and held this role, but not here. Our grandmother Maybelle was a Siphon, then my mother, and now Jules.

Witches and vampires were well organized, each with their own local guilds who held regular meetings at least twice a year. Grims were super secretive. They flew under the radar and rarely stepped out of line. Jules said a different grim showed up at each of the guild meetings, so no one ever knew who was in charge of them. They were . . . odd. The werewolves were a disorganized lot, preferring mostly to live alone and off the supernatural grid, or in packs that moved from city to city. There was no werewolf guild in any region that I knew of.

My family had a reputation for being tough but just, so there was rarely any question about our authority. But like Uncle Ben told Peter Parker, "With great power comes great responsibility." Maybe that's why Jules so quickly changed her tune about this werewolf. Still, it wasn't like her to change her mind so easily.

"Are you serious? I was sure you were going to break out your ten commandments or something. Isn't *No Werewolves* number three?"

She rolled her eyes. "I meant don't *date* them, don't be friends with them, don't become emotionally involved."

"No, I never remember hearing that distinction. Of course, I've never had reason since I've never met a werewolf, so there's that. You won't even let one in the bar."

"Jesus, Evie. That's not true. You're so dramatic. You act like I'm some kind of werewolf bigot."

"Well . . ."

She moved closer to me and set her wineglass on the butcher block. "The reason I wanted you and your sisters to stay away is because they're *dangerous*."

"No more than vampires."

Her stormy eyes glinted with anger. I smiled, knowing what that was all about. Well, sort of.

"Vampires can be controlled. Most of the time." Her nostrils flared. "Werewolves can't. Do you remember what they did—?"

"In the 1400s? No, because I wasn't alive that long ago, but yes, I remember your incessant history lessons about the werewolves helping witch-hunters."

"They're temperamental and often violent." She heaved out a breath and softened her voice, sounding more like Mom than I think she knew. "Tell me, what did this wolf do tonight at the bar that set you on edge? And what's his name by the way?"

"Mateo." Then I muttered begrudgingly, "He almost choked a guy."

"Really?" She raised her eyebrows in mock surprise. "Shocking."

"But it's because of this hex." I hoped Jules didn't hear the defensiveness in my voice even though it was pretty obvious.

"And you're sure it's a hex," she added as a statement not a question.

"It's weird. I can't feel it the way I normally can. But . . ."

"But what?"

"Well, when we touched in the bar, I sensed the block he talked about. His wolf is trapped against his will, that I know for certain. But when I probed, it was much more aggressive. Whatever kind of magic it is."

"So, not a low-cast spell."

"No," I agreed. "Something much more complex. Something I don't recognize. Or maybe it's just I'm not familiar with werewolves enough to recognize it."

"So you think his hex has given him these violent urges."

Again, a statement. I shrugged with one shoulder.

Jules sipped her wine before adding, "And when this hex is broken, and he can shift into a bloodthirsty monster once a month, he'll be perfectly calm and biddable."

I picked at the frayed hole in the knee of my jeans. "Maybe not biddable."

"Ha!" She drained her wine, rinsed her glass, and set it in the sink. "Eveleen Marielle Savoie. Hear me now. We're going to help this guy because it's our job. But you are not to get emotionally attached to this Mateo. I know you have a soft heart, but this isn't one of your strays you bring home to keep."

"Please, Jules. This is a job."

"Exactly. So treat it like one."

Bristling at her condescending tone, I asked, "As opposed to what?"

"As opposed to one of your little fix-it-and-make-it-better projects. Like Mr. Harvey."

This again. I rolled my eyes. "Mr. Harvey was very appreciative of my healing potion."

"Oh yes. He certainly was. That energy elixir you infused with magic finally knocked him out of mourning for his wife and had him chasing after every eligible widow within a six-block radius."

"Well, the elixir worked." I should've kept my mouth shut. But no. I just had to open a door for Jules to point out the specifics of my meddling mayhem.

"It worked so well, Clara had to warn him against crashing her book club every week. Ms. Ferriday was threatening a restraining order, and then he had that incident with Viagra."

"How was I supposed to know that Viagra and magic-infused energy potions were a dangerous mixture?" I snapped defensively.

Jules tilted her head, actually letting out a little laugh as she gave me that look like I was a puzzle she couldn't quite figure out.

"Evie. Just stick to animals for your little projects." She shoved off the kitchen counter, holding my gaze with her gray eyes. "That Mateo is a man. And a werewolf, which means he's—"

"Dangerous. I know."

With an arch of her superior brow and a satisfied smile, she said, "Good. Then we're on the same page."

She flitted out of the kitchen and up the stairs at a quick gait. I let her words sink in before I jumped off the counter. No biggie. I could do my job. Spend a few hours a day with the werewolf, keep my distance and not overstep, then break the hex and be on my way. Easy peasy.

CHAPTER 3

~MATEO~

Waking up to brutally painful morning wood had become the norm since last month. I meant, it was nice to know the plumbing worked, but this was ridiculous. Yet one more problem made worse by this hex.

I rolled out of bed and shuffled to the bathroom, heaving a sigh at the disaster in my boxer briefs.

You gonna do something about that?

Christ. Too damn early for him.

Because you could hammer nails with the tent pole down there.

I was going to go insane. Certifiably insane if I had to listen to him pushing me this early in the morning.

Just rub one off so you don't look like a freak out on the street. Or you could find an actual female to fuck. You do remember what that's like, right?

Shut up.

How about that girl last night? I like her.

I know exactly how you feel about her.

He wouldn't stop yammering about her smell, her skin, her pretty ponytail that he'd like to grip while he took her from behind. I'd almost lost my goddamn mind just trying to have a civil conversation with the girl.

Look, we need her help, so I suggest you behave when we're around her.

Throaty laughter echoed in my mind. **The last thing I want to do around her is behave.**

I stared at my reflection, thankful I didn't look as crazy as I felt. I scratched at the scruff that was bordering on a beard. If I had a split personality disorder, at least I wouldn't know when the other voices took over. That would be my idea of heaven right now. But no, I had to exist on the same plane as my animalistic ego. Or my id. Or whatever part of me my wolf represented.

Alpha. My name is Alpha, and you know it.

Before the hex, I'd only ever heard his voice during the monthly change. I'd have fleeting memories of him taking over and driving me during the shift. But now that I couldn't let him out, he'd beat his way into my psyche, living alongside me every second of every damn day, torturing me with his running commentary on who he'd like to kill and who he'd like to fuck. Which was pretty much every stray dog or human being we came across. I was exhausted by it. By him.

And now he'd zoned in on Evie. The trusting, kindhearted witch who'd convinced her prickly sister to help me. She didn't have to do that. I was well aware of the reputation of my kind among other supernaturals. We were the ones you shunned to the outcast table. Even grims were more acceptable to witches and vampires than we were. Yes, I understood my ancestors had dug our own graves with a long history of witch-hunting and massacre. That's why I was fine living alone, being alone. What I couldn't endure was Alpha dirtying my mind with constant thoughts of his salacious plans for Evie.

After a frigid shower where I ignored Alpha's incessant grumbling, I ate a quick breakfast of fried eggs and sausage, then headed downstairs to my studio. My delivery date for this latest commission was quickly approaching, and I had to find a way to focus if it killed me.

The problem was that it was nearly impossible to channel my muse when Alpha was so present. His urges were violent and hard. My metalwork, while intense in craft, required a sensual hand, a gentle touch. Alpha wouldn't know sensual or gentle if it hit him over the damn head.

Hey. I can be gentle. Go get that red-haired witch, and I'll show her how gently I can smack her ass.

Fucking hell. Save me.

I slammed on my welding helmet, jerked on my gloves, and took the torch off its holder before flicking on the fire. After returning to my sculpt, I moved a dozen stainless steel wires to my worktable, then settled onto my stool. With the welding tongs, I lifted a twelve-inch string of galvanized wire and heated it with the torch. Leaning forward toward the juncture where the ocean waves merged into the leaping mermaid, I set to work, layering the waves with wire and motion.

I'd settled into a flow, placing one heated wire of steel after another, roping the mermaid's tail into an intricate pattern. Then

I changed direction, creating the illusion of a soft torso and silken skin.

He'd actually shut up when I'd found my groove. I'd gotten at least eleven minutes of blessed silence, finally falling into the perfect space between reality and fantasy where my muse took over.

Her tits are bigger.

I exhaled a deep sigh.

What the hell are you talking about?

The witch. Hers are bigger. Make the mermaid's like hers.

"Fuck!"

A perfect handful.

I can't believe this shit.

What? You know you're thinking about her.

I shut off the torch, ripped off my welding helmet, and threw it across the workshop. Spearing a hand into my hair, I contemplated heavy drug use. With my luck, it would just dull my senses and make him even louder.

Why don't we stop playing with metal women and go find a real one? One with red hair.

When was the last time he'd shut up for more than fifteen minutes?

Ponytail girl likes us too. I can tell.

Ponytail girl? She has a name.

Didn't notice. I was kinda distracted.

Evie. It's Evie.

Mmmm. Yeah, that's it. Rolls off the tongue, doesn't it? I like her.

I know you like her. But trust me, she doesn't like you—I mean us—the same way.

Agree to disagree.

Wait. Last night. After we left the bar, he'd shut up for a while. He hadn't said a word all the way to her house or even while meeting her sister. Now that I thought of it, he didn't start his shit again until after we'd left and I'd passed a muscle-head leaving a club. Alpha had wanted me to beat the shit out of him for being a buff male.

He needed to know who was boss.

Come to think of it, even though Alpha had detailed every way he wanted to bend her over the bar, the frenzied buzzing under my skin dimmed the second I had touched her. It still hadn't kept me from almost strangling that drunk, but I remembered feeling lighter somehow by the time I'd left her house. I chalked it up to having a possible solution to this problem, some relief, knowing the witches were going to help me. But . . . what if it was more than that? What if the feeling came from her?

That was it.

That was what?

You're getting your wish. We're going to see the witch.

Sweet. It's time to claim our woman.

She's not ours. Jesus. Would you settle down? We just met her.

A wolf wants what he wants.

I grabbed my keys hanging by the door, locked up, and headed east on Magazine Street. It was just a few blocks to the pub. I knew they served lunch, but it was early. If no one was there, I knew where she lived. She might not want me to bombard her at home, but I was desperate.

I agree.

The coffee drinkers were settled in with their laptops and iPads under the café awnings. I kept my hands in my pockets and my head down, trying to avoid any confrontation. Last month, Alpha had pushed me into a brawl with a morning commuter. I was in my truck, delivering my last commission in the business district, and this asshole sits on his car horn while I was legally parked to unload the sculpture. If he'd just stayed in his car and not gone all road-rage on me, then it wouldn't have ended with him on the pavement with a bloody lip.

You should've torn his throat out.

Are you serious right now?

That low-life scumbag needed to be put in his place for good.

Really? He deserved to die? For yelling at another driver? Nice.

I swear I could feel a furry shrug inside me.

That day was when I knew I was in trouble. I'd never lost my temper and acted in violence. Unless necessary.

It was necessary.

No, it wasn't, asshole.

snort

Anyway, that's when I knew for sure that I was on edge from not shifting. Since then, it had only gotten worse to control my urges.

I wish you'd lose control of your dick, because my balls are so blue you could sprinkle glitter on them and hang 'em on a Christmas tree.

Yeah, well, I wish you'd shut the fuck up, but I haven't gotten my wish yet either.

Not yet, but maybe soon. I walked faster.

I strolled up to the Cauldron and peered in the window. Damn. No one in sight yet or they were in the kitchen. I kept walking past the bar. As I crossed in front of Mystic Maybelle's, I sensed movement on my right. It was some kind of psychic and crystal shop. I glanced in, then came to a sudden stop. Evie. She stood on a ladder, putting something on the top shelf on the back wall.

Mmm. She looks good from behind.

I stepped inside, tinkling a bell over the door.

"Just a minute," she called out.

She was trying to balance a glass orb with a transparent marbleized design on some kind of stand. A decorative crystal ball. Not wanting to distract her, I strolled over to the right wall, checking out what they sold. There was a shit-ton of different kinds of colored crystals and polished stones with names like amber, obsidian, amethyst, ametrine, and blue aragonite. There were small tented cards with labels that read *for joint healing, for anxiety, for meditation.* Another shelf displayed a few books for sale. Titles like *Oracle Guide, Find Your Inner Medium,* and *Unblock Your Chakras.*

I shouldn't have been surprised that witches ran a witchcraft and metaphysical shop, but somehow I was. Humans didn't realize there were *actual* witches living among them. On the second shelf near a display of tarot cards, there was even a stuffed cat. They might've found a better taxidermist because the thing's hair looked coarse and thin, its spine jutting up a bit too far. They could've at least had the taxidermist add some padding to this old pet they'd stuffed.

But then the stuffed cat slowly turned its head and looked at me.

"Fuck!"

Kill it!

"Oh," came Evie's voice.

I heard her coming down from the ladder, but I kept my eyes trained on the aberration. Its glassy orange eyes blinked. One at a time. In a slow robotic way. I gaped at what it did next. It smiled. I'm not kidding. *Smiled.* Like it was seriously wasted or high.

Fucking abomination.

"That's just Z." Evie maneuvered in front of me and lifted the horrifying creature into her arms. She actually cuddled it under her chin. "He's a little shy."

It made a strange sputtering noise, like a small motorboat engine stopping and starting. He must be sick or something.

"Is he okay?" He did *not* sound okay.

"What? Oh!" She laughed, her whole face lighting up. "Yeah, his purr is a little rough. He's kind of old." She scratched behind his ears and his weird purr grew louder. "But isn't he so cute?"

Not exactly the adjective I was thinking of, but I didn't want to insult her right before I asked a huge favor. I needed to test my theory first.

"Will he bite if I pet him?"

"Z? No way." She laughed. "He's as gentle as a lamb."

A deranged, half-dead lamb. Finish it off.

I reached up and stroked a finger over its oddly large head, brushing the top of her hand that lay on his back.

Yes. Immediately, a sweep of calm shivered through me. Instant relief. Like cool water on a hot day. I knew it.

I glanced down at her white T-shirt. This one had the silhouette of a man and woman's hands touching fingertips with #Reylo4Ever scripted in hot pink. I couldn't help but notice how the letters swelled over her breasts. This is probably because Alpha was constantly infiltrating my thoughts. But then again, he hadn't said a word.

I looked up at the creepy smiling cat and chuckled.

"Something funny?" She inched back a little and arched her brows in concern.

"No. Not funny." Pathetic, actually. But I couldn't wipe the grin off my face.

"Well, you've got this kind of crazy look." She thought I was nuts, and I guess I was. "We don't have anything new for you on the hex yet."

I nodded, easing back another step. But not too far. I needed her nearness. "I came for something else. I'd like to ask a favor."

"Another one?"

"Yeah."

"Okay." She set her cat on the counter where he wobbled a second before curling gracelessly into a ball.

I hesitated, trying to find the right words that wouldn't make me sound like a freak or a stalker. Nothing came to mind. Swallowing what little pride I had left, I tucked my hands into my jeans pockets and went for it. "I'd like to pay you to spend time with me."

Her face paled. "Uh, I'm not sure what kind of witches you think we are, but we're not whores."

I choked on my own spit. Somehow, Alpha remained blessedly silent. "No, no, no." I put my hands up in protest. "That's not what I meant. I assure you."

"Then what did you mean?"

"I mean"—I dropped my voice lower—"there's something about you that calms the wolf."

She smirked. "Come again?"

Combing a hand through my hair, I tried to figure out a way to say this without it making me sound completely insane. But there really wasn't one. I'd have to tell her the truth. If there was anyone who'd believe me and understand, it was a witch.

Clearing my throat, I started again. "It's not just animalistic compulsions that I'm troubled with right now."

She stared. Said nothing. Just raised her eyebrows as if to urge me to go on. So I did.

"I can hear his voice in my head."

"His?"

"The wolf's."

Alpha, motherfucker. It's Alpha. Introduce me proper. *For Christ's sake.*

"He actually has a name."

"Which is?"

Exhaling a heavy sigh, I looked at the shelves of quartz and crystals. "Alpha."

When she didn't snicker or laugh, I looked back. Her pretty mouth was tipped up on one side, an expression of pure curiosity heightening her brow.

"I know, I know. If I could lie to you, I would, but then he'd be even louder in my head, and it's hard enough to concentrate as it is."

She placed a hand on the countertop, drumming her fingers, then leaned a hip against it. "He talks to you all the time?"

"All the time."

Her eyebrows shot up further, drawing my gaze to the deep green of her eyes. There were tiny gold flecks circling the pupil, and somehow, I'd never call them hazel. They were such a shocking shade of green, like the new leaves of spring. I lost my train of thought, trying to figure out exactly what they reminded me of.

She cleared her throat. "Like right now?" An amused smile creased her mouth.

I jolted from my musings on her eyes, reprimanding myself for being a creeper, then glanced away for a second. I nodded, trying to come across casual and normal. The opposite of how I felt these days. "He insisted you know his name."

She stepped closer and stared keenly into my eyes, as if she were trying to look through me to him. Funny that she showed zero fear at my supernatural schizophrenic confession. I clamped my jaw tight when Alpha purred a wicked growl.

I knew it. She likes me.

"So he was talking last night?"

I laughed. "Oh yeah. He was running his mouth nonstop last night."

"That explains a lot," she said, tilting her head and examining me intently.

I cleared my throat, nervous. "How do you mean?"

"You seemed, I don't know, distracted. On edge. And don't take offense, but a little weird."

A bark of laughter escaped me before I pressed my lips together with a nod and another nervous rumple of my hair. "I *was* distracted, on edge, a little weird."

She smiled, then her brows pinched together. "I'm confused then. What does this have to do with me?"

"It's hard to explain."

"Try." She crossed her arms, accentuating her assets Alpha loved so much.

Don't even try to fucking fool yourself. You love them as much as I do.

Realizing how creepy my request was going to sound, I eased around her toward Z on the counter, curled in a lumpy ball.

Alpha bristled inside me, rumbling with a low, menacing growl only I could hear.

I reached out.

Don't you do it. He used his gravelly, aggressive tone with me.

Calm down.

Don't touch that hell-spawn.

Fuck off.

I stroked the cat's head with one finger. Its motorboat purr sputtered louder.

"I was trying to work, and he just wouldn't shut the hell up. I've hardly been able to work since last month when he became even more . . . well, just *more*."

She sidled up in front of me, leaning a hip on the counter. In jean shorts, I got an eyeful of her long, well-toned legs. Strange that Alpha let me enjoy the moment without yelling obscenities. He truly was more docile with her around.

"What do you do?"

"Sorry?" I jerked my gaze up to hers.

"You said you can't work. What do you do for a living?"

"Oh. Right. I'm a metalwork artist."

Her tilted smile widened, nearly knocking me out. She was a pretty girl. Straight auburn hair that leaned toward brunette made her emerald-green eyes even prettier. Her face was more round than oval, making her look much younger than she probably was. Of course, witches aged slowly with their longer lives. All supernaturals lived longer than humans. Not immortal—not even vampires as myth would have it—but our life spans were much longer than humans. Her nose was a little small with a sprinkle of freckles across the bridge. Her mouth was perfect, her top lip a defined bow-shape. Distractingly perfect. But it was her smile that elevated her from pretty to beautiful.

"Maybe I've seen your work. Where's your gallery?"

"Not far. A few blocks up on Magazine. The Prometheus Gallery."

Her eyes widened. "I know that place," she said excitedly. "I've window-shopped a bit. Did you make that sculpture of Hermes on flying sandals?"

Smiling, I nodded. "Yeah. That one just sold last week."

"Wow. That is so cool."

A flush of heat rushed up my neck at her compliment. "You like art?"

"Yeah." She eyed me a minute, her thoughts seeming to wander away. "So, how will spending time with me help you?"

I licked my lips, my mouth suddenly dry. Unsure if it was nerves or being this close to her or what, I tried to explain this without coming off like a complete freak.

Too late.

"It's like I said. Being around you calms him somehow. Must be because you're a hex-breaker, I guess. All I do know is that last night, the longer I was with you, the quieter he became. And since I've walked in, he's become . . . less." I eased closer, trying to dial down the desperation I felt. "If you like artwork, I'll create a sculpture for you in payment. If you want. Or I'll pay you in cash. Whatever—"

She held up a hand. "I don't need payment."

"But I'd need access to you every day. Your time is worth something."

"Whatever Jules decides as far as payment goes for the hex-breaking job, that'll be payment enough."

"You don't decide your own fees?"

"I do. We have standard fees for individual jobs. But this will require her input, it seems, so the cost will be hefty enough."

Whatever price they set, it wouldn't break me. What would break me was enduring another day with Alpha's nonstop diatribe of obscenities.

"So you'd do this for me for free?" I asked, disbelieving.

"I'll do this for you as part of the job until we break the hex," she clarified. "And no offense, but I'm not spending all day with you. How about two hours?"

I huffed and stepped closer. She arched a brow at my nearness. And possibly my sudden aggression. I needed longer than that to get my commission completed on time.

Easing away, I countered, "Six hours."

"*Six?* Are you out of your mind?"

"To be honest. Yes."

Her mouth hung open a second before she rounded the counter and pulled her cell phone from underneath. While texting speedily, she said, "Four hours, and that's it. I do have a life, Wolfman."

"Mateo." I winced. "Please."

41

She tucked her phone in her back pocket and propped a hand on her hip. "Fine. *Mateo.* But I've got stuff to do today. It's Wednesday, and I've got a standing date on Wednesdays. So you're coming on an errand with me first."

For a second, I was frozen, basking in the sweet sound of her husky voice saying my name. Such a small thing, but I wanted to hear her say it again. And again.

I'd like to hear her scream it.

He could really ruin any perfect moment. Truly. Shaking him off, I glanced around. "Don't you have to work the shop?"

"Clara had some morning errands, so I was supposed to watch the shop for her. But Violet will be here in a minute. She can take over for me."

"Who's Violet?"

A slim woman with blue hair—taller and less curvy than Evie but with the same fair complexion and shape of face—stepped in from a door in the back.

"Well, well. Who's Mr. Tall, Dark, and Fuckworthy?"

I like her. But sorry, babe, we're already taken.

Taken by whom, I'd like to know?

He snort-laughed in my head. **By the sister. Who the hell do you think I mean?**

Stop obsessing over Evie. She's not mine. Or ours. Or anything.

She will be.

"Mateo, meet my sister Violet. She's got the mouth of a sailor. Sorry for that. Violet, this is Mateo, our newest client."

She sashayed within a foot of me, leaning one hand on the counter, devouring me with her eyes. "Nice to meet you, werewolf." She winked.

Poor sweet thing. She wants us. They can't help it, brother. We've got animal magnetism.

I cringed. *Or you're just a narcissist on top all your other fine qualities.*

Yes, it's true. I do have fine qualities. A consequence of being an apex predator.

Jesus. He didn't even get sarcasm.

Evie grabbed my forearm and led me toward the door, that wash of tranquil bliss bleeding into my veins. I nearly groaned at how good it felt.

"Nice to meet you," I called over my shoulder, but my gaze was locked on the pretty witch swinging her ponytail in front of me.

CHAPTER 4

~EVIE~

MATEO DIPPED HIS HEAD AS WE WALKED. "SO WHO'S YOUR WEDNES-day date?"

"Bam."

"Who's Bam?"

"Actually, it's Bam's Comics."

I dropped his arm, realizing I was still holding on to it. Why I'd grabbed him in the first place was puzzling. Well, not really. If I was going to be honest with myself, I didn't like Violet being flirty with him. She flirted with everybody. It was just her way. But Mateo didn't need her kind of distraction. One that might get his wolf worked up. He needed another kind of distraction. One that suited his artistic nature, which is why it was so perfect that today was Wednesday.

"You like comic books?"

"Like?" I scoffed and rolled my eyes. "Comics are life."

He was silent, striding beside me. When I glanced up, his gaze was yet again on my breasts. Jeesh. Don't get me wrong. I didn't mind his little obsession, but I was definitely about to call him out on it when he asked, "What's hashtag Reylo?"

First of all, he pronounced it *ree-low*. Second, he was apparently obsessed with my T-shirts, not my boobs. Third, how the hell did he *not* know who Reylo was?

Stopping in front of the Boho Chic Boutique, my sister Isadora's favorite shop, I propped both hands on my hips and squared off to him. To his credit, he actually looked concerned, even if he had an extra eighty pounds or so on me.

"You have *got* to be kidding me."

"I'm sorry?"

"You *should* be sorry. Raaaay-lo is the most beautiful pairing ever to hit any sci-fi universe, like ever."

He gave me a complete and utter blank look in response.

Summoning patience, I asked, "You do know *Star Wars*, right?"

"Of course I know *Star Wars*. I'm not a hermit."

"Could've fooled me."

"I watched it once, but it was a long time ago."

"Wait a minute. You watched *it* once? So you've seen one *Star Wars* movie? And that's it?"

He shrugged a shoulder. "Not really into science fiction movies. Or movies in general, for that matter."

"I can't even believe what I'm hearing," I muttered more to myself than to him.

It was like Chewbacca speaking Klingon. Does. Not. Compute. Okay. *Don't freak out on him.*

Last time I was in the bookstore, I overheard a teenager asking for the *Star Wars Rise of the Sith* graphic novel. I accosted the poor guy and proceeded to lecture him on my theories of villain worship till his eyes glazed over. Best not to go there again. Not everyone got my brand of crazy.

"So," I asked lightly, "what do you do all day?"

"I work. And read."

"And?"

"I don't know. Sketch new ideas. I hike and walk a lot."

"Walk?"

"Yeah. And hike."

"Hike? Hike where? All we've got are flat wetlands and snake-infested swamps."

He chuckled, dipping his chin closer to his chest, his longer locks falling forward. God, he had gorgeous hair. It was sexily mussy. It was obvious he didn't even try, and that was tragically unfair.

"If you must know, I drive farther north in between projects or when I need quiet for inspiration. There's a place north of Baton Rouge. Tunica Hills. And I usually spend summers in a cabin in Tennessee."

I thought about that a second. "Of course. You like the woods."

He gave me a self-deprecating smile. "I like the woods."

"Well, if we're going to be spending four hours a day together," I said, marching down Magazine, "then I'm introducing you to what you've been missing."

"I don't feel like I've been missing anything."

"That's because you've been missing it."

Even his sidelong glances were intense. He didn't seem to be aware of how penetrating his gaze was. His looks were like flicks of lightning. When I was a little girl, I used to rub my shoes on the carpet really hard and fast and then zap Jules on the arm. That's what it felt like when he looked at me. Except the shock wasn't at all painful. Just filled with something supercharged and exhilarating.

"Here we are." I gestured toward the small window display spray-painted "Bam's Comics" in graffiti-style lettering.

We entered with the bell tinkling overhead. Bam sat on his stool behind the counter on the right wall, near the cash register. His beatnik style never did quite match his clean-cut hair and lack of a beard. I always thought he'd look better if he'd go full hippie. He was a quirky guy, Bam, with nice blue eyes and a perfect smile. It brightened the second he looked up and saw me. Then it dimmed a little when he caught the shadow at my back.

"Happy Hump Day, Bam."

"And to you, little Evie."

I hated it when he called me that, but he gave me such a fabulous discount on my weekly comic book haul that I let it slide every time.

He stood from his stool and patted today's release of *Farmhand* on the counter. "I've got your baby all wrapped up and ready for you. You going to browse today?"

I decided Mateo could use a little more excitement than walks in the woods, so I opted to browse. "Yeah. I'm gonna look around a bit."

I gestured for Mateo to follow me toward the rows in the back.

"Okay, so since you're an artist, you need to broaden your horizons. The illustrations in some of these are absolutely amazing."

I checked over my shoulder, waiting for him to disagree with me, but his gaze was on one of my all-time faves.

"Oh! That's *Deadpool Assassin*. That's where Wade Wilson is fighting the Assassin's Guild in New Orleans, which is super cool to see him in our city. Anyway, he fights all kinds of villains. My favorite is the knife-wielding speedster called the Harvester."

I grabbed his wrist and dragged him down to another rack. "But take a look at this. *Savage Avengers*. So badass. And Wolverine is back! Gah! *Finally*."

My geeky heart did a cartwheel, so pumped to see Wolverine back on the scene. I picked up the issue I'd bought last week and stared at my lovely, vicious man on the front cover.

"Do you want to get this one?" he asked, peering over my shoulder.

"Got it already."

"Did you just shiver?"

"Yep. Wolverine gives me all the shivers." I gave the cover an air-kiss and set it back on the stand.

When I turned to move on, Mateo stood well in my way, his broad chest blocking the path. Confused, I glanced up to catch a slow roll of yellow across his brown eyes. The subtle shift of color and the penetrating lock of his gaze on me sparked a scary kind of shiver.

"You okay?" I asked, about to step back and put some distance between us.

He shook his head and gave me a tight smile, swallowing hard, his Adam's apple bobbing. "Sure. Fine."

Quickly, he stepped aside, clasping his hands behind his back. I wondered if his wolf was being chatty again. If so, what the hell was he saying to make him go all feral-looking for a second?

I roamed farther down, pointing out another favorite, reining in my crazy this time. "Now, this is awesome too. I freaking love *Wolverine Weapon H*. It's when they combine DNA of the Hulk with Wolverine."

"So what you're saying is you like Wolverine."

Ignoring his sarcasm, I fled ahead, too excited to spout about big W to someone new.

"There's also *Return of Wolverine* and another of my favorites *Old Man Logan*. Oh! That one is so damn good. It's like set in the wastelands of the future. You know, like Mad Max and Road Warrior."

Mateo stared at me like I was speaking Russian.

"That's right. You don't watch movies. Damn. You mean you haven't seen the newest version of *Mad Max: Fury Road?*"

A subtle shake of his head while he continued to stare.

"You have no idea what you're missing. I feel so sorry for you."

I strolled the aisle, pointing out a few of my other favorites like *Star Wars: Tie Fighter*, *Oblivion Song*, *Weapon H*, and *Old Man Quill*. I honestly didn't remember the last time I rambled so much. None of my sisters were into comics. Since Mateo was quiet and attentive, he was just asking for the full-throttle version of my obsession. Or addiction.

When he lifted an issue of *Monsters Unleashed* and focused intently on the illustrated cover, sliding his fingertips over its beautifulness, I said, "I've got that one if you want to borrow it."

"I think I'll get this copy for myself."

I swear I must've looked like the Cheshire Cat, or the Mad Hatter, or both rolled into one. I spotted an issue of *Guardians of the Galaxy*, my brain ping-ponging in another direction.

"You know, I saw this chick in cosplay as Gamora at Wizard World last year. I swear I thought it was actually the actress Zoe Saldana."

"What's Wizard World?"

"Mateo, seriously?" Could he truly be this clueless about the outside world? How lonely he must be. I mean, sure, reading was great. Hiking was nice. But did he have any friends? Who was allowing him to live in this city and hadn't yet dragged him to Wizard World? Sighing heavily, I said, "It's the big Comic-Con every January at the convention center."

"Oh yeah. I have a friend who goes sometimes. I didn't realize that was the name of it."

"So you've never been?"

He shook his head.

Then I shook mine. "You don't know what you're missing. It's where the freaks and the geeks of the world unite."

Chuckling, he said, "Yeah, I guess I'd fit in."

Sighing, I turned him toward the register. "I have so much to teach you, young padawan."

He shot me one of those closed-mouth smiles that gave me all the flutters.

"I've made a convert, Bam," I called out as we strolled toward the front.

"Oh yeah?" He took the comic from Mateo. "This one of your cousins from out of town?"

Last time I'd brought a guy with me into the store, it was my cousin Drew, visiting from Lafayette in the heart of Cajun country. He and his brother, Cole, lived with another warlock named Travis, all members of the Acadiana Coven. They visited a few times a year.

"No." I laughed, glancing at the messily handsome man standing closer than necessary over my shoulder. "Not a cousin."

I'd noticed he had brushed against me more than once for it to be an accident, but I also sensed he needed it. He'd confessed his problem with his wolf, so I figured whatever hex-breaking mojo I was born with helped him just by being around me. Then touch would magnify the calm he needed. Unfortunately, he didn't look all that calm right now. As a matter of fact, he looked downright tense.

"Here," he said, passing his credit card to Bam. "I'll pay for hers too."

"You don't have to—"

"It's the least I can do."

His voice was rougher than it had been when we walked in. As a matter of fact, his mannerisms had shifted as well. Where before he had appeared laid-back and lighthearted, now he was all burning looks and stiff shoulders and rumbly voice. It must be the push of his wolf. The electric charge he was giving off at my back told me I was onto something. I glanced over my shoulder, but his glare was fixed on Bam, who happened to be taking his sweet time swiping the credit card.

I was afraid Bam was stalling, then he proved it by asking, "You two dating?"

Bam was being a little too nosy. Now was not the time to pump me for information, because it was obvious Mateo wasn't in the mood for chitchat.

The problem was, Bam had a thing for me, which is why I was never available for a cup of coffee or a "bite to eat" when he'd asked. Numerous times. He was nice, and I liked him, but Maybelle, my grandmother, always said, "Don't shit where you eat." Knowing that Bam had the best collection of comics in New Orleans, and also knowing I was extremely fickle when it came to men, I decided it best to keep our relationship platonic. A few weeks of dating and some decent, possibly even good, sex wasn't worth me losing access to his comics. Far more valuable.

"Not dating," I said on a laugh, then I leaned forward on the glass and lowered my voice to a hush, looking around with a conspiratorial eye.

Bam leaned forward, too, much closer than necessary for my farce of a secret.

"This guy here is a werewolf, you see. And I'm a witch. He's paid me to break his hex. Now he's doomed to follow me around and do my bidding till I decide to break it."

Bam stared at me for several seconds, then burst out in a braying sort of laugh. Very donkey-ish. "Oh, little Evie." He reached over and tugged on my ponytail. "You've got the craziest imagination, sweetie."

The intense heat at my back made the little hairs on my nape stand up. I didn't need to turn around to confirm that Mateo wasn't pleased about me confessing the truth. I only did it because I knew Bam would never believe me, and it was funny. Or at least I thought so.

While Bam swiped the credit card, I chanced a glance over my shoulder. Yep, he was all fire-eyes and flaring nostrils. I shrugged with a smile. When Bam handed over the credit card, Mateo leaned forward, pressing his chest to my shoulder blade, to snatch it back.

I caught his scowl before he smoothed his expression blank. "You okay?" I whispered.

Those expressive eyes held mine, blinking away whatever fierce emotion they had held a second before. "Fine."

"If you say so." I tucked our bag of new comics under my arm. "Thanks, Bam. See ya next week." Then I left with the werewolf hot on my heels.

CHAPTER 5

~EVIE~

MATEO AND I PARTED WAYS AT THE SHOP. I NEEDED TO CHECK IN AND be sure it was cool before I met him at his studio for several hours. Since Isadora and Livvy were gone, we were taking turns helping Clara man Maybelle's. The second I stepped through the door, my ears were assaulted with a screeching, horrific rendition of "Defying Gravity" from the musical *Wicked*. Yep. Clara was here somewhere.

Clara was my sweetest sister. Sunshine and happiness all the time. No joke. Kind to a fault. And I do mean *to a fault*. She once almost got herself killed while bringing food to the homeless under the interstate bridge. She regularly delivered leftovers—cucumber sandwiches, lemon scones, and French macarons or whatever posh goodies they'd had at her weekly meeting with the High Tea Book Club she hosted.

One late afternoon, she found herself in the middle of a gang shoot-out that had stumbled into the tent city. Before she could use any magic to stop them, she was knocked out cold. Thankfully, she'd woken up completely unharmed except for a bump on her forehead. She never knew what had happened to the shooters. But what was Clara most concerned about? Her homeless friends who had to live among such violence. That was Clara.

So yes, she was possibly the most selfless person I'd ever known. Gifted with beauty and all manner of wonderful attributes. But singing? Holy hell in a handbasket. She was a horrible singer. Interestingly, her twin, Violet, had an amazing singing voice. The problem was, Clara loved to sing. Specifically Broadway show tunes. It made her happy. So, of course, we pretended it wasn't torture to listen to her impromptu discordant, off-key musical performances. We endured and let her do her thing because that's how we rolled. Even Violet—the most brutally forthright of us—never pointed out her twin's appallingly bad singing.

"Clara!" I called out, because I couldn't see her from the front of the shop.

She popped out of the storage room in the back, carrying two stacked boxes full of new tarot cards. "Hey!" She beamed. Her gold hair was braided and twisted atop her head. She stopped suddenly a few feet away and gasped, staring at me with excited interest. "Wow. You have the loveliest blue aura around you today." She said it like she was complimenting my hair or my eyes or something. As if I'd done something on purpose to make my aura all pretty.

"I thought I always had a blue aura?" I stepped forward and took one of the boxes.

She laughed like I'd said something ridiculous. "You do." She examined the invisible light around my shoulders that only she could see. "But today, it's practically vibrating. Beating like a heart.

And so, so blue." She blinked rapidly, then smiled at me before heading to the front shelf to our tarot card display.

I followed. "I didn't know auras could beat like a heart."

"Oh yes. They can pulse, vibrate, spin, even become oozy."

"Ew. That sounds gross."

We set down the boxes and started to pull the individual packs from inside to set out on the shelf.

She knelt to start on the bottom row. "It's typically not a good sign."

Clara was an Aura. Not to be confused with the glowing, pulsing light she saw around others. An Aura was a designation of witch, which meant she could not only sense emotions as an empath but could project her own onto others. It was a cool kind of magic, especially when Violet was in one of her moods. Clara would zap her with some happy juice to make her stop brooding. It was especially funny when Violet actually *wanted* to have her own pity party and continue sucking the joy out of the room, but Clara never let her.

"So do you have a lot of inventory to stock today?"

"Aren't these pretty?" She held up a deck, the cover outlined in gold leaf and displaying a beautiful woman with a scepter.

I nodded, accustomed to Clara's wayward train of thought. "Do you have a lot of new inventory to handle?"

She took her time arranging the new decks perfectly spaced apart. "Not much. I need to infuse the new crystals with some magic, and I've got some sage bundles to wrap with ribbon. But that's it. Why?"

"Well, it's my day to help you out, and I have something I need to do."

Her sky-blue eyes fixed on me as she pulled the second box toward her. "What do you have to do?"

I suppose I couldn't avoid telling her. "Remember the werewolf Jules and I were telling you about at breakfast? He asked a favor."

She knelt, stacking the next row. "What kind of favor?"

Jeesh. I couldn't lie to my sisters, even though I wasn't sure Jules would agree to this. "He asked me to spend a few hours a day with him." I lifted a quill pen from its pewter holder—one of the non-psychic knickknacks we sold in the shop—and twirled it in the air.

"Is that because his inner wolf enjoys your company?"

Putting the pen back in its holder, I stared down at the top of her blonde head. "Come again?"

She put the last of the new decks on the middle row, then stood up. "I'll bet Mateo is more balanced when you're around. Calmer."

"How did you know that? That's pretty much exactly what he told me."

"It seems logical." She gave me that knowing Clara smile. "But I can also read it off you."

Putting a hand on my hip, I frowned. "How can you read it off me? That doesn't make sense."

"Read what off you?" Jules stepped in from the hallway that led to the back courtyard, which connected to the Cauldron.

Dammit.

Lifting the two empty boxes, Clara headed toward the register. "The werewolf Evie is helping needs her company to calm his nerves."

Jules scowled, crossing her arms in her white chef's coat. "What the hell does that mean?"

"Keep him steady," explained Clara. But that apparently wasn't clear enough.

"Evie, what is she talking about?"

"It's no big deal." I met her by the register where Clara pulled out the drawer and started organizing the cash. "Mateo asked if I could just spend some time with him at his studio so he could focus on work. Like Clara said, apparently I calm his wolf somehow. Nothing weird or anything."

Jules arched an eyebrow. "There's so much weird going on, but I believe you. And to be honest, it does make sense. Your hex-breaking magic may counterbalance the effects of his curse. Actually, it might be a good idea for you to spend more time with him."

Wait, what? Shocking.

"Really?"

"Yeah. I'm wondering if you might pick up on something at his gallery or his workshop about the hex. Or the witch who put it on him."

Clara closed the cash register and leaned forward on the counter, her palms down. "We'll need to do a good witch's round before Evie tries to break the hex."

"True," I agreed. A witch's round amplified our power. It would give me a good boost of magic.

Jules bit her lip, her stormy gaze directed out the front display window. "But before that, we need Violet to check him out. Divine him to see what she can discover. Any information will help us."

Tucking my hands in the back pockets of my jean shorts, I said, "Do you not think I can do this? Break the hex?"

I didn't mean for my insecurity to break through, but it did. I cringed at the meekness in my own voice. I'd never failed at breaking a hex, but I'd failed in other areas. And failed to chase my dreams for fear of failure. Yeah. That f-word was the only one that made me wince.

"Not for a second, Evie." Jules sounded put out by my moment of self-doubt. Like it was idiocy. "But from what you told me, this is something new. Something you've never dealt with. The more information we have, the better chance we have of success."

That made sense. "Sounds good then." I turned to Clara. "Are you good on your own today?" I suddenly realized something. "Wait, where's Violet? She could help if you need it."

Clara waved a hand in the air. "She's gone again."

Jules's pensive expression turned into a grimace. "Where the hell does she keep disappearing to?"

"I don't know. You?" I asked Clara.

"No." She smiled, pulling a packaged box from the cabinet below the register. "But it's all fine."

Jules scoffed. "You're not worried?"

"Not a bit. Whatever she's doing, it's not hurting her well-being, that I'm sure of."

If anyone knew, it would be Clara.

Jules huffed, turning for the door while mumbling, "I just don't like secrets."

Clara opened the box with plastic-sealed crystals inside. "Poor Jules. Always worrying about the wrong things."

"What do you mean? She worries about *everything*."

She laughed. "True."

"Well, if you're good, I'll be off."

"No worries." She poured a plastic pouch of purple amethysts into her palm and closed her fingers around them. Then a pulse of her magic sizzled in the air, a dim glow emanating from her hand and fingers as she pumped a joy spell into them. "You go take care of your werewolf. I'll be fine on my own."

"All right then." With that, I headed for the door. "But he's not my werewolf," I called over my shoulder.

Her laughter followed me out the door.

CHAPTER 6

~MATEO~

She'd told me she had to stop in at their shop and then would meet me at the studio later. No way was I going to try again to work on my current sculpt without her there, but I could get some other work done. Stepping through the front door of the gallery, I nodded to Missy behind the long counter against the brick wall running along the back of the gallery.

"Morning. Anything new?"

"Good morning, Mr. Cruz! Not yet, but Kyle did call to say he was switching out some paintings this afternoon."

Her super-shiny greeting rubbed me worse today, and I knew why.

"Would you care for coffee before you head into the studio?" Her sunshine smile beamed.

Missy had been working for me for two years now and knew my routine, but I was off my routine. Way off. I was off my goddamn rocker if I was honest.

"Coffee would be great. I'll be in the office this morning for a while."

I strode on through the studio, noting a SOLD marker on one of Sandra's mixed-media paintings. I hadn't sold much of my own work out of the gallery, but the percentage of commission on the artists who rented my space was keeping the place going. My real income came from private commissions, and the demands were coming faster. But, hell, I was working so much slower with Alpha constantly on my ass.

It always comes back to me, doesn't it? Maybe you've lost your talent.

You don't lose your creative talent.

You sure? Because your new work sucks.

What the hell do you know about art?

I know that mermaid's breasts need to be bigger.

I strode down the hallway and ducked into my small office, then settled in at the desk. I stared at the invoices stacked neatly in my inbox, but my mind strayed as soon as I started leafing through them.

Bam. What kind of name was Bam? *Are you kidding me?* What a poser. Far too pretty and clean-cut to run a comic book shop. Weren't those guys supposed to be shaggy and bearded in tie-dye T-shirts? When he touched her hair—

You should've pulled his arm out of the socket.

Jesus. Can you please just go away for five fucking minutes?

And he better keep his eyes in his skull before I scoop them out with a spoon.

A spoon? Who are you?

A grunt. **I'm Alpha. Haven't we gone over this? Are you getting dementia or something? You're only in your hundreds.**

For a werewolf, that meant I was in my prime, but he had me wondering. I was definitely losing my shit.

"Here you are, Mr. Cruz."

Missy poked her head in with the perfect cup of coffee as usual. I'd tried to get her to call me by my first name, but she'd been eighteen when I hired her and couldn't manage the familiarity, which was fine by me. Her lingering looks warned me early on she had a crush. When I realized that, I stopped reminding her to call me by my first name. Best to keep that barrier up. She was just a baby.

You know who's all woman?

Please not now.

Evie.

"Thank you, Missy," I managed to grit out.

"Are you okay, Mr. Cruz? You seem stressed lately. Is there anything I can get for you?"

Evie.

Stop!

"No, Missy. Just some things on my mind."

You've got to control yourself.

That's the problem. I'm not in control. Not yet. But I will be.

I swear, if I gave you free rein, I'd have a string of STDs by Sunday.

Werewolves don't die of disease. I'll take my chances.

The hell you will. I'm still in charge.

For now.

A primal shiver coursed through my body. His threat of taking over shook me with true fear. My whole life, I'd been in complete control of the beast. Except for my very early days.

As soon as the wolf started rubbing me on the inside each month, I'd pack my things and head for the woods, far away from humans for a week or longer. It was a controlled burn, the release purging the animalistic urges that lived inside me.

But this hex. Christ. As soon as he'd melded with my psyche, intruding on my thoughts in a constant stream, I started to fear what would happen when I was finally able to cut him loose. I was also afraid I might not come back to myself if he took over. The urges and needs and thoughts weren't just Alpha's. They'd become mine too. I'd curtailed my need for blood only marginally by eating semi-raw steak several days a week.

In the shift, I hunted till the bloodlust abated. The carnal lust I'd managed just fine outside shifting, thank God. The problem was I wasn't the dog that Alpha wanted me to be. I was a serial monogamist, tending to keep one woman for a length of time before she bored of me or vice versa. Caroline had moved on about three months ago after she gave me an ultimatum to take our relationship to the next level. I never went to the next level. I couldn't. Ever.

If I did, there'd come a time when I'd have to explain to her why I had to take a weeklong trip alone in the woods once a month, and over time she'd realize I didn't age. I mean, I did, but not at the same rate as a human. I was in my early one hundreds, but I looked thirty. And I'd look like this for another fifty. No. Better to keep a woman for a few months or a year and move on. I could get all I needed just like that.

So where's our next prospect? Your hand can only substitute for so long. We need flesh. Warm skin. That wild witch.

Not going to happen.

"Oh, Missy," I called into the hall where she'd disappeared.

"Yes, sir?" She popped back into the doorway.

"I'm expecting someone. Evie Savoie." I couldn't keep the rough rasp from my voice at the mere mention of her name. "Will you let me know when she arrives?"

"Yes, sir." She ducked out with wide eyes.

Poor girl. She'd been noticing my abrupt moods, but stayed sweet and polite as always.

Back to Evie. Why not her?

Are you a complete idiot? Because she's helping us get rid of this hex.

So.

So?

I put my head in my hands, my knee jumping ninety miles a minute. A growly laugh rumbled in my chest. It was Alpha's laugh, but it found its way out of me.

Seriously. You need to stand down, Alpha.

Foreign language. Don't know what you're saying.

You know exactly what I'm saying. We're not pursuing her. End of discussion.

You want her.

I want her to help us, yes. Break this fucking curse so we can go back to normal.

A rough chuckle. Again, it rose out of my chest, echoing off the small office walls. Mocking me.

And there it was. Another tremble of fear streaked through my body and tightened in my chest with a sharp sting. That ever-present ominous *what if* loomed nearby.

I wasn't just worried about the next shift and what the wolf would do to satiate his craving for blood and violence. I feared he'd take complete control. I feared what he'd do if I let myself go to bed with a woman right now.

Especially one I . . .

I flipped to the next invoice, not even seeing what was on the paper, my knee jumping again with the swift tap of my heel.

God, do you fucking want her.

The happy greeting of Missy's voice came from the front gallery when someone walked in.

"Yes, I'm here to see Mateo."

Evie. A strange coiling sensation stirred low in my belly, a heated burn that buzzed along my skin. I didn't recognize the sensation. All I knew was that I was standing and my feet were moving. Man and beast needed to be near her, and there was nothing in the wide world I could do to deny it.

Her proximity was all I needed. Yeah. I could keep all unwanted thoughts and desires under control.

You can try.

She was shaking Missy's hand with a warm smile when I walked in. That smile. The way her eyes sparkled—actually sparkled—transforming her from pretty to ethereal, radiating some kind of angelic aura. Stunned. I was fucking stunned, bewildered, stupefied by the force of her damn smile. I truly was losing my mind. I was halfway obsessed with this girl after knowing her less than twenty-four hours.

There's no halfway about it, brother.

Anxious to get her back to the studio so I could start working and stop fixating on her heavenly smile, I rushed an introduction.

"Missy, this is my . . . Evie. Evie, my assistant, Missy."

"Nice to meet you," said Evie before I urged her with a hand at her back toward the hallway. The brief brush washed me with calm. She arched a brow over her shoulder. "In a hurry?"

"Yep. I need to work."

"No problem." She patted the leather backpack over one shoulder. "I brought stuff to do while you work."

"Awesome."

"But you only have three and a quarter hours left."

"What do you mean?"

"Four hours a day. That was the deal. We spent at least forty-five minutes at Bam's. And like I said, it won't all be me sitting in some sweaty studio."

I was practically hurtling her through the door at the end of the hall and outside through the small brick courtyard that connected my gallery to my studio and apartment. As we walked through the courtyard, Evie abruptly swiveled around me toward the centerpiece of my patio.

"Whoa," she whispered.

Centered in a square of a small bricked-off garden, which was mostly green plants in mid-October, no flowering blooms this late, stood one of the first pieces I'd ever made. It was Hades, standing tall like the god of the underworld he was with one sandaled foot shifted forward, his tunic flowing in an unseen breeze, one hand gripping his two-pronged bident, the other resting on the head of a waist-high hellhound.

Evie circled the piece, her admiring gaze pulling me closer. But I didn't say a word as she made a second pass, stretching out her delicate hand and tracing the god's arm that held the forklike scepter.

"How . . . how do you make metal look like it's moving?" She shook her head. "I mean, it looks like his cloak is billowing in the wind. It's insane." She dragged her attention away from the sculpture to me, an expression of pure awe written in her smiling eyes and slightly upturned mouth.

I didn't know how to respond. I'd had other artists and critics question me a thousand times on my methods of construction. For some reason, I couldn't quite find the words to respond.

She let her fingers drag across the head of the hound and then walked to meet me. "You're damn good, aren't you?"

A shot of adrenaline pulsed through my veins at her open admiration. At the way she had touched the metal. Swallowing hard, I took two steps to the door and opened it for her. "After you."

She walked through and into my workshop, glancing at the closed door that led to my apartment upstairs, but then took in the surroundings of my workspace.

She whistled, then giggled. "Somebody's a neat freak."

I tried to see what she did, noting my worktable with everything in its place except for the helmet still on the floor where I'd left it this morning. I scooped it up. "I like things in order."

"I see that." She took a long look around the room. I followed her gaze, realizing I didn't even have a chair for her to sit in.

"Oh shit." I headed for the door that led upstairs to my apartment. "I forgot to get a chair for you."

"Don't bother," she said, already sliding to the ground against the wall. "I prefer to stretch out on the floor anyway."

"You sure? I can—"

She waved a hand, already unzipping her backpack and pulling out the comic she bought this morning.

We bought.

Yeah. Small price to pay to have her here. That was the first time Alpha had piped up since she'd arrived. And the mental pressure I felt from his constant pushing had melted away the second she was within inches of me.

I still want to find that Wolverine and challenge him to one-on-one combat.

Yes. You already said this back at the comic book store.

That man-animal thinks he can win over our Evie? He has no idea who he's dealing with.

Look who was calling who a man-animal.

Like I told you, Wolverine isn't real.

But she kissed his likeness and said he gives her the shivers.

Seriously, it was like talking to a caveman.

Only we can give her the shivers.

"All right then," I said, focusing on Evie. "So you're good?"

"I'm good." She glanced up over the rim of her comic and smiled before her gaze returned to the pages.

Those eyes. They looked mossy green in the shadowy space of my studio. *Stop obsessing!*

I'm not obsessing. I'm plotting. Planning.

I wasn't talking to you.

So now you're ignoring me but talking to yourself? Get it together, brother.

You're unbelievable.

Yes, I am. Extraordinary, actually. And once I find that Wolverine, I'll prove it.

Rolling my eyes, I walked over to the opposite side and lifted the garage door, which opened up to my narrow driveway where my truck was parked. The open door let in sunlight and fresh air so the room didn't become too stifled with the smell of melting metal and the heat of the torch.

"You mind if I play music?" I asked.

Her eyes flicked up to me from over the top of the comic again. With a shrug, she said, "This is your place, Mateo. Do whatever it is you need to do." She tapped her watch. "You've got three hours left."

With that, I moved quickly, setting my cell phone on the shelf next to my wireless Bose speaker and hit play on playlist number three. Once gloves, helmet, and torch were in hand, I settled on my work stool in front of the sculpt and got busy.

Jesus. I couldn't believe how easy this felt. It was like her presence whispered to my muse, channeling my energy into my hands and fingers to do the work it was made to do. Heaving out a deep breath, I bent closer and let the music take me to that place where only the art mattered. For the first time in two months, I was actually able to do it without a peep out of Alpha.

Damn, I might need more than four hours a day. But for now, I'd take whatever she gave me.

CHAPTER 7

~EVIE~

Sweet mother of all things holy. How was I going to sit here and stare at that for four hours a day and not drown in a puddle of my own drool?

I'd been just fine for the first thirty minutes or so, completely immersed in my new comic. But after sketching a little on my tablet, I happened to glance up while Florence & the Machine's "Seven Devils" played and nearly had a heart attack.

He was working on this cool but simple sculpture of a mermaid lifting out of the water, her hands braced on a rock, arms straight, the fan of her tail lifting in an arc behind her. It wasn't just his skill with metalwork where he magically melted tiny metal rods into multilayered, three-dimensional works of beauty, but watching the man do it.

So focused. So intense. He was bent close now, his threadbare T-shirt like a second skin to his back and torso. I could actually see the full definition of his obliques as he bent and stretched his arms to work. He set the torch and his helmet aside, still wearing protective gloves and using some metal instrument to shape her breasts. His gloved fingers pressed and stroked up the top slope to indent at her collarbone, becoming more defined under his talented fingers. My skin tingled with awareness of what those hands would feel like on me.

And *why* was I thinking about this?

No werewolves. No werewolves. No werewolves.

Maybe if I repeated it enough in rapid succession, it would seep into my subconscious and take effect. But right now, my body and brain was telling Jules that she and her rules could go fuck off.

He stood from his stool, then lifted the torch and a new string of metal with the tongs. He melted the small steel rods and layered them along the formation of her face, the part most incomplete. As of now, she had a jawbone and a skeletal layer of skull. No hair yet. But he moved with such ease and confidence, I knew he could see her in his mind. Again, he set the torch aside so he could use those fingers to stroke up her jaw and shape the softened metal around her ear.

His hair had fallen back as he tilted his face up to focus, his mouth slightly apart in concentration. The music pulsed, and sweat rolled down his muscled forearms. His biceps tightened with each press of his fingers, the veins in his arms prominent from blood pumping hard in the heated studio. Then he totally did me in.

He went back to work on her mouth, smoothing and pressing, swiping the pad of his thumb along the lower lip. His intense concentration, the way he sculpted with swift, deft movements of his fingers, the unbelievable beauty he created with nothing more than steel and heat and talent, I was completely mesmerized. In awe. And if I had to admit it, a little jealous.

That's it.

Cramming my tablet into my backpack, I eased up the wall and pushed off, heading for the door.

"Where are you going?"

He had stopped with his hands midair, cupping right over her breast as he stared at me with a look of horror. Jeesh. Was my proximity that important that he seemed to look panicked at the thought of me leaving? I licked my lips. His intense brown eyes dropped to my lips and then raised again.

Jabbing a thumb over my shoulder, I said, "Just taking a bathroom and stretch break. You got one in the gallery?"

He nodded slowly, his expression shifting to concern. "Don't be long."

So bossy.

"I won't."

I slipped through the courtyard, noting that his sculpture of Hades stood like a sentinel, watching me pass through. I gave him a little salute and kept going. I found a restroom across from the office in the hallway. After that, I ventured into the gallery rather than head straight back to the workshop.

His assistant, Missy, stood next to a couple who were admiring a sculpture half the size of the mermaid he was working on out back. It was a depiction of a Greek soldier with a sword hanging in one hand. He faced a beautiful woman in a stola, holding one of her hands. Her other rested on his chest as she stared up into his eyes.

Missy was answering their questions. "It was right before King Leonidas left for the battle at Thermopylae. This was the last moment he would look on his wife, Queen Gorgo."

"Fascinating," said the middle-aged man, "how he captured their facial expressions with metal like this."

"It is, isn't it?" Missy was obviously proud of her boss's work, her eyes glistening with adoration. "Mr. Cruz creates one-of-a-kind pieces. He never creates the same Greek character twice."

"Never?" asked the woman, pressing a dainty hand with a rock of a diamond on her husband's arm. At least, I assumed it was her husband.

"No, ma'am. He wants each collector to have a true original."

"Impressive," added the husband.

"He is." Oh boy. Looked like Missy had a bit of hero-worship for her boss. Couldn't blame her. "Are you interested in this piece, Mr. Cooper?"

He bit his lip, staring at the sculpture with crossed arms for a full minute before nodding. "Yes, we'll take it. But we're from out of town. Can you pack it for travel? We fly home Sunday."

"Absolutely." Missy swished around them, her A-line skirt flaring with the turn as she sauntered back to the counter, her pretty curls bouncing on her shoulder. "Let me ring you up, and we'll take care of it for you."

They followed her to pay for the purchase, his wife smiling at the joy she saw on her husband's face. He took her hand, then lifted their joined hands to his mouth. He brushed his lips over the back of her knuckles, before dropping it and tending to Missy. A pang of . . . something squeezed my heart. It was such a small thing. A fleeting moment between two people who obviously had loved each other for a long time. It wasn't a clingy, needy touch, but a swift, careful one that said so much. A deep, knowing kind of love.

It pricked inside my chest. I was thirty-eight, even though I looked younger, and I'd yet to experience anything close to what that couple had. Sure, I'd had plenty of boyfriends in the past, mostly human, which I always ended up breaking off before it got too serious. There was no way I could settle with a human. Even if he accepted the fact that I was a supernatural, I still didn't want to outlive him by a couple of hundred years. I'd only had one serious relationship. That one ended because, well, he just didn't get me.

Derek had moved to New Orleans to finish his residency as a doctor. My cousin Drew introduced him to me and my sisters so he'd have some contacts in the witch world. At first, he was wonderful. So kind and attentive to my interests and my other hobbies. Well, to be completely honest, my artwork wasn't a hobby. It was a dream. He'd thought my obsession with comics and quirky drawings endearing. His words, not mine. But after a year, he started hinting that I should start being more serious, which meant dressing more like a grown-up and doing more adultish things, like attend boring-ass coven cocktail parties with him.

I tried. I really did. But when he finally flat-out told me I needed to stop acting like a teenager and become the kind of partner he wanted to support his lifestyle in the upper echelon of society in the witch world, I had to let him go.

I snickered even though it still stung, remembering the look of shock on his perfect face when I broke up with him. And I do mean perfect, like Michelangelo flawless. To see that serene marble crack into disbelief was more comical than hurtful. He couldn't believe that I—the immature pseudo-artist and waitress—was giving up all the magnanimous wonder that was Dr. Derek Charles Sullivan, wealthy aristocrat and respected warlock. Never mind the fact that he'd used me and my family contacts to be introduced into that society he wanted so badly. Sometimes, I thought that was all he'd wanted from me in the first place.

He'd actually sent me a birthday e-card a few months after we broke up, wishing me well and letting me know he had no hard feelings after the breakup. Pfft. Seriously? But *then* I'd noticed he made sure that he sent the e-card from his professional email, the signature stamped with his title at the bottom, *Head of Coven, Greater Baton Rouge.* He'd climbed the coven ladder and assumed control of Baton Rouge and the surrounding area in less than three months after we'd broken up. He was basically showing me what I'd missed out on after leaving him. It had only made me grateful and more sure that breaking up had been the right thing to do. Sending me that damn card to rub it in my face screamed loud and clear that he was not for me. What a dick. I was relieved to be rid of him.

The world of witches was a small circle, so our choice for spouses was practically microscopic. Hence, the reason my sisters and I were all still single, now in our thirties. Well, Jules was actually forty-two, though she looked younger than all of us with her pixie-size self.

That was what the annual Coven Guild Summit was really all about. It was supposed to be a gathering of coven heads to share the current status of each region. Jules always dragged one or more of us with her. Every head brought an entourage to the final cocktail party to end the summit, which had resulted in more than one marriage over the decades.

Thankfully, Jules had stopped begging me to go for obvious reasons and I was always graciously excused. The last thing in the world I wanted was to have Dr. Derek gloating over me with some model-leggy blonde on his arm.

It wasn't that I missed him. Not even remotely. It was that he'd made me feel bad about my dreams. Made me feel small. Less. And because I'd yet to fully go for and make those dreams come true, I didn't want to be reminded of my failure. It was like his comments about my pitiful attempt at being an artist had stabbed holes in my sails, and I couldn't make myself venture out into open water just in case he was right and I'd end up sinking and drowning.

So I kept those dreams close to my chest, refusing to go too far outside my comfort zone. Jules knew, but she didn't push me. I'd go for it when I was ready.

And standing here, staring at Mateo's insanely beautiful talent in stunning works of sculpture, made me want to curl into a fetal position and hide those dreams forever. Maybe Derek was right. Maybe I was a joke.

"Evie?"

I jerked around and gasped in surprise, not having heard him walk up behind me. Still sweaty, but now with his hair pulled back in a short ponytail, some of it falling free, he scowled.

"You scared the crap out of me."

He eased into my personal space. "Are you okay?"

I glanced around, realizing the couple had already left and Missy wasn't even behind her counter. I'd been standing in a corner of the gallery, staring at some oil painting of a live oak in abstract colors for I don't know how long.

"Of course." My voice was too high-pitched, almost squeaky. "Why wouldn't I be?"

"I don't know." He inched even closer, staring with too much intensity.

I got a good whiff of his natural scent mixed with sweat and some kind of masculine soap that sent my pulse rocketing. Old Spice? Surely Old Spice couldn't smell that good and make me want to lick him.

"Um, I was just admiring this painting." I pointed, trying to draw his overly observant gaze away from me.

He looked at the landscape, burning bright in fiery reds, oranges, and yellows. "That's one of Sandra's pieces."

"Sandra?"

"One of the artists who rents space in the gallery to exhibit their work." His attention swiveled back to me, a frown creasing his brow again. "You seem on edge or something."

"Not at all." I swallowed and stepped back, then glanced at my watch. "Look. I do have a ton of stuff to do before my shift tonight."

"I thought you said you didn't have to work tonight."

"Oh, well, yeah. Jules said she needed me last minute." I shrugged, never having been a great liar.

"My four hours aren't up yet." He looked downright sad.

Guilt punched me in the gut and called me a total asshole. I couldn't bail on him because of my own insecurities, just because I was feeling like a failure while he was amazing in every single way—except for turning into a monster once a month when unhexed.

"Um. Yeah. Right. Well, let's go get that over with." I strolled on back toward his workshop and settled on the floor like before, yanking out my tablet before he even made his way in behind me.

But I didn't work on my art as I should've been doing. My inspiration had deflated faster than Derek's ego the night I'd broken up with him. I focused on my own misery and cowardice while I read some comics on the Webtoon's app for the next hour until my time was up. And I certainly did *not* peek at the sexy werewolf while he created unimaginable beauty out of little steel rods.

Nope. Not once.

CHAPTER 8

~EVIE~

"Four hours." JJ said it like he was repeating a fungus diagnosis—half disbelief, half disgust.

"Yeah. So?" I shrugged and wiped the bar for the third time, my hands moving nonstop since I came on shift two hours ago.

"I thought Jules didn't like for y'all to work with werewolves."

"So did I. But apparently, it's more of a tread-carefully-when-working-with-werewolves policy. Kind of a gray area."

JJ shook his head as he swiped a credit card on the register, gave me one of his looks, then marched down the bar to pass the receipt and card to the customer sitting at the end.

"He doesn't think it's a good idea," said Charlie, sipping his Poison Apple Sangria with a long straw.

Charlie was JJ's best friend. He was always impeccably dressed and had zero filter. He was also one of the few humans who knew what we were.

"It's just work."

He smirked. "You're so cute when you lie."

"I'm not lying."

"See? So cute."

JJ sauntered back, doing that accusing eyebrow thing.

This was ridiculous. I planted a hand on my hip. "What?"

"What do you mean what?" He folded his muscly arms across his perfect chest. "I saw him lose control the other night. For a split second, I thought he was going to disembowel you."

"Oh, please." I waved a hand in front of my face like that was crazy talk. Even as I remembered the flash of yellow in his eyes back at Bam's. "He could only do that if he actually shifted into his wolf. And that's the whole problem. He can't."

Which meant I was totally safe, right?

JJ's gaze narrowed. "I also saw a different look in his eyes the other night."

"Do tell," said Charlie, sipping his sangria with brows raised.

I shifted closer. "Different how?"

"The hungry kind," JJ said. "Not for blood."

"You're imagining things. He needs help. Jules gave the okay, and that's all there is to it."

"That's all there is to it?"

"Yep." I avoided his all-seeing gaze by scanning my tables. Hell, if I didn't know he was human, I'd peg him for a vampire with his supersonic intuition.

"So what did you do with your four hours today?" JJ asked casually, nodding to a new customer who settled on a stool.

Charlie snickered.

"I can't believe you told Charlie."

"It's not a secret."

"It was private," I gritted out.

"Maybe," added Charlie with a superior air. "But the real reason you don't want anyone to know is because you've got the hots for your hot werewolf."

See. No filter.

"Whatever." I shrugged. "We haven't met yet today. We're meeting after my shift." I scrubbed at a nonexistent smudge on the bar top.

JJ chuckled way too knowingly, taking Charlie's empty glass off the bar. "Hang on. I need to hear this."

He popped over to the new customer, retrieved a draft beer and delivered it, then returned to my side.

"Sooo . . . " He drew out the word with a grin. "Why couldn't you meet until after dark? And where are you spending your four hours tonight?"

"You can do a lot in four hours, Evie sweetie." Charlie tossed a bill on the bar.

Rolling my eyes, I informed them in my no-nonsense voice, "Clara needed my help restocking the shelves at the shop, then Jules needed me to run some errands for the kitchen. I mean, I do have responsibilities, JJ."

He stared up and to the left, mumbling to himself, "If my calculations are correct, that would've taken you about three hours. I was the one who delivered the boxes to the shop. Clara's shipment wouldn't have taken long nor would Jules's kitchen errands. So you were either avoiding him purposefully today or you just wanted to wait to meet him for some other nefarious reason tonight."

"Bingo." Charlie grinned.

Damn him!

"You're so wrong." He was so right. "I do have a life of my own." True, but I was totally avoiding Mateo. Honestly, I wasn't even sure why exactly. I just needed some space.

"I'm sure you do," he said snarkily, sharing a look with Charlie. I punched JJ in the arm.

"Ow." I shook my hand, feeling like I'd just hit a brick wall. "You need to slow up on the workouts, Mr. Universe."

"Blasphemer. Shut your mouth." Charlie swiveled on his stool toward me. "His physique is the perfect bait as my wingman."

JJ ignored him, keeping his focus on me. "Stop trying to distract me. What are you doing after hours with him?" His expression had turned serious, stern even. He had his big brother face on, even though we were in no way related and I was way older than him.

"Fine. We're having wild, wolfish sex by the light of the moon."

"Who's having wild, wolfish sex?" Violet practically appeared out of thin air right behind me at the bar.

I jumped at her sneaky sidling. "No one," I snapped.

She grinned. "Oh, Evie. Go, girl!"

"I was kidding! I would never—"

"Oh, yes, she would," said Charlie.

Violet tsked. Her shoulder-length hair was still blue. "Well, you're crazy to not take that for a ride. The artists are always good in bed. Trust me." She winked at me, then turned to JJ. "Two Abita Ambers and a Grim and Tonic."

He nodded and opened the cooler.

Ignoring her question, I switched the subject. "I liked the fuchsia. Why'd you change it so soon?"

Wearing a spaghetti-strap black tank top, she shrugged the shoulder with the blue-and-black inked orchid. "I don't think I'm the kind of girl who can pull off pink."

I snorted. "If anyone can pull off pink, it's you. What? Was it too cheery for you?"

"Fuck off, Sissy."

Violet was the only one who still called me that childhood nickname. I still don't know how I inherited it as the second oldest rather than Jules. Her sassy attitude switched from low to high beams in a flash. She grinned like a fiend and leaned forward on her elbows.

"So what's up with you and that werewolf? Jules won't say shit as usual." She waggled her eyebrows.

"Put your eyebrows in neutral. I'm just helping him with . . . well, I'm not sure how to describe it."

"I do." JJ slid the two beers to Violet, stabbing a cocktail straw in the mixed drink. "Apparently, this werewolf is cursed, unable to change into his wolf for the past couple months. *And*"—he leaned close with a conspiratorial gleam—"he needs to be close to Evie in order to calm the beast within, so they're"—he air-quoted—"spending time together." He smirked like the conspiratorial devil he was. "Every day. For hours."

Violet cackled like a demon, and now they were both waggling eyebrows. Ridiculous children.

With an exasperated sigh, I said, "It's not like that."

"Why not?" asked Violet. "It would be like that if I were you."

"Ditto," said Charlie.

"This is business. That's *all*. End of story." I flipped my ponytail as I focused on wiping the bar again. "He's a werewolf." And he didn't like me like that.

"So you've said," added JJ.

Violet gave me an are-you-kidding-me look, then passed it to JJ who chuckled. They could clown me all they wanted. Mateo was just a guy I was helping. A job. Maybe kind of a friend. But that's all.

I rolled my eyes, propping a hand on my hip. "If you two bitches are done, we actually have customers to serve."

"Yeah," said JJ, humming with appreciation as he leered over my shoulder and bit his bottom lip. "And you just got a new one."

In the back corner booth, Mateo was seated with a menu in hand. The unexpected sight of him knocked me stupid for a second, my pulse hammering hard and fast. He glanced up and caught my gaze, giving me a hello nod. I licked my lips and smiled with a little wave. There was tension in the line of his shoulders and a tight expression on his face, but even so, he seemed glad to see me. No, he seemed relieved.

JJ leaned close and whispered, "Looks like someone couldn't wait till you got off shift."

"Shut up." I pushed off the bar and stood straight, reeling in my wayward feelings of excitement at the sight of his perfect, broody features under the dim lamplight. It was okay to be excited about meeting up with a friend. Totally normal. Maybe being this breathless wasn't, but I'd just ignore that for the moment.

"I so need one of those of my own," said Charlie with a sigh. "Good night, ladies." He waved to all three of us, then headed for the door.

I dropped the rag on the counter, ignoring the two tittering asshats behind me, and made my way around tables to the back booth.

I couldn't miss the way his sultry brown eyes ate up every inch of me as I walked closer. I tried to steady my breathing and paste my casual smile in place. I was failing miserably, but I summoned my best acting skills.

"Hi. I didn't expect you so soon."

"I needed to—" He stretched one hand across the table as if to touch me, then pulled back and gripped the menu like it was a life raft. Staring down, he cleared his throat, but it was still rusty and rough when he said, "I needed to see you. Be near you." He winced. "I know that sounds so creepy."

"Very creepy."

He looked up, horrified. But then he relaxed when he caught me smiling.

"I get it. I've been doing some reading on werewolves."

"You have?"

"I know how your magic works."

"How do you mean?"

Witch magic was very complex. Each witch contained strengths, talents one might have but not another. Even vampires and grims had levels of potency in their magic. While one might be born with such speed it looked as if they disappeared rather than moved blindingly fast, it was different for werewolves. They were all born with the same level of magic, the same curse. And with that curse came a creative gift.

"Well, I read that, the way your magic works, you can't use the gift without the curse. Meaning, you can't work creatively if you can't purge the wolf regularly. So it makes sense that my magic as a hex-breaker somehow dulls the hex that's been put on you. It's just natural." He stared intently. I shrugged. "At least, that's how I see it."

"I think you're right." His hand edged across the table again, but he stopped and whispered, "Do you mind if I touch you?"

I lost all my words for a minute as I contemplated that broad, long-fingered hand with rough calluses touching me . . . everywhere. When he started to draw back, obviously thinking my slack-jawed non-response was a rejection, I jerked my hand forward and covered his, curling my fingers under his palm.

He gave me a tight squeeze, closed his eyes, and smiled. Blowing out a heavy breath, he opened them again. "Thank you."

"It's fine. Touch always amplifies magic much stronger than proximity. It's okay if you need to, you know, touch me from time to time."

No, that didn't sound dirty at all. But seriously, he could touch me anywhere, any time. No complaints here. His eyes flashed gold for a split second, which reminded me . . .

"So how has Alpha been today? He bothering you?"

Mateo's lopsided grin spread wide to light up his whole face. "Constantly."

"Well, you tell him I said to behave."

"He hears you. But he never wants to behave." Mateo's smile slipped, his eyes turning molten. I was suddenly aware of his callused thumb caressing the top of my hand.

"Right." I gave him a squeeze and let go, glancing back at the bar where JJ mixed three cocktails while staring at me like a crazy stalker. I also noticed more customers seated in my section. "So what can I get you?"

He straightened, glancing down at the menu again. "Um, one of your microbrews is fine. Pick a good one for me."

"Sure thing."

I swiveled away and took the drink order for the two guys and girl sitting in the booth behind him, then sped back to the bar.

"Two Grave Diggers, a Spider Bite Martini, and a Witch's Brew. Make sure you get one of the Brews from the back of the cooler where it's ice cold."

"So," he started with the kind of dramatic pause JJ liked to employ while pouring a shot of tequila into each tumbler for the Grave Diggers. "He couldn't stand to wait till closing to see you, could he?"

I stabbed the cocktail straws into the Grave Diggers and set them on my round serving tray. "I guess so," I said nonchalantly. "Or he just wanted a drink after a long day's work."

He chuckled again, flashing me his megawatt smile, the kind that had all the pretty boys lining up for him. "And that's why he's shooting daggers at me right now."

I glanced over my shoulder, catching Mateo's dark glare on JJ. I spun back to face JJ as he set the beer and frosty mug on my tray, then balanced the martini last.

He propped both his arms on the bar and leaned forward, speaking low so only I could hear him. "Remember what kind of a rule you told me it was?"

I had to actually think back to the earlier part of our conversation.

"Tread carefully, Evie. Jules may have given the okay to work with this wolf, but one thing I know well is men. And that look?" He glanced over my shoulder, then back at me. "That's a dangerous one."

Determined to pretend his warning had no effect on me, I turned quickly and maneuvered through the tables, serving the booth behind Mateo before I set his beer and mug before him.

"Are you hungry?" My heart did a triple flip at that seemingly innocent question.

His brown eyes scanned my face, then fell back to the menu. He cleared his throat. "What's good?"

"Well, Jules is a killer cook, so pretty much everything."

"Your sister is the chef here?"

"Yep. A woman of many talents."

He didn't respond, pausing long enough to make it awkward before he dropped his beautiful brown eyes back to the menu.

"So you and your sisters really went for the witches theme, huh?"

"Well, for the drink menu, yeah." I laughed. "Hiding in plain sight and all that. Jules is a tad more serious about her food."

"I see that. I'll take the Cajun chargrilled oysters and the braised beef po'boy."

"Coming right up."

The late crowd pushed in, filling all my tables and keeping me blessedly busy. I couldn't get past what JJ had said. Of course Mateo was dangerous. He was a freaking werewolf. Somehow, though, when I looked into those warm brown eyes, I didn't feel like I was in danger. I felt like I was with a friend. Maybe that was the trouble. He appeared harmless to me, when I knew a beast was caged inside somewhere.

I checked on Mateo as I would any customer, bringing him another beer before he closed his tab and remained in the booth, obviously waiting for me to finish up. He kept himself busy with a sketch pad and pencil.

When I occasionally glanced his way as I served drinks or meandered back from the kitchen, his eyes would always look up from his sketch and snag me for an uncomfortable few seconds. Then I'd force my attention elsewhere and pretend the heat crawling up my chest and neck wasn't caused by his hypnotic, dark gaze.

I cleared my last tab in the register and delivered the credit card to the couple on a round-top near Mateo's booth. "Thanks so much," I said before easing slowly over to him.

He watched me come, unashamedly taking me in. Was he attracted to me? I'd thought so before, then realized he was just admiring my quirky taste in T-shirts. The hot looks he kept tossing my way could make any girl's knees turn to jelly. And I was definitely one of them. I had plans for us tonight, but now I thought it was maybe a bad idea. My lusty imagination was running away from me. He'd been sitting in that booth for three hours. Technically, I only owed him one more hour. I headed closer to his booth, wondering what I should do. Maybe I should—

"What's spinning through that head of yours?" His mouth ticked up on one side.

"What do you mean?"

"You look like you're planning your escape."

"Me? No! I mean, that's so silly." Yes, definitely. Maybe not my escape, but certainly rethinking a night of cozy movie-watching on the couch together. Especially after three hours of his constant lingering looks whose meaning I couldn't decipher. "What would I have to escape from?"

He tucked his sketch pad in a black messenger bag, then unfolded himself out of the booth, shouldering his bag. It was then I was reminded how tall he was. I wasn't a short woman, but he made me feel significantly smaller. He had a broad chest and shoulders with lean muscle, not bulky, but there was restrained power in this body of his. I knew it for a fact since I'd seen footage of werewolves in their beast form. I'd never encountered one live, or I'd likely be dead already. They were the true monsters of the night, the ones that mothers warned their children about. *Don't stray from the path, Little Red.* Because if this kind of wolf caught you during a full moon, that was it. As my grandma Maybelle once told me, "Game over."

I stared up at Mateo and gulped, actually internalizing what kind of monster he'd be when we finally broke the hex. His warm gaze sharpened, as if he knew what was flitting through my head.

"You sure about that?"

What were we talking about?

"Sure about what?"

"Whether or not you'd like to escape."

"I'm sure." I didn't sound sure. "I have a movie marathon planned for us at my house tonight."

His shoulders had stiffened, and not from the mention of a movie marathon. His gaze had shifted over my shoulder toward the bar where JJ polished glasses and watched us. "I don't think your boyfriend would like that."

"My boyfriend?" I glanced at JJ again, then tossed my head back and laughed. "He's not my boyfriend."

Mateo's scowl softened only slightly as he glared toward the bar. "I think he wants to be."

That was it. He was adorable. And all my anxiety vanished like morning mist. I hooked my arm around his and led him toward the door. "No. He definitely doesn't. He's more of a big brother. And if anything, he'd prefer to be your boyfriend. Not mine."

Finally, the cloud lifted from his frowny face, and he blessed me with a dazzling smile. "I'm not his type."

He pushed open the door for me to step through first. I twisted and grabbed his arm again, my ponytail swishing. "Oh? What's your type?"

Why did I just ask that?

I expected him to give me some snarky reply, but instead he stared down at me and hauled me closer to his side. My fingers wrapping his lovely, flexed biceps, he whispered softly, close to my ear, "Ask me another day. Not on a night like tonight."

I smiled up at him as if he'd said a joke, because his words were so cryptic. I wanted to ask what he meant. Like, what was so particular about tonight? My curiosity told me to go ahead and ask, but the tightness of his jaw and the long stride he'd set toward the house told me I'd better do as he said and ask another day. For once, I listened to my sensible side.

CHAPTER 9

~MATEO~

"Just give me a minute. I'm still processing it."

Evie bounced in her seat next to me on the couch, her legs folded underneath her, grinning like a crazy person. An adorable crazy person.

"You loved it, didn't you? It blew your mind, right?" She made the gesture with her hands for her brain exploding.

"Yeah. It kind of did."

"I knew it!" She jumped up and raced into the kitchen, yelling, "We need more popcorn!" I heard the whirr of her air popper being plugged in and the kernels being poured into it. She reappeared in the archway that connected the living room to the kitchen. "Although"—she looked at her watch, a small pinch in the middle of her forehead—"it's well past our four hours, and I'm sure you have to start work early in the morning."

"I'm not going to sleep until I find out what happens in *Return of the Jedi*. So you can kick me out if you want, but I'm taking your DVD home with me."

Her face lit up like a damn Christmas tree. She clasped her hands together under her chin and did a little weird shuffle dance in place before skating away on her socks and disappearing toward the popcorn popper. I couldn't help but chuckle at her baffling excitement over my response to *Empire Strikes Back*. But seriously, Vader was Luke's father? I never saw that coming.

As if she heard my thoughts, she yelled from the kitchen, "I can't believe you never knew Darth Vader was his father. How could you not have heard that over the years?" She returned a minute later with her Storm Trooper helmet–shaped popcorn bowl and plopped down with the bowl between us.

"Like I said, I don't really watch TV or anything."

"And apparently, you follow zero pop culture social media sites."

I shrugged. "Not really."

"It's like you don't even exist in the modern world." She popped back up and walked to the DVD player to switch out the movies. "It's kind of unreal, Mateo."

I shivered, loving my name on her lips.

I'd like something else of mine on her lips.

Damn. He'd been quiet for a solid two hours. I'd almost forgotten about him.

No worries, brother. I'll always be here for you.

To annoy the fuck out of me, yeah.

She dropped the disc on the floor and bent over to pick it up.

Please, no.

Mmmm. God. Damn. Her curvy ass would fit perfectly in my hands.

We've had this conversation. Stop talking about her like that.

Before I could suppress him, an aggressive rumble vibrated up my throat. Evie stood with the disc and snapped her head around, concern etched on her face.

"You okay?" she asked quietly.

I pressed back into the sofa, shifting my gaze away from her to take a handful of popcorn.

"Mm-hmm. Fine," I muffled around a mouthful of popcorn.

There was no way I was letting Alpha loose on a woman while under this hex. No telling what he'd push me to do when my blood was up. Especially not a woman as sweet and soft and pretty as Evie.

Sweet and soft is right. Bet she's delicious and tight too.

Shut up!

I closed my eyes to focus and push him back. It worked sometimes, especially when Evie was around. By the time she'd changed discs and took her seat, I felt almost normal. Even if my pants felt tighter.

"You sure you're okay?"

"What? Oh yeah. Fine."

Her gaze flicked to my leg. I was tapping my foot again. Gripping my knee, I steadied myself and focused on the opening credits, pretending not to notice her staring at me with concern. We both settled in, watching together quietly.

Unfortunately, Alpha had worked on my nerves. Or Evie had. I don't know, but my heart was pumping hard. She repositioned herself on the sofa, her legs folded underneath her, body angled toward me against the sofa back. The scent of her—feminine, powdery, floral—invaded my senses. All I could do was think about how good it would feel to have her wrapped around me, beneath me, on top of me. To touch her was like being struck by lightning— electric but shocking me stone-still at the same time. The aftershock was a racing pulse that made me fear my heart would pound right out of my chest. And at the same time, she calmed my beast. It was the craziest fucking sensation I'd ever known.

Before tonight, it had never felt quite like this . . . like temptation. I was fine with her in public and even at my gallery, in my workshop. But here, on her sofa, in the dim lighting with the house asleep, it gave a man ideas. Very bad ideas.

Fan-fucking-tastic ideas. Roll with it.

By the time Leia strangled Jabba the Hutt, I was curling my fists into balls and breathing through my mouth to avoid smelling her. She was driving me wild. Literally.

Suddenly, the kitchen light went on, and a pretty blonde walked into the living room, long hair grazing her waist. I jumped to my feet.

"Ack!" she squeaked.

Evie jumped to her feet too. But probably at my sudden movement, not the young woman who was obviously her sister standing there, staring with wide blue eyes. She looked identical to the one with blue hair, Violet. Except . . . nicer. She didn't wear a cynical smile or black nail polish.

"S-so sorry, Evie. I didn't realize you had company."

"It's okay," I said, tucking my hands into my pockets to avoid coming across as dangerous. "I—I should get going."

"What do you mean?" asked Evie. "We're not even halfway."

"You were right. I have a lot to do in the morning. It's getting late. I've imposed on you long enough."

She snorted. "If you were imposing, I'd tell you."

That, I believed. She might look all pretty lines and soft edges, but she wouldn't put up with any shit. She definitely wouldn't want a half-crazed werewolf making an aggressive pass at her on her sofa.

Shoving a hand through my hair, feeling it go in all directions, I said, "All the same. I should go."

"You don't have to go on my account," said the blonde.

"This is my sister, Clara. Clara, this is Mateo."

Clara smiled, and for a second I thought I literally saw a halo of light beam around her porcelain face. "You're the werewolf."

"I am. I'll be going."

"Are you feeling well?" she asked, stepping closer.

"I'm sorry?"

"You have a very"—she tilted her head—"erratic aura right now."

"Erratic?" Evie propped both hands on her hips.

I let out a nervous laugh. "Makes sense. I'm feeling kind of erratic."

"What does that mean?" Evie glanced between us.

When Clara stepped closer to me, I jerked back a full two feet. She froze and raised her hands as if warding off a wild dog. I laughed again, but it sounded more maniacal.

"Do you feel like you're about to shift, Mateo?"

Her voice was low and soft, soothing. It made me angry. I wasn't about to blow. Not in that way. She moved even closer, the scent of her filling my nostrils. A growl vibrated in my head, but I refused to let Alpha have any voice in this room. Evie would kick me out and refuse to help me fix this fucking curse. And what a curse. I was seriously losing control.

"No," I said as calmly and evenly as I could manage, but it came out growly all the same. "I'm not about to shift. I just need to leave."

"Maybe I can help," chimed in Clara, her features more elflike than her twin's, her voice sweeter.

She looks like a fucking fairy. Minus the wings.

Without my answer, she crossed the room and grabbed both my forearms. I almost stumbled back, but she held me firm even though I was double her size and weight.

"There now." Her voice had a chime-like quality, but I could barely hear it over the rushing sound in my ears and the overwhelming flood of complete euphoria pumping into my veins. After I don't know how long, she released me. "Is that better?" She smiled, which turned her face angelic.

"Yeah." My voice sounded rusty. "Much. Thank you."

The edge of insanity had receded, replaced by blissful peace and a giddy sort of high.

"What are you?"

She smiled brighter. "I'm an Aura. Have you heard of them?"

"Yeah. You can give—" I pointed my finger between us, back and forth. "Do that. What you just did."

She laughed. "It'll only be temporary. From what Evie told us, you won't be back to yourself until the hex is gone. But I hope it makes you feel better for a while."

"Thanks." I chanced a look at Evie who looked . . . pissed off.

"I'll show you out." Evie marched to the DVD player and ejected the disc.

I headed out of the living room and down the hallway to the front door where I opened it and waited for Evie, sucking in a lungful of air that didn't have her intoxicating scent. She strode up a few seconds later and handed me the *Return of the Jedi* DVD.

"Go ahead and finish it when you have time." She crossed her arms, her frown smoothing a little. "Are you sure you're okay?" Concern edged away her irritation.

"Yeah. I'm good now."

Her frown reappeared. "Do you still want to meet tomorrow?"

"Of course I do. Why wouldn't I?"

"Clara's spell may carry you through the day." She lifted her chin. "You may not need my presence to, you know, focus or whatever."

She stared beyond me, watching a couple heading toward Magazine and the nightlife in full swing.

"Evie." I edged closer, drawing her attention back to me. "I still need to be"—*with* you, *near* you—"around you."

Inside you.

I waved my hand holding the DVD in a circle. "You know, our agreement."

"I haven't forgotten our agreement. I'm just saying—"

"Is nine okay? Or do you have to work at the shop?"

"No, I don't usually work the shop. Clara will handle it. That's really her gig with Isadora. Violet and I work the bar. Livvy handles all the bookkeeping and marketing. Jules handles the kitchen."

"So, nine then?"

"Sure."

She moved to close the door, her mood having plummeted since my little episode when I obviously freaked her out.

Before she could shut it all the way, I put my hand on it to stop her. "Thank you, Evie."

She glanced up through dark lashes, and I swear that spell pumped a new rush of cracked-out bliss into my veins.

"What for?"

I smiled. "For showing me *Star Wars*."

"*A New Hope*," she corrected. She didn't smile, but her features softened. "And *Empire Strikes Back*." She glanced down at the DVD in my hand. "If you don't finish the third one, we can no longer be friends." She said it with a completely serious face.

"We're friends?"

"Of course we are, you idiot."

"Friends." I backed up and released the door, grinning like a, well, an idiot. "Awesome."

"Good night." Her mouth quirked as she shut the door.

"Sweet dreams, Evie."

As I made my way through the streets, I reveled in the realization that Evie was my friend. I wanted to be more, but there was no trusting my wolf to allow *more* to happen. Not right now. Not yet. But maybe after this hex was broken and I was back in control . . . Just maybe.

I knew for a fact that the sensation of euphoria pumping through my veins all the way home and well into the morning, since I couldn't sleep for hours, had little to do with the Aura's spell. And everything to do with Evie.

CHAPTER 10

~EVIE~

"Did I do something wrong?" Clara hovered a spoon over the open carton of Tutti Frutti ice cream clutched to her chest.

I stared at the sweetest sister in the whole wide world.

"No," I answered on a huff. Though I tried not to be a petulant child, I couldn't help it. I wasn't one of those people who could disguise my feelings. I'd been told more than once that whatever I was thinking or feeling was clearly written all over my face.

"Then why are you mad at me?"

"I'm not mad at you, Clara." I definitely sounded mad, rather furious actually, which only made me growl in frustration.

"Did I interrupt something?" She quirked a dark blonde brow and shoveled a spoonful of the rainbow-colored ice cream into her mouth.

"Pffft." I opened the fridge and scanned the containers from the Cauldron's kitchen. Jules often brought home the leftovers, whatever she didn't give away to the kitchen and waitstaff or JJ. Opening one to find her crawfish fettucine, I popped it into the microwave. "There was nothing to interrupt. So don't even worry about it."

"Do you want there to be something to interrupt? He's a—"

"I know, I know. He's a werewolf. No need to give me the same lecture JJ did."

"No. I was going to say he's a nice guy."

I spun in my socks and tilted my head. Not what I was expecting. "Nice?"

She smiled. "Totally nice." She flipped her spoon in the air to gesture. "Well, except for the scary beast he's holding back. I think he wanted to eat me when I touched him." She must've seen some kind of reaction on my face. "Oh, not Mateo. His wolf, I mean. But Mateo, he's very sweet."

"Sweet."

She gobbled another spoonful of Tutti Frutti. "Totally sweet."

I didn't know what to say to that. Yeah. He was sweet. Totally. And beautiful and crazy talented. And adorable in how little he knew about pop culture. I mean, who in the modern age didn't know that Darth Vader is Luke Skywalker's father? Mateo. That's who. Absolutely ridiculous. And completely cute as hell. I had to admit that watching his slack-jawed reaction was the highlight of my entire month. Maybe my whole year.

"You're smiling. So you're not mad at me anymore?"

After pulling the dish out of the microwave, I grabbed a fork out of the drawer. "Clara, I'm not mad at you."

"You were when I cast a joy spell on Mateo. See, you're making that frowny face again."

I twirled a giant bite of fettucine around my fork and shoved it into my mouth to avoid responding.

"Very mature." She smiled and dropped the spoon in the sink and put the ice cream back in the freezer. "You want to know what I think?"

I chewed, swallowed, then stuffed another overly big bite into my mouth. "I'm hungwy," I managed to mumble around a mouthful. Yep. That was me. Super mature. Eating my feelings.

"I think you like this werewolf."

I tried to scoff, but only kind of choked on the pasta. Clara took my bowl, set it on the counter, and patted my back until I managed to swallow and inhale a deep breath.

"And because you like him, you didn't really like your sister helping him in the way that you help him. Because it's obvious your hex-breaking magic has a positive effect on him the way my magic does. Makes him need you somehow." She smoothed her hand down my back. "You just got a little jealous. And that's okay. You like him."

I opened my mouth to protest, but then I realized who I was talking to. Clara could read people better than anyone I knew. It had to do with her gift as an Aura. She just knew shit, what people were thinking and feeling and, holy hell, she was totally right. I was freaking jealous! Which was so stupid.

"We're just friends," I admitted softly.

"Friends," said Clara, as if trying out a new word she'd never heard. She handed me back my bowl of fettucine. "That works, I think."

"You think?"

"You don't want to be his friend?"

"Of course I want to be his friend."

"Then I don't see the problem."

"There is no problem."

"Then why are you scarfing down fettucine at midnight and growling at me?"

"Why are you eating ice cream at midnight?"

"Evie," she said with a laugh in a way that said I was being ridiculous. Because I was. "You know I have a sweet tooth. There's no time limit on my need for Tutti Frutti ice cream or lemon tarts. Or turtle cheesecake. It just happens." She shrugged with a smile like *it's a fact*. And it kind of was.

This was true. Clara had a serious craving for all things sugary. How she remained so thin and willowy was a mystery to me. She and Violet were built like our dad, leaner than the rest of us. It didn't matter how many tarts or pastries she consumed, she remained the same. I didn't mind my curves, but I could definitely tell you that this fettucine was going straight to my ass. I didn't care. I needed these carbs more than I needed a not-fat ass.

"Everyone needs friends, Evie. Especially him."

"Especially him, how?"

"Besides, friends make the best lovers." She pecked me on the cheek. "Night night."

"Why would you even say that?" She giggled and shut the door when I said even louder, "I never said anything about lovers."

Through the window, I watched her shuffle back toward the carriage house.

That's when I noticed Z crouched on the counter staring at me. I scooped him up in my free hand and slung his upper body over my shoulder. He let me carry him however I wanted, never putting up a fight.

"I didn't, Z. I never said a damn thing about lovers. I mean, he's cute and all. I'll totally admit that." Z started his sputtering purr as

I held on to him with one hand and balanced my late-night snack of fettucine for two down the hall to my bedroom on the first floor.

"I mean, okay, he's hot even. I'm not going to deny that at all."

Z let out a scratchy meow.

"Exactly. That doesn't mean I want to sleep with him. I see hot guys every day in the bar. I don't want to jump their bones or anything." Z said nothing. "Clara's right. Friends are good."

I set Z on the foot of my bed. After slipping out of my clothes and into my sleep shirt and shorts with leprechauns drinking green beer, I devoured the pasta, brushed my teeth, and jumped into bed.

"What should I read tonight, Z?" But he was already curled into a ball and sleeping.

I scanned the books on my bedside table. Yes, books. I'd set aside my comics the last few nights in favor of some light reading like *The Demons of the Night*, *The Beast of Gevaudan*, and *Were-wolves: The Origin Story*. I'd raided Jules's library, hoping to gain some insight into Mateo's problem. Last night's reading about the werewolf in Gevaudan gave me nightmares, so I decided to go back to the origins book tonight. Facts were good. And not too scary. Right?

The first part had listed the basics of the life of a werewolf—strengths and weaknesses. Some I knew. Some I didn't. Like the need to balance the curse of the beast and the gift of the arts that dwelled in all werewolves.

The most interesting fact I learned last night, which I absolutely did *not* bring up with Mateo, was the carnal impulses of a were-wolf. Their need for sex and blood was the curse of the wolf inside them. It said they released the beast at least once a month to hunt and satisfy their craving for blood. I also learned that some changed more than once a month as needed. They weren't dependent on the full moon to shift, though many felt the urge strongest at this time.

But it was the facts listed about the sex drive of werewolves that *really* had my eyes bugging out. Words like *insatiable need* and *rough coupling* and *aggressive bed-play*, then finally *pursue his prey until he won her.* First off, wowza. That little lesson got me all tingly. But then I was like . . . huh? I hadn't seen any evidence of Mateo's aggressive sexual nature, like, at all. Which reminded me we were just doing a job together and were friends. Just because werewolves had superhot libidos didn't mean they wanted to bang just any chick. So the truth was that Mateo didn't see me in *that* way.

All cool. No biggie. I was there for him to do a job, to break this hex. I needed to talk to Jules about her plan soon. For tonight, I'd dive into one more history lesson.

On the cover of the book on my lap, the werewolf's eyes, narrowed into slits and hooded, glowed an eerie yellow. A chill spider-walked down my spine as a flash of Mateo on the sofa popped into my mind. When I'd heard him growl, I glanced back, catching the shimmer of fiery gold in his eyes. It was fleeting, mere seconds. But holy cannoli, for that brief moment in time, I wasn't looking at Mateo at all. I was staring at his wolf. And the way he was looking back at me had turned my knees to jelly. If he hadn't recovered so quickly, I might've asked him to leave. But he was so jittery and nervous, I couldn't kick him out. All I'd wanted to do was distract him from whatever was bothering him.

Thank goodness Clara cast her joy spell on him, because I sure as hell wasn't much help. That had annoyed me more than anything. I'd thought my presence was what always calmed him down, but tonight he was more agitated than ever. I couldn't make sense of it.

Sighing, I flipped open the book to the actual origin story. I knew it had to do with a witch who hated her tormentors and had punished him with a curse, but honestly, it wasn't anything I'd been very interested in. Until now. Scanning chapter six, I found what I was looking for.

Ethelinda of Roma descent was one of many witches on the run from the Spanish Inquisition. When finally captured and put into the torture dungeons for her crimes of witchcraft, she was tormented by one particular officer, Capitán Diego Ortega. He was a notorious witch-hunter and gloried in torturing his victims before he eventually killed them. His brutal tactics to force Ethelinda to divulge names of other witches and where other covens were hiding only served to inflame her need for vengeance. While being threatened with an Iron Maiden should she not comply, she conjured a dying curse:

"Men are beasts, Capitán. So be it. Blood of your blood, till the end of time, will curse your name and pay your crime. In every heart, beauty will dwell beside the beast, only the man can tell, who will rule and who will feast. I curse you, Capitán Diego Ortega, and all your male kin."

With the spell spinning in the air, she pressed herself back onto the spikes of the open Iron Maiden, binding the spell with her blood and her death.

Whoa. That was a serious freaking spell. It didn't say what kind of witch she was. What special gift she held. Every witch had a particular power, even though we all had some level of telekinesis and intuitive abilities with nature. I kept reading.

The ironic twist to Ethelinda's tale was that Diego did not stop his witch-hunting ways. Rather the opposite, he became even more feared as the most ruthless witch-hunter during the time of the Inquisition, scouring the countryside, especially in beast form. He gave his wolf free rein and devoured every witch he hunted down, becoming the true beast Ethelinda claimed him to be.

Then there were black-and-white illustrations of women, obviously witches, clothes half-torn, gashes, and mutilation. Yuck. Very similar to what was in the book of *The Beast of Gevaudan.* I shut the book with a quick clap.

"Okay. And that's enough light reading for the night."

Apparently, one of Diego's offspring moved to France to the Gevaudan region at some point a few centuries later. His kin with the curse spread wide. It was pretty chilling when given this sort of evidence that some werewolves truly did let their beasts take over. I turned my lamp off and snuggled down into my covers.

I couldn't imagine Mateo as a bloodthirsty animal, tracking down witches and killing them. I just couldn't see it. He was, like Clara said, a nice guy.

"No way," I mumbled into my pillow, drifting into sleep.

The moon was full and beautiful, shining down on a pool in the warm summer night, stars shimmering on the water like fireflies. It filled me with all good feelings as I inhaled a deep breath and wrapped my arms around myself. The only strange part was a low, vibrating hum in the air.

A twig cracked behind me. Spinning around, I searched the shadows but found nothing. At first. Then, there, two pinpoints of glittering gold pinned me in place. The owner of those feral eyes stepped from the darkness into the moonlight, all nine feet of him in a ghastly, monstrous form. Elongated snout, knifelike teeth, finger-length black claws hanging from his long deformed hands. I noticed, as he stepped closer, the rest of him was covered in sparse patches of black hair, furry only on the ridges of his shoulders and his back.

That low hum rumbled deeper, louder. It wasn't a hum at all, but a vibrating belly-growl coming from the beast stalking nearer. Some survival instinct told me to never run from a hunting predator, but holy hell, my brain shut down and my body took over. Without thinking, I turned and ran straight across the shallow pool, splashing water on my long skirt.

My skirt? I didn't wear skirts. But apparently I did in horrible nightmares. For even through the haze of thinking that this felt way too damn real, I knew I was dreaming. This wasn't real. But the fear pumping my heart into overdrive was definitely hella real.

I ran blindly into the woods, hurdling fallen logs, dodging overgrowth, glancing over my shoulder at the werewolf hunting me, his breath coming out in guttural huffs.

"This isn't real. This isn't real," I mumbled over and over to myself. "Wake up, Evie." I glanced back, catching those golden eyes far too close for comfort. "Wake the fuck up!"

A low-lying branch swatted me across the face, stinging with too much realness. What the hell was this?

Suddenly, I heard the rip and felt the snag of my skirt before I went tumbling to the ground. I rolled over and watched the beast now on all fours, stalking closer, his yellow eyes narrowed on me.

"This isn't real, this isn't real," I murmured, paralyzed as he crawled over my body.

I fell back onto my elbows, mesmerized and horrified by his giant head and hanging jaws and golden eyes. He pressed a giant hand or paw or whatever to the center of my chest, shoving me to the ground, black claws digging through my blouse to prick my skin. My blouse? I didn't *wear blouses. I shook my head as his gaping mouth did something really weird. It, I mean, he . . . smiled?*

"I'm definitely real, baby." His voice was Mateo-like but deeper, like way deeper, like chasms-in-the-middle-of-the-earth deeper. He pressed his snout down to my ear and licked down the column of my neck. "Best not forget it, pretty witch."

ક

I jerked awake, the mid-morning sun streaming through my window. Panting, I looked down at my sleep shirt and felt my neck, thinking there might be claw marks. So stupid. Just a dream. I glanced at my Wolverine clock, his clawed hands pointing at ten and twelve. It felt like I'd just gone to sleep seconds ago, but I'd overslept by hours.

"What the hell?"

My phone vibrated on the nightstand. I jerked it into my lap, my eyes still blurry with sleep and my heart still pounding with the thrilling—no, not thrilling but terrifying, Evie, TER-RI-FY-ING—dream I'd just had. Mateo had texted several times since nine a.m., when I was supposed to be at his place. We'd exchanged phone numbers, but hadn't texted yet. But friends text, right? I scrolled to the top first.

Mateo: Where are you?

Mateo: You okay?

Mateo: I called Mystic Maybelle's. Clara said you were still sleeping. Text when you wake up.

> Me: I'm up!!! Sorry. Overslept. Grabbing
> breakfast then heading over.

Before I could even stumble into the bathroom, my phone vibrated in my hand.

Mateo: Must've been some seriously sweet dream. 😊
See you soon.

"What the—? How did he—?" But no, werewolves weren't psychic. Only witches had that ability. Some of them.

I laughed at my insanity and my ridiculous subconscious for conjuring a dream that did way more than terrify me. Tantalized me, more like. Kind of a wet dream, if I was totally honest with myself. Yeah, now, what would a psychiatrist say about that one?

Yes, well, you see, Dr. Freud, I was a peasant girl running through the woods because a bloodthirsty werewolf chased me. And when he caught me, getting ready to rip me apart, he licked my neck instead and I came in my peasant panties. What's that? Yes, a high-milligram antipsychotic would be agreeable.

No more nighttime reading on werewolves. That was that.

While I took a freezing-cold shower, I couldn't help but wonder what Alpha's voice sounded like in Mateo's head. Somehow, I had a feeling I already knew.

CHAPTER 11

~MATEO~

Evie had been crazy quiet today. She assured me she was fine, but she'd been working on her tablet with her stylus like a madwoman. Completely ignoring me. That also had me wondering what the hell she was working on. But the way she closed her work or pressed her tablet to her chest when I passed by her to get us some waters out of the mini-fridge or find another tool told me it was private. I guess we weren't that kind of friends yet. Still, her behavior was strange, and the way she was looking at me was . . . weird.

Very.

No one was asking you.

You really want to know why she's acting weird?

I heaved a sigh.

Pin her down and fuck it out of her.

Yeah, that'll work.

It would definitely work.

You're so goddamn insane, I can't believe you're actually a part of me.

Believe it. I'm your better half.

That was so ludicrous I didn't bother to respond. I stepped back from the mermaid sculpt and flipped off my torch. Removing my helmet, I stared at her and circled, making sure there were no edges I missed, needing the welds completely smooth. But no. It was just as I'd intended. I couldn't believe it, but I actually met my deadline. By one damn day. And all because of the girl on the futon chair I'd dragged downstairs for her.

I'd noticed she preferred to sit on everything but a damn chair. Bar tops, counters, floors. Anything but actual furniture meant for putting your ass on.

Mmm. Her ass.

Moving on. I didn't want her sitting on my hard garage floor for hours while she waited on me. Even now, she didn't actually sit in the chair like a normal person. She was sideways with both legs dangling over an arm, her tablet leaning against her bent thighs. She never did anything I expected, which I found strangely intriguing. And my little intriguing friend deserved a reward for helping me finish this commission.

After putting all my tools away, I glanced at my watch. Our time wasn't up yet. Strolling over, she immediately closed her tablet cover and sat up.

"All done?" she asked in her perky voice.

I really liked her perky voice. Not the skittish one she had used when she got here today. I told her I didn't care that she was late. She'd waved me off, but somehow she was acting different. Now she seemed almost back to normal. Just . . . quiet.

"I want to take you somewhere to celebrate."

She glanced up. "What are we celebrating?" Then she stuffed her tablet in her backpack.

"I finished the commission, and I owe a lot of that to you."

She stood up and tucked a hand in the back pocket of her jeans, which only accentuated her slim-fitting T-shirt. Today was a graphic of Deadpool riding a bike with a basket full of flowers, holding an umbrella like Mary Poppins with the scripted words *What would Deadpool do?* underneath.

"Oh, come on, you don't owe me anything," she said with an easy smile. Whatever was bothering her earlier seemed to be gone now.

"Evie. When I tell you there's no damn way I'd have finished on time without you, I mean it."

She shuffled a step back with a one-shoulder shrug, a pretty blush pinking her cheeks. "Well, I'm glad I could help."

"Come on. I want to take you somewhere."

"Where?" Her green eyes opened wide. "No! Don't tell me. I love surprises."

"It's not that exciting," I assured her, though something told me she'd think it was.

I grabbed my keys off the key peg on the wall and led her out the open garage door.

"Geez, Mateo. Now you're dumping on the surprise. Don't do that. Let me think it's going to be spectacular."

I smiled and frowned at the same time, pulling the garage door closed behind us. "Then you'd have it built up to be some big thing. I don't want you to be disappointed."

She shoved me on the shoulder and stopped when she caught sight of my truck. "Wow! Vintage?"

Grinning at her appreciation, I replied, "1954 Chevy Classic. Restored her myself."

She rounded to the passenger side, her fingers sliding along the glossy blue paint as she admired my pride and joy. "Very impressive."

"Thank you."

I climbed into the driver's seat as she hopped in on the other side.

She admired the well-kept leather upholstery, sliding her fingers over the seat. I had to look away, the vision of her roaming hands dragging my mind into the gutter.

"I can promise you this," she said. "Any man capable of restoring an old beauty like this couldn't possibly disappoint me with his surprise." She grinned giddily. "I'm just so shocked, because I didn't think you were capable of surprises."

"Wow. Ouch," I said as I started up the engine.

She tossed her head back with a throaty laugh. The arch of her slender neck sent my pulse racing. The pleasant peal of her laughter kicked it up even faster. I forced myself to look away and texted my buddy Scott.

She half-faced me in her seat. "Okay. Give me a hint."

"Nope." I focused on backing out of the drive. "Seatbelt," I reminded her, then headed toward Metairie.

She buckled herself in. "Oh, come on, just a little one."

"No."

She put her thumb and index finger about a millimeter apart and squinted her eyes together. "Just an itty-bitty, teensy-weensy one."

My God, she was so cute. "Not even a teensy one."

She laughed again and took note that we were getting on the interstate. "So tell me something about yourself, Mr. Cruz."

"What do you want to know?"

"Your family." Her voice softened. "You said you didn't have anyone here in New Orleans when we first met, but do you have some elsewhere? Or is that a sore subject? I don't want to pry."

I slid my gaze to her. "Yes, you do want to pry."

She rewarded me with a pretty smile for teasing her.

"But it's okay," I continued. "I'm originally from San Antonio, Texas. I have a fairly proud father, an ornery grandfather, and an asshat of a cousin who I grew up with."

She smiled brighter. "I love them already. Tell me more. Why don't you live and work there?"

Focusing on dodging traffic and the upcoming exit, I realized that I shockingly wanted to tell her the truth rather than the lie I told most people, which was my artwork sold better in a cultural center like New Orleans. While true, it wasn't the reason I'd moved away from home. After a pause, when I could feel her watching me, waiting patiently, I told her.

"It's the wolf inside me. I can't be around another dominant werewolf for long without . . . without wanting to fight him."

I gripped the steering wheel tight, scared of what she'd think of me after this conversation. It was hard to admit something so shameful, that I lacked control. It was also what drove me to seek Evie's help, so that I could regain the control slipping away from me. I never wanted the wolf to take hold of me like it had that first time.

"You mean your father? Or your cousin?"

"My father." A stiff jerk of my chin. "That's the thing about werewolves. Especially those with alpha tendencies." And I certainly was an alpha among my kind.

Fuckin' right.

"You mean . . . you and your father didn't get along?"

I merged right to get off on Clearview Parkway. "No. We actually get along fine. I mean, he loves me as his son. And I love him. But our wolves? They're both alphas. And when the need to shift came, we both became aggressive toward each other."

I gulped hard at the memory, the incident that happened right before I decided I best move away.

As if she could see what I was thinking, she asked, "Did something happen?"

"Yeah. You could say that." I veered toward Scott's restaurant. "The first full moon after my eighteenth birthday, I uh . . ." I combed a hand through my hair. "I attacked my dad right after I shifted. He was still in human form."

"Oh no, Mateo. Did you hurt him?"

The pain pricked my chest. "Not badly. Physically, anyway. I clawed his chest and . . . he didn't even shift to beat me back. Just stared at me like he couldn't believe it. Hell, I couldn't believe it."

I remember it so clear, that expression of disappointment burned in my brain. I'd run away that night after he gave me that look. My shame chased me away.

"I took off. My shift lasted for days where I remembered close to nothing. I woke up almost a week later on the bank of the Rio Grande River." I was naked and bloody from killing rabbits and deer, having found two stag carcasses nearby, even a mountain lion. I'd become completely wild for almost a week. "After that, I went home, I apologized to him and my mother, packed my bags, and left."

I turned down the street toward a strip of trendy new restaurants, a sushi and seafood place on either side of Scott's restaurant.

Wanting to lighten the mood, I admitted, "You'd love my grandpa."

"Oh yeah?"

She watched me, but I kept my eyes on the road. "When I hit puberty, which is also unfortunately when a werewolf first starts to feel his wolf coming on, I used to growl all the damn time. For no reason. And Grandpa, who lived with us and cooked most of the meals, he found me prowling the kitchen while he was prepping dinner. He popped me on the nose with a spatula like I was a dog and said, 'Mateo Francisco Cruz. If you growl one more time, there will be no empanadas for you for a solid month.'"

Evie laughed. "And I guess you behaved after that, eh, Mateo Francisco?"

I didn't mind her teasing. "Yep. Grandpa could always put me in line."

"What about your cousin?"

"I left the house before he hit puberty and his shift came on. We get along, even though he can be an arrogant dick sometimes. Nico thinks a lot of himself." I chuckled, thinking of the smart-ass boy who became a cocky man. "I haven't seen him in a while. He's been traveling out west for a few years."

I swallowed the pang of regret of not being able to live closer to my father. Even now, my hackles rose when we spent too long together.

"So puberty is rough for a werewolf?" she asked teasingly.

"Puberty is a fucking nightmare."

She laughed as I finally found a spot on the street.

I was glad to move away from my sad little past. But then she said, "I'm sorry, Mateo. I can't imagine what it's like not to be near your family."

I gave her a smile. "Don't be sorry. This is just the way it is for us. Part of the curse. I like being alone. It isn't a burden or anything. And now, when I visit on holidays and weddings and stuff, everything is fine. Though we all still miss Mama. She was human, you see, and has been gone for a while."

Evie's gaze saddened. "I'm sorry."

"Don't be. She lived a full life. I just always feel bad because she worried about me, you know?" I shrugged.

"Why did she worry?"

I stretched my arm across the headrest of her seat and looked over my shoulder as I backed into the parking spot.

"She was a mother. Before she died, she wanted to see me find a girl, settle down, be taken care of. Not be lonely." I laughed.

"Why is that so funny?"

"Not funny. It's just . . ." I put the truck in park and turned it off, staring out the windshield. "I don't need to be taken care of. Most werewolves are loners. Just part of our DNA makeup. Some move in packs, but those guys tend to be total douchebags. Criminals, typically." A flash of Nico running with a pack of particular assholes popped to mind. That was the only time I'd pushed against him, wolf to wolf, but it had to be done. I didn't regret it. "Anyway, I've always known I was meant to be alone. But I'm not lonely. I'm happy with my life. Mama, God love her, she worried for nothing."

I finally looked at Evie, expecting that look of pity my mother often gave me, not believing me when I told her I was fine on my own, time and time again. But that wasn't how she was looking at me at all.

"I get it. I mean, I understand," she said, chewing her lip thoughtfully. "Sometimes, my sisters drive me batshit crazy, even though I can't imagine living without them. But . . . I get it. While I don't have your, you know, alpha thing, I get that you enjoy being on your own."

Baby, I can't wait to show you my alpha thing.

"Come on." I glanced over her shoulder. "Let's go eat."

"Where?"

I pointed out her window to the right. "At Gotham City Grill, of course."

She gasped, flinging her ponytail when she twisted her head so fast. "Oh. My. *God.*"

"I know it's DC Comics, and you seem to prefer Marvel, but I thought you'd get a kick out of this place. My friend Scott owns it."

"Wait, wait, wait." She closed her eyes a long second and held up both hands in front of her, palms out. "You know the difference between DC and Marvel?"

"Pshht." I waved her off. "I'm not that ignorant."

"Please marry me."

My heart stuttered, then I let out a loud laugh. "Come on. There's more inside."

She popped out before I could even make it around to her side, my instincts telling me to open the door for her.

"There's *more*?"

"Much more. Hold on to your panties. You're about to be blown away."

I'll hold on to her panties if she loses them.

She hooked her arm through mine, now a familiar move of hers when we walked together, which felt oddly . . . wonderful. What made me feel better than the spell her sister put on me last night was the beaming smile Evie shot me, a sudden jolt of pleasure I wasn't expecting. Why? Because I'd put it there.

CHAPTER 12

~EVIE~

"I want the Holy Bat-bacon Burger." I ogled the menu and wanted to spank it and make it my bitch. It was the finest thing I'd ever seen. "How have I never known about this place?"

Our waiter Joe laughed, but it was Mateo who responded. "You're just not as cool as me."

I scoffed so loud, the girl at the next table whipped around and gave me you're-a-weirdo eyes. "Coming from the guy who didn't even know Darth Vader was Luke's father?"

Mateo grinned, unruffled as usual by my dig at his piss-poor pop culture knowledge. He perused the menu. "You wanna split some Daredevil fries?"

My gaze fell back to the most amazeballs listing of food in the history of menus. "Daredevil fries?"

"Right there." He reached over and pointed at the bottom of my menu. I couldn't help but notice the bulging vein wrapping from underneath his forearm to the top of his wrist.

Gah! Why was I such a forearm whore? Was there such a thing as arm porn? Or man-veins porn? Because if there was, I needed a monthly subscription, like yesterday.

"They're covered in pepper jack cheese and jalapenos."

"Sounds good."

"They're spicy."

"I like spicy," I said, clearing my throat.

Mateo turned to the waiter. "I'll have a Gotham Goliath. And can you bring us an order of Suicide Squad Sizzlers for an appetizer?"

"Sure thing. I'll be right back with your iced teas."

I devoured the decor of the restaurant, the industrial-style architecture that matched the slick, urban style of the DC comics. But what caught my eye the most was the oversize charcoal artwork hanging on the walls. I mean, comics were meant to be rendered in bright and varied colors, but these black-and-white charcoal drawings were just completely breathtaking.

"You like the artwork?" he asked.

"It's insane. I mean, look at that one."

There was one titled *The Dark Knight's Watch* hanging on the corner wall behind Mateo. It was as tall as one of his sculptures. Batman's cape arced out, his body filling the entire canvas. But almost camouflaged in the wings of the cape was the outline and pinpoints of light of Gotham City.

"Pretty good, right?"

I snorted. "Pretty good? I'd die to meet the artist."

"No need for that," said someone stepping up beside our table. "Hey, man." A tall but gangly bearded guy with piercings in his eyebrow and tattoos roping his arms reached out and shook

Mateo's hand. Then he turned and offered to shake mine. "You must be Evie?"

I couldn't hide my surprise. "You know my name?" I glanced at Mateo as I shook the guy's hand.

He chuckled and nodded to Mateo. "As of about thirty minutes ago, yeah."

"Evie, this is Scott Berard. He owns Gotham City Grill, which also happens to be his very own gallery."

"Dude, you cook *and* you're an artist?"

"Nah. My uncle is the chef and runs the restaurant. I just own the building and the, well, the branding and decor."

I heaved a sigh of relief. "Good thing. I'd have to divorce Mateo and drag you to Vegas."

He laughed again. "Well, before you cancel those plans, consider that I do make a mean omelet." He winked before rocking back on his heels, arms crossed, accentuating all the black ink swirling his biceps. "So when did you get married, man?" he asked accusingly. "You didn't tell me?"

"Oh no." Mateo leaned forward on a nervous laugh, elbows on the table, gaze skating from me to Scott then back to me. "We're not married. That's just Evie being . . . Evie."

"Ah. Gotcha."

Fidgeting with the napkin in my lap, I cleared my throat as heat flamed up my neck. I was the one who'd laid it out there like Mateo and I were a thing. Well, more than a thing, then left Mateo to bail us out. And Jesus, did I hate uncomfortable pauses. Thankfully, the sudden awkwardness didn't seem to bother Scott.

"So, Mateo texted me you're a DC fan?"

"Then Mateo lied like a dog." Whew. Awkwardness gone.

"No, I said she was a comic book fan," corrected Mateo.

"Oh, hell. You're one of those Marvel fanatics, aren't you?"

"Guilty," I said proudly, with a high arch of my eyebrow and haughty lift of my chin.

Scott heaved an exaggerated sigh. "You're forgiven. Since you seem to have good taste in artists." He gave Mateo a sly grin, which made my insides do all kinds of crazy, melty things.

He was still under the impression that Mateo and I were a couple. This time, before Mateo could correct him, the waiter popped up and dropped off our iced teas, both with lemon. Saved! Thank you, Joe with the crew cut.

"Well, I'll let you guys enjoy your meal. But hey, we're still doing the Voodoo Festival booth, right?" he asked Mateo.

"I've got it all reserved. I'll have Missy message you the details."

"Cool. Nice to meet you, Evie."

"You too," I said sincerely.

He sidled off, and I took a long drink from my iced tea, hoping Mateo didn't feel weird now with my whole marriage/divorce joke debacle. Apparently, it didn't bother him at all because he gave me a playful smile and asked, "So is this a good surprise?"

"This is the epic-est surprise ever."

"Epic-est?"

"Definitely."

"And you like his artwork?"

I rolled my eyes. "It's crazy good. And badass."

He played with the straw in his drink, stirring the ice around, gaze flitting from his glass to me. "Better than mine?" His voice had dropped softer even though he still gave me the playful eyes.

"Are you jealous I might like his work better?"

He squeezed the lemon wedge that had been sitting on the rim of the glass into his tea, dropped it, then licked his thumb. "Maybe."

I blinked a few times, trying not to get distracted by his mouth and his fingers. "You are jealous. Oh, man. Maybe I should draw this out."

His eyes darkened to dangerous. Sexy, playful dangerous. "You'd torture your own friend who just gave you the epic-est surprise ever?"

"In a heartbeat." I slid my gaze back to the giant charcoal Batman. "Mmm. I think Scotty has amazing skills."

"Scotty?"

"Yeah. We're best friends now."

"Since when?"

"Since we bonded over omelets and art."

He took a deep swallow of iced tea and set it back on the table. With a swift lick of his lips that I felt zing between my legs, he then said, "Scotty isn't the only one with amazing skills, you know?"

And suddenly, the temperature shot from AC-breezy to Mordor-scorching. I averted my eyes and sipped my tea, needing to move away from this, whatever it was. Mateo won. He was way better at teasing than me. "You do know your artwork is insanely good, right?"

"Yeah, I do. But I want to know what you think." He leaned forward again, his upper body kind of swallowing the table space. His biceps bulged all pretty in his T-shirt. "What *you* think of my art," he said low and sensual-deep.

My stomach proceeded to step up to the diving board and do a triple somersault, while I tried to come up with a response that didn't sound all throaty and stupid-sexy. Because Mateo's playful side felt dangerously like flirting. But that couldn't be, right? I was 90 percent sure he was pleased as punch when I accidentally friend-zoned him last night. I hadn't actually meant to, but it just came out my stupid mouth. Then he was all "friends" and "awesome." And I was like, *fuck, what did I just do?* But then Clara said friends was a good thing, even though she made that weird comment about friends and lovers. And then my nighttime cocktail of reading werewolf horror—I mean history—with carb-loaded fettucine somehow gave me psychosexual dreams about Mateo's wolf. So here I was, staring at friendly Mateo looking entirely too adorable with that silly grin on his face, trying desperately not to make an ass out of myself, like telling him I wanted to marry him *again*, and—

"Here you are. Suicide Squad Sizzlers."

Thank God! Saved by Joe again. I loved Joe. He was the best waiter in the whole wide world.

"Careful." Mateo put his napkin in his lap while I did the same. "These are super hot."

"Well, yeah, I kind of got that from the whole sizzling on the skillet thing."

"Okay, smart-ass. I meant spicy hot."

I picked up a fork and stabbed a big juicy shrimp in the buttery red sauce, then dipped it in the avocado-lime aioli on the side.

"Mmmm." I closed my eyes on the first bite. "That is freaking delicious." When I opened them, Mateo had frozen with his shrimp halfway to his mouth. He blinked heavily, then shoved a bite in his mouth too.

"Sure is." He chewed, then reached for his tea, glancing elsewhere. His jaw clenched hard with each bite.

I forked another big one, the jumbo-size tail too big to fit in my mouth in one bite. After I bit it awkwardly in half, Mateo looked up and grinned at me.

"What's so funny?"

He stared at my face and laughed.

"What?"

He picked up the napkin dispenser, which was silver chrome and shiny as a mirror, and held it in front of me. Apparently, in my attempt not to overstuff my mouth, I'd tipped my nose in the red sauce coating the shrimp.

I went to grab a clean napkin from the holder, but he was already reaching across the table. "Come here, Rudolph."

With a quick swipe, he wiped it clean, even though I leaned close to the napkin dispenser to double-check. All while he continued to chuckle at me.

"You didn't see that," I huffed at him.

"I definitely saw that."

"Well, there goes my record of perfection in your eyes. I suppose we should dispense with this friendship here and now. How can you continue to worship me after this tragedy?"

"No worries, Evie. I'll still worship you," he teased. Yes, definitely teased. Even so, his words curled in my belly like a warm cinnamon bun straight out of the oven and melted just as sweetly.

Our food followed right after. Thank you, Joe. Again. I might want to marry him, too, before this lunch was over.

Then I marveled at Mateo eating double half-pound patties. Medium rare, mind you. Gross. But again, werewolf. So I got it. My burger was cooked well done. Crispy and deliciously juicy on the inside. And the Daredevil fries? Holy shitballs. What a meal.

"I might sell my firstborn to have those fries delivered to my doorstep every day." I walked ahead of him toward the exit, glad I'd worn my stretchy jeans because I was hella full. My food baby needed room to grow.

"Happy you liked it," he said from close behind me before he held the door open and let me walk through first.

"Your surprise wins at least four gold stars."

"Four? Out of how many?"

I rolled my eyes. "Out of five, of course."

"Why only four?"

"Oh, Mateo." I angled my head and gave him my bless-your-poor-little-heart look. "If it were a Marvel-themed grill, then it would've gotten you five perfect stars."

"Well, then." He unlocked the truck and opened my door, not giving me much room to pass him by. And just as I ducked by him, he added close to my ear, "I'll have to think of another way to get those five stars."

He gave my ponytail a firm tug, which sent a delicious tingle skating down my body all the way to my toes. As he closed the door and rounded the hood, I realized I was in big, big trouble. Friends shouldn't make your toes curl from a platonic ponytail tug. Bless my poor little heart.

CHAPTER 13

~EVIE~

"WE MISS Y'ALL!" ISADORA COOED TO ME FROM THE DESKTOP WE KEPT in the corner of the kitchen. "Is Clara holding down the shop okay without me?"

"Yes, don't worry. I've been helping her in between shifts. Violet, too, if you can believe it."

"Really? She isn't sneaking off per usual?"

"I don't sneak off!" Violet yelled behind me as she walked into the kitchen, then popped her head in front of me, filling up the screen. "Is, I've told you I'm not sneaking. Sneaking implies there's shame involved. And there's no shame in what I'm doing."

Isadora rolled her grass-green eyes, the same shade as my own. "Then why don't you tell us what you're doing?"

"When I'm ready." Violet winked at me, then strolled into the kitchen where Jules was stirring her shrimp creole. Then she popped back, sticking her blue-haired head in front of me again.

"If you want something juicy to discuss, ask Evie about her were-wolf who's coming to Sunday dinner."

"Go away." I shoved Violet on the shoulder.

"What werewolf?" Isadora leaned closer excitedly, her blonde-haired, big-eyed face filling up the screen. "You have a werewolf? Coming to *our* Sunday dinner?"

"No. He's not *my* werewolf." Though lately, I had this irrepressible wish that he was. "And you and Livvy won't be here," I remarked. "So what's one more mouth to feed? Jules is used to cooking for all six of us."

Jules made a disgruntled noise from the stove.

"Besides," I went on, "he's really coming over to discuss how we plan to break his hex, so I just asked him to come to dinner beforehand."

Violet was there again, putting her big head in my way. "Also so Evie can spend her four-hour-a-day minimum time allotment with him." She waggled her eyebrows and drifted toward the pantry.

"What the hell have we been missing?" Isadora asked. "Why does all the excitement happen when we leave?"

"It's not that much excitement," I assured her, even as my tummy did a nervous arabesque and twirl.

"Has anyone seen Fred pass through here?" asked Violet from the walk-in pantry.

Jules placed the lid back on her Magnalite pot and propped a hand on her hip, wooden spoon in the other hand. "And why the hell would I have seen Fred pass through here?"

Violet stared at her, blank-faced, then said slowly as if to a child, "Because you have eyes and might have seen him walking through." She used two fingers and walked on air to demonstrate.

"He isn't allowed in the house, smart-ass, and you know it."

"I still don't understand this rule. Z is allowed in the house."

"Z is potty-trained."

I tuned back to Isadora who had her head tilted, listening to Jules and Violet going at it. "Well, nothing has changed here. Tell Livvy sorry I missed her."

Is smiled big. "I sure will."

"Hey, cousin!" Drew's head popped on-screen next to Isadora, all tanned skin and bright blue eyes.

"Hey, Drew. Y'all taking care of my girls?"

"You know it. Cole took Livvy to a Gumbo Cook-off downtown. Travis and I are about to take this one down there."

"Don't wear them out. They have a flight to catch tomorrow afternoon."

Isadora and Livvy left early for their trip to see Mom and Dad, deciding to visit with our cousins before they ventured overseas to Switzerland.

Drew rolled his baby blues. "Don't worry. We got it. How's NOLA?"

"Loud, crowded, hot as hell. Nothing new."

He chuckled, his bright white smile so infectious. He was the prettiest warlock on the planet, I was sure of it. And he knew it.

"Well, we expect to be fully entertained on our next trip to make up for the demands of these two. They're so high maintenance."

Isadora shoved him with her shoulder. I rolled my eyes. "My sisters are not high maintenance. Well . . . maybe Isadora."

"Hey! I am not!" she protested, then turned sheepish. "Well, not very much."

We all laughed, even Is. Because she was the queen of list-making and guilty of organizing trips down to pee breaks.

"You guys ready to go?" asked Travis, his giant form coming up behind them before he lowered his sandy blond head into view. "Well, if it isn't pretty Eveleen."

"Don't do it, Travis! Don't—" But he started singing anyway, off-key and horribly.

"Eveleen, Eveleen, Eveleen, Evelee-eeen! Please don't take my heart away just because you can."

Yep. To the tune of Dolly Parton's "Jolene." It was such a bad joke, but the doofus couldn't help himself. Every. Damn. Time.

Isadora laughed while she made googly eyes at me. Drew and Cole were our cousins. Travis wasn't. He was just the superhot warlock who lived with them. He was a ridiculous flirt, but I never entertained him as anything more than a friend since he lived with Cole and Drew. I would've enjoyed dating a fine-ass hot guy like Travis, but that's just the thing. I knew Travis was the kind of guy I'd have tons of fun and most definitely hot sex with, then we'd break it off. And there would be that weird awkwardness every time we saw each other. Besides, they lived two and half hours away, so dating him wasn't even much of an option.

It still didn't stop him from being an insane flirt whenever I saw him.

"Hi, Travis." I waved.

"Hey, beautiful. When are we getting married again?"

"We're not."

"You're sure?" He smiled, skyrocketing from handsome to hose-me-down hot.

"Quite sure."

"Fine then." He sighed heavily like I'd really put him out. "The least you can do is save me a dance at the Coven Guild party. I won't take no for an answer."

"Right." I shook my head, grinning at his ruthless flirting. "I would, except I don't go to those things with Jules. Not anymore."

Drew frowned. "But you have to go to this one. You're hosting it."

A spike of adrenaline shot through my veins, rushing like flame through my blood. I glanced up at Jules who was giving me her oh-shit look. I rarely saw it because Jules didn't need this look. Her resting bitch face was pretty much what she wore 90 percent of the time. But right now, she knew she'd screwed up. "I can explain."

"Uh-oh," said Is.

"Wear something hot," added Travis. "Strapless."

"We'll call when we land in Switzerland." Izzy blew me a kiss and clicked off the video app before the guys could even wave goodbye. That's because Isadora knew what shitstorm was about to go down.

"Why in the hell are we hosting it?" I asked Jules, clicking off the app, then rounding the counter toward her.

"I was going to tell you, but I just needed the right moment."

"There isn't a right moment."

"The summit has rotated to other covens for years now, and it's our turn. I can't tell all the leaders we can't host because you're still pissed at your ex."

"I'm not pissed at him. I broke up with *him*, remember?"

"Good. Then there's no reason to avoid him."

"You can take our other sisters. They'll be enough to play hostess with you. You don't need me there."

"Evie." Jules sighed and tucked her straight dark hair behind one ear. "It will look strange for my closest sister to not be there. Especially since you've been avoiding the Summit for *years*. They might suspect trouble within our ranks. We can't allow that."

Dammit. I leaned my back against the counter and crossed my arms. She was right. There was no question that Jules was the most powerful witch in all of the New Orleans region, but if there was any suspicion there was tension in our household, which could lead to volatile results for witch covens, it would be bad news. The entire Guild could investigate us, interrogate us, and move some other witches into power.

I'm not going to say that Jules is a control freak, but Jules is a control freak. It wouldn't matter if they investigated us, but what would I say? *No, my sister and I are fine. I'm just being an immature child and don't want to stare at my ex's arrogant ass all night at a cocktail party.*

"You don't have to come to the coven meetings. Just make a quick appearance at the cocktail party so you can smile and greet the rest of the Guild, then you can leave."

That didn't sound so bad. Then why did my stomach twist into a knot just thinking about it? I knew exactly why, of course, but I didn't want to think about him. Or the way he'd used me to get what he wanted, all the while belittling me for what I wanted.

"Like an hour tops," she pleaded and then added in her maternal voice, "Evie, please. Come on."

The doorbell rang. *Mateo.* And just like that, all thoughts of douchebag Derek were gone. I schooled my features so Jules wouldn't see how excited I was about the man on our doorstep.

"Fine," I huffed all begrudgingly. "One hour."

Then I marched out of the kitchen and practically ran to the front door. I swung it open, then almost choked on air. I'd become accustomed to Mateo's tall and utterly stunning beauty in his worn-out faded jeans and clingy T-shirts, but this version of him made me a tad weak-kneed. And by a tad, I mean I had to suddenly grip the doorjamb to keep myself in a standing position. In a long-sleeved, jade-green button-down that somehow made his brown eyes softer, prettier, and fucking hypnotic, and wearing dark blue jeans that fit far too well on his muscled thighs and no doubt his fine ass—once I got a good look from behind, I'd confirm that—he looked completely dreamy. If that wasn't enough, his dark, wavy hair was pulled back in a short ponytail except for a perfect wispy strand that dangled at the most sensual angle on the outer edge of his right eye that amped him from superhot to sex god. And his smell! What was he wearing? Some kind of werewolf pheromone cologne? Where did they sell it? Could I buy enough to bathe in it?

I glanced down at myself in jean cutoffs and my newest Wolverine T-shirt, feeling utterly underdressed. For my own Sunday dinner.

"You didn't have to dress up," I said, while wanting to cut out my own tongue the second I said it. Because him dressed this way made me want to lay him out on the dinner table instead of Jules's shrimp creole.

Friends-friends-friends. Friends-friends-friends. Maybe if I chanted it enough in my head, it would sink in.

"I didn't want to look like a slob for your family."

"Well . . ." I blew out a breath as I looked him over one last time. "Goal achieved."

He glanced away, a flush of color filling his cheeks. Was he blushing? I wanted to eat him up.

"Can I come in?" he asked with a shy smile.

I realized then I was just standing there, blocking his entrance, staring. Ogling, really. Probably drooling. I needed to carry a handkerchief with me nowadays to prevent such embarrassment.

"Of course. Come on in."

He handed me a bottle of merlot as he stepped inside.

"Mateo. You're good. Buttering up my sister, eh?"

He put both hands in his front pockets, an innocent gesture he seemed to do in order to make his tall, lean-muscled frame appear less threatening. Silly werewolf.

"I know she wasn't crazy about this idea in the first place, of helping me, so I thought it couldn't hurt."

"Smart man. And it's the exact merlot she loves the best. How did you know? Are you stalking her?" I play-frowned.

"Nah." He pointed to his nose. "I figured out which one she was drinking that night I met her. Just a stroll down the wine aisle is all it took."

"That's some impressive olfactory senses."

"I can be pretty impressive sometimes."

"And so humble."

When I nudged him with my shoulder, he looked down with a timid smile. A loose strand of hair fell forward, then he tucked it behind his ear before locking on my gaze again. Those warm brown eyes held me captive as always.

Distracting from the sudden heat passing between us, I said lightheartedly, "As long as you're not stalking her then."

"If I was going to stalk anyone, it would be you, Evie."

While we both laughed, there was a thread of nervousness rippling between us. When I looked up as we stepped through the living room, his smile slipped, his expression shifted, darkening so fast I almost missed it. A primal shiver zinged through my bones, then we were standing by the dining room table and his polite smile made an appearance again. The dining room overlooked the brick courtyard and opened up to the kitchen.

"Welcome, Mateo," said Jules.

"He brought wine," I said cheerily, passing it to her.

"Thank you." Her face actually softened when she saw the label. "That was kind of you. Go ahead and have a seat."

"Hi, Mateo," said Clara sweetly, coming in the back kitchen door. "Good to see you again."

"And you."

"You can sit here," I said, pointing to the seat Isadora usually occupied right next to me. "I'll get your plate."

"Where's Violet?" asked Jules.

"She was right behind me." Clara pointed to the door she'd left ajar.

And that's when all hell broke loose.

CHAPTER 14

~MATEO~

Fucking hell!

The blur of motion and sudden squeal of females jarred me so badly I didn't even think. I grabbed Evie around the waist and jumped back toward the living room, watching the streak of black, followed by a puffed-up rooster. Then Violet whizzed by.

"Goddammit, Fred!"

The black streak, which I recognized quickly as Evie's cat Z, moved faster than I thought was possible for the old bag of bones. He leaped up onto the kitchen counter, leaving the rooster to squawk and cluck angrily from below. The cat sat and stared, his twitching tail the only sign he was agitated by the chase.

"Violet!" yelled Jules. "If that rooster loses one feather in my kitchen, I'm going to wring his neck and fry him for dinner."

Violet gasped, then scooped the rooster off the floor and pulled him close to her chest. "Don't even say such things. Fred will be—"

She stopped, clutching her rooster who happened to be wearing a purple polka-dotted bow tie, then swiveled her gaze to me. That's when I noticed everyone had stopped and was staring at me. That's also when I noticed I was growling. Well, Alpha was growling. I was also clasping Evie in a death grip around the waist and the front of her shoulders, pressing her to me with an insane amount of force.

"**Back off.**" The deep, rough voice of Alpha rumbled up my throat and out of my mouth.

Clara gasped. Jules took one step forward, her palms facing me at her sides, fingers spread.

Oh, fuck.

That's right. Daddy's got his girl.

Stop growling, motherfucker, before they cast a spell or something. Let Evie go.

As soon as the threat is gone.

There's no threat, you Neanderthal.

I will protect her from all foul creatures.

It's a rooster and a damn cat!

"Wait," I begged Jules, my voice almost back to normal, hoping she didn't zap me with her magic before I could rein him in.

After one more rough huff, the growling in my chest stopped. My pulse was racing. No. That wasn't mine. That was Evie's. I could hear it and feel it drumming against my forearm that was still pressed to her upper chest. The swift beat of her heartbeat made me want to lean my head down and lick her pulse. Then the rest of her.

"I'm sorry," I said to her, releasing her so fast she stumbled. I grabbed her arm to steady her. "Sorry."

"It's okay," she whispered and gave me a pitying look, though there was a thread of trepidation in her voice. To think that I'd put it there sickened me.

"I didn't mean—" What didn't I mean? To grab her at the first sign of danger and clutch her to my body like she was mine? To allow Alpha to take over and scare the shit out of the witches who were trying to help me? Who was I kidding? I was losing control over him. Slowly but surely.

And the looks her sisters were giving me, especially Jules. Not good. Thankfully, the attention swiveled back to Violet when the cat let out a yowl.

"Get that damn rooster out of here," ordered Jules, steel in her voice. Whether it was for me or her sister, I wasn't sure. "I'm warning you, Violet. He's two steps away from being chicken pot pie."

"He's a rooster. Not a chicken." Violet scowled, shushing the clucking bird.

"He'll taste just the same."

"Ignore her, Freddie," Violet crooned to him.

"*Now*, Violet," said Jules with unrestrained annoyance, pointing toward the door.

"I'll get Z some milk," said Clara, quickly pouring a saucer and taking him to the pantry, her gaze flicking to me with the same sympathetic look Evie had given me a second ago.

When they'd both left to take care of the party crashers, Jules turned her gray gaze on me. "I'm sorry, Mateo. I realize now that even small mishaps can cause your wolf to exert himself."

She hasn't seen nothing yet.

"No. I'm the one who's sorry." I swallowed hard against the shame of losing my shit and acting like a possessive psycho over nothing at all.

Jules waved a hand at the door where Clara and Violet had left with the animals. "It's not usually like this."

"It's usually much more chaotic," said Evie, her voice lifting lightheartedly, though a glint of sad compassion still sparked in her eyes.

Jules gave Evie a look. "I just meant we don't typically have barnyard animals running through the kitchen at dinnertime."

Evie mouthed, *Yes, we do.*

I glanced down, studying my shoes for no reason, willing away the shame. Evie stepped closer and nudged my elbow with hers. "It's okay," she murmured just for me. "You should see the freak show this place is when all my sisters are here."

She was trying to lighten what had happened, which I appreciated, but it just proved to me how bad off I truly was. Evie's quick forgiveness went a long way to smooth over my awkward embarrassment at grabbing her like a maniac to protect her from a rooster and a half-dead cat.

"Have a seat," said Jules, sounding more curt than polite. Her heavy, observant gaze sent off some alarm bells. She apparently wasn't quite as forgiving. Understandably. While Evie walked over to the stove to serve our plates, Jules asked quietly, "Does that happen a lot? Your wolf taking over the man like that?"

There was no reason to deny it. "Only since this hex. I've *always* been in control before then."

"Always?" she asked with a skeptical arch of her brow.

"Yes," I said a little aggressively, forcing myself to remain calm. "Always."

"Have you ever hurt anyone physically since this hex was put on you?"

Pressing my lips together, I didn't want to tell her the truth. But I certainly wasn't going to lie. "Only once." Like only one incident of violence was okay. Clearing my throat, I told her, "I had a delivery for a client and was parked legally on the side of the street. But some guy with serious road rage got out and jumped in my face, screaming and cursing me out for blocking his parking spot."

"What did you do?"

"It was a quick reaction. Instinctual. I punched him in the nose."

Damn straight, we did.

"I see."

I put a napkin in my lap and held her examining gaze so she wouldn't think I was hiding anything. Which I wasn't. "I'm able to keep things in check most of the time."

"Except when startled." She nodded again to the door where her sisters had left a minute ago.

"Exactly."

She glanced beyond my shoulder where Evie was, then said low, "My sister can handle herself, but be warned that I'll have to step in if you threaten her in any way."

Feeling that warning like a lock on my bones, my muscles clenched at the danger. "I understand. I would expect nothing less."

She nodded, her lips pressing a tight smile, telling me she was glad we agreed on the matter.

Evie returned to the table and set a plate in front of me. "Help yourself to French bread." She gestured toward the basket at the center of the table, her gaze flicking between me and Jules, obviously picking up on the strained vibe.

Jules left to fix two plates and set them down at empty places at the table, her lips still compressed into a tight line. It didn't take a genius to detect the tension had less to do with the circus animal act and more to do with my sudden possessive aggression toward her sister. Winning over Jules would be a major undertaking. Evie's sister was important to her, so I had to try.

I'd thought to push this friendship with Evie to the next level once this hex was broken, but now I was wondering if Jules would try to prevent even friendship. I suddenly wished Clara would hurry up and return. Something about her mere presence lifted any dark vibes.

Which one is she? The one who pisses glitter and shits rainbows?

Not even entertaining him right now.

"So where did he get the name Z from?"

Violet and Clara filed in right then. Violet snorted as she took her seat. "It's short for Zombie Cat."

"Zombie Cat?" I forked a spoonful of shrimp, spicy tomato sauce, and white rice.

Clara beamed, reaching for a slice of French bread. "Z is special. He's thirty years old."

I looked at Evie. "Thirty? How is that even possible?"

She smiled sheepishly. "Our sister Isadora is a Conduit."

Whoa. I'd heard of them before but had never met one. This kind of witch could transfer energy from any source into another. Apparently, even energy to extend the life of a cat.

"Yeah," added Violet. "Evie tried to call him Oliver once upon a time, but Isadora dubbed him Zombie Cat after she started giving him 'treatments.'"

Evie rolled her eyes at Violet's air quotes. "You're such a hypocrite. How old is Fred now? Hmm, let me see . . ."

"Shut up, Sissy."

"Mateo, where does your inspiration for your art come from?" asked Clara, completely out of the blue. But it kind of seemed her style.

"Um, mostly mythology. And history."

"That's interesting. Any particular reason?" She sipped her tea, her inquisitive brows raised.

"Not really. I've just always been drawn to it."

"I don't think that's entirely accurate." Her accusation was pronounced so sweetly it took the sting out of the rudeness.

I opened my mouth to tell her I knew my own mind, but then a sudden wash of memory swept me back. Mama lay in the bed with me, cuddled close, reading the story of Perseus to me. It had been so long ago, I hadn't thought of the memory in ages.

"My mother," I admitted. "She was fond of the Greeks. I believe that's where it started for me."

Clara smiled brightly. "Well, that's lovely."

Evie gave me a smile of her own, much smaller and more crooked, but it was enough to ease the remaining tension from my shoulders.

"The shrimp creole is delicious," I said to Jules.

Jules nodded, spooning a bite from her bowl. "Thank you."

Violet checked her watch. "Yeah, well, this is nice and all, but we need to speed it up. I have a three o'clock appointment."

"With whom?" Jules injected some venom in her question. I was glad it was no longer turned on me.

"None of your business. You're not my mother, Juliana."

An electric current rippled in the air, raising the hairs on my arms. Alpha rumbled a deep growl at the sudden presence of magic.

"No, but everything that affects this coven needs to go through me."

"This doesn't affect the coven," Violet snapped back.

"Why are you being so—?"

"Oh, for fuck's sake, Jules. You can't control everyone and everything." Violet rolled her eyes. "Drop it."

Clara reached over and placed her hand on Violet's forearm; a pulse of yellow light flashed, then was gone. Almost like the flash of a camera, but cameras didn't leave a sizzle of electricity in the air. Clara's magic hummed against my chest from across the table, a pleasant vibration. Strange.

"Don't bother," said Violet, standing with her empty plate. "I'm not angry. Just ready to get the show on the road." Then her piercing gaze landed on me. "If you're done, Wolfman. Let's do this."

Jules popped up, then Clara, carrying their plates to the sink. Evie stood and picked up my empty plate too. With a shrug, she said, "Sorry. They're not usually such assholes."

"Yes, we are," said Violet, heading through the living room and out into the hall toward the back of the house.

"What are we going to do?" I carried mine and Evie's glasses to the sink behind her.

"Violet is a Seer. She wants to divine you to see if she can find the witch who put this spell on you."

"So you're sure this wasn't some kind of accident? Like residual magic, a spell meant for someone else that bounced off me?"

She faced me at the sink, a somber expression I'm not sure I'd seen before. Except maybe when I told her about my family life.

"No. Since I've been spending time with you and what I've read, this is a binding spell. Someone meant this for you."

Hearing confirmation of it shocked me to my bones. Who had it out for me that he'd want to smother my wolf, make me literally lose my mind? Because that's what was going to happen if this hex wasn't broken.

"Come on," she said, taking my hand and leading me back through the living room.

I squeezed her delicate hand gently, her touch grounding me with that sweet, familiar balm I craved every second of every day. She led me down the same hallway she had the first night we met. Right before we approached Jules's study, she dropped my hand. A sharp pain pricked inside my chest, but I didn't grab for her again.

"Take a seat here," said Jules, pointing to a large wingback at the foot of a long mahogany coffee table.

I did. Violet sat on the floor on the opposite side, a polished, wooden bowl filled with water in front of her. Evie picked up a pair of scissors and walked toward me.

What the fuck? Attack!

I clenched every muscle in my body, gripping the armchair with brutal force. I had to remind myself this was Evie.

"It's okay," she said with a smile, raising her other hand to rest on my shoulder as she looked down at me. "I just need a few strands for Violet. I promise not to damage your pretty hair."

It wasn't what she said but the gentle thread of her voice and the soothing sweep of her hand on my shoulder up to my hair that eased me.

I held perfectly still as she snipped just a few strands, walked to Violet, and dropped them into the bowl of water. Evie set the scissors on the bookshelf, then returned to my side. She leaned against the side of the chair, her heat wonderfully close, and placed a hand on my opposite shoulder. Someone might even think she was wrapping her arm around me in a kind of embrace, but I knew better. She was grounding me with touch.

"Relax," she whispered down to me. So I tried.

Clara lit a tall, slender candle and placed it at the center of the table, then sat to Violet's left. Jules had been busy lighting a stick of incense. She whispered something, then walked a full circle around the table, then around me, then behind Violet before stabbing the stick into a small bowl of black sand to the right of the divining bowl. She took a seat across from Clara.

Violet had been seated, cross-legged, with her eyes closed the entire time. Now, she opened them, her sky-blue eyes shining with supernatural light as she stared into the pool. With a swirl of her purple-painted fingertip above the bowl, the water moved in a circle. I could see the few strands of my hair sitting on top, slowly sinking as the little pool rippled around.

The second my hair slipped into the water, a sharp pulse of energy punched the air. It came from Violet. Alpha growled despite Evie's calming force at my side.

"Shhh," she whispered. "You're safe."

I knew I was safe and these witches were here to help me. Even so, the magic in the room felt like a threat, and I had no idea why.

"Show your master," Violet whispered to the water.

The water swirled and swirled as she circled her finger in the air above the water's surface, faster and faster, images seemingly to flit by in the ripples. Violet snapped her fingers. The water froze as if we were watching a television show and someone pressed pause.

Above the still water, a droplet suspended in midair. Beneath that on the surface of glassy water was an image of my artwork in the gallery. A bust of Medusa, her hair like living serpents hissing at an enemy.

Violet snapped her fingers, and the water swirled again, so fast that some of it was slipping over the edge.

"Show me your master," she commanded louder, her voice dipping to an unnatural register as she snapped her fingers again.

The water froze like before, but this time the image was of myself working in my studio shirtless. The focus of the frame was my naked torso, my arms and back muscles flexed as I worked on a sculpt. I often worked shirtless in the summer months when the heat was just too unbearable. Evie's hand clenched on my shoulder.

What the hell was this? I wasn't the one who put this spell on myself. Why was it showing images of me and my artwork? It made no sense.

When Violet snapped her fingers again, the water swirled in a frenzy, rippling wildly as if a beast surged beneath the surface. She put her palm in the air facing down toward the bowl.

"Enough," she whispered with guttural menace. "Show me your fucking master."

The water swirled and lifted out of the bowl, raising out of its holder, still circling insanely fast. The blur of an image inside the water, a streak of gray and red. My wolf? Blood? What was it?

"Show me!" Violet's voice vibrated with aggression.

Clara jumped at the force. Evie clenched my shoulder so tight I could feel her nails digging in.

The image bled black, turning the water muddy. With a sudden crackle of magic, the bowl flipped in the air and landed face down with an audible thwack. The black water had snuffed out the candle, and the burning incense hissed when it sizzled out.

Violet panted, scowling down at the mess, her fists balled on the table. Clara reached over quickly with both hands and put them on her sister's arm, her skin lighting with that golden sheen like the other night when she put that happy spell on me.

Jules turned a scowling gaze on me. "Someone definitely means you harm, Mateo."

"I have no idea who."

Violet snapped up into a standing position, brushing Clara off, telling her, "I'm okay." Then her electric gaze moved to me and Evie. "Whoever it is, she's a strong bitch."

"You mean witch," said Evie, calm as ever.

"No, I mean bitch. She's not only cast a binding spell on him, she's bound the fucking spell itself so we can't see in. She doesn't want anyone seeing in. If it is a she. Could be a he for all the fuck I know."

"Violet—" started Clara.

"I'm fine," she snapped, then more gently to her twin. "Really. Don't worry about me. You should all be worrying about this werewolf. This is a powerful witch, whoever he or she is. Anyway,

I've got to go." She raised her hands and slapped them against her jeans. "This mess."

"I'll clean it up," said Clara. "Go on."

Violet didn't wait. She left in a huff. Clara smiled at Jules. "I'll go get some towels."

Jules aimed her gray gaze at me. "You don't know of anyone who would mean you harm?"

Frustration ripped through me. "I told you. I have no enemies."

"I'm afraid you do," she snapped back.

Leaning forward with my elbows on my knees, I combed my hands into my hair. "Look. I don't know of anyone. I've told you."

"What about business rivals?"

"Business rivals? I'm an artist. In a rare market of metalwork. The other artists I know don't even have the same clientele. Our work is so different."

"What about an ex-girlfriend?" she asked.

Evie flinched at my side, removing her hand from my back where it had slid when I leaned forward. I wanted to grab her hand and put it back on me, feeling the separation like a bone break.

I thought of Caroline, meek and mild as a lamb who had stuttered out an apologetic plea for us to move in together. I shut her down so fast it made her head spin, then I severed all ties. Last I heard, she'd already started dating some dentist in Metairie, so she obviously wasn't that brokenhearted.

"No." I shook my head. "I've only dated humans anyway."

"Humans hire witches to cast spells all the time."

Growing more frustrated, I rephrased, "I don't let girlfriends get attached."

Jules scoffed. "You're a very attractive guy, Mateo. Handsome with a thriving business. A sensitive artist. Some women would get very attached. Whether you want them to or not."

When I glanced up from boring a hole into the floor, I caught her looking over my shoulder at Evie, not at me.

"Trust me when I tell you, it's not an ex-girlfriend. I break it off long before they can get attached. Before they can get their hearts tied into it. I'm a loner, okay. Yes, I fucking love sex, but I prefer it with someone I know, not a random hookup. But I always break it off as soon as the newness has worn off. I can promise you women never stand a chance with me."

I felt Evie go rigid behind me. I knew I sounded like a cold-hearted bastard, but it was the truth. And I wasn't going to let her sister think for a second that one of the timid, submissive women I'd dated in the past could be the culprit here. It would just waste time finding the real target.

Jules simmered for a second, apparently thinking over my words. "It would help us if we knew what kind of witch cast this spell. Especially since Evie has never tried to break the hex of a werewolf."

I glanced back to find Evie leaning against the bookshelf, avoiding my gaze. I wanted to force her to look at me, but Jules kept talking.

"We'll perform the spell on the night of the full moon next week. I think attempting the hex-breaking spell at the time your wolf will want to come out the most would be best. Especially now that we know we have a powerful witch on the other end of this binding spell."

I nodded, grinding my jaw shut. Something about this whole experience had my hackles rising. But the only thing that really had me pissed off was the fact that Evie had withdrawn from me, and I didn't know why. Well, sort of. I'd talked about women like they were disposable, and that made me look like an asshole. But it was the way life had been for me. The way I wanted it. Until now.

Evie walked toward the door, still avoiding my gaze. "Come on. I'll show you out."

Show me out? The hell she would.

You tell her.

She was going to talk to me whether she liked it or not.

And if talking doesn't work, I have better ideas.

CHAPTER 15

~EVIE~

BY THE TIME WE GOT TO THE FRONT DOOR, I'D ERECTED A STONE fortress, complete with battlements and a moat filled with crocodiles, around my silly, soft heart. Yeah, Mateo had told me he didn't do relationships, but something about the way he said *women never stand a chance with me* doused the inferno that had combusted when he'd said *I fucking love sex.* I had to let go of the small inkling of hope that *we* could become an *us.*

There was always the option—after we broke this hex, of course—that we could have a purely sexual relationship for a few months. I could do that. Scorch-the-earth sex with Mateo, then . . . then what? Then he'd toss me to the curb like his other ladies so I wouldn't get too clingy. Because let's face facts, I was already getting clingy. Right now, I loved just hanging with him. If we let sex muddle it all up, we wouldn't even have the friendship thing. And goddammit, I really liked him as a friend. But . . . hot, melty, lickalicious sex with Mateo?

"Did you even hear me?"

"What?" I snapped back to the man spinning my brain into mush.

Standing on the porch, he chuckled, but his expression was tight. I didn't blame him. That shit show in the study was pretty freaking intense.

"Come have coffee with me. French Truck Coffee makes a mean espresso."

I glanced at my watch, not even reading the time. "Nah. I should get some more reading done. Looks like I have my work cut out for me with this hex of yours."

"But we've still got two hours left."

I shrugged one shoulder. "Just kind of tired."

"Tired? Or angry?"

"Why would I be angry?"

"I don't know. You tell me."

"I'm not angry."

"And you're a shitty liar."

"Well, now I'm angry." I crossed my arms. "For your information, I'm a phenomenal liar."

"Oh yeah? Prove it."

"Like how?"

He eased a step closer, his hands in his front pockets. "Pretend you're happy and come have coffee with me."

He was using that gentle tone with the vulnerable puppy dog look in his eyes. Damn, he played dirty. Even though I was stewing about his I'm-a-loner bullshit, I really couldn't resist him. So I raised the drawbridge, letting my hungry crocodiles snap in their moat, and said, "Fine."

He held out his arm. I'd become accustomed to hooking my arm through his while we walked. Right now, I was staring at it like it was a poisonous viper ready to strike. He smirked, tilting his head. "Such a bad liar," he whispered.

Inhaling and exhaling a deep breath, I slipped my arm through his and let him lead me down the walkway to the street. I could be an amazing actress when I focused, so I did just that. Strolling lightly alongside him like I usually did.

"So, dinner was pleasant, right?" I injected a bit more sarcasm than was necessary.

I felt a rumble of laughter through his rib cage to my arm but didn't hear it.

"Lovely. I've never had a predinner animal act. That was a nice touch."

"We aim to please. Especially with such an illustrious dinner guest as yourself."

We walked on, but he went silent for a second. I suppose I could've held back some of the bitterness in my voice. But okay! I wasn't a good liar! Happy now?

"Evie. I upset you."

YES! "*No*. Not at all."

He grunted. "So the fact that I mentioned past girlfriends has nothing to do with this."

"Mateo, what you do with other women is your business."

"Mmm. Right." He flexed his arm, tightening his hold on me. "Look. I know I sounded like a dick, but I was frustrated, all right? Your sister was onto the wrong lead. And I'd told you before I never stuck with one woman for long."

"Yes. You told me. That's fine."

"I'm not a complete asshole, Evie. I'm honest and up front."

"I don't doubt that for a second."

"So you're just angry because what? Because I'm honest?"

I was being an idiot. He was right. I blew out a breath and pulled us to a stop, angling to stand in front of him as a troop of lady shoppers paraded by, their bags taking up most of the sidewalk.

"I'm not mad at you." And now it was true somehow. How could I be mad at him for being who he was? He was still the same Mateo. Honest, genuine, and maddeningly beautiful. I just had a much clearer picture where women stood in his life. This little hissy fit of mine proved one thing to me. I'd rather be his lifelong friend than his temporary girl. I smiled and held out a hand to shake. "Friends?"

He stared with such intensity I thought he'd zoned out. His lips parted to speak but nothing came out. After a slow blink, he took my hand and pulled me against him in a semi-hug, wrapping his other arm around my waist. His voice was rough, his mouth close to my ear. "Friends."

I let myself lay my head against his shoulder for a few seconds, knowing good and well I was going to need a double-moat. Before I could sink into the warmth and scent of perfection, I pulled away. We walked on without touching but in a more contented silence.

A cool breeze swept down the street, raising goose bumps on my bare legs. I crossed my arms, realizing the weather was finally taking a turn for fall. Good thing since October was almost over.

Before long, we were stepping up to the bright yellow café, French Truck Coffee. He held the door open for me, and we slipped in.   ·

"Dinner was on you so coffee is on me," he said. "Anything in particular?"

"I love their Crosstown Espresso."

"Got it."

While he stood in line, I found a two-top and settled in. Because I was too busy people watching, I didn't notice when Mateo started talking with a woman in line behind him. She spoke animatedly with one hand, her other arm loaded with an oversize Saint Laurent handbag and a Pilot and Powell shopping bag. I'd stumbled into that store once when Livvy was looking for something to wear to a Mardi Gras ball. We stumbled right back out after looking at one of the price tags.

The woman was probably in her forties, well-styled blond hair just past her shoulders, and the mannerisms of someone with good breeding. Someone accustomed to money and all the wonderful things it could bring. I glanced down at my T-shirt and shorts as he waited with her for their, I mean *our*, coffees to be ready. I squirmed in my seat, not happy with how natural he looked next to a woman like that. I then had the awful feeling that maybe she had been one of his lovers that he'd let go.

No. I was being paranoid. Ridiculous. He smiled at her with genuine fondness.

He walked over to me with her at his side. She carried her coffee in a to-go cup.

"Evie," he said, setting our espressos on the table. "This is Sandra Blake, one of the artists who exhibits in my gallery."

I was a total idiot. I held out my hand with a smile. "Do you paint the abstract landscapes?"

She took my hand and gave it a genuine shake, not a feeble, girly one. That made me like her and feel even more like an asshole.

"Guilty, I'm afraid." She wasn't just a lovely-looking woman as I'd thought from afar, but was stunning. To-die-for bone structure and a flawless complexion that was just downright sinful on a woman past thirty. "I wish I had more originality like Mateo here, but I'm one of those who paints what she sees."

"Like the Impressionists," I added.

"Yes. You know your art." She gave me a kind smile.

"Well, I know my artists." I glanced at Mateo, then said to her, "Your work is beautiful." And I meant it. She'd painted the silhouettes so familiar to Louisiana but in brilliant colors and with bold, intense brushstrokes.

"You're too kind, Evie. But thank you."

"You must have a beautiful home."

"I do, but I owe it all to my Gene, God rest his soul. You and Mateo should come and have tea with me sometime."

I laughed to myself, thinking of Clara and her weekly book club where they had a high tea and broke down their latest historical romance. Though a bit younger than her book club members, she'd love Sandra Blake.

"That would be nice, thank you."

"Well, I won't keep you." She turned to Mateo. "So I can send Missy my commission request?"

"Of course," he replied, a soft smile curling his lips. "But Sandra, let's just make a deal on gallery rental space. I don't feel comfortable invoicing you."

She waved a diamond-befingered hand. "Please. You'll invoice me the full amount, and that's all there is to it. Your time is valuable." She leaned in, and he bent for the perfunctory kiss on the cheek they both seemed familiar with. "You two kids enjoy your Sunday. Pleasure meeting you, Evie."

Then she was off out the door, and Mateo settled across from me.

"Wow," I said. "I'm not sure what I was expecting of your fellow artists in the gallery, but it sure wasn't her."

"How's that?"

I froze a minute, trying to find the words.

"Don't tell me," he teased. "You're expecting them all to be bohemian, tattooed, and pierced to the nth degree. Like your *best friend*, Scotty."

"Well, I wouldn't say that, but—" I sipped the espresso. "Mmm, this is delicious. Better drink it up before it gets cold."

He chuckled, taking a sip and eyeing me from under his dark lashes before he set his cup down and said, "I do believe you're an artist bigot, Evie."

"I am not! I just, I mean, she doesn't look like the kind of artist I'm used to around here. But she's good."

"Yeah. She's truly talented. She was actually the first artist I met in the area at another exhibit uptown. I told her I was looking to buy a gallery, but wanted other artists to join in to rent show space. She invested to get it off the ground until I could pay her back. Her connections got another artist, my friend Kyle, on board. And with some others like Scott, who exhibit from time to time but not on a regular basis, I've been able to do quite well."

I smiled, happy to see that Mateo had found success here after he felt forced to leave his family and home. But I couldn't keep my mouth shut when I asked, "So, did you and her ever . . . ?"

"Ever what?"

"You know." I gave the universal twirly hand signal that meant to fill in the blanks. In this case, I insinuated sex.

"Me and Sandra?" He sounded almost appalled. "No way." He chuckled and frowned at the same time.

"Why so shocked? She's a very attractive woman."

"She is. But she started as my business partner. Any thoughts I might've had in that arena ended way back when."

"Then you're admitting you *did* have the hots for her."

His heavy gaze and lopsided smirk told me he knew I was fishing too hard on this. My jealousy was showing like a stupid bright beacon. A Batman-size beacon.

"Yes, she is a very attractive woman." He placed a forearm on the table, leaning closer, his voice dipping intimately. "But she's just a friend."

"Like us."

"No." He blinked heavily, his gaze drifting to my mouth. "Not like us. We're very good friends."

Mouth gone dry, I needed to drink down my coffee and shut up. "Well, cheers to Sandra Blake." I held up my cup.

He tapped his to mine. "And to very good friends," he said low and soft and with complete adoration as he lifted the cup back to his lips, his dreamy brown eyes hooked on mine.

I smiled and drank, knowing full well the warmth curling in my belly had nothing to do with the coffee and everything to do with my very good, swoony, heart-melting friend.

CHAPTER 16

~MATEO~

"I have another surprise for you," I told her from the other side of the bar top at the Cauldron.

"What!" Her look of pure joy jerked the breath out of me. Funny how she always tilted her head slightly to the side when she smiled like that. Her almond-shaped eyes crinkled like she had a secret. No, like we shared a secret. I wanted to wrap her in a hug and lift her off the ground, bury my face in her neck, but that would be kind of crazy.

She nudged my elbow. "Is this better than Gotham City Grill?"

"I'm not sure. Maybe."

"You're not sure?" She reached back and tightened her ponytail, then blew a loose strand that had fallen in her face.

Again, my instinct was to touch her, tuck that auburn hair behind her ear, trace the shell with the pad of my fingers, feel the silkiness of her skin.

"How can you not be sure? It's your surprise!"

"Yeah." I glanced away for a second, curling my fingers into fists, willing myself not to touch her. "But I'm not sure if you've been here before, so it might not be all that exciting."

"Oh, now I'm *super* intrigued." She rounded the bar top, grabbing her brown leather jacket off a hook. "Am I dressed right?"

I took in her tight skinny jeans, her pink Converse, and long-sleeved T-shirt with Deadpool wearing a Jason mask.

"You're perfect." Indeed, she was. "How many Deadpool T-shirts do you have anyway?"

She grinned and ignored my question. "Whatever you have planned, it must not be Halloween-related."

"Why not?" I shielded her from a rowdy group of guys pushing toward the bar where JJ was serving up drinks fast.

"Because it's Halloween, doofus." She let me wrap my arm around her shoulders and push through toward the exit. "And you're not in costume," she added.

"That doesn't mean it's not Halloween-related." We pushed out onto the street, buzzing with partyers. "I can't believe you were able to get off tonight."

"Ha!" She skipped a step, her ponytail swinging high, her hands tucked into her jacket pockets. "We're on annual rotation for Halloween night. Because of our pub's theme, we tend to draw in big crowds this time of year. And none of us want to work the crazy party people. This year, Violet and Clara pulled the short straws. And Belinda, our other server, is there. They can handle it."

I opened the passenger door of my truck parked on the street. She flashed a small smile and hopped in. I jogged around to my side, more excited than I thought I'd be for tonight. Maybe it was because this past week Evie had been more withdrawn. She'd joined me in the studio every day, as promised, but she wasn't engaging as much with me. Even though she said everything was fine after that interrogation gone bad by Jules, I felt like something was off. I had hoped my plans for tonight might bring her back to me. This past week, she'd either stretched out on the floor or cozied up on the futon, her head bent and focused on her tablet as she worked with her stylus, ignoring me. I should've been focusing more on my own new sculpt, but Evie had become both a balm to my manic thoughts and spark to newer, more sensual, ones.

I had my suspicions on what she was working on, but hadn't found the right time to ask her about it. There was no doubt she was being secretive, wrapping up her work quickly whenever I approached. No matter. Her intense focus allowed me uncensored glimpses of her in deep thought. It was perfect to help with my new commission.

Sandra had sent over the parameters, which allowed more creative license on my part than most. Her request was simple: a young, beautiful woman in a flowing gown and a hooded cloak with an expression conveying hope, strength, and love. She'd given the size requirements and the deadline she was hoping for if I could make it happen. Other than that, she'd only written, *I want a beautiful, powerful piece. Follow your muse, Mateo.*

With that, Sandra had opened the door for me to create what had been stamped in my brain, and possibly on my heart, for a short while now. Having access to my living and breathing muse for this sculpture, to watch her daily, to mark her expressions, to channel her soft beauty into heat and galvanized steel, felt like fucking heaven.

You know what else would feel like fucking heaven?

Not even you can drag me down, Alpha. Things feel too good right now.

It was almost as if the hex had been frozen or stalled. The feverish thoughts and anxiety had lessened considerably. Alpha kept his mouth shut almost entirely when I was around Evie.

That's because I like her.

This isn't a news flash.

I also want to fuck her.

Again. Nothing I didn't know.

Just you wait. The time is coming. Jacking off isn't going to cut it much longer. I need flesh.

The last was punctuated with an otherworldly rumble that sharpened my senses and shot a chill of fear down my spine. That's when I heard the growling rumble filling up the cab.

"Are you okay?" asked Evie next to me.

"Oh, sorry. Yeah. All good."

"Just Alpha being grumpy again?"

She likes me.

"Yeah," I answered with a nervous laugh, combing a hand through my hair. "I think he's a little testy with so many people out and about."

"People make him nervous?"

That's funny. *No one* makes me nervous.

"Not exactly." I wasn't sure I could put it into words. It was like the feeling I got when it was time to shift, a push toward the animal. Like being shoved in the back by something big and primal. "I think it's just the energy in the air."

"Maybe because the full moon is almost here."

"Maybe." I glanced at her and kept my thoughts to myself.

She was quiet a minute as we neared City Park.

"We've got the hex-breaking ceremony soon." She stared out the window as if to avoid looking at me.

"Are you worried about breaking it?"

"No." She shook her head before facing forward. "I can do it."

"Then what is it?"

The thickening crowds cleared enough to see the banner-size signs marking where I was taking her. "Oh my God! The Voodoo Festival!" She unsnapped her seatbelt and launched herself across the seat to hug me.

"Whoa!" I laughed, giving her a one-armed hug as I maneuvered down a side street to find parking.

"Mateo! I can't believe it." She bounced back to her side.

"So you've never been?"

"Yeah. But it was a few years ago." She's beaming as she spits out, "Violet is the only one who likes concerts as much as me, but for some reason something always comes up around Halloween."

"Might be the whole witch business."

"Ha ha. Funny guy." She laughed. "But you're probably right. Somehow, there's always some crazy crap going on in the magic world this time of year."

I had to park a few blocks down. We hopped out. She was actually bouncing, giddy with excitement. I couldn't stop grinning while I waited for her to meet me on the side of the street. When we started walking, I maneuvered to the outside on the street side. Some drivers didn't give a shit about pedestrians. If they didn't move in time, they got hit.

I'll smash their car into dust if they try to hit me or my woman.

Okay, Hulk. You do that.

"I never pegged you for a concert guy," she said excitedly, giddiness in her voice.

"I have a booth here every year. We'll stop by there first."

"Do you need to work it?"

"Missy takes care of sales. Me and Kyle and Scott always leave it in her hands. Pop in to check on things. But one of us always helps break down the booth each night."

"That's cool. I hope you're paying her overtime for working the whole weekend of the festival."

"She's paid well for her hard work, and she earns it. But let's get back to your little comment and my concert preferences." The back of my hand brushed hers, sending a sizzle of awareness along my skin. "You know, there's a lot you don't know about me."

She grinned. "Ooh, big mystery man."

I waggled my eyebrows teasingly.

She giggled in a throaty sort of way that made me want to grab her and kiss the fuck out of her.

Finally! That's a start. *Go* **with this feeling.**

I shook my head to shake him off. More and more, Alpha's little nudges sounded like perfect sense, and that bothered the hell out of me.

"Let's play Two Truths and a Lie." She beamed a teasing look at me, not noticing my derailed thoughts.

"Two Truths and a Lie?" I put my hand on the small of her back as a loud muscle car sped by.

"Yeah. I tell you two things that are true and a lie about myself. And you guess which one is a lie. Then we switch."

"What do I get if I win?"

She laughed. "Whatever you want."

Oh, sweet baby of mine. Daddy's ready.

"Within reason," she added. "But it could be a tie."

"Okay." I glanced around, watching for cars. "You go first."

Music pumped in the near distance. Another car powered up the street. I wrapped a hand around her hip and pressed her close then released her when they passed. I didn't mean to be handsy, but I couldn't stop myself either. My primitive nature seemed to be sweeping forward tonight. And there was no doubt my wolf thought of Evie as mine to protect.

Fuckin' right.

She took a minute before finally saying, "My favorite memory of my dad is when he wore my mom's apron and sang Diana Ross's 'I Will Survive' while baking Christmas cookies." She glanced up at me. "That's memory number one." The soft glow of the streetlight shimmered over her profile. "A boy in elementary school punched me in the stomach when I knocked his lunch over."

Kill. Him. Find him and tear him limb from limb.

Overkill.

That's the stupidest word in the English language.

"Violet punched him back and bloodied his nose," she added, then skipped a step. "And finally, Violet won a recording contract for a song she wrote in high school, but she turned it down because she thought a singing career wasn't challenging or fulfilling enough. Okay, which is the lie?"

I thought for a second. "I think the second is the lie." I hoped so, because thinking of some dickhead hitting her, even in elementary school, made me see red.

"Dammit. Yes! You guessed it."

"Pretty creative on the lie, though."

"Actually most of it was true. Benny Davidson was such a bully. But it was Jules who punched him in the nose."

"Really?" I fisted my hands, trying to cool my overreaction to a long-ago memory of some little twat who pushed my girl around. My girl? What the fuck? I had to get Alpha out of my head. "So she isn't just all bark and no bite, your sister?" I added.

"Not at all." She laughed.

Take note. Benny Davidson is officially on my top five kill list.

Oh yeah? Who else is on there? The guy who had road rage on me last month?

That douchebag is number three.

What about the dude who cut in front of us at Subway last week? He definitely deserves to die for delaying our footlong steak and cheese.

Nah. Giving him a pass.

Who's number one then?

I'm saving that spot for when someone really pisses me off.

So you've only been moderately pissed off by the others so far.

That's right. But the time is coming when they'll all pay. As soon as I can shift and you step out of my way.

A shiver trembled through me, the fear and need and craving for my next shift promising danger. Yet another reason to cool my jets on this possessive streak that I was feeling way too hard.

"Your turn," said Evie. She glanced up at me. "You okay?"

"Of course." I forced a smile. "Let's see." I thought a minute. "Okay. My cousin Nico joined a Lycan motorcycle gang. But he fought the leader for alpha status and lost, so he left the gang."

"Whoa. That's a doozy."

"Memory number two." I winked. "My grandpa taught me to make meat pies. I got so good I won three contests, including first place in the San Antonio Amateur Bake-off, savory category. Twice."

"Ohhhh, man." She shook her pointer finger at me. "You're good at this."

"Number three. I once spent a year in the wilds of Alaska, living off the land."

She smirked up at me. "That last one is a no-brainer. I'm surprised you only spent a year."

I nudged her so hard she lost her balance. But I grabbed her forearm and pulled her quickly to my side, both of us laughing. I let my hand reluctantly slide away, fingertips grazing her skin.

She glanced at me out of the corner of her eye, then cleared her throat. "Okay. Let me think. All I know about your cousin is you said he's an arrogant asshole. So would that kind of personality join a motorcycle gang? Because I'm not sure he'd want to follow anyone."

I shrugged and made my face as blank as possible.

"But if he also challenged the alpha, that seems to line up more with the overconfident guy you described. However, maybe you're trying to use reverse psychology on me."

"Great analytical skills. I didn't realize this game was so complex."

"*Or,*" she dragged out in exaggeration, "you gave me a somewhat plausible lie as the truth and a ridiculous truth as a lie. Depends on which psychological tactics you're using, really."

"Me baking award-winning—no, first place award-winning—meat pies is ridiculous? I'm so hurt." I palmed my chest and gave her a sad face.

"Please."

"Stop stalling. I want an answer."

She narrowed her gaze on me suspiciously as we stopped at the four-lane we had to cross to enter City Park. I arched a brow at her and waited.

"Okay. The story about Nico is the truth and that pie story has to be a lie."

A crazy wave of excitement flushed through my body, like a shot of adrenaline. Why was I so excited that she was wrong?

Because now you get a reward.

"Wrong." I grinned like a villain. "My cousin did join the gang, but he left after I beat his ass and told him to stop being a fucking idiot, not because he lost a challenge to the alpha."

"Are you kidding me?"

"Not at all."

"You beat up your cousin? You don't seem like the kind of guy who would use violence to win an argument."

Oh, baby. Violence is my beloved friend.

Her smile slipped, as if she'd heard Alpha. I knew she couldn't. She'd just forgotten I was a werewolf for a minute there.

"Like I told you before, I keep a tight leash on my temper. But Nico wouldn't understand anything other than brute force at the time."

"Wait a second. So that means you're actually a meat pie award-winning baker?" She was shrieking so loud, I eased forward and playfully covered her mouth with my hand.

It wasn't meant to be intimate, but my other hand was on the bare nape of her neck. The press of her lips against my palm. The pulse of her heartbeat beneath my fingertips. The closeness of our bodies. God, I felt like I was drowning in sensation from something as innocent as this. I was in so much trouble. Her green eyes dilated, and all I could think of was what it would feel like if I peeled my palm away and replaced it with my mouth.

Alpha said nothing, but his purring growl was enough.

Counting backward from ten, I managed to speak without sounding like I'd swallowed a rusty can. "Believe it, Evie. Like I said, there's lots you don't know about me."

I dropped my hands from her and eased back. She stared a minute, her mouth partly open. Maybe in shock, because there was no denying the charge sparking the air seconds before.

She cleared her throat and glanced at the thinning traffic. "Well, then. I guess you'll be making me meat pie for dinner soon."

"*I* won the game. That means I get the reward, not you."

"Mateo Francisco Cruz." Her sass was back. Thankfully. "You do not throw out a detail like that and not allow me to be the judge of your award-winning skills. You're making me meat pie."

I grabbed her hand and led her across the street through a break in cars. "If you're going to beg me, Evie," I said, shooting her a wink, "I'll give you my meat pie."

CHAPTER 17

~EVIE~

I'M IN WAY OVER MY HEAD. YEAH, I WANTED TO EAT HIS MEAT PIE, NO doubt about that. And I was not imagining things. There was definitely something going on tonight. He'd be all bestie friendly one second, then suddenly look at me like I was one of those double-stacked Gotham burgers the next. But maybe that was all Alpha's fault?

That made so much more sense. I mean, I wasn't blind that he was physically attracted to me. I knew that look, though there had been few men who could make me shiver with longing when they gave it to me. But he hadn't acted on those feelings, and that was for the best.

Definitely for the best. Because friends was better than nothing. And after a few months of mind-melting sex, that's what we'd be when he cut me loose.

"Here."

He stopped me close to the entrance gate and pulled out two purple plastic bracelets from his pocket—our tickets for entry. He wrapped one around my wrist, his fingers brushing the tender underside as he snapped it close to my skin, but not too close. Without much effort, he ripped off the excess without hurting me. Mateo seemed so at ease, so calm all the time, that I really did forget he was a werewolf sometimes. But then he'd do small things like that, and I'd remember. Humans nor witches could snap that kind of plastic like it was a toothpick.

"VIP tickets?" I studied the bracelet and arched a brow at him.

He just smiled, giving me all the tingles, as he put his own on.

"What does Loa mean?" I asked, noting the word in eerie script on the bracelet.

Our heads were bent, me looking at my bracelet, him snapping his on. "Loa means *spirit* in the Voodoo religion. The one you call upon for special requests." His voice was low and husky as he peered at me from his lowered head. The melting brown flared with a shock of gold beneath his lashes. "So if you have any requests, tonight is the night to ask." He took my hand and led us inside.

Yet again, I weighed the two options, friends or temporary lovers, wondering if it was worth crossing that line. Then he laced his fingers with mine and aimed his beaming smile at me, tugging me toward a row of tented booths set up in the park.

No way. I'd miss this. I wasn't sure how, but Mateo had become essential to my life. I liked having him around every day. I'd miss him if he wasn't. And that shocked the hell out of me.

"Wow, I've never seen all this before." We meandered past tents with all kinds of artwork, most of them shutting things down for the night.

"Check that out." He pointed to a giant screen with some kind of live feed of an unbelievably beautiful beach with crystal waters and silvery fish swimming around. The view kept swiveling from a focus on the water then to the land. I noticed a petite girl standing to the side with a virtual reality headset on.

The vendor stood behind a control panel. He punched something and the beach disappeared, now a dark castle in a thunderstorm looming ahead. The girl wearing the headset walked forward, the castle's door drawing closer. When it opened on its own, a gruesome ghost popped out.

Everyone watching, including myself, jumped. The girl with the headset screamed and pressed hands over her laughing mouth. The crowd laughed too. She reached out to the air. On the large screen, the gruesome ghost evaporated into mist. She froze, staring at a set of rickety stairs.

"Do it!" yelled a slim guy next to her. "Come on, Lacey. Don't be a chicken."

She swatted the air beside her but her friend jumped out of reach.

"Come on, Lace," said another girl. "Go see what's up there."

Mateo smiled at me and tugged me on. There were other cool booths that seemed to be just opening up while the arts and crafts booths were closing down. We passed a video game simulator with live action and a giant screen in front of the two players. They stood in front of some sort of video monitor that tracked their movements as they aimed kicks and punches in the air. On the jumbo television screen, two muscle-bound opponents were mimicking their actions as they fought each other.

"I'm going to kill you, dude," said the player wearing a backward hat.

"In your dreams, bro."

We moved on as their friends and the crowd cheered them on. The atmosphere was fun and festive, the bands cranking up on the three separate stages in the distance.

"I didn't see any of this last time. Violet and I just came for the bands."

I noticed he was holding my hand again, but very casually, like we did this all the time. Somehow, it felt like we did, even if I was cognizant of every time he squeezed me tighter, moving us through the crowd. His constant small touches tonight kept spiking my adrenaline, my heart steadily beating faster than normal.

"There are all kinds of vendors in the music and video industry who show off their new tech here. Come check this out."

He stopped at a tent marked Loa VIP Lounge. We scanned our bracelets and then entered. There were plush chairs and sofas spread around, a cash bar in the corner with specials for VIPers, free water and soda station, even some snacks set out. In one corner, there was a tarot card reader bent low over her cards, only the scarf wrapping the top of her head visible. A few people stood around, partially blocking my view as they watched her give a blonde girl a reading.

"You want a reading?" he asked with a smirk.

I shook my head on a laugh. "If I wanted one, I'd get Violet to do it. She's far more accurate."

"You're a tarot reader snob." He poked me in the belly. Rather than tickle, it only heightened my awareness of him, of his hands on me.

I rubbed the spot and batted his hand away. "No. But—okay, well, maybe I am."

"So you don't believe in readings?"

"Of course, I do. They're completely legit. With the right witch or human psychic anyway."

He nodded, his gaze lingering where I still had my palm flattened to my stomach. That heightened awareness shot into the cosmos, his gaze raking my body, my face, settling heavily on my eyes.

His looks were like a tangible caress sweeping over me. But rather than satisfy, it was the kind of phantom touch I could become addicted to. His heavy looks made me wonder what his talented hands would feel like if they traced where his eyes tracked over me. My pulse pounded harder, drumming in my throat. Suddenly, the cool night air wasn't enough to keep the sweat from dampening my neck.

"You want a drink?" His voice—gruff and husky—pumped my blood even faster. "Water? Beer?"

A tight nod. "A cold beer sounds good." A little alcohol to take off the edge would do me good right now.

"Preference?"

"Anything Abita if they have it."

He nodded and headed to the bar. I wandered over to the tarot reader, unable to help myself. The closer I got, I sensed the sizzle of magic in the air.

Oh. She was a *real* witch. Not just a human psychic. This, I had to see. As I maneuvered through the crowd, I recognized the sharp features of Beryl. Her dreadlocks were tamed back with a purple scarf wrapped around the top of her head, the ends streaming down one shoulder. I couldn't help but smile when her amber eyes caught mine. She held my gaze for a second, then went back to finish her reading.

Beryl had been my mom's closest friend for ages. There wasn't a time I don't remember her being in our lives, popping in to spend time with my mom in her study, which was now Jules's study. Beryl was the one who taught us girls the best herbs in making our own smudge sticks. I can still hear her sharp instructions on wrapping the lavender and bayberry together, the cedar and sage, the sweetgrass and myrrh.

We rarely saw her these days unless Mom was in town. Keeping to her professional persona, she pretended not to know me as I approached. The Chariot card was upturned in front of the girl.

"So hold fast to the opportunity. When it comes, go. You're meant to take this journey."

"It will be like a real journey? Like a vacation?" the wide-eyed girl asked.

I pinched my lips together so I wouldn't laugh. Beryl was restraining from calling her a fool. This was a paying customer, so she had to show more restraint than she would with me or my sisters.

"Possibly. Keep your eyes open," Beryl told her.

Then she swept the card back into the deck, mixing them with supernatural speed. I noticed some cards shuffling between others of their own accord. Beryl was a Seer like Violet, but her magic poured out through cards more than the divination bowl like it did for my sister.

"That is so cool," one of the blonde's friends murmured as they watched Beryl shuffle. "It's like magic or something."

"It totally is," said another friend.

"Y'all are full of crap. All sleight of hand and shit," said the guy with glasses waiting for them. "Let's get to the stage."

He made me want to laugh most of all because it was totally real like her friend said. That girl had a journey coming. Beryl never missed.

The group meandered off. A brunette hopped in the chair but Beryl held up a palm, the bangles around her wrist jangling. "Not yet, my dear. First, that one." She pointed to me.

"But I was here first," the brunette pouted.

Beryl aimed a withering look at the girl. "When Spirit speaks, we must listen. Spirit wants to message her."

The small gathering of about five swiveled heads to me. I think the last time Beryl read the cards for me, she'd pulled the Major Arcana card, The Fool. This was right before I started dating Derek. I didn't heed her warning, and look where that had gotten me. A year of mediocre sex and a hard kick to my self-esteem.

"I'm not here for a reading, Madame Beryl," I said, smiling at a woman who'd had dinner at our house a hundred times.

"I'm not asking." She snapped a finger, her bracelets jangling again. "The Spirit demands. You must listen."

With resignation and a roll of my eyes, I settled into the chair. I knew she needed my hand on the table, so I faced my right palm down, fingers spread like she'd instruct if I didn't do it. She narrowed a maternal look at me, feeling my sass through my body posture and movements.

Inhaling and exhaling a deep breath to release my anxiety, I let her know I was opening up for her. Otherwise, she'd cause a scene by telling too many secrets about how the Spirit thought I was willful and disobedient like she typically told me.

"Both palms, dear," she commanded.

"Oh, come on, Beryl."

"Both," she snapped.

I ignored the whispers of those watching and pressed both palms to the table. She wanted to be sure I was open. Fine. I was open now. *See*, I seemed to say with a jerk of my eyebrows up, crinkling my forehead.

She began to shuffle the cards again in her tawny, long-fingered hands. The cards moved faster, many shifting without her touch, floating in between each other with frightening speed. With a resounding thunk, she flattened the deck to the table with her palm, jarring the tea light candles on the table.

The brunette waiting beside me squeaked, clinging to her friend. That's when my breathing became labored, too loud in my head, everything else too quiet, like sound sucked into a vacuum. Beryl wouldn't move her palm, her sharp eyes on the downturned deck, a frown pinching her brow together. Oh, hell. This wasn't good.

"Flip the card, Beryl."

When she lifted her palm, the card flipped itself, her magic so attuned to the cards that they did what they were supposed to whether she used telekinesis or not. Something told me the cards were in charge right now, not her. Or Spirit was. Especially when she flipped over the card of—

"Death," murmured Beryl.

The brunette and her friend gasped, round-eyed. But I didn't freak out. I knew this card had more than one meaning besides the obvious. Beryl knew I did, too, but she had to keep putting on her show for the bystanders.

"Death isn't just about endings. It's about beginnings as well. It can mean birth and rebirth. Change and transformation. Could there be a new beginning or a change coming in your life, dear?"

"Maybe," I whispered, and yet my gaze was hooked on the skeleton in knight's regalia, riding a white horse and carrying the five-petaled white flower.

Could it mean my part to play in Mateo's transformation? Could it be a new beginning in my secret dream I kept close to my heart and was still too afraid to chase? I didn't know. All were possibilities, but then all I could focus on was the skeleton head, my breath coming faster as a coldness swept over me, like being kissed by a dark angel. This card wasn't presented as a lofty interpretation of renewal. It was a message directly from the skeleton knight riding on the card.

In a fleeting blur, the knight moved, the horse galloping in place, the flag of the white flower billowing in a nonexistent breeze. The skeleton knight turned his skull's head toward me, his mouth opening into a soundless scream. The hairs on the back of my neck rose. Then suddenly, the card was still, snapped back to the unmoving original design, the knight in profile. When I looked back up at Beryl, I realized she'd seen it too. We must've been the only ones. What did it mean?

"Eveleen," she whispered, but then I felt him.

Mateo's heated presence at my back sent prickles of awareness along my skin. My body just knew when he was near, craving him to come closer. Beryl had her palms flat on the table. The deck shuffled itself, the cards floating high into the air. The watchers gasped. But I held my gaze on the cards, fluttering back down into a ridiculously even stack. Like a knife shooting from an assassin's grip, a card flew out of the deck, flipped, and landed below the card of Death. I closed my eyes at the sight of it, sucking in a deep breath.

"Lovers," said Beryl, her frown smoothing into an accusing look.

I stared at the card with a naked man and woman reaching their arms out to each other.

"Beware of the Lovers card, dear," she said, eyeing the man I knew was at my back. "The Lovers card can hint that you are at a crossroads. One cannot take both paths," said Beryl, her gaze only on Mateo standing right behind me. "Study your options and make the wisest choice." Finally, she looked at me, a flicker of— what was it—fear crossing her face. "Bear in mind, the Spirit gave you two cards at once for a reason."

I couldn't say, *Oh, Beryl. This is ridiculous.* Because for a Seer, Spirit wasn't silly. It was the guiding force that gave her true messages from the metaphysical world. I nodded. "Thank you, Madame Beryl."

I went to pull a bill from my back pocket, but she shook her head. "Go, dear. I can take nothing for that reading, and you know it."

Beryl worked as a tarot reader for tourists for money, yes. But when Spirit took control, she said she couldn't accept money for the message. It must be freely given and accepted.

With a stiff nod, I stood and turned to Mateo whose grim expression was hard and fixed on the table.

"Let's go," I murmured, taking one of the Abita Purple Haze longnecks from him.

"Eveleen," came the softer voice of Beryl. When I looked over my shoulder, she said, "Be careful."

It was no surprise her gaze landed on Mateo yet again. It couldn't be any clearer. *Don't fuck the werewolf! Danger, danger!* Like, was I going to actually die if I did? Was that the message? That's the only thing about tarot readings. I always had more questions than answers afterward. I preferred Violet's divining pool of hard-core images.

Mateo followed me out of the tent, and I stopped to guzzle a third of my beer.

"You know her?"

I dabbed the back of my hand on my lips where a drop of beer dribbled. "She's one of my mom's best friends. Known her forever."

He grunted and swigged his beer, too, looking back at the tent. I expected him to comment on the cards on the table or say something else about Beryl, but he said nothing at all. His deep frown told me his wheels were spinning, though.

"Come on." He gestured toward a row of exhibit booths.

I walked alongside him, both of us drinking down our beers pretty damn fast in silence as we went. I couldn't even take in much around me, still absorbing whatever the hell that was back with Beryl, until we stopped in front of a twelve by twelve tent. Missy was wrapping a familiar charcoal drawing matted in deep red. One of Scott's works.

"Oh, hey!" She beamed her sweet smile at Mateo. "I was just wrapping things up. Kyle already packed yours in the van."

The table was nearly clean with only a few easels standing empty. I walked over to the last one still propped up. It was a brightly colored abstract with hard black contour lines. At first it looked like a burst of jagged sunbeams, like broken glass, but on closer look, I noticed the subtle shades of blue among the fiery reds and golds. The blues together formed a woman's face, though the pieces of color were spread out. It was sort of an optical illusion.

"Wow, this is cool."

"Thanks, pretty lady."

I turned and almost jumped out of my skin. A tall, lanky guy stood behind me, his face painted like a voodoo king, the skeleton features bright white against the black. His look was complete with a tall black top hat and a red velvet coat with tails. His eyes were electric green, almost glowing in the shadowy light around the tent, obviously contacts. Though he looked supernatural, there was no hint of real magic emanating from him.

"Jesus, Kyle," said Mateo, standing closer to me, his hand once more at the small of my back. Without a thought, I leaned into him. He rubbed a small circle with the flat of his palm. "What the hell is this getup?"

He laughed, his big white smile gleaming against the black painted on and around his lips.

"I'm the doorman at the haunted house." He motioned with a jerk of his head. "We've got a mini-version of the Seventh Circle Haunted House to advertise for the big one downtown. Who's your girl?"

"This is Evie. Evie, this is Kyle Montgomery." Mateo didn't bother to protest that I wasn't his girl this time, and I wasn't sure how I felt about that.

He extended a long-fingered hand, which looked super creepy with skeleton bones painted intricately on the back. "Nice to meet you, Evie." He grinned. "Pretty creepy, huh?"

I laughed on an exhale of breath I hadn't realized I'd been holding. "Yeah. You look legit, though. Like a real voodoo priest."

"Just call me Papa Legba."

He winked before turning back to Missy who'd been watching us and packing at the same time. She'd already cleared the whole table except for the painting of Kyle's I'd just been admiring.

"You okay with the last of it?" he asked Missy.

"Yep. All good. You got my keys?"

He passed them over. "The cop at the gate said it would be fine, but don't take too long."

"No worries. The cart has wheels. I'll take care of it."

"You sure?" Mateo asked her.

"Y'all act like I can't take care of things. Haven't I always taken care of everything for you, Mateo?" She seemed a little exasperated, aiming him a sharp look.

"If you're sure."

"Go. I promise I've got it." She waved them off, sliding Kyle's painting into a portfolio carry-case. She heaved it onto her shoulder and took hold of the cart on wheels. "Go have fun." She gave me a tight smile and headed out.

"She's bossy," said Kyle.

"Missy?" Mateo sounded shocked. "She's never bossy."

"You don't know the Missy I know then." He shook off whatever he was thinking and turned back to us. "Hey, why don't you two come check out our haunted house?"

"We were getting ready to head over to the stage."

"Aw, come on, man. Unless you're scared."

Mateo rolled his eyes, which made him look adorable. I'd never seen him make a face like me before. He dipped his head lower to mine. "What do you think?" The weight of his hand on my hip shocked me stupid for a second.

"Yeah." I grinned up at Kyle, unable to meet Mateo's eyes right now. "I love haunted houses."

CHAPTER 18

~EVIE~

Kyle had left us at the entrance and disappeared inside for a few minutes before returning. His grin looked more sinister with the skeleton face paint, and I was getting too many eerie vibes from the repeated imagery of skeletons tonight. I was suddenly rethinking going through the haunted house, but I wasn't about to admit how freaked out I was. And I really did love haunted houses. So why was I so on edge?

"You guys can go in," said Kyle, pointing our way with a gold-tipped cane in his hand. "Don't piss yourself, Cruz."

Mateo gave him a rough shove that knocked Kyle back a step. He just belted out a loud laugh.

"You have really interesting business partners."

"Keeps things from getting dull." He smiled down at me while pushing me ahead of him with a hand on my waist.

"Oh, so I'm going first?"

He smirked. "Ladies always go first."

"Oh my God. Mateo, are you really scared?"

He laughed, but it was sort of breathless, as we were now about a yard from the dark entrance. "It isn't that I'm afraid. It's just—"

"Don't worry." I grabbed his hand in both of mine, tugging him through the arched doorway. "I'll protect you."

"I bet you will."

We entered a pitch-black tunnel, horror sounds in the distance, but here it was quiet. I clung to Mateo's arm, giggling to myself.

"You were saying you were going to protect me?" he whispered against my ear.

I just kept laughing to myself, readying for the first—

"Ahhhhhh!"

A black creature that blended with the wall leaped out with arms raised. I screamed, then threw my head back laughing as I pulled Mateo through a mesh-like door to the next scene. His hands moved over me, one across my neck to grip my shoulder in a loose chokehold. Another coasted from my waist to my hip, squeezing and shooting my adrenaline into the stratosphere. With the added exhilaration of the haunted house, I felt almost high. Completely touch-drunk by Mateo, and I didn't want it to stop. I'm pretty sure I was addicted.

We walked through a sort of graveyard, the mist and wrought iron gate surrounding aboveground crypts. We passed the first, waiting for something to leap from the shadows, but no one did. We passed another on the right, but nothing. When we passed the third, five zombies stumbled out of the mouth of the crypt.

Not only did I jump and practically crawl up Mateo's body but I pushed one zombie back with a telekinetic punch. The dude fell backward onto his ass, then he sat up, shaking his head.

"Crap. Keep going!" I hauled Mateo past the zombies.

"Did you do that?" he muttered in my ear, his lips brushing the shell.

Heat pooled in my middle. "I couldn't help it!" I yelled over the thunderstorm sounds coming from the next room. "He got too close. It just happened."

He gripped my waist with both hands, pulling my body back close to his so I could hear him over the noise. "Be good, little witch."

I had no smart comeback because my brain had left the building and my body wanted to rub up against him like a cat. He nudged me through the next door where there was indeed a simulation of a thunderstorm all around us. No rain, but a fine mist and strong winds whipping the moss-laden fake trees along a winding path. There were eyes peering from the dark, blinking and disappearing. They were canine-like. Then a howl erupted and carried on the wind.

"Oh shit," I said, realizing what kind of creatures were in this "forest" we walked through.

I glanced over my shoulder at Mateo, who'd slowed his walk. His dark eyes were glowing with that inner fire. The feral gleam of his wolf, of Alpha. Fuck. His wolf was readying to fight an opponent.

"Come on." I tugged him harder, pulling him along the lit path.

But when the dude in a werewolf costume jumped out in front of us, I knew we were in deep shit if I didn't do something fast. I turned abruptly and wrapped my arms around Mateo's waist underneath his coat. His body was a steel wall, a murderous growl rumbling in his chest.

"Mateo," I said. "It's okay."

He didn't hear me, his now otherworldly gaze on the fake werewolf making all kinds of stupid snarling and howling noises, swiping the air with his fake claws. This dude was about to get beat to a pulp, and he didn't know it.

"It isn't real." I pushed a hand into Mateo's hair and tugged, forcing his gaze down so he'd look at me. "It isn't real." I shook my head. "He's human. You know this. Reach out."

I wanted him to reach out with his magic, to feel there was no danger. His taut body eased some, his narrowed gaze assessing, his head tilting. With a deep sniff of the air, his body relaxed further but not fully. We could always sense other supernatural creatures. Mateo was able to override his wolf and recognize this for what it was. Thankfully, the fake werewolf made one more little howl and leaped back into the fake forest. Smart move, dude.

I pulled Mateo along, knowing we had to be coming to the end. His body practically thrummed with magic, emanating a sizzling electricity I hadn't sensed on him before. His skin was fever-hot. We needed out of this damn haunted house. This had been a bad idea.

We walked through a mad scientist's lair where deformed creatures hobbled around, chained and in pens, reaching out to touch us. I wasn't even fazed, completely focused on finding our way out. I could see the final arch up ahead, right through one more doorway.

"Almost there," I muttered more to myself, feeling the tension rippling off the werewolf behind me.

As we walked through the last doorway, which was strangely shaped and about three feet deep, a wooden door sealed shut in front of us. I spun to see a wooden panel slam shut behind Mateo. Then I recognized the shape—a coffin. We were standing in an oversize, upturned coffin. I spun back around as people banged on the outer walls, circling us with screams and maniacal laughter. All part of the spooky vibe of a haunted house. Except what the spookers on the other side didn't know was that I was now trapped in a very small box with an amped-up werewolf.

It wasn't fear that jack-knifed my pulse from zero to sixty in a millisecond. It was the wall of steel behind me and the sexual charge snapping off him like a dropped power line.

"Mateo?"

His roughened hands gripped my wrists and pressed my palms to the door in front of us. I was breathing fast and hard.

"Mateo?" My voice shook now.

I felt his head dip, but he hadn't touched me other than to place my hands on the wall, his hard body a wall of heat at my back.

"Don't. Move."

Holy shit. His voice. It was all gravel and rust. Deep and feral. I wasn't talking to Mateo anymore, and I knew it. Long fingers skirted around to the front of my waist, then traveled down over my jeans until he cupped my vagina in a possessive grip. Not moving, just holding.

I jumped. "Oh my God!"

"Shhh."

His other hand fisted around my ponytail and tugged my head back and to the right with a sharp pull. Not enough to hurt me, but enough to make me obey.

Then I felt the heat of his breath just below my ear. And his tongue. Fuck, his tongue. He trailed a line down the column of my throat, sloping onto my shoulder where he bit down with teeth. Enough to sting. His body was aligned with mine, his thighs to mine, his hard cock against the cleft of my ass, his broad chest to my shoulders.

"**Fucking delicious.**" Again, that rough voice that wasn't Mateo, but also was, vibrated against me. A voice that reeked of naughty, naughty things.

The people trying to scare us on the outside bled into nothing. Their stupid screams only amplifying the sensation taking place inside this coffin, this box of dark need and hot werewolf.

His tongue licked a line back up till he gave me a hard suckle just below my ear on a deep, rumbling groan. I bit my bottom lip, but still couldn't stifle the moan of . . . of what? Pleasure? Fear? Both?

"**Yeah,**" he growled in Alpha's voice. "**My girl is fucking delicious.**" He scraped his teeth along the side of my neck, like scoring paper with a knife, outlining where he intended to make his mark. "**Bet you taste good everywhere.**" He rubbed his hand where he cupped me between my legs. A chill shivered down to my toes. For a second, I honestly wondered if he planned to *actually* eat me. Then he tightened his hold on my ponytail, pressed his nose to my skin and inhaled deep. "**Fuck, it's gonna feel good when I finally sink into you.**"

Aaaand, my knees buckled. I pushed against the wall, my fight or flight instincts punching me in the gut. He pressed his body harder, keeping me upright and trapped with far too much ease. His hand on my hair tightened.

"Mateo?"

A rough chuckle against my ear. "**He's left the building, baby.**" He punctuated that with a rock of his pelvis and a grind of his hard dick against my ass.

"Alpha ... please ..."

A hot chuff against my neck. "**Yeah, you'll be sayin' that a lot.**"

He released my hair and skimmed his long fingers around to grip the front of my throat. I froze. This was the moment I knew I was in danger. The wolf's need for both blood and flesh was about the same according to my late-night readings. I could punch him across the room telekinetically but *not* when I was enclosed in a coffin with him. If I pushed him with my magic now, it might make him lose his shit and hurt me.

"**You wanna know what the worst thing is?**" he asked, all husky and carnal.

He brushed the rough pad of his thumb along my pulse. His hand between my legs moved, sliding his long fingers back then forward before he cupped me again, keeping a tight, possessive grip. This insane experience felt more intimate than any sex I'd ever had.

"What?" I asked, resting my forehead against the wood door, the sounds of the banging and laughter outside slowly receding. Thank God. Almost over.

"**When I see a guy looking at you, wanting you ... I want to rip his throat out. Push you to the ground ...**" His hot breath was at my ear, fanning the flames licking in my blood. "**And claim you for all to see. So the world knows you are *mine*.**"

I saw spots for a second, overstimulated and hazed with lust and a small amount of hysteria. Okay, maybe not so small.

"But Mateo, that coward, he won't even entertain the idea."

"I like Mateo," I whispered on a shaky breath.

"Give me one night, and you'll like me more."

The weight and heat of him, the heady sensation of his mouth on my skin, his dominant hold on me, was about to make me spontaneously combust when the door swung open and we both stumbled out into empty air. None of the people who'd been banging and screaming on the coffin were there. Without even looking back, because I couldn't, I jogged ahead for the exit, sucking in a deep breath when we were finally outside and standing on the grass, the upbeat tempo of a band playing nearby.

I breathed in and out for a few seconds, trying to erase the hot brand of his hands on my throat and lady parts. Now I knew why Mateo was so worried about Alpha taking him over. Oh shit. Mateo?

I spun around to find him. For a second, I thought he'd run off, but no, there he was with both hands pressed against an oak tree, arms stiff, his head hanging low. He looked like he had the first night I met him when he'd lost control with that customer and nearly choked him to death. He'd retreated just like this, obviously trying to regain control. I knew he'd be embarrassed because Mateo didn't like to lose control. He'd probably be humiliated by what had just happened. I wasn't embarrassed. I was—well, hell—I was aroused. I wonder what a psychiatrist would say about that.

Well, Doc, apparently I get turned on by being pinned down and helpless, with a bloodthirsty werewolf's hands around my throat and on my pussy without my permission. Is this normal?

I was starting to wonder if my fascination with the bad boys of comics was a healthy thing. Right now, I needed to fix whatever just happened with me and Mateo, because there was no doubt he was in some emotional pain right now.

I eased closer. When I pressed a gentle hand to his back, he flinched. I pulled away.

"Mateo." I sucked in another breath of air, knowing he was back. If he wasn't, I don't think he'd be blocking me out. Alpha would have me on the ground and— Okay, not going there. *Stop* thinking about it. "Mateo, it's okay."

"*No.*" God, that voice. "It's *not* okay."

Holy shit. He was in serious pain.

"Yeah. It really is. I mean, we probably should've thought about what might happen in that haunted house."

He didn't answer, still stiff as ever. He rolled his head up toward the night sky. "I lost myself, Evie."

The anguish in his voice. It cut me so deep my heart clenched.

"Not for long," I tried to reassure him with a soft, friendly tone.

Finally, he turned to me. I winced at the agony etched in the tight lines of his face, the misery in his eyes. "We *have* to break this spell. I could hurt someone. I could've hurt you or . . . worse."

He licked his lips, glancing at mine, then looked away, despair drenching his features. He wouldn't say it, but I knew what he was worried about. And we weren't going to ignore the ginormous elephant in the room. Like Eleven said in *Stranger Things*, "Friends don't lie."

"You think Alpha would've had his way with me?" I asked lightly. Yeah, he might've, but I'm pretty sure I wouldn't have resisted. And that said a whole hell of a lot about me.

He snorted and squeezed his eyes shut, spearing both hands into his hair until he gripped the back of his head.

"He wouldn't have hurt me," I said.

Somehow, I knew this to be true even though Mateo seemed to believe otherwise. I mean, I'm not saying I didn't consider for a second that he gripped me a tad too hard around the throat, but when Alpha told me about his little fantasy, he didn't mention harming me at all. I didn't want him murdering random strangers for looking at me, mind you, but I was almost positive he wouldn't have hurt *me*.

Mateo finally met my gaze, his arched brow and half-grunt full of cynicism. "He would've—" He cut himself off, clenching his jaw so tight I heard something pop.

"No. You're wrong. I know it."

"You *don't* fucking know. What he wants."

Actually, he'd been kind of explicit, but I didn't think repeating it would help right now.

He shook his head, looking helpless and furious at the same time. "He would've done whatever he wanted. Without your permission. He's a fucking animal, and he's a *part* of me. God, when I think—"

My pulse pounded insanely fast. Not out of fear, but from some other emotion overwhelming me as I watched Mateo crumbling in on himself, hating himself. I stepped in front of him and took his hand gently in both of mine. This time, he didn't flinch away.

"Hey," I said softly. He looked at me and swallowed hard. I squeezed his hand. "We're going to fix this. I promise."

He shook his head. "I'm sorry if I scared you. You have to know that I'd never hurt you. But Alpha?" He gulped hard, his Adam's apple bobbing. "I have no idea what he'd do."

"It's okay." I stepped closer, gripping his shoulder and giving him a squeeze so he'd look at me and hopefully see the truth in my face. "I'm fine. We're okay. Right?"

After several painful seconds of absorbing the agony in his eyes, I tugged him out of the shadows. He still hadn't answered me, but he was letting me lead him, and that was good enough.

"You promised to show me some amazing bands, Mateo."

"Yeah," he agreed roughly, his mouth quirking on one side. "I did."

"So stop pouting and come on."

No, he wasn't pouting. He had reason to be stressed out, to be afraid of what might've happened. But I couldn't let him dwell on it and beat himself up any more. That's not what friends did.

As we headed toward the stage, I was sure of two things. One, I had to break this hex, because two, he had good reason to be afraid.

CHAPTER 19

~MATEO~

I was fucking chicken shit.

No argument here.

The morning after the Voodoo Festival, I texted Evie and told her we should take a break until the night of the full moon when we'd do the hex-breaking ceremony, whatever that entailed.

I hope it's a bunch of witches dancing naked in the woods.

Shut up. You're the reason I got into this shitstorm in the first place.

Me? What did I do?

He actually sounded completely innocent. Utterly clueless.

You scared the hell out of Evie, idiot, and I'll never forgive you for it.

A rough snort. **She wasn't scared. I can promise you that. She was down for a wild ride. And you cockblocked us again.**

I couldn't reason with him. Ever since that night when he'd had control for those few harrowing minutes, when I'd experienced true, bone-shaking fear, I'd forbidden myself from seeing Evie. This self-imposed punishment was sheer torture. Not only had Alpha been prominent in my thoughts constantly without her nearby but I . . . I missed her.

I missed her smirky smile, her smart mouth, the sway of her ponytail when she walked, her teasing games, her pretty face.

Her tight, curvy ass.

I wasn't sure what Evie thought when I'd told her let's just wait till the hex-breaking ceremony to see each other again. She'd texted back, worrying about me getting behind in my current commission for Sandra. But I told her a few days wouldn't kill me.

I was such a goddamn liar.

I felt like I was dying slowly. Painfully. Every hour felt like a millennium. That's why I was showered and dressed and pacing my apartment, trying to convince myself not to go to the Cauldron, knowing she was on shift tonight.

Why are you debating this shit? You know you're going.
I shouldn't.

You totally fucking should. She wants us to. She misses us.
She's probably thanking God I gave her a reprieve for a few days.

I mean, she hadn't texted me at all since I'd told her we needed a break.

If I remember right, you texted her, *I need to stay away from you for a while.*

That didn't sound good the way he put it. I mean, I had texted that, but I'd also told her it was because I was worried about what had happened at that haunted house. She'd said she understood, then silence. Nothing. For three days. I was dying. Was she? Did she miss me?

You blew it. She's moved on.

She can't move on when there's nothing to move on from. We're just friends.

Keep telling yourself that. In the meantime, put on your fucking boots and go find her.

This had been my life for three days. I'd even avoided Missy, knowing I was slowly slipping back to the manic, nervous guy I was when I'd first met Evie. I hadn't realized how much I truly needed her to calm the beast.

Blah, blah, blah. Yada, yada. Fuck off. Let's go.

Fine!

I shoved on my boots, grabbed my black hoodie, and headed out. Hands in my pockets, I wove through the night crowd roaming the sidewalk. The cool weather had pushed people out of their homes and onto the streets. They wandered from one haunt to another, laughing and enjoying the company of friends. It made me lonely.

I stopped in my tracks. When had that happened? I'd never been lonely. I was a self-professed loner, a happy bachelor, and supremely contented introvert. Since when had this pang of loneliness filtered into my life?

I'll give you one guess. Starts with an *E* and ends with an *E*.

No way.

You're so slow. Catch up.

I didn't want to think too hard about that. Right now, all I could think of was . . .

Hot as fuck, curvy witch.

Jesus. I walked faster, hoping for the love of all things holy that he'd shut the fuck up once I'd reached her. I was now moving like a man on a mission. It didn't surprise me that two young women leaped out of my way, giving me crazy looks, as I barreled down the sidewalk. I couldn't help it. Now that I'd given in, I had to get to her as soon as possible.

The fear that she'd had more time to think about the haunted house and all the fucked-up things Alpha had said to her had me losing my mind. I had heard every word and felt every sensation when he was in control. I can't imagine what was going through her mind when we handled her that way. Said those things.

She liked it.

If anyone drove her away, it's you, asshole.

That witch has been lying in bed every night, dreaming of what happened in that box. She was so primed and ready, I could smell her.

Great. Now he had me thinking of Evie touching herself in her bed, and I was hard as a hammer.

Throaty laughter echoed in my head.

I weaved past the crowd outside Ruben's Rare Books heading to the alley entrance to the Green Light. The vampire who ran the bookstore, the dungeon behind it, and the vampire coven of New Orleans, Ruben Dubois, was a private man. Perhaps more private than me. I'd never had dealings with the vampires, but I knew their haunts. Seemed business was booming at their dungeon tonight, where humans could mingle and play with the pretty immortals. Actually, vampires were no more immortal than me, but they did live longer than most supernaturals.

"Excuse me." I pushed past the tall, lean guy smoking a cigarette and leaning against a gaslit streetlamp on the corner of the alley entrance. A sudden wave of melancholy washed over me, like being kissed by emptiness.

Back off, fucking grim.

"Did you get that hex broken?" asked the grim, his dark eyes resting on me as he took a drag of his cigarette.

"Not yet," I said over my shoulder before I realized I'd never actually told him I needed a hex broken that day I met him.

Moving on, the morose feeling slipped away. Apparently, the vampires had hired a grim reaper to help with business. Made sense. Their emo aura could make the right kind of human more susceptible to the pleasures in their dungeon. If I hadn't had that epiphany about my own loneliness a few blocks back, I'd blame it on the grim. But I couldn't. The truth was that for the first time, I wasn't content by myself. I yearned for her.

Speeding the last few blocks, I slowed down and exhaled a shaky breath when I caught sight of the Cauldron, the strumming of a guitar coming from inside. Hauling open the door, I eased inside. The place was pretty packed, the booths and tables filled. There were a few empty stools at the bar, so I pulled up to one and straddled it, trying to find Evie in the crowd. My foot was tapping, my knee bobbing like crazy as I frantically searched for her.

"What can I get you?"

I jumped. JJ stood in front of me, scowling with both his hands braced on the bar.

"Whatever you've got on draft."

"Imported or domestic?"

"I don't care."

He left to pour my beer. I kept scanning the room, panic starting to take over. I needed to see her or I was going to lose my mind.

JJ plunked the frosty mug down. "You looking for Evie?"

"Is she working tonight?" I tried to sound casual, but I'm pretty sure I sounded as desperate as I felt.

Right when I asked the question, Evie darted out of the swinging door leading to the kitchen, carrying a tray stacked with food. I swear, a rush of adrenaline and relief shot through me so fast my limbs went limp. I set my beer back on the bar and rubbed my sweaty palms on my jeans.

"Hey." JJ jolted my attention back to him and his crossed arms. "I need to know what your intentions are with Evie."

I almost laughed but realized he was serious. I arched a brow and bit my lip to keep from telling him what Evie and I did was none of his business.

He leaned closer, a hand on the bar. "If you're planning on fucking and forgetting her, I need you to know that werewolf or not, I'll kick your ass."

Yeah, right.

The guy was packing a lot of muscle and carried himself in a way that said it wasn't all just for show.

I shook my head. "That's not my plan."

"Then what is your plan?"

I chuckled and drank a gulp of beer. "Honestly, I don't know. But I can tell you it in no way includes hurting Evie."

"All right then." He held out his big paw for me to shake. "Then I'm JJ. It's nice to meet you."

I shook it, somehow happy that Evie had this big brotherly guy looking out for her. "Mateo."

"I know." He nodded over my shoulder.

Right as I turned, Evie popped up beside me, a tilted smile quirking one side of her mouth. I had the craziest urge to lean in and kiss her.

"Hey! I didn't expect to see you till tomorrow." She set her tray on the bar, and JJ took it back to the kitchen. There wasn't even a hint of awkwardness or embarrassment coming from Evie for what happened last time.

"I just needed . . . I mean . . ."

What did I mean? Think, think, think. Shit, I hadn't thought of what I'd tell her exactly. I just needed to be near her, to see her, drink in her pretty eyes, her prettier smile. Holy hell, I was staring at her mouth again. Stop! *Fuck*, what did I say?

"I wanted to come by and sort of look at you, I mean, see you. Hang out with you." That was the stupidest fucking string of words I'd ever put together.

She laughed. My heart soared. "You just couldn't live without me, could you?"

You have no fucking idea.

I shook my head, smiling down at her and so goddamn happy right now I might burst into song. She didn't hate me. Somehow, she didn't hate me. Unable to resist, I reached up and coasted my fingers around her slim wrist, then down to her hand. With a quick squeeze, I said, "It's so good to see you."

I must've looked like a sad, heartsick teenager, but I couldn't help it. She wore a pink T-shirt with Princess Leia holding a blaster that said *Don't mess with a Princess*. She was too adorable for words.

She huffed out a breath on a sweet smile. "Listen, I've only got an hour left on my shift, then I can hang with you awhile."

"Cool." I let her go, which took every ounce of my being, then she wound back to her tables.

Turning around backward on my stool, I watched her shamelessly. I loved the way she smiled and laughed with customers. I loved watching the way her customers were drawn to her when she spoke. I couldn't blame them. She was magnetic. Fun, flirty, beautiful, hypnotizing. I was so far gone, and I hadn't even noticed how it happened. When had this started?

One second, I was thinking friends was good, then I thought maybe more than friends could work, and now I was sure I couldn't go a day without her in my life. I wanted her, not just as my lover or my friend, but as my one and only.

She chatted with a brunette, making some kind of gestures with her hand as she told a story, then they both tossed their heads back in laughter. My gaze sharpened on the soft curve of her throat. God, I had it so bad. I wouldn't overwhelm her tonight, though. Not so soon after that nightmare in the haunted house. But I could reassure her I was back to normal and Alpha was well-contained. I could hopefully touch her a little more and feed my need for her sweet scent and soft intimacy.

I'd vaguely heard a guitarist strumming an instrumental piece in the background, but then I heard a familiar voice speak into the microphone from the small stage in the corner.

"Hope you like my rendition of 'Black Hole Sun.' Here goes."

"You've gotta be kidding me," I whispered to myself, staring at my cousin Nico onstage. "What the hell?"

I watched him sing a rather haunting, slower version of the nineties favorite, drained my beer, then headed up toward the stage. He caught my gaze halfway there, smirking at me with a nod. Funny, I hadn't sensed another werewolf in the vicinity when I came in. Apparently, I was so obsessed with Evie, I hadn't even noticed. Of course, the magic electrifying the air from her, Violet, and Jules in the kitchen sort of nullified my awareness of him. Until now.

He strummed the last riff as I finally reached him. I hadn't seen him since Christmas three years ago in San Antonio, not since he'd wandered away from home for a while.

He leaned toward the mic. "Ten minute break, and I'll be right back."

A high-top of ladies not far from the stage whined. But then he gave them his signature wink and grin, and I swear they nearly fainted. He removed the guitar to step down, then wrapped me in a brotherly hug with a slap on the back.

"What in the hell are you doing here?" I asked, not in anger but in actual shock.

"Good to see you too, bro." He scratched the scruff at his chin.

I shook my head in disbelief, grinning at this crazy bastard. "It's great to see you, Nico. But I thought you were still in Austin."

His small smile gave away nothing. "I wanted a change of scenery."

"So, New Orleans?"

"Why not? All you ever do is brag about it being the best place on earth."

His gaze trailed behind me back to the table of ladies. When I looked over, I noticed Violet serving them another round of fruity cocktails. Violet shot a death-glare at Nico, then moved on with a sharp sway of her hips.

"You know her?" I asked, a little dumbfounded.

"Not really." He laughed, which could've meant anything for Nico. Like, they'd hooked up one night and he knew her intimately, or he'd passed her on the street and trailed her here to do some hunting. He was a likable guy but hard to read, keeping all his outer emotions friendly and easygoing. That way, you never really knew what he was thinking.

"You know she's a witch, right?"

His gaze was on her again, hotter than before. "I know."

Wanting to steer him away from eye-fucking Violet, I grumbled, "I still can't believe you're here in New Orleans and you didn't even give me a goddamn call."

He shrugged. "I figured I'd find you."

"How long have you been here?"

"A little while."

That was so fucking Nico. If I didn't know he was born with Spanish blood in his veins, the same as mine, I'd swear he was a nomad. He roamed wherever he wanted, and life just seemed easy for him. Still, there was a heavier glint in his eyes when he cast them toward Evie's sister.

"You gonna tell me how you know Violet?"

That got his attention. He snapped back to me. "How do you know her?" There was a threatening growl in his voice, which I know he hadn't intended to reveal, and a possessive glint in his eyes.

I actually tossed my head back and laughed. "What is this? I mean, how?"

His dark, assessing gaze was trained on me. I raised my hands in surrender. "Trust me. I have no designs on her. But her sister . . ."

I nodded toward Evie who was bouncing from table to table, her ponytail swinging. "I definitely have designs on her."

And yeah, I heard the throaty sound of my own wolf in my voice when I staked my claim. I might not have done it for real with Evie yet, but I sure as hell needed this werewolf in the room to know, blood relative or not.

His easy smirk was back. "She's a pretty one."

Back off. She's ours.

This was one time I agreed with him.

"So how long are you here for?" I just realized having Nico here was a stroke of luck. I wasn't one to talk about my problems, but maybe he'd heard of this sort of hex before.

He shrugged. "For a while."

"You've got a lot of gigs lined up?"

He nodded. "I've also got some other business to tend to."

His smile didn't ease, but a flicker of fire in his gaze told me his business wasn't all that good. Nico had run with a bad bunch for a while and had made some enemies along the way. I'd never interfered too much. Once he was out of that fucking Lycan gang, I didn't poke around more than was needed. He was a grown man after all.

"You're good though, right?" I asked, knowing he would know what I referred to.

His smile stretched, flashing the smile that made women drop their panties for him. "I'm great, cuz." He nodded back to the stage. "Better get back to it. Let's catch up later?"

He clapped me on the shoulder and resumed his spot on the barstool. "Text me tomorrow."

I meandered back to the bar, wondering what had brought Nico out this way. It might be nothing, just my cousin the wayfarer, wandering to a new town as usual. I also wondered how he'd met Violet and why the hell she seemed to hate him already. I also knew that Nico wouldn't tell me. For such an easygoing guy, he was a secretive bastard.

People thought I was a loner, but I actually stayed in one place and had friends, had planted some roots. I was pretty fucking sociable for a werewolf. Nico wasn't a loner; he was a wanderer. And so his connections were thin and ever-changing.

But those thoughts fell away as the crowd started thinning and the hour ticked down and finally Evie wandered over to me wearing a smile that slayed me.

CHAPTER 20

~EVIE~

"How about a drink before we go?" I hopped up on the stool next to Mateo.

I needed some liquid courage, I had to admit. Seeing Mateo after three days of deprivation was like spiking my bloodstream with a shot of something fizzy and fantastic. And now I needed an actual shot of something to calm me the hell down. Especially when he looked at me the way he was. I was half-drunk already off the smoldering smiles and the heavy-lidded eyes he'd been shooting me all night.

I was nervous. I wasn't quite sure why, but I could feel that something fundamental had changed since Alpha had gone rogue the other night. I could also sense something coming.

"A Witch's Brew?" asked JJ.

"Nope. Blood Orange Old Fashioned." JJ gave me one of his looks. That damn man always saw too much, so I turned to

Mateo. "You want one? JJ is a fabulous mixologist. He makes his own bitters and marinates his own cherries. *Amazing.*"

JJ rolled his eyes and started working his magic. Yeah, though human, his talents behind the bar made us famous all over the city.

"Uh, sure," said Mateo, a frown pinching his brow for a second.

"I saw you talking to our new live music guy. Jules just hired him today, and I almost fainted because he's a werewolf. It's like she's being open-minded and all, and it's freaking me out a little. Anyway, you know him?"

He chuckled, probably at my diarrhea of the mouth. JJ slid two of his wonderfully potent drinks in front of us, jabbing mine with a straw in a way that said *drink it slow.*

"I do know him. Actually, you do too. Sort of."

"Huh?" I glanced back at the werewolf strumming and crooning an Evanescence song, his masculine version sounding sexy as hell.

Three wide-band silver rings dragged my attention to his long, masculine fingers moving effortlessly over the strings. A musician's hands. Wearing a black T-shirt that highlighted his well-toned chest and bronzed biceps, as well as some black ink peeking out and swirling his forearms, he held himself like a man who knew his hotness had conquered many a woman. If I'd met this guy before, I wouldn't have forgotten him. Trust me. Interestingly, his hotness still didn't compare to Mateo's, but that probably had more to do with my stupid heart than my eyes.

"It's Nico," he said, hooking his boot on the lower rung of my barstool, his knee pressing against my outer thigh.

"Your cousin?" I plucked the cocktail straw out of my drink and dropped it on a napkin before taking a nice, deep gulp. JJ could suck it. I wasn't going slow tonight. Mateo's proximity was already doing swirly, fluttery things to my tummy. "The arrogant ass?"

"The one and the same." He took a much more leisurely sip of his drink, his smile over the lip of the glass making me warm and melty, more potent than the bourbon.

"You didn't tell me he was coming."

"I didn't know." He glanced over at the stage, then back at me. "Typical Nico."

"Well, I guess you want to, you know, catch up with him tonight? Instead of hanging with me, that is."

He shook his head so fast my pulse lurched again. "He's working till closing, I'm sure. We'll get together tomorrow." He propped his arm along the back of my chair, leaning in. "Tonight, I want to be with you."

The dawning realization that he missed me as much as I'd missed him began to sink in. The incident at the haunted house had scared me. But not for the reasons he might think. I could handle his wolf. It was these feelings of intense attraction keeping me awake at night, spinning that sensual memory in the coffin on constant replay, that frightened me most of all. Could he feel the same way?

I fiddled with the cocktail straw on the napkin, rolling it under the pad of my index finger. "It's only been three days."

His expression grave, he edged closer and said quietly, "It's been an eternity."

He perused my face like he needed to memorize it. Like he was looking for something. An answer to a question. I licked my lips, his gaze following the movement. The seriousness of his words and his expression, hunger darkening his eyes, told me that I definitely wasn't alone in my nightly fantasies. I couldn't breathe.

I gulped another deep swallow of my drink, the cinnamon and whiskey lingering on my tongue, shooting bravery down my throat. I stared down into the glass and whispered, "It sure felt like it."

He swept his hand behind my ponytail, the pads of his fingers sliding along my nape in slow, tantalizing brushes. The same soft but sure way he did when he was tracing the details of one of his sculptures, pressing and forming till it was perfect beneath his capable hands. Like it was precious and important. Like *I* was precious and important.

Nico strummed the beginning of a song I recognized. I couldn't move, paralyzed by the intense hurricane of pleasure devastating my insides, laying waste to all my doubts and insecurities about Mateo. By the time Nico started singing Nirvana's version of "The Man Who Sold the World," I was humming with desire.

Mateo stood, his presence a wall of tempting loveliness beside me. I still was staring at the bar when he whispered close to my ear, "Come dance with me."

He squeezed my nape, then skated that hand down to my own and tugged me off the stool. I downed the rest of my drink before he pulled me through the crowd to the very small square near the stage that served as our dance floor when we needed one. There was only one other couple taking advantage, but I really didn't care. I was about to be swaying in Mateo's arms and pressed against his body. And while I'd experienced that intensity from Alpha, I was hella ready to see how Mateo would hold me.

After that last incident and our three-day break from our "friendship," I thought Mateo would be tentative, careful, and pull me into a safe, platonic embrace.

Jesus. Not even close.

One hand skimmed along the small of my back and wrapped to my opposite hip, crushing me to his hard frame. The other landed between my shoulder blades, fingertips grazing the skin above my T-shirt. I was so shocked at the intensity of his hold, I merely curled my fingers around the belt loops at his waist, needing a second to adjust.

His mouth was at my temple, his words soft and intimate and sincere. "Nico and I used to play this song over and over."

I couldn't speak, so I just listened to him.

"Honestly, it was like our anthem in those days of learning about ourselves when the wolf came."

His hand between my shoulder blades rose and wrapped tenderly at the base of my neck, the sensual weight catapulting my heart into space. I slid my hands around his waist. Nico sang with heavy emotion, his eyes closed.

Mateo's lips brushed my temple as he spoke. "That's how it felt, you know. This song. When the shift would come over me, it was like passing my wolf on the stairs, like seeing an old friend and brushing by him with a nod. I counted on him to take care of us, to purge his dark needs without fucking us up, without losing total control."

His hand cupped my nape, feeling different than when Alpha had gripped me by the throat in the coffin, but also frighteningly similar. Possessive and sure.

"Except for that one time with my father, he'd kept his end of the bargain, Evie. But the other night . . ." His arms flexed, tightening around me. "He pushed me out and handled you, said things to you in a way I never would."

I tipped my head up so he could hear me, his mouth still brushing my hairline. "I'm okay. You didn't hurt me."

"Listen to me. I have to say this." He inhaled a deep breath before going on. "It wasn't that what he said wasn't true, that it wasn't something I didn't want. My wolf is a part of me, Evie."

Emotions. So many emotions. A flock of butterflies took flight in my belly. Then he kept talking, and my brain fizzled.

"I would never act on those cravings . . . unless you wanted me to."

Was he really saying this? Thank God I was in his arms, because my knees buckled, my body sagging against him. His arms squeezed me tighter, pressing my body to his chest. His jaw brushed my forehead when I angled my face toward his neck, inhaling a deep breath of him. He smelled like citrus and soap and beautiful man. Mateo. His hand on my nape gave a little squeeze, his mouth against my temple. "And I would never hurt you. Not on purpose."

"I know." I eased back and looked up at him, stricken by the stark adoration in his heated gaze. I wanted that look on me for the rest of my life. The realization knocked me senseless for a split second before I assured him, "You didn't hurt me."

His hand slid from my nape to cup my jaw. "What I'm saying is that I want you—" He shook his head, closing his eyes for a second. "The past couple of days, I kept praying I wasn't alone in this. Hoping that you might want more than friendship too." His fingertips curled tighter on me. "*Please*," he begged, "tell me I'm not alone."

I swallowed hard, the thickness in my throat making it hard to answer. Adrenaline shot through my blood like lightning. I tipped my head up higher, speaking against his granite jaw, the scruff tickling my lips. "You're not alone." My voice was husky with emotion. My heart hammered out a new beat, yearning for him to match my tempo, to harmonize with my body, to melt against my flesh, and make me his own. There was nothing else but the soul-stirring want humming along my skin, vibrating through flesh to my bones.

"Thank fucking Christ," he murmured against me, exhaling a shaky breath.

For another minute, he squeezed me closer. Not even a ribbon-thin slice of air between us, our bodies happily pressed together in perfect alignment. His heart drummed against my chest, answering my own. I smiled to know I wasn't the only one losing my shit over this.

He whispered, "I'm afraid, though."

I finally looked up. Fear skated over his face, tightening his jaw.

"What are you afraid of?"

He huffed out a laugh. "That next time I won't be able to push Alpha back again."

"You will."

"That you'll change your mind and won't want me that way."

"I won't."

"*Christ.*" He cupped my face, pressing his forehead to mine. "Evie," he breathed on a groan, still swaying to whatever song Nico was playing now, having moved on to another. I couldn't hear anything but Mateo and my overloud thoughts shouting things like YES and THANK GOD.

I couldn't focus on anything but the miracle of words spilling out of Mateo's mouth. He wanted me. *Gah.* It was almost too much for me to handle. My gaze was fixed on his wide, sensuous lips, imagining what devastation those lips would do to my body, leaving me a wreck of want and completion. I was suddenly very aware that I needed a vag landscaping appointment ASAP.

"Evie." A subtle warning. When I looked up, his eyes were swamped with heat, his dilated pupils full and dark. "We need to wait to pursue this until after the hex is broken. I don't trust him."

I didn't need to ask who *him* was. It was more than apparent how little he trusted the wolf. Tomorrow night. I could wait that long. Maybe. Even though I wanted to tell him I was pretty much okay with everything Alpha had said—except the whole ripping guys' throats out who glanced my way—I didn't think now was the right time.

"I think we should test the boundaries a little." I clasped my hands around his neck, luxuriating in the silkiness of his hair on the backs of my fingers and the fact that it was okay for me now to luxuriate in it.

"What do you mean?" He couldn't keep his eyes off my mouth either. So this wasn't going to be hard.

I shrugged one shoulder. "I think you should kiss me."

Pause. His throat worked, then he licked his lips. Yellow rolled across his eyes, promising that Alpha was present and watching me. Very aware of my request. Rather than instill fear, it sparked a desperate hunger that sizzled along my skin, heating me in low, delicious places. I wanted whatever Mateo *and* Alpha had to offer.

"Just to see if we have any chemistry together. I mean, we might want to keep it friends only if there's nothing there. Ya know?"

No freaking way would there not be bombs and explosions going off when his lips were on mine. He stopped our swaying, his hands now on my hips, fingers curling in tight.

"I'm not sure that's a good idea." But he was already breathing fast. We were so doing this.

"You think I can't handle the big bad wolf?" I arched a challenging brow, wrapping my arms tight around his neck and pressing my breasts to his chest. Another roll of gold washed over his eyes, a keen look of pleasure. And feral hunger. I dropped my voice to what I hoped was a sexy whisper. "You tell Alpha that if he doesn't behave, he'll get no reward." I skated one hand under his hair, grazing my nails along his nape. "He isn't the only one with claws."

His eyes closed on a groan, a frown pinching between his eyebrows. I was sure he was going to protest again, but then he unclasped my hands from around his neck, laced his fingers with mine, and pressed the back of my hand to his lips before he walked off the dance floor, tugging me behind him.

We were headed back toward the bar, but then he took a sharp left down the hallway that passed the restrooms and a supply closet, not stopping till he was pushing open the last door into the storage pantry. The second we were inside, I was off the ground, my ass on top of the beer cooler, his pelvis pressed between my legs, his hands gripping my thighs. And then, his mouth. His fucking gorgeous mouth ghosted over mine.

Jesus.

It was a barely-there brush, a slow, airy sweep. I leaned forward on a whimper, seeking his mouth, needing a hard, blistering kiss. But he quickly backed away out of reach. Lifting a hand, he slipped his fingers around my nape and took hold of me in a firm grip.

"Let me lead, Evie," he growled against my mouth, his voice so deep and dark, I whimpered. A soft but definite command from Alpha, not Mateo. He needed control. Got it.

"Uh, okay."

I was sure I looked like a lust-crazed idiot, jaw slack, pulse pounding, my eyes fixated on his mouth. A teasing smile spread across his face a split second before he leaned in again.

Then he finally put those sensuous lips to really good use. More sweeping and slow nips. His mouth coaxed me gently, but his hands held me hard. I combed my hands into his dark, silky hair. That was all it took to earn me a groan and some tongue. And some aggression.

Yes!

I felt like the Incredible Hulk trying to break out of my skin, but instead of angry Hulk, I was horny Hulk. I hummed on the first taste of him, the flavor of whiskey and cinnamon and dominance blazing into my senses. I stroked my tongue inside his mouth and scraped my blunt nails against his scalp.

"Fuck." His hand on my thigh tightened, then he jerked me forward till he was seated between my thighs, pressed up against me.

Oh yes, yes, yes. This is heavenly.

Arching my back, I pressed my boobs against his chest and locked my ankles right above his perfect ass. He couldn't get away if he tried. I'd just hang on like a monkey. But he wasn't trying to get away. No. His drugging kisses morphed into the bruising, brain-melting kind. A throaty groan rumbled from his chest to mine, putting my girls on full alert. My nipples saluted with gusto. I rubbed against him, needing friction, really not giving a shit if I was acting like a cat in heat. He didn't seem to mind.

"Evie, Evie." Another thrust of his tongue, then a nip of my lip with his teeth. "What are you doing to me? *Christ.*"

I didn't recognize myself, my blinding desire for him driving me like a freight train on fire. One kiss from him had unlocked a closeted vixen who wanted and needed only him. Mateo was the key. Alpha was the welcome mat. And I was loving the hell out of walking through this door, pushing my werewolf over the edge. I wanted us to go together.

His hands were everywhere. He ground his pelvis against me. *Wowza!* His dick was hard and ready and right there. It had been a long time, so my little lady was getting really excited about where this was going. Was I really going to have sex on the beer cooler in our bar pantry? Hell yes, I was!

I jerked his T-shirt up enough to slide one of my hands over his chiseled abs. He hissed in a breath and grabbed my wrist.

"Evie, we should—"

The door to the pantry popped open, letting in light from the hallway. We both jerked our heads to the door, our bodies and arms still tangled all over each other. Violet stood there with a shit-eating grin on her face, one hand on her hip.

"There you are, sis." She took in the scene with casual nonchalance. "Seriously hate to break this up, but it's about that time."

I stared at her, blinking, trying to remember what day it was. "Time for what?"

She snorted. "Jules said thirty minutes." Then she closed the door.

I let my forehead drop to his chest. He slid his hot palms up and down my back, one hand easing up to the back of my head below my ponytail.

"You have plans tonight?" he murmured into the crown of my head.

When I could finally think through the horny fog in my brain, I remembered what Violet was talking about. "We just need to do a round tonight."

I pulled back, catching confusion glinting through the lust darkening his expression, his breath still coming hard.

"Like a witch's round," I explained, still reeling from unfulfilled need. "For energy."

Licking his lips, he massaged his hands down my back with soothing sweeps. "You do this often?"

I'd never had a friend who wasn't a witch and didn't already know what this was. Sure, I'd had human friends, but other than JJ, none of them knew what we really were, so that information was privileged. There was a kind of contentment warming my middle in sharing this part of me with Mateo.

I unlocked the death grip my ankles had on his ass and let my feet dangle down. Sorry, beer cooler. No sex for you. Or me, unfortunately.

"We do it monthly, actually. It helps center our magic, rejuvenate."

He inched back, but not too far, sliding his hands from my shoulders down to my hands where he held on to them. "I didn't know witches had to do that."

"Not all do. My sister Isadora is a Conduit, so her magic allows her to move energy any time she wants and from anything. The rest of us need a little group help."

He rubbed his thumbs at the center of my palms, and I swear, I instinctually squeezed my thighs against his hips on the shock wave it pulsed between my legs. I had no idea that the center of my palm was an erogenous zone. Actually, I'm pretty sure it wasn't. It was just him. Anything he did with those hands made me crazy. The way he handled me in our make-out session had my imagination running stark-raving mad, thinking of how well he'd handle me in bed.

I cleared my throat and my wayward thoughts. "But you're right. We want to be sure we're powered up for tomorrow night."

He gripped my waist and lifted me off the cooler to stand in front of him. Taking my hand, he tugged me toward the door. "Let me walk you home."

Very reluctantly, I followed behind him. Nico was still playing on the stage in the corner. He and Mateo exchanged one of those manly head-nods, then we cut through the crowd and out the door. We walked in silence, taking a right at our shop on the corner. It wasn't until we were at the gate and Mateo held it open for me that he said something. "So, I think we have good chemistry together."

"Sorry?"

He chuckled, pulling me to a stop on the front porch. "You wanted to test our boundaries, remember?"

"Oh, right."

"Do you agree?"

I shrugged one shoulder, pretending indifference. "Yeah. I guess we can give it a go."

"Just a go."

"Sure." I pressed my lips together to keep the smirk from breaking free, because it was practically impossible to play it cool after my Mount Vesuvius–level explosion of lust and feelings back in the storage closet.

"Hmm. So on a scale from lukewarm to scorching, how would you rate our chemistry?"

I made a good show of pretending to figure out where we'd end up, squinting one eye. "I'd say maaaaybe like a simmer."

He bit his lip, trying to keep from smiling, because he knew I was a big fat liar. "I see." He dropped my hand and pulled away, putting a few steps between us. "Maybe it's better we don't give it a go then and just keep this"—he gestured between us with one hand—"nice and platonic. What do you say?"

I leaped onto him and wrapped my legs around his waist. He staggered back, laughing, his shoulders hitting the wall beside the door, one palm on my ass, the other under my thigh.

"Don't you even think about it, Mr. Wolfman," I said, nose to nose before I crushed my mouth to his.

He was still laughing until I slid my tongue along his and clenched my legs tight around him. Electric heat sizzled up my spine. He sucked on my tongue and groaned, skating down to kiss my neck. I arched for him, giving him *all* the access he wanted.

"Mr. Wolfman needs to get the fuck out of here," he muffled into my skin. "You're killing me, woman."

His voice was edged with a growl. Pushing him in this arena wasn't a good idea. As much as I wanted to tear his clothes off, I didn't want Alpha showing up. For one, he scared the shit out of me. And second, I couldn't stand to see that look of helplessness in Mateo's eyes like I did after the haunted house debacle. I straightened and caught a flicker of gold flash before his eyes cooled to brown again. Yep, time to be a good girl. Detangling my legs, I dropped back to the porch and cupped his face, both of us heaving.

"I'll see you tomorrow night." I pressed a closed-mouth kiss to his devastating lips.

He pressed his forehead to mine, eyes closed for a second. "Tomorrow night. We break this curse."

"Then your life can go back to normal."

"Back to normal," he repeated, catching my gaze and holding it. "Except you'll still be in it."

I grinned, pecked him on the lips, and backed away toward the front door. "I'll text you the details in the morning. I'm sure Jules has a detailed plan and color-coded chart to go along with my spell."

He laughed and shoved both of his hands into his jeans pockets, swallowed hard, and licked his lips with a deep nod. "Tomorrow then." He jogged down the steps and loped toward the front gate as I opened the door.

"Hey, Mateo!"

He stopped and turned to me.

"Molten lava."

His brow scrunched into the cutest frown. "What?"

"On the scale." I flashed him a grin and made the explosion gesture with one hand. "Volcanic, seismic activity."

His grin slid away, replaced by a hot look that made me squeeze my thighs together. Then he touched two fingers to his lips and tipped them up in my direction before sauntering off down the street.

Hmph. A big, bad werewolf just blew me a kiss. That was the sexiest and cutest thing I'd ever seen.

And now to face the firing squad. Unless I could get Violet to keep her big mouth shut and not tell Jules. Somehow, I knew there was no way that was happening.

CHAPTER 21

~EVIE~

"WHAT!"

"They were practically clawing each other's clothes off," said Violet, checking out her new OPI nail color, Vampsterdam black. I'd moved her new polish off the kitchen counter this morning so Jules wouldn't rip her a new asshole. But now I was plotting to *accidentally* spill last week's Berry Fairy Fun purple on Jules's butcher block. "If I hadn't interrupted, they'd definitely be fucking on that freezer."

"We would not be fu—" I ground my teeth together before snapping, "You are the suckiest sister on the planet, you know that?" I picked up a throw pillow with my magic and launched it at Violet's face.

She fell back onto the sofa, laughing like a goddamn hyena. No, I mean literally, she sounded like a braying donkey or hyena when she laughed full force like this. It was so unattractive but strangely endearing. Except when she was laughing at my expense. Like now.

"What did I miss?" Clara walked in, cuddling Z to her chest and wearing her gauzy white sundress.

"Evie is having sex with that werewolf," blurted Violet.

"I am not!"

But I would be soon. If everything went well.

"All right, all right," said Jules, completely annoyed, her maternal scowl permanently fixed. "Enough, Violet. Sit down, Evie."

Jules and I had gone over tomorrow night's plan, waiting for Violet to end her shift and close up with JJ. Everything was fine and dandy till five minutes ago when she walked through the door and said, "Evie is doing Mateo."

"First off," I said, retaking my seat on the overstuffed chair beside the sofa, "Mateo and I aren't sleeping together."

"Yet," added Violet with a waggle of her eyebrows.

"And if we do, that's no one's business but our own." I aimed the last at Jules. She may be my older and wiser sister and all that shit, but she didn't own me and couldn't dictate who I could have a relationship with.

Jules kept her all-seeing stare on me, moving over my face for several seconds before she took a sip of her red wine and smoothed her features back to calm-as-the-Dead-Sea. "You're right."

"I am?"

"She is?" Violet leaned forward with shock and awe brightening her face.

"Look, Evie. You're obviously a grown woman and can do whatever you want. My only concern was, and still is, the volatile nature of werewolves." She paused and tilted her head toward me. "However, I've noticed how different you've been lately. You seem so . . ." She waved a hand, searching for the word, like she could pluck it out of the air.

"Happy," said Clara.

Since when wasn't I happy? I mulled over Clara's observation, which both thrilled and saddened me at the same time. "I wasn't happy before?"

"Of course you were," said Jules. "But something's changed."

This actually kind of pissed me off. I wasn't a doom-and-gloom kind of girl. If anyone was emo, it was Violet, or high anxiety, it was Isadora.

"I'm always happy."

"Not really," supplied Clara. "You're a very content person, Evie, it's true. Nothing bothers you or sets you off. You're the most even-keeled of all of us. But it's also true that you've come more alive since you and Mateo became friends."

Clara was right. I had been smiling at everything and laughing far too easily these days.

"All I'm saying," interjected Jules, "is if you're happy being with him, then I'm of course not going to stop you. I just caution you to be careful. Especially with this hex. We still don't know what we're dealing with."

At least I knew what his alter ego was like. I wasn't going to lie and pretend that Alpha couldn't be dangerous. While I was certain he'd never hurt me, I was fairly sure he could and would hurt someone else if he managed to overtake Mateo in an uncontrolled environment. It was just one more reason to help Mateo get rid of this damn hex. He needed to shift out in the woods where Alpha could run and hunt to his wolfish heart's content.

"Fine. Warning heard loud and clear. Now, let's get this round moving."

Jules nodded, apparently content now that she'd given me her motherly advice on the matter. We filed out into the courtyard. Clara left Z inside.

"Is Fred in his pen?" asked Jules.

"Yes." Violet sighed. "I double-checked, don't worry."

We always made sure the animals were locked up because the amount of energy we conjured could actually do damage to other living creatures. I mean, this was all positive, life-force kind of energy, but we never knew if a wayward zap could give Z or Fred a heart attack. Better to be safe than sorry.

We opened the wrought iron gate wrapped in ivy that led to the back garden. The enclosed space jutted out from the back corner of the house—quiet and out of the way. Jules struck a long match and lit the candles in each corner as we took our places around the witch's wheel chalked at the center. Well, Jules, Violet, and I sat, but Clara remained standing at the top of the witch's wheel scrawled with the season, Yule. Violet sat beside her at Samhain, even though Yule was her birthday month too. I took the place opposite at Midsummer with Jules beside me at Beltane. The two spots for Isadora at Imbolg and Livvy at Lugnasadh were left open.

When Mom introduced us to the witch's round when we were between five and ten years old, she'd placed us on the wheel at the season in which we were born. It had become our natural place whenever we summoned Mother Earth's energy ever since.

"Did you re-chalk?" I asked Jules.

She was already cross-legged, her eyes closed, hands on her knees. She nodded.

I'd asked Mom why we didn't just paint the wheel on the cement, but she'd taught us that the spell of building the wheel with chalk needed to be refreshed every month to keep the magic close and bound to it.

Since we recharged faster when all six of us were here, it meant we'd need to spell-cast a little longer tonight. Not a problem. I was ready for the hex-breaking ceremony right freaking now. Especially since I knew a hot love affair waited for me on the other side of it. Well, I don't know about love. I just meant hot and sex and Mateo. So, yeah, time to get this show on the road.

Clara opened the little box at her feet and dragged out her ceremonial items. Yes, she had actual props for this shindig. It was entirely unnecessary, but Clara was Clara.

As an Aura, it was always best for her to lead the spell-casting of a round, her magic putting our minds in the positive, calm mindset we needed to seep into the magic.

Clara was a bit theatrical. And ever since she watched the *Divine Secrets of the YaYa Sisterhood* with her sixties-and-up book buddies one wild and crazy Friday night, she decided our witch's round needed more flair.

She removed the garland from the box and placed it on her head. It was adorned with silk rosebuds and dangling with pink and purple ribbons. She'd bought it on our last outing to the Texas Renaissance Festival to replace the bedazzled, ceremonial crown she usually used. She took out her wand—yes, you heard me—handcrafted according to her Pottermore-assigned wand as 14.5 inches long, made of vine wood with unicorn hair core.

I'd asked her what her craftsman had used instead of unicorn hair, because unicorns weren't real. She'd just laughed at me like I was silly and naive. So I left it alone.

"Mother Moon, Goddess Earth." She raised her hands outward, tilting her eyes to the night sky, pooling her magic so she glowed.

The effect was quite striking. With her waist-length blonde hair, sheer white dress, beribboned garland, and ornate wand, she looked like a fairy queen about to summon spirits or nymphs or her pixie army.

"To your breast we're forever bound. Light within, magic out, feed us in your witch's round."

"Mmm. I like that one," whispered Jules, her eyes still closed, her voice almost sleepy.

"Thank you." Then Clara spun around three times—we never knew what the significance of the spinning was—before she floated down into a sitting position. Her wand in her lap, she closed her eyes, then finally so did I.

The rest required little talk. But sometimes, whatever charms lit up our skin made us mumble nonsense into the circle. The magic had a will of its own, especially when we settled into this kind of trance, pulling magic from the world around us and sucking it into our bodies, our minds, our blood.

"Remember, ladies," said Jules, "focus on moon magic. She holds the soul of the werewolf."

For some reason, that made me angry. That any element of nature or the cosmos held power over Mateo. But then again, that's what he was. A werewolf. The creature condemned to always be part man, part beast, no matter what form he showed the world. And I needed to remember that.

"Careful, Evie," warned Clara, her angelic voice vibrating along my skin. "Summon only the light. None of the dark."

That made me wonder yet again what kind of witch had cursed Mateo. Or was it on accident somehow? Had he accidentally stumbled within the circle of a spell-caster and the ricochet effect was this block to shift? A pulse of white serenity punched into my chest, simmering into my limbs. I gasped.

"Okay, okay," I told Clara. She was getting pushy, slapping me with her happy spell.

Then we were all quiet for some time. Violet mumbled "bridge of black" once, then later "stone flowers . . . bone towers." Clara let out a sudden, throaty giggle like she was being tickled, then it went vacuum-like quiet right after. Jules spit out a length of nonsense that ended with, "And then all will walk on Trouble's heart." If any outsider ever walked in on this, they'd think we were tripping on heroin or something. Communing with our magic was like a drug, though, pulling us from reality, carrying us into other worlds.

One might ask, what other worlds were there? What we'd learned over the years was that there were many. Just because you couldn't see them didn't mean they weren't real.

The humming of the circle building with power resonated between us. I realized that everyone had fallen in deep, but I was still holding back, resisting magic's pull to the round.

"Let go," whispered Clara, sounding nothing like her jovial self and more like she'd channeled some serious maternal spirit. She probably had channeled Mother Nature herself.

So I did. Letting my head sag, chin to chest, I stopped resisting and fell.

As always, I stepped through a door of light into the unknown, like Alice down the rabbit hole. Except in this Wonderland, there was always some story to teach my heart. I'd never feared the round until now, when our sole purpose and focus was on my werewolf. I was afraid of what I'd find through the door.

Stepping onto plush grass—no, not grass but green moss—I followed the sound of water trickling nearby. I walked through woods made of purple-trunked trees with blue leaves. Yeah, it was as trippy as always, just like Wonderland, except I wasn't on an acid trip like the author of that story. I was high on magic. Pure, pooled magic.

Walking over giant tree roots jutting out of the ground, I finally found the source of the water. Except it wasn't really water. It was shimmering white, a fountain of witch magic streaming through a fantasy forest. For a second, I thought I'd somehow slipped into Clara's vision because this was totally something her subconscious would conjure. I looked around, waiting to spot a unicorn or fairy or something. Slowly, I waded into the pool, then dove underneath, the sizzle of energy flowing all around me. When I finally came up for air, I looked down to see that I was wearing Clara's white gossamer dress. Except now it was soaked through and completely transparent.

That's when I heard the growl. That familiar, chilling sound I knew all too well by now. I stared into the shadows to my right, expecting the frightening form of a werewolf. But what stepped out was worse. It was Mateo, but it wasn't. He was completely naked, and wow did my subconscious have a wonderful imagination. Sweat was slicked over every flexed muscle as he came closer. His eyes burned fire-gold, but his mouth was twisted at a sinister slant.

"This isn't real," I told myself. "So I'm not gonna run."

He laughed, but the deep-belly sound wasn't Mateo's. He waded in toward me, splashing the liquid magic. I was thigh-deep, but I knew this was just some aftereffect of the haunted house. This kind of crap could happen when you went deep into a trance in a witch's round. Especially when every waking and sleeping moment, you were fixated on a particular werewolf.

"It's not real?" he asked, his gravelly voice raising goose bumps on my arms.

"You're just my imagination."

"Is that so?"

He stood directly in front of me, his heat so intense I started to sweat. But you can't sweat in a dream, so I was imagining that too.

"You're not the real Mateo."

He wrapped his hand around the back of my loose hair and pulled a little too hard until his sweaty, hard body was pressed against mine, his heat seeping through my transparent, wet dress.

"You don't know the real Mateo."

He smiled and leaned in. I thought he was going to kiss me, but his mouth kept widening until a primal shiver shook through his body and he blurred into the werewolf, all wide, fanged mouth and malevolent, piercing eyes.

"No," I whispered on a shaky breath.

"Too late," came a voice on the wind. A hissing, feminine voice I didn't recognize. Then the creature who held me lunged for my throat with a snarl and razor-sharp teeth.

"Evie!"

I opened my eyes to find my head in Clara's lap and Jules and Violet bending over me with concerned frowns.

"Wh-what happened?" I croaked.

Jules stared at me hard. "Clara broke the round when she sensed your emotions dip into something—what was it?"

Clara stared down at me. "Something icky."

"Icky?" I sat up, dizzy, sensing the euphoric energy of doing the round, but also having a pounding headache. That wasn't normal. "Can you be more specific?"

"It was just gray and oozy. That's how it felt." She peered deep into my eyes, and I was afraid she would see the images my subconscious had dragged up. All of that was just my fears brought on by that damn scene at the haunted house, and I wasn't going to worry them for nothing.

"What did you see on the other side?" asked Clara.

"I can't remember," I lied, feeling like a total shitbag for it. "But I feel good. Like I'm ready for tomorrow." I turned to Violet with a smile. "How about y'all?"

Jules leaned back and exhaled a deep sigh. "Are you sure you're okay?"

"Yeah, yeah." I stood and plastered a smile on my face. "That was a good round. I just went deep, I think. Really deep. I don't know."

All three of them stared at me. Hard.

"I'm fine! The important question is, are y'all pumped and ready to go?"

Pumped with magic, that was.

"I'm good," said Violet.

Jules finally gave a heavy nod. "I'm ready. You just have your werewolf at the meeting spot tomorrow night."

"Sure thing. No problem." By some miracle, I sounded perfectly normal.

I blew out the candles while Clara gathered her things back in her box. Violet walked on toward the carriage house while Jules and I went inside quietly.

"Good night," I said cheerily, heading toward the hallway.

She gave me a funny look and nodded as she went up the stairs. "Night."

Once in my bedroom, I shut the door and leaned back against it, blowing out a heavy, shaky breath.

"It wasn't real," I whispered.

If it wasn't, why did it feel like it had actually happened?

CHAPTER 22

~MATEO~

"YOU MEAN THOSE WASTES OF SPACE CALLED THE BLOOD MOON Brothers?"

I couldn't help but smile at Nico's hard tone. Once upon a time, he had been one of those wastes of space.

"Nah, man. They shift multiple times a week. They're more wolf than man, to be honest."

Let's join them. Sounds like my kind of guys.

Don't start with me. Those fuckers are criminals of the worst kind.

But you heard him. They shift all the time.

After tonight, you'll have free rein. We'll stay in the wetlands for a week so you can hunt till your heart's content.

I'm starting to like you.

Nico drank down the rest of his beer and set it on my coffee table. "Besides, if one of them went dormant or couldn't shift, he'd be in some deep shit. Roman, the president of the Brothers,

won't abide any kind of weakness. He'd make that guy disappear."
He winced. "Not that it's a sign of weakness."

"No worries," I assured him. Those Lycan gangs had creative
ways of making people disappear. "Want another beer?"

He glanced at his watch. "I've got time for one more, but then
I've got a gig at El Gato Negro in the Quarter."

I pulled two more Abita Ambers from the fridge, popped the
tops, and handed him one, spreading myself out in the overstuffed chair next to the sofa.

Nico leaned forward, elbows on knees, frowning down at my
hardwood cypress floors. "I mean, you can't think of anyone? An
old girlfriend you pissed off?"

I blew out a breath. "Man, if I did, I would've chased her
down by now. It's so fucking frustrating, you have no idea."

"I can't imagine." He rubbed his lip with his index finger, back
and forth, thinking it over. "And you said your wolf talks to you?"

"All the time. Twenty-four seven." I took a pull on my beer.
"Except when Evie's around."

Nico's mouth tilted up on one side. "The hex-breaker, eh?"

**He better get that lusty look off his fucking face, or I'll
punch it off.**

"Yeah."

"So why hasn't she broken the hex already?"

"We're meeting tonight, actually. They, uh, hadn't worked
with werewolves before so Evie and her older sister needed to do
some research."

He chuckled darkly. "I got that impression when I hit up the
oldest one, Jules, for a gig at the Cauldron."

I sat up straight, curious at that. "They didn't advertise? You went to Jules?"

He tapped his fingers on his knee like he was playing a tune on the piano, a nervous habit he had as a kid. "Yeah. I had no idea you knew one of those witches, though."

"I'm kind of shocked Jules hired you, to be honest. It wasn't easy for her to agree to let Evie help me."

"She didn't seem to care much for werewolves." He took a swig of the longneck. "But I was able to charm her into it."

It was true Nico could charm the pants off just about anybody, but Jules was a no-nonsense witch. What was probably closer to the truth was that she'd opened the door for me and maybe thought she'd try to be more open-minded by the time Nico had come around looking for work.

"Hello?" Evie's voice called from down below as two sets of feet stomped up the stairs from my workshop.

"Come on up!" I headed over to the landing where the stairs opened right beside my kitchen.

My apartment was almost a completely open floor plan. Only my bedroom and bathroom were sectioned off from the large living and kitchen space. The vaulted ceiling with cypress beams elevated the space even more, especially with two sets of glass French doors that opened onto a narrow balcony. It was the perfect space for me.

Nico growled, or should I say his wolf did, a deep-chested rumble that faded almost as soon as I'd heard it.

What the fuck? Am I going to have to beat the shit out of your cousin again?

I got my answer as soon as Evie stepped up onto the landing with, Violet. That rumbling growl wasn't for my Evie. It was for her sister. Nico was already standing, his beer forgotten, his hands loose at his sides, but his relaxed posture was a lying bitch. A ripple of alpha waves bounced off me. I glanced over my shoulder with a chill-the-fuck-out look. He looked at the floor and cleared his throat.

"Hey," said Evie, all sweet and shy. I wanted to kiss the fuck out of her. I wasn't sure how she'd respond in front of an audience, so I satisfied myself with a swift peck on the mouth. I licked my lips, that cherry Chapstick she wore, pummeling my ability to keep my hands off her.

"Hey." I slid a hand around her waist and gave her hip a tight squeeze.

"Hey," she said again, grinning like a maniac.

"For the love of God, can y'all just go scratch your itch in the bedroom," snapped Violet as she pushed past Evie. Then she froze, catching sight of Nico by my sofa.

I have to say it was really entertaining to see the mouthiest chick I'd ever met stunned stupid and completely *silent.*

"Evie, this is my cousin, Nico. Nico, this is Evie and her sister Violet."

"Hi." Evie waved politely, leaning her body along the side of mine. I choked back the groan of satisfaction.

Nico ate up the few steps between us, shaking Evie's hand quickly, then holding out his hand for Violet. She crossed her arms and tucked them under her armpits, leaving him hanging. He dropped it with a smirk, then tapped a tune out against his thigh.

"Seems you two already know each other," I added.

That snapped Violet back to attention. "Know each other? We don't know each other."

"We've met," said Nico, his tilted smile and sharp gaze fully on the crazy sister.

"Briefly," she spat. "That doesn't mean we know each other."

"Y'all met after his set at the Cauldron last night?" asked Evie.

"No. Please. Not even." Violet rolled her eyes as if that were the most ridiculous thing she'd ever heard. Someone was overreacting.

"Soooo, where did you meet then?" Evie raised an eyebrow at Violet.

Nico opened his mouth to say something, but Violet practically shrieked, "None of your business!"

Evie rolled her eyes. "Violet, what are you? Twelve? Why is it top secret?"

"It's not." She stared daggers at my cousin. "It's just none of your business. Can we go now?"

"Jeesh." Evie glanced up at me. "Ready?"

"Do y'all need some help?" asked Nico. "I could come along if—"

"Absolutely not." Violet snorted and scoffed at the same time, sounding like a pig sneezing. "No one is allowed at a hex-breaking ceremony but us and the hexee."

"Well, then." Nico grinned. "I'll see myself out." He walked toward her, brushing his arm aggressively against Violet's as he passed, even as she tried to step out of the way.

I stared down and bit back a smile, knowing full well what that meant to a werewolf. Overt touches, brushes of the body or hands on skin in casual settings, especially in front of any kind of audience, was a way a werewolf staked his claim on a mate.

My mind came to a screeching halt at a sudden realization. I'd been touching Evie constantly since the very beginning. Had I been staking my claim before I even knew it? I'd been wrapped up in my need for her touch because of her hex-breaking mojo or whatever, but what if it had more to do with my need to imprint myself on her? What if the calm I felt when she was near me had nothing to do with her hex-breaking magic and everything to do with the fact I wanted her, that my wolf saw her as . . . ?

Mine.

Whoa.

"Ready to go?" Evie squeezed my hand she was now holding, looking up at me all bright and cheery, not realizing my world just rocked sideways. I couldn't move for a second, frozen by the discovery that Alpha had been staking his claim all along.

"You okay?"

I shook myself, then grabbed my keys off the counter. "Let's go."

After locking up, we exited through the garage. Evie slid into the middle of the bench seat of my truck with Violet on the other side. I'd gone mute, processing this new discovery. If it was, in fact, a discovery.

I was stunned silent for a while as I drove onto the interstate. Violet had put the address in her GPS on her phone. We bumped along quietly until Evie squeezed my arm just below my biceps.

"You sure you're okay?"

I held her green gaze, pulse quickening at the sight and scent of her this close. I remember my father sitting with me on the back porch in San Antonio when I was eighteen, not long before I left home. He was smoking a cheroot, the sweet smoke still imprinted in my memory. I'd asked him about how he met my mother and how he knew she was the one for him. At the time, I was infatuated with a girl in my senior class. My hormones were raging, and I couldn't tell if I was in love with the girl or just her mile-long legs and fantastic rack. So Dad, his eyes squinted from the cigar smoke swirling around him, looked over at me and said, "Son, a man can fall for many women, but the wolf falls only once."

Is that what this was about? Was she the one?

Nothing.

What? NOW you shut up?

A husky chuckle in my mind.

I hate you.

You hate yourself?

You're not me.

Ohhhh, yes, I am. Just because you like to block me doesn't mean I'm not every bit a part of you. You know it's true.

This was the first time I'd initiated a discussion with the asshole. I was suddenly regretting it because I was the one who sounded unhinged.

"Are you nervous about the ceremony?" Evie asked softly. "You shouldn't be."

I huffed out a laugh. "I'm fine."

Fine? I wasn't fine. I just realized she was far more than a friend to me, and it hit me like a brick to the head. Now I was terrified. What if she didn't want something this serious? What if she just wanted to play around? I was no longer playing. She was it for me.

Thankfully, her attention was drawn to her sister. "And what was that back there with his cousin, Nico?"

"I don't know what you're talking about."

Evie laughed and butterflies—yes, fucking butterflies—burst into mayhem in my stomach. I had to play this cool. Jesus. We just slipped over from friends to dating *last* night. And now, Alpha was giving me caveman thoughts. Lots and lots of them. The most prominent was me kidnapping her and putting her in a castle, high in some faraway mountains.

A simple cabin will do.

This was madness.

A rough chuckle. **When we've claimed her enough times to plant our seed, then maybe we can come down from the mountain.**

Fuck! He was insane!

I don't think I'll be satisfied till she's swollen with our cub.

This isn't the prehistoric age, you Neanderthal.

I've told you before. A wolf wants what he wants.

Nice. I don't even know if she wants kids. Shit! Why are we even discussing this? We haven't even gone on one single fucking date.

If you'd let me take over, I'll make her ours. She wouldn't complain. I can promise you.

You're not getting one goddamn second alone with her. Not again. Not after last time.

Coward.

"I think you know exactly what I'm talking about. What's going on with you and that werewolf?"

"Nothing. Why don't you just shut up about it?" Violet pointed. "Get off at this exit."

I exited toward the sign to Bayou Sauvage. Evie had texted me and told me we'd conduct the ceremony in the woods because when I shifted, I'd have some stored bloodlust to take care of. I'd need to stay in the woods and hunt for at least a week. I'd given instructions to Missy that I would probably be gone for a while so she should take care of the gallery. It wasn't anything new for her since I did this at least once a month on the regular.

"Oh, now look who wants to shut up," said Evie, smiling. "I think Jules would totally enjoy hearing about your reaction to her new live music guy."

"Sissy, come on. There's nothing to tell." Violet jutted her chin in the air, trying for nonchalant. Wasn't working.

Evie laughed. "There's *loads* to tell. Mateo, didn't you see the way Violet totally overreacted at your place?"

"Yep." I was going to support whatever came out of Evie's mouth. "Not to mention Nico's obvious interest."

"Fine!" yelled Violet, her cheeks pink with anger. "What do you want?"

Without a pause, Evie said, "You take my closing shifts for a month."

"A month!"

"*And* clean Z's litter box."

"That's ridiculous." She huffed, arms crossed over her chest as she stared out the window. "How long for Z?" she mumbled.

"I think a month will do."

"That's really shitty, sis."

"Well, so was what you did last night to me."

"What did she do?" I asked, concerned now.

"Nothing!" said Evie, shooting Violet a glare.

Violet's cat-eyed gaze narrowed, but she smiled like the bad kitty she was. Then we all were focused on the road. Violet pointed, so I veered onto a gravel road heading deeper into a wooded area. Bayou Sauvage was part woods, part wetlands and swamp. It would indeed be a good place for me to get lost once I shifted. Even now, tension hardened my muscles with the simple thought of shifting and hunting.

"There." Evie pointed to a silver SUV parked along the side of the road where a hiking path led into the trees.

I parked, then we piled out and headed toward the well-worn path. I could see just fine in the dark, but Violet shone the flashlight on her phone ahead of us. Evie gripped my hand, lacing her fingers with mine and squeezing. I felt the constriction all the way up to my chest where it tightened around my lungs and breathing became difficult.

"Don't be nervous," she whispered. "Though I've never done a spell like this, I know it will be fine."

"And what happens when . . . if . . ." I licked my lips and cleared my throat. "What happens when I shift? You'll need to protect yourself."

I felt like a fucking asshole. I was warning her against what was essentially myself.

Now, you finally admit it.

"I'll be fine. Don't worry. If things go awry, Jules can null you temporarily. Then we'll leave you here to, uh, take care of wolf business."

You'll need to stay, love, if I'm going take care of all my wolf business.

I forced a smile at her and squeezed her hand. "Good to know."

We walked side by side into an opening. There was a circle of tall white candles but nothing else.

"Hi, Mateo!" Clara waved, beaming a sweet smile.

Jules gave me a stiff nod in greeting and stepped closer. "Glad you made it on time."

I glanced up at the full moon in a clear night sky. "Are we going for a certain window to do this in?"

She shrugged. "I just hate it when people are late."

"She's got a long list of pet peeves," said Evie at my side.

Jules frowned. "I just like people to be respectful of others. And, yes, maybe I'm particular about the way things are done."

Evie raised her brow, glancing around the clearing. "Yeah. We know."

"Well, let's do this," said Violet, moving to stand on the opposite side of the candlelit circle where Clara was.

Jules took up a position farthest away.

"Take off your shirt." Evie held out her hand.

I froze for a second, not registering why.

She smiled. "I need the connection. Your DNA, your smell."

Ah. Gotcha. I pulled the long-sleeved black T-shirt over my head and passed it to her.

"Nice," whispered Violet.

"Shh!"

That must've been Jules, but I couldn't take my eyes off Evie because hers were eating up my torso in rapid detail. Her pulse quickened at the base of her throat, and I wanted to lean forward and suck it. Then find and kiss and suckle all her pulse points.

"This might not be the right time," I whispered, stepping closer.

She hugged my shirt to her chest. I waited for her gaze to sweep back up to mine, wanting her eyes on mine before I went on.

"But I'd like to ask you over to my place for dinner after this is done."

Her green eyes looked brown in the dark, but her pale skin glowed under the moonlight. "A date?"

"A date," I confirmed.

Rather than tell me yes, she eased closer and lifted onto her toes. I was leaning down for her when she swept a kiss to my lips. To say I was shocked was an understatement.

"Aren't you breaking the 'no werewolf' rule?" I asked, nodding behind us where her sisters watched.

She grinned. "But you're worth it."

My God. This girl.

She stepped back. "Now, get your"—she waved her hand to indicate my chest area—"wolfy self into the circle."

"I'm not wolfy yet. That's the problem, remember?"

She huffed out a breath. "Move it, Mateo."

"Yes, ma'am."

I didn't know how this worked, so I stepped over the tight wall of candles and moved to the center of the circle then turned to face Evie again. She put the T-shirt to her nose, closed her eyes, and inhaled a deep breath. I'm not going to lie. It was kind of erotic.

Kind of? I want to see her make that face on her knees in front of me.

Shut it, Alpha. You'll have free rein soon to go hunt and kill to your heart's delight.

Not soon enough.

She whispered a chant I couldn't quite make out, catching only a few words—*unbind, nature's toll, right the wrong, wolf in chains.*

Her sisters glowed with their magic, somehow amplifying Evie's as she did her work. A sudden wind whispered through the grove where we stood, circling us, guttering the candles but not blowing them out. Evie's muttering grew more feverish, and my body felt suddenly limp. As if I'd just run a marathon, my legs wobbled and buckled beneath me. My knees hit the cool ground, the dewy grass soaking through my jeans. My muscles felt soft, my bones heavy, my mind adrift, floating in the soft waves on the wind.

Evie spoke louder, her voice resonating with trembling magic. "Show your mark and loose his soul."

Pain! Spine-cracking, gut-punching, mind-numbing pain.

CHAPTER 23

~EVIE~

I SUCKED IN A SHARP BREATH. MY SISTERS AND I ALL JUMPED AT ONCE at the piercing howl of agony bellowing from Mateo's upturned mouth. His hands were in his hair, his face contorting with excruciating pain. But he *wasn't* shifting. He was writhing. I couldn't stand to watch. It was unbearable. I almost choked on the final command to break the curse, but I summoned it again.

Willing the magic piercing and binding him to obey me and not its maker, I raised a hand out to him, the other still clutching his shirt close to my breast.

"Show your mark and loose his soul!" I screamed into the whirling wind.

I gasped. So did my sisters—taking a step back—as a blinding red flash burst from Mateo's body, illuminating hundreds of signs etched in magic on his skin.

"Oh my God," breathed Jules, her words sucked into the wind.

"Mateo!" I cried out, steam rising from his skin where the glyphs had burned.

His eyes snapped to me—full fiery gold with a wolf who was mad as hell. He actually snapped his teeth, though other than his eyes, he was still a man. Nothing had changed. He hadn't shifted. The wolf was still trapped, and he was fucking *pissed off.*

The signs sizzled on his skin in red light. They were witch symbols, crawling all over his skin, but I only recognized one. He wasn't just cursed. He was dipped into the batter of a very, very dark spell. Something I'd never seen before. It was common for the curse to illuminate when I probed with my gift to break the hex, to set the cursed person free. But I'd never, ever seen something like this before. It was horrifying. *He* was horrifying. I stood there, shaking, not knowing what to do.

His predatory gaze was fixed on me, his teeth bared, then he launched himself over the candles and into the air.

"*Pas un geste!*"

Jules used the sharp command in French. It did its work. He froze in midair, his arms reaching for me, hands spread like claws, in full attack mode. My nightmare swept back to me, and again I heard that witch whisper on the wind. She was powerful, whoever she was.

Clara had already leaped over to Mateo's side and placed a hand on his shoulder, his body still telekinetically frozen in the air. She pushed into him with her joy spell, probably dialed up to a thousand. Jules and Violet joined me at my side.

"Don't hurt him, Jules. Don't take anything away." A tear slipped from my eye. I didn't want her to punish Mateo by siphoning his powers. "It's not his fault."

"I know." She wrapped a hand around my shoulder. "I'll just put him to sleep for a while."

"*Aller dormir,*" she whispered softly, curling the "r" in the French tongue.

Mateo's eyes drifted closed immediately, his limbs going limp, his head lolling forward.

"What the fuck was that?" asked Violet. "Did you see all that witch sign? Like, holy shit!"

I swallowed down a new fear I hadn't thought of. What if this witch, whoever he or she was, had some darker intent with this curse? A million questions flitted through my brain.

"I've never failed to break a curse," I said dumbly.

"Come on," said Jules, waving her hand and moving Mateo through the air back toward the car.

I gripped his shoe since he was floating head first. Not that I could hold him up by the tip of his shoe or like Jules would drop him. Our telekinesis strength would shock the shit out of people if they knew how powerful we were. I just needed to have my hands on him. For my own reassurance more than anything.

"Clara and Violet, you two can get the candles. We'll get him home where he can sleep off the spell."

"You mean the spell that didn't work," I said. "Did you see how much pain I put him in?" I choked on a sob.

"No." Jules squeezed me closer. I wrapped an arm around her shoulders, my other hand still clinging to the toe of Mateo's shoe. "This wasn't your fault. We're dealing with something I've never seen. Far more powerful than we thought."

"God, Jules. I hurt him."

"Stop saying that. It wasn't you who did that. It was the curse that blocked your magic. We had no idea. We need to find out more before we move forward."

I nodded as we came out of the woods. Jules had successfully levitated Mateo all the way to our two vehicles.

"Put the seats down in the SUV," she said, maneuvering Mateo to the back hatch.

I flattened the second and third row so there was room for him to lay down. Even so, when she pushed him in, I helped her ease his head to one side, bending backward over the driver's seat as his body was still too long to fit straight. She put him down gently, then we both physically bent his legs so he was curled on his side.

"He won't wake from my null spell, but I want to ride with you just to be sure. Give me a second." She felt into Mateo's jeans pocket and pulled out his keys, then scooted out the hatch and ran back along the path.

I twisted around and brushed his long locks away from his face. His skin was hot, burning up, but at least the symbols had faded from his skin.

"I'm sorry, Mateo." I swallowed the lump in my throat, wishing I was more powerful than the man or woman who'd done this to him. "We'll figure this out. Don't you worry."

Jules opened the driver's side door. "I'm driving. You can't drive right now."

I didn't argue. I walked around and hopped in beside her, put on the seatbelt, then we were on our way. "Clara and Violet will drive his truck back to our place. He'll need to stay the night to be sure he doesn't wake up and have some residual effects."

"Like lunge at my throat again or something?" I asked with too much snark when she cranked the car.

"Well, he did lunge at your throat," she added dryly.

"That wasn't him, Jules. He would never hurt me."

We remained silent as we bumped off the gravel road and back along the highway. Neither of us spoke for some time, both absorbed in troubling thoughts, still processing what had just happened. As we veered onto the interstate toward Magazine Street, I glanced back at Mateo. His face was calm and peaceful, completely beautiful. Then the image of that violent flash of dark magic filled my mind.

"It wasn't just the symbols and his screaming pain that has me so shaken," I said into the quiet cab.

"I know."

"You felt it?"

"Yes. Definitely." Jules looked at me. "It was like a living malevolence, wasn't it?"

"Yeah." I wiped a tear roughly away. "It was fucking horrifying."

Jules wasn't the comforting sort too often, so when she reached across and squeezed my hand, I knew I was a hot mess.

"It's going to be okay. We'll figure this out."

She steered with one hand, holding mine with her other. I squeezed hers in appreciation. "We have to."

"We will."

When we pulled up to the house, Jules backed far up the drive so no one on the street could see us levitating a body from the back of the SUV. There weren't many people out anyway.

"I'll do it," I said, wanting to lead the lifting of him. Needing to.

Gently, I pressed my magic toward him and lifted. Jules opened the back door and pushed chairs out of the way as I held his head in my hands, levitating him feetfirst through the house.

"Where are you taking him?" she asked when I passed the sofa in the living room.

"To my bedroom."

"Evie, that's not a good idea."

I gave her a sharp look and kept going.

"Okay. Fine."

She squeezed past us down the hall and opened my bedroom door. I pushed him through, then lowered him onto my bed. I had a queen-size bed, but it somehow looked so tiny with him in it. His long limbs and broad shoulders and chest—broad and naked—ate up the space.

"I'll sit with you awhile."

I didn't argue. I didn't want to be alone right now. I removed his shoes and socks, then sat on the edge of the bed, combing his hair back away from his eyes. His dark lashes formed perfect black crescents on his cheeks. That sensuous mouth, which had snarled at me in rage an hour ago, was now soft and slightly ajar in slumber.

We heard the back door slam, then Clara and Violet were both in the room. Violet leaned her shoulder against the doorjamb, but Clara walked to the opposite side of the bed. She put her hand on Mateo's forehead and closed her eyes, assessing his inner emotions, another aspect of her gift as an Aura. When she opened her eyes, I asked, "Well?"

She smiled. "He's fine. Like it never happened. All cool and calm in there now."

"Well, we need to talk about that shitshow back there in Bayou Sauvage." Violet's wary gaze was fixed on Mateo.

"Has anyone ever seen witch sign like that?" I asked.

"Never," said Clara, a little breathless, her clear blue eyes wide and round.

Violet shook her head. "That was the darkest curse I've ever seen."

Jules stood, both hands on her hips with her thumbs forward, fingers back. "We're obviously dealing with something serious. Someone serious. I recognized some of the signs, but I need to check Mom's grimoire to see what they mean."

"Not tonight, you aren't." Clara stood from the bed. "All I can feel from the lot of you in the room is extreme exhaustion. You all need rest." She glanced back at Mateo. "He's fine now."

With Clara's joy spell and Jules having nulled him, there was no way he was a danger.

"Fine," agreed Jules. "Everyone get some sleep. Evie, just take Isadora's room tonight if you want."

"No." I stood and went to my dresser to get a sleep shirt and shorts. "I'm staying right here. He might wake up and . . ." Be afraid? Be hurt? Need me? "I need to be here when he does."

Jules's assessing gaze flickered over me, then landed on him, then back to me. With a stiff nod, she went for the door, pushing Violet out ahead of her. Clara walked around the bed and squeezed me in her arms so tight I could hardly breathe.

"Don't you worry, Evie. He's going to be perfectly fine." She pecked me on the cheek, then sauntered out. Eternally optimistic. I wish I was.

I stared down at the man who had commandeered a place in my heart somewhere along the way. "I hope so."

CHAPTER 24

~EVIE~

No matter how hard I tried, I couldn't sleep. After I'd changed into my raining-cats-and-dogs sleep shirt and shorts, brushed my teeth, and slipped under the covers, I lay there curled on my side facing Mateo. I'd left him in his jeans and pulled up the covers over him.

I spent about an hour illustrating on my tablet, even sketching some character profiles with the inspiration lying in bed next to me. But after a while, I closed the tablet and put it aside, unable to get those images out of my mind.

The witch signs—curves and glyphs and hash marks—archaic in origin but familiar in some of the books Mom used to read. The only one I recognized was the scimitar-looking glyph, which represented murder. Not death or killing or revenge or harm to your enemies. It was a very straightforward symbol that meant *only* murder. I couldn't imagine what this symbol, among the others, was doing burned into his skin with dark magic. For there was no question that we were dealing with black magic.

Heaving out what must've been my hundredth sigh, I propped my head in my hand on my elbow and looked at my sleeping werewolf. "Who did you piss off so badly?"

I brushed at the wayward lock of hair that always liked to fall in his eyes, sliding my fingers over his forehead to tuck it aside. He snatched my wrist and his eyes popped open, then I was under him.

"Mateo, it's me, it's me!"

But there was no fire behind his eyes. No signs of his wolf running the show.

"Evie," he whispered, holding his weight off me. "What are you doing here?" He looked bewildered, his chest heaving, pressing down against mine.

"In my own bed? I was trying to sleep, but having trouble." I wiggled my body but was pinned tight beneath him. "A little stressful night."

He blinked in confusion, glancing around the room. He released my wrist and settled on his side, one of his heavy legs still draped over both of mine.

"What am I doing here?"

"You don't remember?"

His brow furrowed, those deep brown eyes moving over my face. "I remember going to Bayou Sauvage. Walking through the woods and stepping into the circle of candles." He swallowed hard, staring beyond me at the wall, trying to recall what had happened.

"Nothing else?"

He shook his head and glanced back at me with a mixture of horror and relief. "Did I shift? How long have I been here?"

Part of me was relieved he hadn't remembered the episode. But another was scared as hell. I'd read in my nighttime study of werewolves that they rarely lost complete memory when they shifted. Only when the man was suppressed so deep that the wolf had full and autonomous reign. Something about the curse and me trying to crack it open had pushed Mateo to the back and dragged his wolf to the very forefront.

"I'm sorry." I sat up, the covers sliding to my waist. "I couldn't break the curse." It took a hell of a lot for me to admit that. "This hex . . . It's got traits of something." I licked my lips, finding it hard to say it aloud. "Of black magic."

Mateo's intense gaze swept over my face and my hair, skimming past my shoulders to the tops of my breasts, down my pajama top, and then back up.

"Are you sure?"

I half-laughed. "I wish I wasn't."

He scooted back to the headboard and pushed both his hands into his hair, combing through it in frustration. His abs tightened and flexed with the action, drawing my gaze to the perfect eight-pack he was sporting under all that bronzed skin.

"Black magic?" he asked, as if he'd never heard of such a thing. "But why? I haven't done anything to anyone."

My heart clenched because I knew that was true. For all his strength and the fierceness of his wolf, Mateo was gentle. Kind and creative. Beautiful and benevolent to a fault. I couldn't imagine him doing someone harm intentionally. Not ever.

"Apparently, someone thinks you have." I placed a hand on his jeans-clad knee. "But don't worry. We're going to figure it out. It's not something we've seen before, but we've got a ton of resources. One of whom is our mother."

"And she'll help?" His vulnerable gaze, almost boyish, melted something inside me.

I nodded with a smile. "I know she will."

He inhaled a lungful of air and blew it out softly, surveying my room. There wasn't a whole lot to see. A dark wood dresser, a desk filled with a Mac desktop computer and a printer/scanner, my open closet bearing a wall-to-wall shelving unit with my categorized comics, a chair in the corner with some dirty clothes haphazardly draped on it, but his gaze landed on the nightstand on my side. I hitched in a breath when he leaned over and reached across me, but was relieved when he took one of the books stacked there.

He flipped open the hardback cover and arched a brow at me. *"The Beast of Gevaudan?"*

I shrugged a shoulder, drawing his attention there. "Research."

"I see." His dark eyes caressed down my hair to my shoulders before he dropped the book on the other side of him and reached out, smoothing a strand between his fingers. "I've never seen your hair down before."

Suddenly self-conscious, I squirmed a little. "It's just easier to wear it up."

"So soft." He fanned his hand from the base of my skull and let the strands drift out of his fingers. "So pretty."

"Th-thank you."

I was still sitting up, but he scooped an arm around my waist and tugged me down and underneath him, taking up that position hovering over me again. "You're stressed?"

"A little."

"I'm sorry."

"It's not your fault."

He grunted. "I think it is." His fingers continued their exploration of my hair, combing his fingers through, the sensation zinging from my scalp all the way down to the netherlands. He leaned closer. "This isn't how I imagined I'd get in your bedroom whenever I finally got here."

"Oh?" Breathless. Heart hammering. "You've imagined being in my bedroom?"

He swept my hair away from my neck, his fingers trailing over my pulse. "A lot. Specifically, your bed." He dipped his head and swept a kiss over my collarbone, lips nipping a sweet trail.

My brain checked out, and my body began humming with want, my blood roaring in my veins. More. I needed more.

"You said you couldn't sleep?" A languorous lap of his tongue to the hollow of my throat.

"Uh. Yeah." A riveting conversationalist, I was tonight.

"I know a way to help you sleep."

Whoa, boy. Though my body was screaming yes, I wasn't ready to have sex. Not after tonight's sad debacle. I was still jittery from it all. But my body was protesting my brain, putting up a blockade with signs and chants like, *We want sex! Sex is good! Sex, yes, sex!* All super creative chants, by the way.

Jeesh. I couldn't even form coherent thoughts with his hot mouth working up the column of my throat.

"I'm not sure if—"

His mouth was on mine, coaxing with a teasing brush of his sensuous mouth before he licked inside. He'd wedged himself between my legs, and I let them fall open like the starting gate to a horse race. He settled right where my lady parts wanted him. A carnal groan rumbled from his chest to mine, tightening my nipples beneath my superthin tank with its cute cats and dogs inside raindrops pouring down.

Mateo curled two fingers in the tank of my shirt, sliding it down my shoulder, kissing the flesh he exposed along the upper slope of my breast.

"I just want to make you feel good." He lifted up over me, sliding the material lower until cool air hit my naked breast, tightening my nipple into a bud. Still, he looked only into my eyes. "Nothing more," he promised. "Let me make you feel good, Evie."

The way he asked it, like a sweet plea, there was no way I could say no. And who didn't want a hot werewolf to make a girl feel good? I wasn't an idiot, so I nodded dumbly. His gaze slid to my exposed chest. He hissed in a breath. I thought I'd seen the look of lust on this man before, but it was nothing to what I saw now. He dipped his head and circled the nub with his warm tongue. Arching on a gasp, I pressed up into his mouth, clutching one fist in his hair and clawing my nails into his biceps with the other.

"Oh God, Mateo."

His large hand swept under my tank, splaying across the flat of my stomach, roaming to one side, then the other, caressing the skin there right above my sleep shorts. Back and forth, his fingers dipped barely under the waistband, all the time his lips nipped and sucked my nipple, forcing my hips to rock up against his hard, jeans-encased cock.

Then his mouth lifted away, the cold air against my wet breast tightening the tip even further. I moaned in frustration until he eased his head down my stomach, opened his mouth, and bit the end of my tank between his teeth. Holding my gaze, he slid it up, exposing my stomach, ribs, both my breasts.

He was so fucking sexy the throb between my legs warned me I wouldn't last a millisecond once he touched my clit. I wanted him too badly. He felt too good.

I rocked my pelvis up again, right at the same time he curled his fingers underneath my shorts and panties and pulled them down. Actually, I was pretty sure he timed it, watching my body, knowing when I'd lift up to rub against his erection. He knew exactly when the perfect time would be to pull them down my thighs. He lay half over me, his weight on his left forearm as he dipped his head to the breast he hadn't touched yet. His tongue flicked the tip at the same time his middle finger brushed between my folds and circled my clit.

"*Mateo.*"

"Does it feel good, baby?" he breathed against my sensitive skin.

"Fucking fantastic."

He groaned when he slipped his finger farther down, finding me ultra slick. Like embarrassingly so. Still, all I could do was moan and pump my hips like a greedy porn star. A porn star in puppy dog and kitty cat pajamas.

"There you go," he whispered against my nipple, voice husky, lips brushing, tongue tasting. "Take what you need."

His words just spurred me on. I brushed his hair out of his face so I could watch him working my breast. He pulled his hand from between my legs.

"No, no, no," I begged, clenching my nails into his scalp and his bare shoulder where I held on.

He chuckled, holding my gaze as he inserted his index and middle finger all the way into his mouth, sucking them clean. His moan vibrated into the side of my rib cage where he leaned his weight against me, skin on skin.

"Fucking fantastic is right." He stared up at me and slipped those two fingers back down along my pussy, a glorious slick glide down to my entrance, then he pumped inside.

"Oh shit, oh shit."

Two deep thrusts of his fingers up to his knuckles and I was coming already. I bit my bottom lip, trying to hold on, but there was no way.

He launched up over me, still stroking his fingers deep. "No you fucking don't. I want to hear you. Let me hear you come on my fingers, Evie."

Arching my neck and my hips, I let out a throaty moan as the greatest orgasm *ever* rocked my world. His hot mouth was on my neck with a swift bite, then his tongue was in my mouth, stroking hard, devouring every sound. His fingers were thrust deep, holding still as I throbbed around him. His kiss was rough and thorough and wonderful. He kept kissing me down, swallowing my little sounds, my panting breaths.

"So glad we're out of the friend zone," I muttered.

He laughed into the curve of my neck before planting a kiss there. He curved his palm over my mound, his fingers still partly inside me. He lifted his head from my neck to gaze down at his fingers working me. Those dark eyes promised a world of heady pleasure, and when I wasn't wrung out from a super-speedy orgasm like a wet noodle, I planned to partake of all those promises. Right now, all I could do was lay there and stare back at him, catching my breath.

He grazed his nose over mine. "Did that feel good?"

I laughed. "You know it did."

"That was the sexiest fucking thing I've ever seen." He gave my little lady a firm squeeze, like a good handshake that says I'll see you again soon, then he eased his fingers out and pulled my panties and sleep shorts back up my hips. "I was planning to do that a little differently, but . . ."

"Differently how?"

He shrugged a shoulder. "I was getting ready to go down on you and let you come on my tongue."

My brain fizzled a second, imagining what glorious heaven that would feel like.

He made sure my shorts were right, then he lowered my tank and slid his hand up over the material to leisurely cup my breast. It wasn't a sexual touch, but it definitely was a possessive one.

"You just went faster than I thought."

I swallowed my pride because, hell, I hadn't been with a guy in a long time. And I sure as shit hadn't been this turned on in like forever. "Sorry," I muttered.

"Don't be sorry." He blew out a breath, then licked his lips as he stared at my mouth. "I'll take care of that fantasy of mine next time."

"Next time? There will be a next time then?"

A pause for a soft, sultry kiss, then his voice, all smoky baritone, rumbled, "There will be many, many next times." Another dip and melding of mouths without tongue. "Now roll over and get some sleep. Hopefully you won't have trouble now."

It just hit me like a dummy that he gave me that fantastic orgasm so I could relax. And sleep. Jeesh.

"You know, for a big, bad werewolf, you sure are sweet."

He rolled my body to face away from him, then pulled me completely flush into the curve of his body, his bare chest pumping major heat into my back. It felt delicious.

"You sure you don't want some, uh . . . you know." I nudged back with my bum. "Reciprocation?"

His mouth was on the slope of my neck and shoulder. I swear I felt his cock twitch, but he made no move to thrust against me.

"No," he said calmly, pressing the sweetest, softest kisses to my neck before nuzzling his nose into my hair and squeezing his arm tight around my waist. "This is all I need right now."

"Just this?"

"Yep. Just this."

"You sure?"

He tightened his hold. "Very."

I settled my head onto the pillow, but couldn't help but ask, "Because if you want—"

His fingers dug into my ribs, tickling, and I squealed into the pillow with a huff of laughter. Then I felt teeth on my neck, and I stilled.

"Sleep, Evie," he whispered, kissing me where he'd bitten.

I let out a contented sigh, wondering if I could possibly fall asleep with this gorgeous hunk of man pressed up against me from behind. Funny, even after I'd met Mateo's wolf firsthand at the haunted house and knowing there was a scary-ass witch who'd put a black magic curse on him, I still felt safer in his arms than anywhere else.

I fell asleep faster than ever.

CHAPTER 25

~MATEO~

I woke up alone to the screeching sound of what I thought was someone singing. Very badly.

In the kitchen, I could hear the chatter of Evie and her sisters, as well as one of them singing—or trying to sing—"Think of Me" from *The Phantom of the Opera*. Might as well roll out of bed since there was no way I could sleep through that.

Swinging my legs over the side of the bed, I remembered the night before and smiled. Even though my morning wood was as painful as ever, I was somehow satisfied.

What? No cocky, asshole-ish remarks?

I'm not talking to you right now.

Fine by me.

I was rested, content, and strangely relaxed. There was no question that it was all because I slept with Evie in my arms last night.

Imagine what you'd feel like if you'd fucked her like I told you to *before* you fell asleep.

I thought you weren't talking to me?

Silence again. Good.

I glanced around the room, taking in her bedroom. It was simple with a dash of quirky. Like her. I chuckled at the unicorn-farting-a-rainbow lamp and the Wolverine clock on the night-stand. Warmth pooled at the center of my chest, especially when I saw her cute pajamas tossed on a chair. My cock stiffened more when I remembered sliding my hands into those pajamas last night.

I looked around and found my shirt from last night folded at the foot of the bed like Evie wanted me to find it. After shrugging into it, I caught sight of her tablet on the nightstand. Glancing at the door, I tuned in to the voices in the kitchen, able to make out the distinctly deeper voice of Jules, the throaty, friendly voice of Evie, and the higher-pitched, sweet voice of Clara.

I stared at the tablet and walked over to the nightstand. I shouldn't invade her privacy. I really shouldn't.

You really should. Why's she keeping secrets from us?

She isn't keeping secrets. It's just private, whatever she's working on in here.

Doooo it.

Having Alpha whisper in my ear all day was like having a devil on my shoulder.

That's right, bitch. I'm your devil. Now open it.

The problem was, there was no angel on the other shoulder. And sometimes, Alpha was so fucking hard to resist.

I snatched up the tablet and opened it, surprised to find it unlocked. It was already open in a software program called Clip Studio Paint Pro. The file at the top read *Witches in the City*. It was obviously her own artwork.

"Wow."

It was an illustrated comic, currently at fifty pages long. I started flipping to the next screen and the next. Some were divided into full-page spreads, others were half and quarter with amazing different angles. After being completely stupefied by her talent, I slowed down and read some of the story. It was Fred, their rooster, strutting into a ballroom, wearing a black silk bow tie next to a woman with pink dyed hair in a black cocktail dress.

They swaggered into the party with upturned chins, or actually one upturned chin and one beak, while the onlookers gasped in shock. It was obviously Violet, though the host of the party greeted her as Lily.

Just. Wow.

It was about her and her sisters. I skimmed through the rest, completely blown away by her skill. Why wasn't she publishing these? Were there more?

I closed the file and scrolled down to some Adobe Photoshop files in a folder called *Works in Progress*. My heart pounded out of my chest when I saw a folder titled *Mr. Wolfman*.

"No way."

Clicking it open, I sat back on the bed and skimmed through sketch after sketch . . . of me. Close-ups, angles from above, profiles, long distance of me on the street, of me working in my studio, clothes on, shirtless, and a lengthy portfolio study of my arms and hands.

Yeah, baby. Someone wants Daddy's hands on her.

I was floored and shocked and turned on all at the same time. A lot of the sketches were nothing but rough drafts, but some had been detailed and fleshed out with layers of color and contour lines in Adobe.

The giant printer next to her desktop on the desk could also double as a scanner. Closing the tablet, I went to the desk and pulled out the top drawer on the right. It was deep and filled with single-page sketches. The one sitting on top made me drop into the desk chair.

I lifted the black-and-white sketch of me walking down Magazine—I could tell because French Truck Coffee was behind me—wearing my hoodie, one hand in my jeans pocket and the other holding a short leash that was attached to a wolf at my side.

Besides the fact that she'd obviously been studying me with unbelievable detail these past few weeks, I couldn't get over the mastery of her craft. Her skill in drawing and technique in facial expression was easily better than most professionals in this trade.

Granted, I wasn't a comic book expert like her, but I knew the art form well enough. Scott's artwork was similar, though he only used charcoal medium. I couldn't get over this.

Evie was a true artist, and yet she'd been hiding it.

Why?

Plates and forks clanged in the kitchen, and I heard the snarky addition of Violet to the boisterous voices. I wished I could have Evie alone so I could tell her how absolutely amazing she was, but it seemed that conversation would have to wait.

Tucking the sketch back into the drawer, I ducked into the hallway bathroom, took care of business, and found an extra, unopened toothbrush in the drawer, which I took the liberty to use before heading into the kitchen.

"That's not what I said," grouched Violet, sitting at the table and tearing into her breakfast.

Clara plopped down prettily next to her with a plate. "Don't be so grumpy."

"I'm not grumpy," she yelled around a mouthful of food. "Evie just needs to watch her fucking self with that were—"

That's when she looked in my direction and pointed her fork toward the living room where I stood in the entryway.

"Wolf," I completed her sentence. "Yes. I've heard we're dangerous."

Violet swallowed, visibly embarrassed, which was a brand-new expression I'd never seen on her.

Evie sauntered over to me, perky and beautiful in jeans and today's T-shirt—black with Darth Vader saying, *Welcome to the dark side. We have cookies.* She made no hesitation about wrapping her arms around my neck and pulling me down for a swift kiss on the lips.

"Good morning. Ignore Violet. She's overreacting as usual. Have a seat."

I pulled up a chair with Violet scowling at me.

"No offense to you, Wolfman."

The name immediately made me think of the discovery I'd made in Evie's room. She took a plate from Jules who was prepping at the stove, the smell of ham and eggs and something else delicious making my stomach growl.

"None taken." I poured a glass of orange juice from the pitcher on the table and gulped it down.

"What I meant was, you were out of your fucking mind last night. You looked like you were going to kill Evie."

I almost choked on the orange juice. "What?"

That dampened my good mood fast.

What is she talking about, Alpha?

We might've jumped at Evie with the intention of attacking her.

What do you mean 'attack'? You were going to hurt her?

I don't think so.

You don't think so! Well, what DO you know?

I know that I felt this wicked pain, and I wanted it to stop.

Violet snapped her fingers in the air over the table. "Earth to Mateo. Are you listening?"

"It doesn't matter." Evie set a plate in front of me. She whispered in my ear, "She likes you."

I looked at Evie like she was nuts.

She giggled and pointed to Jules at the stove. "Her, not Violet."

"How do you know?"

"Because she cooked eggs Benedict. You're getting the special breakfast treatment."

"Maybe it's just my last meal before execution."

She laughed in that husky way she had, forcing me to smile. Clara giggled across the table, watching us with a twinkle in her eyes.

My mouth watered as I forked a bite of the layered English muffin, Canadian bacon, poached egg, and hollandaise sauce. A mound of cube-cut spicy hash browns and slices of cantaloupe completed the dish. I couldn't suppress a moan as I chewed the first bite.

Jules sat at the head of the table with her plate and smiled. A genuine one, not a placating or pitying one as she'd given me before. "So, how are you feeling this morning?"

I swallowed a bite of melon. "I was great until I found out that I tried to attack Evie last night."

My stomach sank as I slid my gaze to her. She reached under the table and squeezed my knee like it was no big deal.

"Did you have any luck with the symbols?" Evie asked.

"A little." Jules took a sip of coffee. "I sent a pic to Mom to see if she could help."

"Wait a minute." I set my fork on the plate. "A picture?"

Jules pulled out her phone. "I snapped a picture last night when it happened." She glanced at me guiltily. "Are you sure you want to see?"

I actually had to think about it a second. And why was Alpha being so fucking quiet? My brain had derailed at spending an entire night pressed to Evie. Was it her touch that tuned him out so much? If so, I might have to beg her to start sleeping at my place.

"Yeah. Let me see."

Jules flipped through some photos, clicked one, then passed it across to me. Evie had her hand on my thigh and squeezed reassuringly. But nothing could prepare me for what I saw.

"Jesus," I mumbled.

"Exactly!" Violet wiped her mouth with her napkin and balled it on her plate. She hopped up to come around and look over my shoulder. "See. You look like a fucking deranged animal."

"Violet! Shut your hole," Evie snapped.

I cleared my throat. "No. She's right." I stared at the image of me leaping toward Evie, her eyes round with fear, my flexed body poised to come down on her with force. And the red-lit symbols covering my exposed skin. What the fuck? "To be honest, at this moment, I'm more animal than anything else." I passed the phone back to Jules, not wanting to look at it any longer. "But I didn't shift."

Evie turned in her seat toward me. "Part of the curse that's been put on you includes a block. Like a really strong wall. It's preventing me from penetrating through to break the curse."

Jules tucked her short, cropped hair behind one ear. "I recognized that symbol. The hammer-looking glyph." She pointed to the photo where the symbol appeared on my forehead, chest, and shoulder.

"So many," I muttered. "So you think your mother will know what they mean?"

"Maybe not all. But she can advise us where to go from here."

A ringtone echoed from the countertop area. That's where a desktop was set up, facing diagonally out from the wall.

Jules popped out of her chair. "And there she is now." She hurried to the desktop, hitting the accept call button.

Evie walked around and stood over her shoulder. Clara and Violet followed. I stayed put, watching as an attractive woman popped up on-screen. She had dark auburn hair the same shade as Jules, darker than Evie's, and looked to be middle aged, but I knew she was likely much older.

"Hello, my lovelies," she beamed.

A chorus of hellos shot back from the four of them.

"Livvy is absolutely furious with all of you."

"Why?" asked Evie.

"Because you all waited till she and Isadora left town to have all the *dangerous fun*, as she calls it."

"Well, our dangerous fun is standing in the kitchen," said Jules, pointing over her shoulder.

"Oh really?" Her voice held a maternal authority, but was also edged with the love she felt for her daughters. "Go ahead and introduce me to your man, Evie."

I didn't know what Evie had told her mother about me, or whether it was Jules who had been relaying info, but the fact she had tagged me as Evie's man had me grinning like an idiot. I put my napkin on the table and stood. Evie met me halfway and pulled me to stand in front of the monitor, edging Clara and Violet to the side.

"Mom, this is Mateo Cruz. Mateo, this my mom, Serena Savoie."

"Hi, Mrs. Savoie. It's a pleasure to meet you." I gave a little wave.

She stared at my eyes for what seemed like a lifetime, measuring me well, before she gave a stiff nod. She had the kind of eyes that could be light and merry or burrow into your soul, depending on her mood. On the surface, she was whimsical, but this woman, this witch, held power. It eked off her from thousands of miles away.

"Yes. Yes, I like you, Mateo. You have kind eyes. You'll do just fine."

Sweet. Mother's approval. Now we can officially claim Evie.

Not now. Please not now.

Of course not. I don't want you to bang her on the kitchen table in front of Mom. What kind of a guy do you think I am?

Just, shut it. Go back to sleep or whatever.

"Mom." Evie, her face and neck pink, interrupted her mother's blatant examination of me. "Where's Dad, Livvy, and Isadora?"

"He dragged the girls into town to shop for birdhouse materials."

"Birdhouse?" asked Clara.

"He's built and painted three already for a family of Blue-throat larks taking up residence. I swear he wants to make our backyard into a bird sanctuary. But you know how your father is with animals."

"How lovely." Clara clapped her hands together, a jolt of joy pulsing off her like radio waves.

"Speaking of, how are Z and Fred? He'll want to know since he missed talking to you."

"They're fine," said Violet off to the side. "Except Jules isn't near as sweet as Dad is about the house rules."

The sisters exchanged glares.

Mrs. Savoie's green eyes sparkled with joy. They were similar in shade and shape to Evie's. "He would love it if Fred retired to Switzerland. That'll be next on his agenda. Making our twenty acres into a running farm. To tell you the truth, I've seen him eye-ing sheep for sale recently."

The girls laughed, but then their mother's face turned serious.

"Now, let's get to the matter at hand." Her voice was a sharp blade, her eyes darkening with severity. I'll bet she was a formi-dable leader when she once ruled as Head of Coven of New Orleans. "The first thing I can tell you is that this curse you're trying to break isn't a curse at all."

Evie leaned in. "Mom, it has to be. It's preventing him from using his magic."

"Not exactly," said her mother. "You're right that it's black magic. The red glyphs say as much, but what this looks and sounds like to me is a blood magic spell. Very different from a hex."

"What do you mean?" asked Jules. "What's its purpose then if Mateo is unable to shift and it's causing him . . . problems?"

That was as good an explanation as any.

Mrs. Savoie leaned closer to her monitor and looked at me. "Mateo, we don't practice blood magic. It's forbidden. My knowledge is limited because even reading the spells can be harmful." Her gaze flicked between Jules and Evie. "Listen to me, girls. Blood magic is sentient, just like our white magic. Its desire is always malevolent. Its intent is to seek a powerful conduit to attach itself to. That's why even reading some of these spells can be dangerous. The magic wants to seep into a host and latch on."

"So, if you had to guess, what do you think the purpose of this spell is? And why is he unable to shift?"

Mrs. Savoie squinted her eyes as if in thought. "If it were a regular hex, then Evie would've broken it. She's the most powerful hex-breaker in North America."

"Mom, I don't know if I'm—"

"Evie, darling, your power surpasses even your own recognition." Her voice had gone soft and maternal, her eyes full of adoration for her daughter. I knew that feeling. "Just because you don't see it, doesn't mean it's not there. The reason you couldn't break it is because it's not a curse. Not exactly. The blood magic spell has chained Mateo's wolf, not as the reason for the spell, but as a side effect."

"So how do we discover the reason? Its purpose?" asked Jules.

"That's the crux, isn't it?" She bit her bottom lip. "I don't want any of you researching and studying blood magic spells. Not only is it unbelievably dangerous, especially with the magic coursing through your veins, but it's highly illegal. I recognized some of the witch sign burning on Mateo's skin." My own skin suddenly prickled and itched. She went on more earnestly, "There is a book that details all witch sign without the risky addition of the spells."

"But what good will that do us?" asked Evie. "We need to know what it is in order to conduct a counter-spell."

"Not necessarily. The Coven Guild Summit is coming up in New Orleans, right?"

Jules nodded. Evie scowled, blowing out a frustrated sigh. What was that about?

"End of November."

"Good. Then get the book, match the witch sign you have that was marked on Mateo, then ask Clarissa in person."

"Excuse me," I butted in. "Who's Clarissa?"

Evie's mother answered me. "She's the president of the Coven Guild. She should have some helpful advice." Then her gaze swept back to her daughters. "This isn't something that needs to be batted around on cell phones or email. You don't want anyone reading them and thinking you're dabbling in blood magic. Clarissa will know you're telling the truth. Besides, I'll give her a heads-up before the summit."

"But Mom," said Evie. "A blood magic spell? Should we be worried this is over our heads?"

The pretty woman laughed, a throaty sound like Evie's laugh. "Don't be ridiculous. Yes, you should show extreme caution because this witch means business. Her spell is tight and strong. But every one of you is more powerful than any blood witch." She narrowed her eyes on Evie. "Even you, love."

Again, I was jarred that their mother seemed to be bolstering Evie's confidence. I'd never once thought of Evie as lacking assurance. If anything, she seemed more sure of herself than anything else.

"Sounds like a good plan." Jules sighed. "But Mom, what was the title of the book? You didn't say."

"Oh! Sorry." She laughed again. "It's called *The Etymology and Definition of All Known Witch Sign* by Marigold Lord. Clever title, eh?"

Evie and Clara laughed.

"And Jules, you'll need to ask Ruben for it. No one else will be able to acquire a copy as quickly as him. You need a copy fast."

Violet snickered behind her hand. "This should be interesting."

Evie grinned, but made no comment. When Jules spoke again, her voice was tight and strained. "Mom, what about Beryl? Surely she's got a copy."

"Doubtful. She shuns anything even close to blood magic." Mrs. Savoie turned thoughtful again. "You don't understand. I'm not kidding when I say that dark magic has a voracious appetite and will hook into a host as soon as she or he lets her guard down." She snapped her fingers in front of the monitor. "That's another thing. Once you've gotten the information you need, burn the book. Don't argue! Not one of you. Or you can tear the section on blood magic out and burn that portion. That's what all true magic wielders do."

Violet snorted. "I guess we now know why you'll have to go bargain with the rare book dealer." She nudged Jules.

"You mean make a deal with the devil," she mumbled back.

Mrs. Savoie flashed a beaming smile. "Okay, girls. I think you have what you need. I need to go finish up my lamb and sausage gumbo."

"Ew. Lamb and sausage?" asked Clara.

"Quite delicious. Always best to use what's fresh and local. That goes for witchcraft *and* cooking, you know that." She winked.

"Bye, Mom. Thank you," said Evie.

The others followed suit.

"Goodbye, my lovelies. I'll send your sisters back right before Christmas. Goodbye, Mateo. Don't worry. My girls will take good care of you. You'll be right as rain before you know it."

"Thank you, Mrs. Savoie. Your daughters are quite . . . remark-able." I couldn't help but look at Evie.

Mrs. Savoie's motherly grin grew wider. "That, they are." She blew a big kiss, then the screen went dark.

Bye, Mom. I heard a smacking kissy sound and a rough chuckle. **She likes us.**

Evie turned to me and gave my forearm a squeeze before tangling her fingers with my own. "Well, at least now we know more of what we're dealing with."

I exhaled a heavy breath. "But now I'm more worried than ever. I mean, blood magic? What the hell?"

She squeezed my hand. "The sooner we can get to the bottom of it, the better off we'll be. If my mother says we can handle this, then we can. Trust me."

"I do." I held her gaze for longer than was necessary, trying to tell her without words how much I already trusted her. Not just with this curse. But with my heart, my soul. My everything.

Clara brushed my shoulder in passing with a friendly tap and a zing of happiness. "Don't worry. It will all work out. I'm going to open the shop." Then she sauntered out the back door through the courtyard.

Violet huffed out a laugh. "Jules, you better get to calling Ruben so he can get that book."

Jules stood at the window, her arms crossed as she stared, or rather, glowered into the courtyard.

I leaned down to Evie. "What's going on?"

"She and Ruben don't get along," she admitted with a smile.

After a long, tension-filled minute, Jules spun around. "Fine." She whipped out her phone and started texting feverishly.

"If she doesn't like him, why does she have his cell number?" I asked.

"She has the numbers of all the supernatural leaders. Ruben is head of the vampire coven. Or master, overlord, whatever." She was whispering, but then she lifted her voice to Jules. "Don't they call him Master of Coven NOLA?"

"Yes," she gritted out while she waited for a response.

I took the quiet moment to whisper, "What's the Coven Guild Summit?"

Evie's mouth tightened into a line. "An annual meeting of the witch covens of Louisiana."

"What's wrong with it?"

"Nothing." Her green eyes were flinty.

"Then why are you angry about it?"

She huffed out a sigh. "It's not the summit. It's the cocktail party celebration at the end. I don't want to go, but Jules is making me this year."

"Why don't you want to go?"

A ping announced Ruben's return text.

"Later," she said, but I knew it was a brush-off.

Jules read the message greedily, then shouted, "That motherfucker!"

Evie gasped. "Jules!"

Violet tossed her head back and laughed. "Such language from the head of household. I thought you were above cursing."

"What's wrong?" asked Evie, more urgent now. "He won't get the book for you? He doesn't hate you that bad, does he?"

"No." Her flinty gaze shot up to us. "He'll get it. But on one condition."

She was grinding her teeth together so hard it was giving *me* a headache.

"Well?" Evie walked over and tossed up both hands, asking for more. "What's the condition?"

She let her head fall back with a loud sigh. "If I go on a date with him."

Violet jumped up and clapped. "This is the best. I love that fucking vampire."

"Shut it, Violet." Jules started texting back furiously. "Fine. I'll play your little game." She seemed to be talking directly to him through clenched teeth.

I shared a look with Evie who only smiled and shook her head. "Their feud has been going on for a long time."

Jules hit send, lifted her head with a pasted-on, brittle-as-hell smile. "Go grab your jackets. You two are coming with me for my *coffee date*"—she paused to make exaggerated air quotes— "with that asshat."

"Now?"

"Now."

Evie beamed up at me. "Our first date?"

I ushered her out the door, my hands on her hips and dipping my head low to her ear. "This is *not* our first date. I have plans for that."

Fuckin' right, we do.

Put your dick back in your pants. I'm in charge of date night.

No problem. I'll be in charge in the bedroom afterward.

I wasn't going to debate this shit with him. I honestly had detailed plans for my first date with Evie. I'd been thinking about it for a few days and had some special things shipped from Amazon to make it special for her. Some things I knew would put that pretty smile on her face. And no matter how badly I wanted to discover every inch of her hot-as-hell body, I wanted to discover her mind even more. After finding her artistic talent she's hiding from the world, we had lots to talk about. And I wasn't going to be satisfied until I knew everything about my pretty little witch.

CHAPTER 26

~EVIE~

RUBEN DUBOIS REEKED OF SOPHISTICATION AND SWAGGER AND SEX.
So did his bookstore, Ruben's Rare Books & Brew. Yes, he also
had a café at the front of his store, but it looked more like a sleek,
vintage hotel lounge. There were overstuffed blue velvet love
seats and silver-brocade chairs with artfully crafted, round-top
tables tucked here and there. Jewel-tone Tiffany style lamps with
soft warm lighting gave the lounge a sultry mood, which leaked
into the rest of the place with its art deco vibe and softly playing
big band music.

And it didn't seem to attract the same hipster, bohemian
crowd as the other coffee shops along Magazine Street. Nope.
The people who stretched out with their books, not laptops or
other electronics, seemed to fit here. Even Beverly, the cashier/
barista behind the counter, looked like she walked off a pin-up
poster in her tight black pencil skirt and silky red blouse with a
floppy bow hanging at her well-endowed and well-lifted bosom.

Her fire-engine-red lipstick matched her blouse, accenting her pearly pale skin. Her blonde hair was pinned up in a twist to complete the ensemble.

Beverly was definitely a vampire and was also apparently enthralled with vintage clothes like Ruben. Or she was just trying to keep her employer or lover happy. I wasn't quite sure what her relationship was with Ruben because she always looked at him like she wanted to bite him. But how could anyone blame her?

As the man of the hour sauntered into the lounge area where we were seated, I remembered why he took my breath away every time I saw him. He was so . . . so . . . put together. Handsome was too inadequate to fit him. Regal was too feminine. He was just so . . . Ruben. Dressed in tailored charcoal pants, white starched shirt with silver cuff links, and a black vest with a gray stitched design, he looked like he just stepped out of the 1940s, except he forgot his hat, coat, and tie. Somehow, I was sure he'd have all those accessories and more for a nighttime event. Since this was a daytime coffee double date, no need to go all crazy and dress full formal, right?

Like all vampires, he was stunningly handsome. His sandy blond hair fell in a perfect wave across his brow. His blue-green eyes shifted in different lighting, dipping closer to dark green in the warm glow of his lounge.

Those ever-watchful eyes swept over me and Mateo, then landed on Jules and stayed there. Rather than look irritated that Jules hadn't come alone for her "date," he seemed completely amused, his pretty mouth sweeping up as he drew closer.

"Hello, Juliana." He leaned down, took her hand, and swept a kiss over her knuckles.

Jules scowled, but I wasn't sure if it was at the kiss or his use of her full name. She snatched her hand back and tucked both between her legs.

"I didn't think you'd mind if I brought company, seeing as the book I need pertains to them."

"Not at all." His smile never slipped as he shook my hand with both of his. "Pleasure to see you again, Evie." He turned and shook Mateo's hand. "I'm Ruben Dubois."

"Mateo Cruz."

"I've stopped into your gallery a few times."

"You have?" Mateo seemed shocked. Makes sense. Ruben was a powerful figure among supernaturals, even among human society. Surprising that Mateo never knew he'd visited his gallery without notice. Then again, he was a vampire, one powerful enough to use glamour to hide his comings and goings.

The only place for Ruben to sit in our circle was the chair opposite Jules at the long mirrored coffee table. She had done it on purpose, to keep him at a distance. I tried not to laugh when he stepped over to a two-top with armless chairs, lifted one, and plopped it right next to Jules. Super close.

"You're an exceptional artist," continued Ruben, leaning an arm on the blue velvet arm of Jules's chair, invading her space.

"Thank you. I had no idea you were a potential customer." Mateo stretched his arm on the sofa back behind me. "I would've greeted you personally."

"No need to go to the trouble for me."

For a powerful vampire who ruled the largest population of his kind in the Deep South, he acted rather humble. Even in his dapper threads, he looked relaxed and friendly. Oh. Until I got a good look at the tiny design repeated in gray on his black vest—a boa constrictor seductively draped and wrapping the body of a naked woman, her throat arched back for him, her eyes closed in rapture. The design was repeated several times on the vest. There was no doubt that Ruben had his clothes custom made.

"If you're interested," continued Mateo, "I'd be happy to give you a behind-the-scenes tour. Show you some pieces not in the gallery."

"That would be much appreciated." His gaze had been on Mateo as they had their little exchange, but then that penetrating gaze swiveled to Jules. "Would you care for some coffee?"

"Sure." She was trying hard not to be rude, I could tell. After all, we needed a favor.

"Beverly." He raised a hand. The bombshell glided from behind the counter and into the nook where we were.

"Yes, sire?"

Sire? I forgot the formality among vampires. Jules stiffened, suddenly interested in her fingernails.

"Is espresso good for everyone?"

"Fine," said Mateo. I nodded. Jules pretended to be invisible. It was so strange. My sister was a powerhouse, a badass witch Enforcer and culinary chef extraordinaire who managed not only our witch business but the Cauldron as well. She wasn't shy. Ever. But right now, she looked like she was trying to sink right into her velvet cushion and become a part of the fine upholstery.

"Right away, sire."

As Beverly glided away, swinging her curvy hips, Ruben turned back to Jules. "How have you been, Juliana?"

"Fine." She avoided his heavy and attentive gaze. "How's the blood-sucking business going?"

"Bloody as ever." His voice dipped, rolling to a sexy lilt. "How are things in the kitchen? Still hot?"

"Enough to burn you to a pretty crisp."

He grinned. "You think me pretty?"

She chuffed, rolling her eyes and staring at the ceiling.

"And the knives, Juliana? Still sharp?"

His sultry tone insinuated all kinds of things, but I had no idea what the hell this was all about.

"Very. I use a magic whetstone these days to make sure they hit their mark. All unwanted intruders."

He smiled wider. "Good. Remind all the other suitors they better keep their distance."

Suitors? Only Ruben would use archaic words like that. And why was he so interested in Jules's dating life? Not that she had one.

She rolled her eyes. Again. The action became comical in its redundancy. "There are none, Ruben."

"That's because they're all afraid of you. But I'm not."

"No. You've made that quite clear. Besides, I have no time for *any* suitors."

He just smiled serenely like they were talking about the weather, then turned to us. "Now, what is the book you're looking for?"

Jules straightened, downgrading her tone from murderous to business professional. This was my sister's comfort zone. *The Etymology and Definition of All Known Witch Sign* by Marigold Lord."

Ruben's smooth forehead puckered into a frowning expression I'd never seen him make. Granted, I'd only been around him a handful of times when he'd come to the house or the Cauldron to speak business with Jules. But nothing seemed to ruffle the dude.

"I'd think that would be a well-used staple already in your library." This was directed to Jules.

"It's not a necessary tool. We don't need witch sign for our magic."

"Really?" Ruben leaned in, genuine interest in his expression. "Why not?"

Mateo leaned forward too.

Jules glanced at me with a question. This wasn't something we discussed outside the house or the company of other witches. It wasn't a secret, really, just knowledge only witches needed to know. Or cared to know. I shrugged and nodded.

Jules angled in her chair to face Ruben, which actually put her farther away from him. Definitely on purpose. "Witch sign is used in casting spells outside a witch's natural order of magic. Meaning, if a witch is conjuring magic that isn't an innate gift of his or her own, they need to send the message to the magic with witch sign. It's like . . ." She motioned with her hands in a circular way, her eyes sparkling as they always did when speaking of magic. "Like having a conversation."

"You mean, speaking to magic," clarified Mateo.

I turned my knees toward him. "Think of it this way. You don't need any kind of help talking to your wolf, right?"

He scoffed. "I can hear the bastard loud and clear. Especially lately."

Ruben looked like he wanted to interrupt, but he didn't.

"Well, I don't need any help talking to my magic. I can summon it at will. Same for Jules and all my sisters. But let's say I wanted to do, oh, I don't know, a love spell."

"You can actually do those?" asked Ruben, his gaze swiveling to Jules. Her face burned pink.

"More like infatuation," she clarified. "Love isn't something magic can make happen. But surface feelings—lust and fascination. Yes."

Mateo leaned close to me, teasingly. "Have you used this spell on me?"

I slapped his chest with the back of my hand. "*Anyway*, if we did want to use this spell, we'd have to use witch sign in a casting circle with all the other ingredients."

"What other ingredients?" asked Ruben. "Animal sacrifice or something."

Jules shivered. "Please. It's not that primitive. A lock of hair or something of the owner. But that's not the point. The thing is, spell-casting can be extraordinarily complex. The more complex, the more witch sign that's used."

"Hell," said Mateo, leaning back against the sofa back. "Then the one cast on me is majorly complex."

Beverly sidled up and set a tray down with four espressos in white china cups with blue rims, small silver cream and sugar decanters, and four teaspoons.

Ruben gave her a smile. "Thank you, Beverly."

She nodded, then left.

Mateo leaned back with his long fingers wrapped around the cup. "So witches don't need witch sign for their natural-born gifts of magic."

I blew on my espresso before taking a sip. "Like telekinesis. Most witches have some level of innate ability. We don't have to cast for that. We can do it at will."

"Yes, I know all about that," said Ruben, flashing a smile at Jules, showing a little fang.

"Really?" I asked. "How do you know?"

"Your sister once threw a raw rump roast at my face. Telekinetically."

Mateo coughed on his coffee. I barked out a laugh, then stifled it. My sister was practically purple with the deepest blush sweeping up her cheeks. Ruben was all smiles as he sipped his coffee with casual grace.

After calming myself, I asked, "Why in the world did you do that, Jules?"

She shrugged and sipped her coffee. "We had a disagreement."

"About what?" I asked.

Ruben opened his mouth, but she gripped his forearm still lazily draped over the arm of her chair. "It was business. No need to discuss it."

Ruben's gaze darted to her hand on him. He seemed to ponder for a second, then said, "A business disagreement." Jules removed her hand and tucked it back in her lap. Ruben set his empty cup on the table. "So you've enraged a witch, have you, Mateo?"

I found it interesting that Ruben never remarked on Mateo being a werewolf.

"Apparently." I'd set my coffee cup back down, so Mateo took my hand, lacing his fingers through mine. "Whatever spell she put on me, I can't shift."

"Damn."

Ruben sat forward, elbows on his knees, long fingers loosely clasped together. A silver signet ring with some kind of crest adorned the index finger of his right hand. He truly was polished from head to toe. I felt a little schlumpy in my T-shirt and jeans.

"You don't know who cast it?"

Mateo exhaled a sharp breath, his hand sliding absently over my upper back, tugging on the end of my ponytail. "I wish I did."

Ruben's gaze glimmered more blue than green. "I'll ask around and see if I can find anything."

"That would be great. I'd appreciate it."

If anyone could dig up information about a witch casting black magic spells around here, it was Ruben.

Ruben kept very exclusive company with ties to celebrities, politicians, even more *organized* businessmen. Aka the mafia. Or so the rumor went.

"I'll access my resources and get the book delivered as quickly as possible," he said to Jules.

Mateo stood. "Thank you for your help. If you ever need a favor, you know where to find me."

Ruben smiled, then stood with Jules and me. "I'll take you up on that." He shook Mateo's hand, then turned to Jules. "I'll text you about our date."

Jules's face went white. "This was it. We just had it."

Ruben's laugh was all deep and seductive and melty like decadent chocolate, traveling in a sweet slide down my spine. I'll bet he had dozens of women lined up to be his blood-host.

"This wasn't our date." He splayed his long-fingered hand over his vest, smoothing it, the other tucked casually in his pants pocket.

"Yes, it was," she snapped, eyes sparking with defiance. "Besides, you don't want to date me."

"You have no idea what I want." His tone was serious, almost severe, his expression even more so. This time, Jules didn't look away, holding his gaze with the same intensity he'd been staring at her this whole time.

Mateo nudged me toward the door, his hand at the small of my back. I glanced over my shoulder to see Ruben moving into my sister's personal space, speaking low and soft, but then we both ducked out the door, and I didn't get to hear what he said.

Pulling me against him, locking his arms at the small of my back, he whispered against my temple, stirring the little hairs and giving me a shiver. "Speaking of dates, I'd like to take you on one."

"I'd *love* it." Excited, I wrapped my arms around his waist and squeezed. "What'll we do?"

"Dinner and a movie?"

I tilted my head and quirked a brow. "Not very original."

"I'll see what I can do to help that." Grinning, he asked, "Tomorrow at six?"

I rose onto my tip-toes. He leaned down and met me halfway for a very not-friendly, butterfly-inducing kiss. "It's a date."

CHAPTER 27

~MATEO~

"I thought we were going on a date," said Evie as I tugged her through my courtyard past the Hades statue.

"We are." I pushed open the workshop door.

"You promised dinner and a movie."

I pulled her to a stop. "All upstairs waiting for you."

"You cooked?"

"Don't look so surprised. I told you I could."

"I'll be the judge of that." She glanced toward my workshop table. "Whoa. You've been working a lot without me." Heading over to the still-headless sculpture for Sandra, she then walked a circle around it.

"She's already so lovely. Her gown." She crouched and ran her fingers over the steel waves, a skirt billowing in an unseen breeze, pressed against the leg my dream girl had put forward, her bare foot peeking beneath the metal gown. One of the sculpture's arms was at rest by her side, the other was raised, reaching out toward something or someone. Long, delicate fingers I knew so well.

Evie twisted around, her brow pinched. "I thought you couldn't work with Alpha in your head."

"I couldn't. Before."

"Before what?"

"Before you."

She blinked and swallowed hard, staring back at the unfinished piece. She traced the square shoulder and long arm on one side. "How?"

"I'm not sure. It's not like he leaves me completely alone, but he's much quieter since I've been spending time with you."

"Why do you think that is?"

"I don't know." But I did know. I just wasn't ready to tell her. Or scare her off. "Come on."

I led her upstairs, not bothering to flip on the lights. I watched her face as she took in my living room.

"*Mateo.*" She stood there and stared, her eyes growing brighter by the second until she belted out a laugh. "What on earth?"

She rushed to my spread on the floor set up in front of my seventy-two-inch plasma TV.

"Oh. My. God."

I smiled as she practically vibrated with excitement. The giant Death Star sleeping bag spread out on my Persian rug, a stack of furry Ewok throw pillows, the room lit only with red and blue tall candles set in lightsaber candlesticks, a domed serving tray in the shape of R2-D2's head, the tall glasses with Han's and Leia's faces etched on the side, a pitcher of margaritas, popcorn-filled Storm Trooper helmet bowls, chips, salsa, and guacamole in a Millennium Falcon chip-n-dip tray, and sugar cookies with chocolate icing shaped like Darth Vader.

Evie stood there with her mouth hanging open, staring with gleeful wide eyes. "I can't even."

"The best surprise is this." I took a seat on the far side of the sleeping bag and lifted the R2-D2 dome to reveal a stack of perfectly baked golden pies.

"Are those . . . ?"

"Only first place award-winning meat pies for you."

She stood there speechless, shaking her head.

"Do you like it?" I don't know why I was nervous, but I was, rubbing a palm on the side of my jeans.

She stumbled to the middle of the blanket and sank to her knees, still staring at it all. "You had me at lightsaber candlesticks."

Laughing, I picked up the remote and pressed play on the movie I had frozen and waiting.

Her head jerked at the opening music. *"The Force Awakens?"*

"Of course." I made her a plate with two meat pies, some chips, salsa, and guacamole, and handed it over. "I have to know what happens next." I poured her a margarita, then fixed my plate.

She settled against the pillows with her plate on her lap, the prettiest smile spread over her face. "You're like the perfect man conjured from my nerdiest fantasies. I couldn't have made you better in a *Weird Science* experiment if I tried."

Trying to be casual when my heart was drumming hard, I held out my glass for a toast. She raised her own. "May the force be with you." I clinked mine to hers.

She shook her head with a heavy sigh, her loose hair around her shoulders gleaming in the candlelight. She'd worn it down for me. I knew it was for me. "That does it. You win."

"What do I win?" I drank a gulp, set my drink down, then scooped some guacamole with a chip and took a bite.

"All of it. You just win all the things."

"You haven't even tasted my meat pie."

The flash of pink that filled her cheeks had me grinning.

Oh yeah. She's gonna taste our meat pie.

Settle down. Go back to sleep.

I wasn't asleep. Just watching this epic fail at seduction.

I wasn't trying to seduce her.

Good. Because you've got no game.

You have no idea what Evie wants. You think all a girl needs is a hot tongue and a hard dick.

Am I wrong?

Yes! Yes, asshole. You're completely and one hundred percent wrong.

We'll see.

"Mateo, you okay?"

I shook him off and cleared my throat. "More than okay."

She picked up a meat pie and took a bite, then closed her eyes as she chewed it. She gave me the biggest smile. "You totally deserved that first place award."

I grinned, biting into my own.

"It's perfect that you cook because I don't. That'll come in handy if—" She stopped herself and averted her eyes nervously before gulping some of her margarita.

"Come in handy if what?" I asked.

"Let's watch the movie. You'll be lost if you miss this part at the beginning."

I let her off the hook for now. She was thinking if we ended up as a couple, like something long-term, then we would fit. We'd match. And we did. We so did.

I was an introvert. She was the opposite, dragging me out of my workshop, even when I didn't want to. I was too broody and introspective. She was light and funny and kind and so fucking gorgeous. I was caged away in my own little world, and she opened my eyes to so much more. She made me think, made me smile, made me laugh, made me *want* like I'd never wanted anything in my whole goddamn life.

I tried not to get overwhelmed with the emotions that swamped me every time we were in the same room, but it was hard. And now, here she was, sitting in my apartment, eating my food, lying on my floor. It was enough to make my dick rock-hard. That dominant part of me taking hold.

Yeah, I'm here.

Yeah, him. He wanted her in every possible way. We both did, truth be told. *Patience,* I told myself.

After her third meat pie, which made me unbelievably happy for some insane reason, she put her plate aside and settled onto the pillows. I moved the tray of food onto the coffee table behind us, stretched out and bent one arm behind my head, then pulled her into me with the other. She cuddled against my chest, her slender arm draped across my waist. For a while I was distracted by the perfection of how she felt next to me, then the movie sucked me in.

Evie was the first to start the ongoing commentary that had happened during our first *Star Wars* marathon.

"Don't judge, but all of Kylo Ren's angry stomping is hot."

"You find a man with anger issues hot?"

"No!" She slapped me over the rib cage. "Don't be ridiculous." She laughed, snuggling closer. "There's just something about that dominant, clomping walk that does it for me."

"Soooo, you'd find Frankenstein hot? Because it's very similar."

"Frankenstein doesn't look like Kylo Ren."

"So it's only okay to have anger issues if you're good-looking."

"That's not what I mean." She tapped me again with those long, delicate fingers. "And the way he looks at Rey. Jeesh."

I squeezed her hip where my hand draped lazily. Naturally. This was so . . . easy. I couldn't quite get over it. The women I'd dated in the past, even the relationships I'd let go on for too long before breaking them off, had never felt like this. Everything was work. Or a debate that felt like arguing, disagreeing—not playing, like it did with Evie. Debating with Evie felt like a game, one I never wanted to end.

"You do realize he's the villain," I commented.

She reached behind her for a handful of popcorn, which she pooled into a little pile on my stomach and ate one piece at a time. Her fingers plucked a piece and popped it into her mouth, over and over. I hoped she didn't notice the raging hard-on she was giving me from eating popcorn served on my abdomen.

"Not . . . necessarily."

"Evie, he's conspiring with that Snoke guy."

"True. But—"

"And they just blew up that planet for funsies."

"They're the Empire." She peered up at me and stuffed a piece of popcorn in my mouth, her fingers brushing my lips. "That's what they do. Blow up planets."

"Exactly." I chewed, trying to ignore my body's reaction to her innocent playfulness. "He's the villain."

"Right now he is."

Suddenly, I rolled over on top of her, the few popcorn kernels left rolling off and squishing between us. "Did *you* just spoil the next movie for me? I can't believe you did that."

"I didn't!" she cried, laughter in her eyes.

"You did, you little witch."

"Well, I am a little witch. But I didn't spoil anything!"

"You just implied he's not a villain in the next movie."

"I did not. Besides, he's still a villain in *The Last Jedi*."

"See, you admit that I'm right. He's the villain."

"Regardless"—she shrugged—"he's still hot."

I quirked a brow. "Do I need to start throwing temper tantrums, stomping around my workshop, and throwing shit to get you hot and bothered?"

She shook her head and bit her lip. "You don't have to do a thing." Her dark green eyes zoned in on my mouth. "You just have to breathe and I'm . . ." Her lips went slack, half open.

Dipping my head so I could lick her bottom lip—buttery and sweet at the same time—I whispered, "You're what?"

She wouldn't answer. Just stared at me. Intently. I slid my lips up her jaw. "You're what?" I nipped with my teeth. "Turned on?" No answer, so I slid lower, licking a trail down to her collarbone. "Aroused?" Still nothing but heavier breathing. I gave some attention to the hollow of her throat and the delicate indentions of her clavicle with my lips and tongue. "Because if you're half as hot as I get just when you walk into a room, then I'm a happy man."

Her fingers combed through my hair, then slipped to the nape of my neck. "Then you should be a totally blissed-out, high-as-a-kite happy man."

I crushed my mouth to hers, angling so I could go deep, needing to taste, to devour, to show her what she meant to me. Because, holy fuck, she meant so much to me. How did this happen? How did it go from a brief, casual friendship to me not being able to function without her near me? To wanting to rip her clothes off and fuck us both into oblivion.

Now we're talking.

As much as I wanted that, I didn't want to push what was happening here. I didn't want casual sex or for her to think it was. Because there was nothing casual about the way I felt about her. So I restrained from doing what I wanted, from dipping my hand into her jeans, feeling how wet she was for me, stripping, and sliding between those fine fucking legs.

I really, really hate you sometimes.

Besides, I had something important to talk to her about tonight, and that would probably dampen the mood. Whenever I got the guts to bring it up.

Dramatic music and screams pulled me out of my kiss-hazed stupor. I rolled to the side to see what was happening on the screen.

"Are you fucking kidding me?" I gaped. "I can't believe he just did that."

"I know. Isn't it terrible?"

I glared down at her. "How can you think he's hot? Kylo Ren is irredeemable after that move."

"Maybe it needed to happen for the plot and proper character motivations for later on. Maybe he'll turn good in the end." Her eyes glimmered with humor and something else, maybe the lingerings of lust I'd put there.

"Oh, I see. You're one of those who has no problem torturing and killing off main characters for a dramatic finish."

"Dramatic finishes are epic. Have you seen any of *Game of Thrones?* Take the Red Wedding episode, for example. Wait, why am I even asking that? Okay, that's next up on our agenda. I have so much to say about—"

"Shh." I wrapped my hand around her waist and pulled her tighter against me. "Lightsaber battle."

She snuggled closer. "I love that you love lightsaber battles," she whispered. "Now *that* is hot."

I slipped my hand under her shirt, but kept it at her waist, brushing my thumb back and forth over silky skin. Then we watched the rest of the movie in contented silence. I found myself digging my fingers into her waist as Rey marched up the island and handed over the lightsaber to—

"No. Fucking. Way!"

"Yes!" Evie popped up and clapped her hands together like a giddy girl. "Can you believe it!"

"Chills, man." The soundtrack started with the rolling credits as I shook my head in awe. "That was . . . wow."

"*Right?*"

"To be honest, I think I have new inspiration for my art."

"No way!"

"There are dozens of scenes that would make a terrific dramatic sculpture."

She shook her head, biting her lip, an expression of elated disbelief lighting her face. She leaned over and picked up her margarita. "I'm excited it inspired you." Then she swigged the rest of it down.

"What can I say? You've created a monster."

"I knew you were cool." She tossed a piece of popcorn up and caught it in her mouth, then laughed at my ogling. Because I definitely was. Everything she did captivated me. She sobered, tilting her head the way she did sometimes. "You know you really are an amazing artist."

I sucked in a deep breath, then took the plunge. "So are you."

Her brow puckered as she sipped her drink, then set it down. "What do you mean?"

"The comics you're drawing are absolutely amazing."

She froze, eyes wide and fixed on me. But she didn't respond.

"You obviously have a gift."

"What . . . when did you see them?" Her chest rose and fell quickly.

"In your room. I saw the sketches in your drawer. And on your tablet."

"You opened my tablet!" Her gaze was angry, flinty. "Do you always go snooping in other people's private stuff?"

"Never. And I probably shouldn't have done it. But I also couldn't stop myself, and I'm glad I did."

She curled up with her knees to her chin, glaring at me over the top. Guarding herself. "Well, this isn't a side of you I knew existed."

"You're mad because I saw something you've been hiding, but Evie, you shouldn't be hiding it. Are you hearing me?"

She stared at her knees, jaw clenched tight.

"*Why?*" I walked on my knees till I was right in front of her, sitting back on my feet. I gripped the back of her ankles to make sure I had her attention. "Why aren't you publishing? You have a series already started. Not to mention . . . the other one."

"You saw the sketches? Of you?" Her face flushed a darker shade of pink, embarrassment bordering on humiliation. My stomach sank.

I nodded, concern tightening a knot in my gut the way she appeared almost distraught. She'd been observing me so closely all this time. Very closely. And the way she'd rendered me with the wolf, the way she saw me . . . *Flattering* wasn't even close to the right word. Dumbfounded. Humbled. Stupefied. Those came closer to the mark.

"I did. You should be out there publishing these, sharing them with the comic-loving world. What's going on?"

"It's not as easy as you think."

"You can self-publish. You don't have to depend on a publisher. I mean, you're already using software to create it in the aesthetic of modern comics."

"I know." Her chin was set at a stubborn angle away from me.

"Then what's going on? What are you afraid of?"

"*Everything*, okay? I mean, you say I'm good, but you don't know that." She raised her hands, palms up, gesturing wildly. She glanced away, now rubbing her palms on her jeans. "Did you read my whole series?"

I hadn't had that kind of time. And frankly, I did feel a little guilty about sneaking a peek into her tablet, so I'd cut my spying session short. "No," I finally admitted.

"Sure. My illustrations might be okay, but my story might suck." Her gaze fixed on the blanket beneath her where she picked at a loose thread. Shrugging, she added, "People might laugh at me and think it's ridiculous."

"Violet and Fred going to a cocktail party together was kind of ridiculous." I squeezed my hands around her ankles, which were pressed together. She was a tight ball of tension, curled in on herself for protection. "But in a good way. A funny way. The way you intended."

Her mouth quirked up on one side. "That's just one little part. The rest might be complete and total shit." Tears were pricking in her eyes now, from complete and total fear. The bitter tang of it pierced the air.

"Hey, hey, hey." I eased forward, gripped her hips, and pulled her body between my thighs. Even if she was still curled into a tight ball, I felt better with her in my arms. I spread one hand on her back, the other I used to tip her chin up to look at me. "You're *really* afraid. This isn't like you. Not my Evie."

"Maybe you don't know Evie."

I laughed. "Oh, I do. You're just being stubborn and refusing to talk to me. Our first date *and* our first fight."

"We're not fighting. I'm just telling you that you don't know what you're talking about. You don't have all the information, so you can't just blindly tell me my work is great."

The bitterness in her voice and the pain in her eyes pierced me with a sharp sting in the middle of my chest. I lifted a hand and cupped her cheek, forcing her to look at me.

"Number one," I started gently. "I'm not blind. I saw enough to make a good, sound judgment of your artistic ability. And two,

I'm telling you that you're full of shit and you're better than great. That means we're arguing. Arguing equals fighting." I said all of this with the most tender voice I could manage, seeing as my heart was panicking at the sight of her in pain.

Just like that, she shut down again, angling her head away from me to the TV, which was now looping on the home screen of *The Force Awakens*.

"So what if some people hate it," I added. "That's what artists do. They create and share their artwork with the world. Some people love it, admire it, become lifelong fans. Others hate it, trash it, and call it dog shit. That is honestly the way of the world, especially with the free-speech-loving society we live in."

"I know that."

"Then what's going on?"

She heaved out an exasperated sigh. "There's more to it than just that."

"Tell me."

"No. You'll think I'm an idiot."

"Well, I think you're an idiot for not publishing, so it can't get any worse."

She scowled deeper and backhanded my leg before clasping her arms tighter around her knees.

"Evie," I whispered softly, brushing the pad of my thumb over her cheekbone. "Pretty, pretty Evie." She rolled her eyes, but a little smile flashed before she could hide it away again. I leaned forward and cupped her face, forcing her to look at me. "Talk to me. I'm your friend, remember?"

"My friend?"

"Your best friend."

"When did we become best friends?"

"The minute you saw the *Star Wars* extravaganza I made for you tonight."

Her smile spread wider as she hooked me with those soulful green eyes. But then she sobered almost as quick. "I'm embarrassed to tell you."

"Best friends can tell each other anything. And nothing will change. Don't you know that?"

She stared at me for a minute longer, then I saw the shift in her gaze when she decided to confess this terrible, shameful secret. Whatever it was.

"It's because of a guy."

"A guy?" My stomach twisted. Acid burned. "What guy?"

"His name is Derek Sullivan." Annoyance wrapped around his name when she said it. "He was my boyfriend for a while. He's a witch." She glanced at me. "Do you really want to hear this?"

"If it affects the reason you aren't pursuing your art, then yes." I already wanted to throat-punch him just for existing, but unlike Kylo Ren, I could control my temper. Unless Alpha got involved.

Oh, I'd do more than throat-punch this fucker. Derek Sullivan. Sounds like a pansy ass.

"Anyway," Evie went on, "we were pretty serious for a while. I really liked him and things seemed to be progressing."

Gut him with a spoon.

We're back to the spoon, are we?

Though I was having murderous thoughts of my own without Alpha's homicidal commentary.

"Derek was finishing his residency at UNO, and he wanted to take our relationship to the next step."

"Which step is that? He wanted you to . . . ?"

I couldn't even say the words *marry him* without wanting to vomit.

"He wanted us to move in together, but he kept telling me I needed to give up my hobby of drawing and pursue a serious career, maybe look into owning my own business since Jules legally owns the Cauldron and manages it. But I never wanted to do that. He was into social climbing in the coven and all that bullshit, and I wasn't." She blew out an exasperated sigh. "Actually, I'm pretty sure the reason he first asked me out was because of my connections. Or my family connections."

"He used you?"

A dull spoon.

Agreed.

"In the beginning, I think so. Jules teases me for always having my 'projects,' as she calls them. I wanted to help him fit into witch society here, so I introduced him to everyone. Including my mother and grandmother, two of the most influential witches in New Orleans history. Their friends."

She glanced at me, then away quickly. I continued to hold her close, let her know it didn't matter what that asshole had thought or said or done to her. He was in the past. But I sensed she needed to tell it all, so I waited.

"Later though, I was sure he had genuine feelings for me. As much as Derek can have for another person. But I didn't fit his ideal, and I was unwilling to change for him."

"Good for you." I swept my palm up the center of her back and gave her nape a gentle squeeze. "He didn't deserve you."

The satisfied smile on her face did something to tamp down the fury burning in my gut.

"I take it he said more about your drawing than you're letting on."

She shrugged a shoulder. "It was early on when I was really getting started in Adobe Photoshop. It was new, and I was learning. He saw some of my first work."

She twisted a frayed thread on the seam of her jeans, refusing to look me in the eye.

"And what did he say?"

"He, uh, laughed at them." She yanked the thread out of the seam, then finally looked at me. "Said my drawing was mediocre at best and would never be good enough for publishing. Then he added that it wouldn't fit into *our lifestyle* together anyway, so I should give it up."

I think I'll cut out his eyes first.

I'll help.

Yes, brother! Welcome to the pack!

"And what did you tell him?" Yeah, my voice had dropped to that deeper register.

"Nothing. I dumped him."

I pulled her even closer. "Good." I blew out a breath. "But since you obviously knew he was full of shit, what's stopping you now?"

She sighed heavily again. "That's the thing. I'm not so sure he was full of shit. I mean, yeah, I know I'm good. Like maybe better than good. But then, maybe I'm not?"

That was it. I pried her arms from around her knees. "Come here."

Stretching out my own legs, she allowed me to pull her sideways onto my lap. I needed her close.

"Listen to me. First off, Derek Sullivan is a total dick."

"No argument there."

"Secondly, he's not an artist and has no basis for judgment on your craft. However, I happen to be an artist. An amazing one, in fact, according to my girlfriend."

"Your girlfriend?" Her sweet eyes lit up, and there went that tumbling of butterflies in my stomach again. I swear, the girl made me feel like a heartsick teenager. "I thought I was your best friend."

"You're both." I pressed a firm, closed-mouth kiss to her lips. And though she returned it easily, that teasing look in her eye told me she didn't know how serious I was about this. About her. "My girlfriend happens to be an excellent judge of art. Like me. She should know that I know what the fuck I'm talking about."

"You're also a little biased."

"Maybe." A shrug of one shoulder. "The truth is, Evie, it doesn't matter what I think. Or what anyone thinks." I spread my fingers through her silky hair, loving the texture against my palms, cradling her skull and forcing her to look up at me. "No one can tell you your artwork is worthless but you. And no one can tell you it has value but you. Will you get ridiculous trolls who write heinous, soul-crushing reviews? Yes. You will. But you'll also get readers who love your work and appreciate your efforts. Above all that, you'll be achieving your dreams and sharing it with the world. And that's what matters."

She leaped up onto me, coiling her arms around my neck, pressing her head into the crook of my shoulder. "Why didn't I meet you sooner?"

Holding her tight and rocking side to side, I squeezed her to me, loving the soft lushness of her body against mine. "We met when we were supposed to."

"I wish we could figure out what witch cursed you so I can thank her."

I chuckled, then pressed a long, languorous kiss to the side of her neck. "I wish I knew too."

The mention of this Derek asshole being a witch reminded me of something. "I'm guessing that Derek attends these coven summits, doesn't he?"

She hung limply against me and grumbled, "Yes. That's why I don't want to go to that damn cocktail party."

"Then don't go."

"I have to. It's kind of complicated, but basically witches can be gossipy bitches and highly suspicious. So if I don't show up, rumors could spread there's trouble in our household. And Jules could be in danger of losing her position. It's not likely, but Jules doesn't deserve any more headaches than the ones she already has to deal with."

"Just because you don't go to a party?"

"It's a very important party in the eyes of the Guild. And pretty much every witch, actually. I definitely don't want to make things hard on Jules for any reason. She does everything to keep things running smoothly. So I'll go to the damn party and pretend his presence doesn't bother me."

I hated the idea of Evie feeling uncomfortable in any possible way, especially because of an ex who had demeaned her talent and her dream. I hated him more for knocking her self-esteem, her belief in herself, than I did for actually having the privilege of being an important part of her life. How could a man have Evie and throw it all away? One thing I knew for sure, if I was lucky enough to make her mine, I'd never let her go.

"Come on." I set her away from me, stood, and took her hand, guiding her toward the door. "Let's get you home."

She stopped, her gaze flicking to my bedroom door. "I thought . . ."

Shaking my head, I pulled her body to me, rocking her gently with a brief kiss to her temple. "Not tonight."

"Why not?" She gestured to the spread on the floor and coffee table. "You wooed me with *Star Wars*. I'm pretty ready to let you into my pants."

FUCK YEAH! Finally. Let's go.

"Not tonight, baby," I repeated. Apparently, I didn't need to explain—she simply stared at me a few seconds, then nodded and walked ahead of me down the stairs.

I didn't want her to think I'd brought her here for our first date just to get her in my bed. Yes, I wanted her in my space, my domain, probably the territorial wolf in me, but I wanted even more than that. Besides, the night had ended on an emotional whirlwind, and I wasn't an idiot. She'd be brooding for the rest of the night about her decision, her regret to let Derek have any say-so over her own personal choices. And there's no way in hell I wanted her ex to have any room in her head the first time I took her to bed. When there was no space for anyone else but the two of us up there in that beautiful brain of hers, then I'd take her. Then I'd make her mine.

I swear, you want our dick to fall off, don't you?

My dick is perfectly safe from falling off.

Not so sure.

When we walked through the gallery and onto the street, hand in hand, she said, "Thank you for my wonderful first date."

"You're welcome. My pleasure." Then I couldn't help myself. "Does it beat all your other first dates?"

"Definitely."

"Even with Derek?"

When she pulled me to a stop, the couple walking behind us almost plowed into us. She cupped my face, brushing her fingers over the scruff I needed to shave. "It beats all the dates."

"All the dates? Ever?"

"Every one."

"So I guess I get five stars then. As opposed to only the four I got for the lunch at Gotham City Grill."

She laughed. "Oh, you get five gazillion stars for this date."

"Wow. I'm honored." And I meant it.

Then we were kissing hard and making a spectacle of ourselves on the street, but we were both lost in each other. Unaware or not caring who saw us or what they thought. Our bodies perfectly aligned, her soft breasts pressed to my hard chest. I skimmed one hand down to cup and squeeze her curvy ass. She moaned.

"Get a room," said a guy, laughing with his friend as they passed.

That jarred us apart. A little. Her lips kiss-swollen, her cheeks flushed, her eyes shimmering with desire, she was completely stunning.

"You know. You made a promise about *next time*."

I didn't have to think too hard to remember the promise she was referring to. My cock twitched and strained harder against the zipper of my jeans. Just the thought of licking her pretty pussy made my vision haze. I craved her with maddening need.

"Yeah," I said, hearing the raw huskiness in my voice. "That's a promise I plan to keep."

"Next time." She threaded her fingers through mine and tugged me back along the sidewalk.

Next time.

CHAPTER 28

~EVIE~

THE FACT THAT OUR FIRST OFFICIAL DATE WAS SO PERFECT MUST'VE pissed off the universe. Because right after, we were waylaid with a series of events that blocked us from having a second date or even getting any time alone.

First off, Jules's new sous chef, Mitchell, didn't close the freezer all the way on a Monday night, the butcher's delivery day, and we lost the entire stock inside. Granted, it wasn't Mitchell's fault since he wasn't aware you had to put the steel peg in the door every time you closed it or it had a knack for popping back open. It was one of those things Jules would hammer home a thousand times to any new employee. But ever since we had coffee with Ruben, she'd been an absent-minded dingbat.

On top of that disaster, a tomcat had gone after Fred, and Z had come to the rescue. Clara and I were stupefied when we heard the racket one late afternoon and found Z tumbling in the courtyard with the orange tabby. Fred was fluttering around like crazy, his rainbow bow tie dangling loose around his neck. By the time we ran over, Z had scared the tomcat away. But Z had a few bleeding gashes on him and was limping on his back leg.

I rushed him to Beryl's house. She was the best witch healer in the city. After mending his fractured leg with a suture spell and patching up his puncture wounds, she swiveled to me with a maternal and condescending scowl. "You need to let this cat live out the rest of his life naturally."

"He is. Just with a little help."

"Isadora can't keep him alive forever."

"No," I agreed aloud but not in my head, "but maybe for another twenty years or so?"

A really heavy sigh. "It's unnatural. Cats don't want to live that long."

I eyed Z, whose sputtering motorboat purr rumbled under my palm. "How do you know?"

She arched a superior brow. I glanced around at her menagerie—three cats, a toy poodle named Fitzy, a cage of canaries, a ferret, and her pygmy goat named Matilda—then turned back to her with a sigh.

"Yeah." She was the Dr. Doolittle of witches, so I guess she had a point. "Maybe you're right."

She put a gentle hand over mine where it rested on Z's back in my lap. "It doesn't have to be now, but maybe have Isadora ease up."

I nodded. "Okay." I swallowed hard at thinking of letting Z go, but Beryl was right. She was always right.

"So what about the werewolf?" Her cocoa-brown eyes watched me the way my mom's used to. Studying with too much awareness and knowledge.

"What about him?"

"Are you lovers?"

"No," I admitted, avoiding eye contact. "Not yet." Then I glanced up at her. "Why? Do you think I'll die if I do, according to the cards Spirit pulled for me?"

I was hoping she'd laugh at me or shake her head, but she shrugged. "I don't know."

"Beryl . . ." I licked my lips, deciding to go for it. "I care about him. A lot."

"I know. The death card, the transformation, most probably has to do with him."

I scoffed. "That's just it. A witch has him tied into a complex spell where he can't shift. He can't transform. More than three months now."

Her sage expression puckered into a serious scowl. "That's not good."

"It isn't. His wolf is . . . causing him problems."

"No, that's not the problem." Matilda was chewing on the ends of the long scarf that wrapped around Beryl's waist and dangled to the floor. She shooed her away and stood to walk to her window overlooking an English garden of herbs and medicinal flowers. "The witch who has cast the spell has blocked him for a reason, and it's not so his wolf will drive him crazy."

"What do you mean?"

She tapped a long finger to her lips. "It's the nature of the werewolf she's trying to harness for some reason."

"His nature? To become a beast?"

"His lust for blood."

I stood with Z in my hands. "That makes no sense."

"Not to us." She spun to face me. "But it does to her. Or him. Whoever they are." Spinning toward her wall of shelves, she pulled one drawer out and flipped through several little envelopes the size of seed packets before lifting out one and handing it over. It was one of her many herbal concoctions she put together. "I take it you'll be doing a hex-breaking spell soon."

"We tried already, but it didn't work."

She stopped, glared over her shoulder, then went back to flipping through her packets.

I continued, "We need to know more about the witch sign, the spell put on him. Jules is on it, and we'll be asking Clarissa at the Coven Summit."

"Good." She found what she was looking for and turned back to press the packet into my palm. "Take it with a cup of hot tea. It won't remove the bitter taste, but it will mute it."

"Thanks." I stared at the small white packet with barely a bump inside filled with her powdered concoction. "I don't think he's a tea drinker, but he'll do it if I ask him."

"It's not for *him*. It's for you."

"Why for me?"

"I don't know. Spirit is telling me to give it to you."

"To drink it now?"

"No. Spirit says you'll know when to take it."

I stared down at the packet. "What's it do?"

She cupped my face in her hands, gazing at me with more kindness than was her norm, something she hadn't done since I was a little girl. "It will take away the fear and give you the focus you need."

Clearing my throat, I whispered, "Okay."

That told me absolutely nothing. But no matter. Whenever the time was right, I'd know. Strange, but I felt it in my bones.

Beryl leaned forward and gave me as tight a hug as she could manage with Z in my arms. "Take care, love."

I pressed a kiss to her cheek. "I will, Beryl. Don't worry about me."

I slipped the packet in the outside pocket of my backpack as I walked to her screen door and opened it. With a glance back and seeing the concern etched in the tight lines of her face, I repeated, "Don't *worry*. It'll all be fine."

But as I plopped Z in the pillow-lined box on the passenger seat, then drove back toward Magazine Street, I wondered if it would be.

After that day, I was feeling a little protective about Z, staying close to the house and helping Jules catch up in the kitchen as we got closer to Thanksgiving, which was a *huge* deal for Jules. Mateo had been holed up in his workshop every day, finishing his commission for Sandra. He managed to come by for dinner and a drink in my section a few nights. He behaved like a gentleman. Far too much for my liking, quite frankly.

For some reason, he'd been able to handle Alpha much easier lately, and I couldn't figure out why. When I asked him, he just shrugged and smiled that secret smile that made me all melty. We were still waiting on Ruben to find us a copy of that book, but we weren't worried. If anyone could find it, it would be Ruben.

Then before I knew it, Thanksgiving Day had arrived. I'd been slaving in the kitchen doing meal prep alongside Clara the day before and all morning. I wasn't lying when I said Thanksgiving was a big fucking deal to Jules. I think it had more to do with a holiday surrounding a decadent meal than it did being thankful. But that's how Jules showed her love. She wasn't an openly affectionate person, even with me and the rest of our family, but I knew she'd kill or die for us. For her, cooking a fantastic meal was like giving the biggest, best hug she could manage. So the Thanksgiving meal was like a ginormous, lovey, snuggle-fest hug.

Clara and Violet had pushed all the round-top tables to the wall and brought in the portable tables that we shoved together to make one long one to fit all our guests. The long table was draped in white tablecloths and decorated with orange and yellow gourds, silver candlesticks, and Clara's cute little turkeys made out of tissue paper along with the silver stemware and crisp, burgundy napkins. The table was splashed with the colors of autumn.

"Wow," said Mateo when he walked in the door and stared at the pretty table.

I hooked an arm through his, thankful for one thing more than anything else this year. "Just wait till you see the menu."

Jules always outdid herself in the kitchen for this day, experimenting with all the new recipes she discovered or created herself.

"Oh really?" He cocked a brow. "Let me hear it."

I grinned. Actually, we were both grinning like complete idiots. I'd missed him, and I couldn't control my mouth muscles not to smile so insanely because I was so damn happy he was here.

"Today, we'll be having herb and citrus butter–roasted turkey, apple, walnut, and chicken stuffing, oyster dressing, roasted acorn squash with maple bacon drizzle, green bean casserole with fried shallots, roasted sweet potatoes with goat cheese and scallions, tangerine-cranberry jam, cracked pepper and marble rye dinner rolls, brussels sprouts, red pepper, and avocado salad." I took a deep breath. "Then finally for dessert, we'll have pumpkin bread pudding with whiskey cream sauce and chocolate-chunk pecan pie."

"Damn," came the velvety voice behind Mateo. "Now I'm starving."

Nico stepped in with a hand to his stomach. I offered my hand to shake. "Welcome to the best Thanksgiving meal you'll ever have."

Nico's mouth tipped up on one side, looking a lot like his cousin for a second.

"Unless you happen to come back next year, that is," I added. "In which case, she'll top this. She always finds a way. It's kind of ridiculous. Y'all come on in."

"Everybody," I said to the crowd still at the bar where JJ was mixing drinks. "This is Mateo and Nico. Guys, that's JJ, our bartender who you know; his friend Charlie; Elsie and Sam, two of our awesome line cooks; our new sous chef, Mitchell; and my fellow girl in the trenches, Belinda, who you've seen working tables with me, I'm sure." Belinda waved a flirty hello. Then I swiveled to my sisters, exiting the kitchen, carrying the last of the trays of food to put on the sideboard set out so we could serve buffet style. "And you know my sisters Jules, Clara, and Violet."

Violet's eyes widened in surprise since I hadn't warned her Nico was coming. I mean, Jules always says we should invite whoever we want who might not have a family table to go to on Thanksgiving. Nico fit this description. I could've warned Violet, but I didn't. She was evil and deserved some payback.

"Welcome, everyone," said Jules. "Why don't you all put your drinks wherever you want." She gestured to the table. "Then fill up your plates. We've made plenty."

Mitchell, who'd been working overtime to make up for his first-day blunder, eased to the sideboard behind Elsie and Sam who were positively gleeful at the aromatic spread. He was a handsome guy with clean-cut dark hair and a trimmed beard. Sidling close to Jules, he said, "I wish you would've let us help you cook the meal. This"—he gestured with one hand, shaking his head—"was an enormous amount of work in the kitchen."

Jules smiled, her arms crossed but loosely and relaxed. "That would defeat the point, Mitch. This is my day to give back to those who work so hard for us. For the Cauldron family."

"Yeah," said Violet, setting her glass of something whiskey-colored on the table. Probably straight whiskey, now that I thought about it, her shifty eyes flicking at Nico. "She's got us for slave labor, so don't you worry your pretty head."

Mitch nodded, his cheeks flushing pink, then took his plate and started to serve himself. "Well, I appreciate it."

"Of course," said Jules. "You just moved into town, and we consider our employees as family. Glad to have you."

He nodded, using the tongs to pick up a slice of turkey. "Where's Finnie and Barb?" Finnie was our dishwasher and Barb was our third line cook.

"With their families," said Jules. "Finnie's grandmother would kill him if he didn't go to her place, and Barb always has a gathering with her family in Metairie. But we'll still need to fix some to-go plates with leftovers."

Sam took a seat at the table. "I don't think that'll be a problem."

"I don't know," said Nico, getting in line. "I can eat a whole lot."

"Hungry guy, are you?" I asked.

He winked, then slid his gaze to Violet. "Very."

I rolled my eyes. Werewolves.

"Oh, Mrs. Ferriday!" Clara squealed and rushed to the door. "I'm so glad you came." She hooked her arm around the elbow of one of the older ladies I recognized from her book club. "Everyone, this is Mrs. Ferriday, who will be joining us today."

"Please, just call me Miriam." She was a vibrant-looking woman in her seventies, wearing a dress that matched the fall decor and a shimmery gold scarf around her neck.

"Come on in, Miriam," said JJ. "What can I get you to drink?"

"Can you make a Tom Collins?"

"Coming right up."

She raised a warning finger to JJ. "Don't skimp on the gin, son."

"I wouldn't dream of it." Heading over to the bar, he flashed one of his pretty smiles, which made her withdraw her hand and flutter with her scarf. Looked like JJ found another admirer. Not shocking at all.

"Where's Clara going?" asked Mateo, frowning as my sister left the bar and skipped across the street. His plate was piled so high I was afraid he'd have an upset stomach after he ate it all.

Violet snorted. "Don't worry. She must've spotted a vagrant."

"Don't be an ass," I told Violet.

"What? I'm being serious. She loves taking care of the homeless."

Charlie sidled up to get a plate next to her. "We know. It's just that everything that comes out of your mouth makes you sound like a bitch."

That was true. Violet sounded snarky even when she didn't mean to. It was kind of shocking she and Clara were twins. Yes, they were pretty identical in skin tone, eye color, and shape—though Clara was thinner—but their differences were huge and drastic. If they hadn't been split from the same egg, you'd never know they were sisters.

While everyone was filling their plates and finding a seat, I peeked out the window as Clara stepped lightly up to the tall guy leaning against the corner of the bakery, Queen of Tarts, which was closed today. He watched her approach, taking a long drag on a cigarette. I'd seen him around plenty.

"She's asking a grim to Thanksgiving dinner?" I murmured to Jules, who watched with me.

"Apparently."

"That'll be interesting."

Clara talked animatedly, using her hands, the way she always did. Though I couldn't see her face, I was sure she was beaming a smile up at him. The guy, his black bangs hanging in his face and almost covering one eye, just watched her, smoking his cigarette. Clara took her time with her spiel, probably about how we liked to welcome anyone, including strangers, to our table for Thanksgiving. Hell, she might've given him a mini history lesson on the pilgrims and the Native Americans, an idealistic version for sure, and how it was our civic duty to welcome all the lonely wanderers of the world to our table. Nothing would please Clara more than to feed all the hungry people in the entire world.

The grim watched her, focused but casual, still leaning against the brick building, his cigarette dangling loosely in his fingers. Clara was still going and apparently even laughed at something she'd said, not in an embarrassed way, because she didn't embarrass easily, but in a isn't-that-funny kind of way. The guy looked up the street, blowing smoke to the side, and then said something with his head turned before meeting her gaze again.

She nodded and gestured with her hands as she talked, then gave him a little wave and skipped back across the street, the traffic practically nonexistent today. He watched her make her way back to the bar, then dropped his cigarette and crushed it with his boot before he sauntered in the opposite direction, hands in pockets.

"No grim reaper this year," I whispered to Jules.

"Thank God," she replied, joining me to get our plates, the last ones besides Clara. "Two werewolves is all I can handle at the moment."

I shot her a dirty look but caught the smirk she was trying to hide. "Admit it. Mateo is a nice guy." I spooned an extra-large helping of the oyster dressing. It was to die for. "Except when he's reacting to a wicked witch's spell."

"Except for that." She sighed, scooping some of the tangerine-cranberry jelly for her marble rye roll. "Ruben texted and said he's found a copy. He should have it within the week."

"A week? Why so long?"

"Apparently, it's with a witch who lives in the Carpathian Mountains. A healer. One of the vampire covens there knows her really well. But she lives off the grid, so he's sending one of his men in to find her and get the book. And it's dangerous, so . . ." She shrugged a shoulder.

"Dangerous how? Does she practice blood magic?"

"No, not her. She's a healer, Evie." I should have known better. Healers couldn't channel their magic if they dabbled in the dark arts because their magic came from the earth. Healing magic was inherently good. "The Carpathian Mountains are full of other covens and a rough pack of werewolves. Not the kind who follow rules." She glanced over at the table. "Not like your Mateo."

My heart fluttered at her compliment. *My* Mateo.

I forked a slice of the roast turkey onto my plate. "So Ruben has to send in someone who can fight a pack of werewolves? For our book?"

"He said he has a guy."

"Damn. Sounds like a scary guy."

"A very skilled one, according to Ruben. Anyway, if all goes well, we'll have the book soon."

I eyed Mateo, who was laughing at something Nico said. "Good. That'll be before the next full moon. Hopefully."

Clara dinged her spoon on a glass of white wine. She was standing next to Miriam, who was seated next to JJ, getting her flirt on. The murmur of voices and clanking of silverware died down as I took a seat between Mateo and Nico. It didn't escape my notice that Violet had forced Elsie to switch places with her so she was no longer right next to Nico where he'd put himself.

"First, I'd like to thank my sister Jules for preparing this amazing meal for all of us." A chorus of cheers went up. "But I'd also like to continue our tradition of going around the room and sharing one thing you're thankful for."

"Come on, Clara." Violet groaned. "*Must* we do this every year?"

"Yes. We must." She raised her chin and glared at her twin. "But since Violet likes to moan and groan about this tradition, I thought I'd compromise to ease her pain a little. Let's share in only one or two words something you're most thankful for this year."

"That's easy," said Mitchell. "New jobs."

Jules smiled and raised her glass to him across the table. "New employees," she added.

"Hey! Wait a minute," said Sam, gesturing to himself.

"And old ones," she added. A few laughs rounded the table.

"New friends," said Nico with a tip of his glass to the table.

"And old ones," added JJ, smiling at Charlie.

"To best friends," said Mateo next to me, his hand sliding under the table, long fingers wrapping my thigh.

My mouth went desert-dry as he snagged my gaze, his intense expression holding me captive, his large hand squeezing my leg. Without a glance at the table, I repeated dumbly, "To best friends."

I think someone laughed at us, and yeah, everyone kept talking, adding their words of thankfulness. But I didn't hear a damn thing. I was lost. Completely and utterly lost in the beautiful brown depths of Mateo's eyes, the insanely compelling expression on his face, the tummy-twisting strokes of his fingers up and down my leg. Even in jeans, I could feel the heat of him, the magnetic pull of his touch, of his gaze, of his body, of his mind, heart, and soul. It was true. He'd caught me. Reeled me in with kind words and soft touches and hard kisses. And it wasn't enough. I wanted more. I wanted it all. I wanted everything.

Yes, I was thankful for my sisters, for the roof over my head, for the blessings in my life. But most of all, I was thankful for one thing and one thing only. And he currently had his hand wrapped around my thigh and his will wrapped around my heart. I knew then and there that he'd put the most powerful spell of all on me. The one that launched a thousand ships and waged wars and toppled kingdoms. The one that compelled kings to forsake their oaths for a woman. The one that would beguile me to do anything—*anything*—for him. I recognized this emotion for what it was and tried not to tremble as it swept through me on a tidal wave.

I gulped, forcing myself to stuff this three-star Michelin meal into my mouth, hoping he couldn't somehow detect what had just happened. It was wonderful and terrifying at the same time. What if he didn't feel the same way?

"What is it?" he whispered close to my ear, his lips brushing the sensitive shell.

I shivered. "Nothing. Just . . . happy you're here."

"There's no other place for me to be," he said, his hand still possessively on my leg.

"Good," I said to my plate, unable to look at him right now. My emotions were raw and swirling.

Then his lips brushed my cheek before he pulled away. A simple kiss. Nothing sexual or intense. But at the same time, it felt . . . permanent. Like he knew where his lips belonged. On me. Somehow, that eased the tension in my spine, enough that I could hope—maybe, just maybe—his feelings were falling in the same direction.

CHAPTER 29

~EVIE~

"Clarissa said that she wasn't well-versed in witch sign either," said Jules, "but she knew two of them. The bridge sign was a sort of gateway symbol, typically used to combine spells. That's why she said this one was so complex. The spell put on Mateo is actually layered."

"You mean, more than one?" I asked Jules as we crossed Canal Street, one block from the parking garage to the Roosevelt Hotel, where the Guild cocktail party was being held. Clara and Violet walked a few paces behind, laughing about something. The traffic buzzed by, the city even more alive at night.

"Yes. The bridge symbol locks them together. The other sign she recognized was that infinity-looking one. Do you remember it?"

I clenched my black clutch to my stomach. "It was all over his chest."

"She said that can mean eternal life."

"Like immortality? I thought that was impossible."

Her brow pursed together. "I did too. Maybe this witch, who-ever he or she is, found a way. Or thinks they did."

"What the actual fuck, Jules? It makes absolutely *no* sense for Mateo to have immortality and death signs all over his body!"

My voice bounced off the high rises framing us as we walked up Roosevelt Way. My anger and frustration was obviously boiling over. Someone had serious ill intent toward this man I cared about so much it was hard to breathe air in the same room as him, and I was a goddamn hex-breaker who couldn't help him. It was driving me nuts!

Jules linked her arm with mine for comfort, her skin to skin contact calming me. We'd both decided to leave our coats at home. It was chilly but not so much we'd freeze in the short walk to the hotel in our cocktail dresses. Jules had opted for a deep red, skintight chiffon dress that hit her at the knee, giving her petite size the illusion of height. What wasn't an illusion was the undeniable killer body my oldest sister had, which she typically hid under chef coats and baggy pants.

I'd chosen my go-to wedding/party dress, determined not to spend one damn dollar on a new dress for this shindig. Besides, my green silk dress with the ruched top at my breasts showed off my cleavage, and the mid-thigh length showed off my toned legs. This dress always made me feel confident and beautiful. And that's how I needed to feel for this particular party. Not that I was trying to show Derek what he was missing because I could give a rat's ass what he thought. I just needed the kind of feminine armor that screamed, "I am woman, hear me roar."

"Don't worry," whispered Jules. "We're going to figure this out. If anyone can—"

She flinched next to me, slowing our pace. I followed her gaze to the hotel up ahead. Propped against the wall under the gold-filigreed gaslights at the bottom of the stairs to the Roosevelt was Ruben. And daaaaamn, did he look good. Wearing a black tuxedo with a white satin scarf draped along the lapels, his hands in his pockets, one ankle crossing the other, his blond hair gleaming under the warm glow, he looked like a model in a magazine. A magazine for sexy-as-fuck vampire billionaires. I had no idea how wealthy Ruben was, but he currently looked like a gazillion dollars' worth of beautiful man.

"Holy hell in a handbasket," muttered Violet behind us.

Jules straightened, holding on to me even tighter, as we drew closer. Ruben watched us approach, his gaze lingering on Jules. Well, lingering was putting it mildly. He was roving, calculating, imagining things with my sister I didn't think I wanted to know about. When I'd once asked what was up between the two of them, she growled with complete disdain, "There is absolutely *nothing* between us but pure hatred."

While watching Ruben get an eyeful of her with a lusty half-smile plastered to his face, I thought I might need to remind Jules that she might not understand what hatred looked like. Because that wasn't it. But now wasn't the time. Especially when he pushed off the cream-colored stone of the Roosevelt's entrance and pulled out a book from inside his jacket.

"Oh," I muttered, quickening my steps to close the gap between us.

"Good evening, ladies," he said with a small bow, making eye contact with all of us, even Clara and Violet who stopped at our backs. "Here is the item you requested."

"Come on, Violet." Clara dragged Violet's ogling self toward the red-carpet-lined stairs. "We'll see you both inside."

I waved at them, shaking my head at Violet's slobbering expression.

"Thank you," said Jules, taking the small hardbound book in her hand. The leather cover was green with gold script lettering on the front. "You weren't planning on attending, I hope." Jules gestured toward the entrance to the hotel with a superior tilt of her chin.

He chuckled. "I don't think a vampire would be welcome at the Guild's cocktail party. Besides, I wasn't invited."

Well, that's the damn truth. Actually, it was the reason I hadn't invited Mateo either. Another reason I wasn't a fan of these Guild parties was because they were so pretentious. Witches only and all that. I always wished the Guild would be more open and accepting of other supernaturals. They were the most uppity of the different races. Yes, it was put upon witches to enforce that supernaturals obeyed the laws of magic, simply because an Enforcer was more powerful than any and all of us, but it seemed like most witches held an elitist, superiority complex because of it.

"Unfortunately," said Ruben with his intense expression focused heavily on Jules, "I have other plans."

Her gaze dropped to the book in her hands. "Did your man have any trouble acquiring it?"

"None at all."

"That's a relief," she added. "I was worried he'd have a run-in with that Lycan pack you told me about."

Ruben now had both his hands tucked loosely in his tuxedo pants pockets. "Oh, he did have a run-in with them."

"He wasn't hurt, was he?" I asked, feeling suddenly awful for Ruben's friend or business associate or whoever he was.

Ruben smiled, his blue eyes darker than usual. "Like I said, he had no trouble."

"So he's not hurt then?" asked Jules.

The vampire laughed, and for the first time I think ever, I saw Ruben's canines extended. Vampires didn't usually extend them until they were ready to feed, from what I understood. The look of this insanely gorgeous man laughing with a glint of sharp fangs before he hid them away again made my brain haze for a second.

Jules was statue-still next to me, probably calculating how fast she could stun him if he tried to bite her. But Ruben wasn't an idiot or a violator of rules. He wouldn't take blood from an unwilling host, no matter how much he wanted it. And right now, looking at my sister, he wanted it pretty damn bad.

"Not even a scratch on Devraj." He glanced at the book in her hands as she tucked it inside her clutch. It was actually just small enough to fit. "So now you owe me that date."

She scoffed. "We already discussed that. It's not happening."

"Oh, Juliana," he practically sang in his velvety voice, moving in lightning vampire speed till he was just inches from her, brushing a gentle kiss to her cheek. "It's so going to happen."

Then he vanished, leaving a rush of wind in his wake, which pushed my long hair over my shoulder.

"Damn, he can move fast." I looked both ways. No sign of him. "He's really powerful, isn't he?"

She cleared her throat and turned away from the street toward the stairs. "Yes."

"How old is he?" I asked as we entered the glass doors to the grand foyer of the hotel.

"Two hundred something."

"*Really?* I had no idea he was *that* old."

Jules didn't respond, clacking across the shiny floor toward the reception hall where the party was being held.

Of the supernaturals, vampires had the longest life expectancy, around seven hundred years old. Werewolves were second in line, averaging around five hundred, which made me wonder how old Mateo was. Funny, I hadn't asked before. Why was I so curious now?

Oh yeah. Because I wanted to spend the rest of my life with him, which would be about another three hundred years if I was lucky. I was still quite young for a witch. Was he? Or was he far older than he appeared like Ruben? What if he was older than Ruben? My mind was on a manic spree of what-ifs as we walked through the door to the cocktail party.

"Eveleen!"

I knew that voice coming from the cluster near the bar where Violet and Clara were laughing with my cousins. Jules slipped off toward Clarissa and her cronies at one of the round-top tables. Travis met me halfway across the room and swept me into a hug, lifting me off the floor.

"Damn. You smell good." He put me down, grinning like a fiend. "Is that for me? You wore that for me, didn't you?"

"No," I said, play-slapping him with my clutch and pushing him back a step. "I have a boyfriend."

My heart jumped into orbit at the thought of Mateo, wishing I'd invited him now. I mean, so what if we got a few looks from these snobs, right? But it was too late.

"No!" Travis clutched at his heart. "I can't believe you're cheating on me."

"Oh my God, I'm not cheating on you." I punched him in his Armani jacket-covered biceps, which felt like hitting a rock. "Come on, I need a drink."

"Yes, you do." He smiled like the devil he was. "I plan to get you drunk and have my evil way with you."

"Travis." I shot him a disgusted look. "That's not even funny."

For a second, he looked confused, then shocked. "No! Not that. Jesus," he said, looping his arm around my waist and guiding me to the others. "I mean making you dance with me."

I laughed, accepting the glass of champagne from Clara. "I'm pretty sure you don't need alcohol to ply women anyway."

"Well," he drawled out, "maybe it's true I haven't been lonely much." He gave my waist a squeeze.

"Shocking." I rolled my eyes.

"Don't you look amazing," said Drew, flashing his brilliant smile and giving me a squishy hug. Drew was a hugger. He was an Aura like Clara, so it wasn't a surprise. He just gushed wonderfulness like she did.

"Thank you. So do you. But you know that." I sipped from my glass, glancing around the room at the array of beautiful, leggy witches in the room. "Looks like you've got a nice selection this year."

Travis laughed at something Violet was saying, the two of them looking like criminal conspirators at prom, contriving who would get the bucket of blood dropped on them at midnight.

"I think our visit to New Orleans will be fruitful," agreed Drew with a wink. Unlike Clara, he played his beauty and charisma to the hilt with the ladies.

I shook my head. "You're really working your Aura magic tonight, aren't you?"

"Never," he denied with a smile, sipping his drink from a glass tumbler. "We don't need to use our magic, do we, Clara? It just happens naturally."

"What's that?" asked Clara innocently. Truly, my sister looked like a goddess in a white sheath dress that molded to her thin frame, her blonde hair cascading in ridiculously perfect waves down to her hips.

"You know? It's totally unfair," said Violet.

"What's unfair?" asked Cole, stepping up to our group with a beer in hand, his resident scowl in place.

"The fact that she got the Aura magic. It's a complete waste on her," complained Violet with a flick of her hand. "She doesn't even use it to reel in the hotties. Hell, I don't even know when the last time was that she brought a man home or got laid."

"Violet," Clara chastised calmly but with a frown, which wasn't often. "This isn't the time or place to blast my personal love life to the world."

"There is none," she scoffed. "That's what I'm saying."

"I can help you with that." Travis grinned down from his bearlike stature at Clara's side.

"I'm sure you could," she said, flashing him a smile that probably wasn't intended as flirty but had a devastating effect anyway. "I can take care of myself in other ways."

"Gross," said Drew. "That's a picture of my cousin I don't want in my head."

"I don't mind it." Travis sipped his drink, mischief in his eyes. Such a flirt.

"So are you guys here for a while?" asked Violet. "We can take you guys out like last time."

"Afraid not." Drew cased the room, probably looking for his annual coven hookup. A few couples danced on the small dance floor set in the middle of the room, swaying to a slow Billie Eilish song. "We're still playing catch-up at the brewery from when Isadora and Livvy visited. Orders have been stacking up."

The three of them owned and ran Bayou Brewery just outside Lafayette. That's actually where we got our specialty beers like Witch's Brew and Gator Trail. And of course, we got the family discount.

"Evie," Cole whispered to me and pointed. "Jules wants you."

"You can *receive* messages too?"

Cole was an Influencer, what used to be called a Warper, like Livvy. Influencers had the gift of planting thoughts in other people's heads so they thought they were their own. An additional part of their magic, if they were strong enough, allowed them to speak telepathically to other people. But it was a one-way connection, unless it was two Influencers communicating back and forth.

"No." He chuckled. "She waved over here and pointed to you. But I did confirm." He tapped his temple. "She needs to speak with you."

"Excuse me, guys." I made my way across the room, around another cluster of guests—coven members from north Louisiana—till I was standing next to Jules, Clarissa, and an older gentleman I'd never met. If he was graying as a witch, that put him in the upper two hundreds at least.

"Eveleen, I'd like you to meet my father, Perry Baxter," said Clarissa. "He's visiting from London."

He shook my hand. "Pleasure to meet you." He was all polished aristocrat, his accent making him sound that much more sophisticated.

"Nice to meet you too." Jules had already warned me that Clarissa's father, a powerful leader of the London Coven, would be here.

"He was just saying what an exciting city New Orleans is," added Clarissa.

"Yes, I enjoyed a show at the Saenger Theatre last night and dinner at Commander's Palace. I'm not sure if I've had a better meal in all my life."

"That's definitely one of our finest restaurants," said Jules.

"What show did you see?" I asked.

"*Waitress.* Very good show, even though it wouldn't have been my first choice."

"Dad," Clarissa chastised him. "Be nice."

"I'm always nice," he said with a gleam in his eye that told me that wasn't necessarily true. "I just prefer the classics. Give me *Les Miserables* or *The Phantom of the Opera*, and the night would've been perfect."

"Why'd you choose to go to that one?" I asked, wondering why he'd picked it if it wasn't his style. Not that the Saenger had a lot to choose from, but there was definitely other entertainment in the city than going to see a show you didn't care to see.

"We were graciously hosted last night for dinner and the show," said Clarissa.

"By whom?" asked Jules.

"I'm afraid I'm the guilty party," came the familiar voice over my shoulder.

I swept closer to Jules to put a little distance between us, but Derek imposed himself by drawing closer inside our circle. And yes, of course, he had a tall, gorgeous black-haired beauty on his arm. Even so, he dropped her arm to pull me into an awkward embrace and drop a kiss on my cheek. "So wonderful to see you, Evie."

"You too," I replied, biting back what I really wanted to say, feeling my lips tighten in irritation. It wasn't just that he had to insert himself into our conversation, but he had to act so familiar with me. Like he still had a right to invade my personal space. Even now, he leaned to the left, brushing my shoulder with his own. But I didn't want to be rude in front of Clarissa or her father.

"Good to see you too, Jules." He leaned across me and shook her hand rather than kiss her hello. He should've greeted me the same way. Yeah, we'd slept together for two years, but it was pretty clear after we broke up that our friendly days were over. But I could be civil, as long as he was.

"Aren't you going to introduce us to your friend?" asked Jules, nodding to the woman at his back.

I swear, Derek was actually blocking her. So rude. If you're going to bring a date, then treat the poor girl like a date and not your luggage.

"Forgive me. Perry and Clarissa had the pleasure of meeting my fiancée, Millicent, last night. Darling, this is Jules and Evie Savoie." He stared at me as he swept a hand around her tiny waist. "Millicent, this is the Evie I told you about."

"Am I missing something?" asked Perry, a calculating gaze sweeping between us.

Before I could change the subject or say something polite, Derek piped up with, "Evie and I were lovers for two years when I lived in New Orleans. Inseparable, at the time, actually. Weren't we, sweetheart?" He touched my bare elbow with the tips of his fingers, sliding them up the back of my arm until I inched over to break the contact.

Wait. *What did he just say?* He was going to throw that out in front of *everyone*? Rude!

"Oh," was all Millicent could manage as she looked me up and down.

I actually felt sorry for the woman. You bring your fiancée to her first Coven Guild Summit and then embarrass her in front of the president and her father, a bigwig in London? There was no need for him to go into that detailed description of our former relationship. If I didn't already hate the sight of his face, no matter how good looking he was, I did now.

"That was a long time ago," I said with bite.

Leaning over to set my empty champagne flute on a tray as a waiter passed, I grabbed another and used the movement to ease away from him so there was a good two feet of distance between us as I faced him.

"Doesn't feel like it," he said smoothly. "I can still remember everything clear as a bell."

He did not just look at my breasts. Douchebag!

Clarissa laughed, albeit a little nervously because this was fucking uncomfortable. "Witches have excellent memories."

"Too true," said Jules. "I remember the day Evie broke up with you, Derek. I'd never seen a warlock look so shocked in my whole life."

I loved my sister with all my heart. Loved her to the moon and back. Because he shifted uncomfortably, tightening his hold on his still-mute fiancée.

"Evie," he said lightly, which warned me something nasty was coming, even though he seemed distracted, glancing toward the entrance to the hall. "Do you still do your little comic drawings?" He chuckled, and it was a mean chuckle, telling the group he was laughing *at* me, not with me. "Still chasing that little dream?"

Furious heat flushed up my neck and filled my cheeks as I ground my molars together. His ridiculous smirk told me how much he was enjoying this, flaunting something so private of mine in front of this particular audience, the upper echelon of Coven society who he'd wanted to mold me to be like.

In that minute, I realized how wrong Derek was for me. How absolutely miserable I would've been if I'd tried to become the kind of woman he wanted. The silent, pretty trophy like the one standing there and taking his shit right now.

Even more infuriating was that I was angry with myself. If I hadn't let this asshat get to me the way he had, I'd be published already. Diving into that dream of mine without fear. And though I'd gotten the ball rolling since date night at Mateo's, it wasn't anything to really brag about. Yet. So instead of snapping back, I stood there and took it, remembering the only reason I was miserable right now was because I allowed it to happen. It was my own damn fault.

His smile slipped, and Millicent's eyes shifted over my shoulder. Then so did everyone else's, their jaws dropping, frowns forming. Except for Jules. The death glare she'd been shooting at Derek vanished, replaced by an arrogant smile. What the hell?

I turned, realizing the room had fallen to a hush. Then I spotted the devastatingly fine man walking across the room straight toward me, and I knew why. Not just a man, a werewolf among witches. My werewolf. And sweet baby Jesus in a basket, Mateo in an all-black, well-tailored suit, striding through the parlor with purpose, his beautiful face set in a dangerous expression as it flicked to Derek behind me.

All I could do was watch him stalk closer in all his glory. When he finally sidled up to our group, he pressed his palm to the small of my back—a firm, comforting pressure—before he leaned in and brushed a slow, closed-mouth kiss to my lips, his dark eyes riveted on mine. It was the kind of kiss that told everyone else in the room they didn't matter. That they could go to hell. Because all he was here for was the woman in his arms. A riot of feelings erupted in the vicinity of my heart. I'm not going to lie. I wanted to cry on the spot.

"So sorry I'm late, baby," he said loud enough for the others to hear. "I got held up at the gallery." Like I'd invited him, and it was his fault he wasn't at my side, defending me against the dickless wonder standing there with his jaw hanging open.

When Mateo finally pulled away, his palm at my back slid up my spine, behind the fall of my hair, and wrapped gently around the back of my neck. I didn't bother to look at Derek then because I could feel his eyes burning into my face. I'd also lost my ability to speak since I couldn't even manage to introduce him. Thank God for Jules.

"Everyone, this is Mateo Cruz, renowned metalwork artist in New Orleans. Mateo, this is Perry Baxter of London, his daughter Clarissa, our Guild president, and this is Derek Sullivan and his fiancée, Millicent."

Mateo kept his position at my side with his gentle but possessive fingers wrapping my nape. He extended his hand to shake each one as Jules went around the group, but he didn't move a muscle to lean into them. Nope. He made them come to him. And when he shook Derek's hand last, there was no mistaking the vibration of a deep, feral growl rumbling in Mateo's chest. It was low and menacing, not the kind that said he was about to attack, but put Derek on alert that danger had him in its sights.

"I've heard all about you," said Mateo. Somehow he managed to sound more than civil while also sounding disgusted. What a gift my werewolf had.

I almost laughed, but then I caught the flare of gold in his eyes. Uh-oh. Clarissa and Millicent gasped, probably expecting him to shift right here and now. If it weren't for the hex, I thought he just might. Then Derek decided he needed to reinsert his manhood with his résumé.

"It's actually *Dr.* Sullivan. I'm also the president of the Greater Baton Rouge—"

"I don't care." Mateo cut him off quickly in an even, pleasant voice. "I would apologize, but I'm not sorry. I didn't come here for you"—he swept his gaze to the rest of the group, then looked down at me—"I came here for her." He unclenched his jaw, his expression softening just a tad. "Dance with me, love."

Love?

I mean, he didn't mean it like *love* love, but still. The endearment with the heartfelt look in his eyes, the serious tenor of his voice, and the grip of his hand on me was enough to make my blood race like a fever through my veins. I couldn't take my eyes off him. "Yes."

His stoic expression morphed into something dazzling and unearthly. Like someone had dialed the night all the way up, making the stars too bright, too brilliant to gaze on. I was utterly mesmerized. Then the hand on my neck slid to my hand, where he laced his fingers with mine like lovers did. Like real lovers. The kind that meshed in every way, needing to be bound together and wanting the world to know it.

When he swung me to face him, his strong arms went around me, one wrapped all the way around my lower back, his fingers curling around the opposite hip. His free hand enveloped mine with our arms out, waltz-fashion. And our bodies, well, they were pressed so hard together you'd think we were completely alone in the room. I held on tight, dizzy with the heady mix of suit-Mateo and Alpha-wolf.

I didn't care who watched, which was probably everyone at the party because, honestly, this was a witches-only event. We didn't have bouncers who'd kick him out, but I did worry Jules would get some nasty emails afterward. Right now? I couldn't care less who was there and what they thought. So did Mateo from how he was looking at me right then. His penetrating gaze shimmered with an edge of amber-gold, his lips hovering inches from mine. In my heels, I was perfectly aligned to his body, allowing him much better access to my mouth. But right now, all he did was stare at me, drink me in, his jaw clenching and unclenching.

"Mateo," I choked out.

"Yes?"

"You're my fucking hero."

"No." He let out a self-deprecating kind of laugh. "I'm your slave." The rough pads of his fingers slipped to the bare skin in the middle of my back, circling and raising goose bumps on my skin. "I'll do anything you ask. Go anywhere you go."

"Even to a cocktail party for witches only."

"I'd go to hell for you if I had to."

"Well, this isn't much different."

He chuckled, then let out a shaky breath. His eyes turned molten. "Not from where I'm standing." Sweeping down my face to my chest, his hands holding me tighter, he pressed me so close I could feel the hardness of him everywhere, specifically in his pants. "This is more like heaven." Then he whispered, "You're so fucking beautiful, Evie."

His mouth took mine—slow and sure—a dominant sweep of his tongue, and I couldn't hold back the moan. My bones liquefied, but he held me up, kept me close. I was in very capable hands, so I let him do all the work. Kiss the living fuck out of me in front of the entire Guild, their family and friends, and my dickwad ex. When he broke the kiss, his nostrils flared, a look of determination tightening his jaw.

"I think it's time for *next time.*"

Shocked that he suddenly had me thinking very dirty thoughts in a room full of witches, all of whom were probably watching our every move, I opened my mouth to say something but he cut me off.

"Evie." His voice dipped into a desperate timbre. His hand on my back speared up into my hair, cupping the back of my skull before he tugged down so I was looking straight up at him. "I need to lick you and touch you and suck you. Every inch. Before I fuck you hard."

I didn't miss the flash of Alpha in his eyes, but I also had zero power against the onslaught of Mateo's sexual magnetism. I was done for, already boneless from the promise of what he planned to do with his mouth, his hands, his cock. There was only one thing for me to say.

"Yes."

CHAPTER 30

~EVIE~

WE DIDN'T SPEAK. NOT A DAMN WORD ALL THE WAY HOME. I SAT next to him on the bench seat of his truck, my body vibrating, humming for him. He didn't try to kiss me or touch me, grope me on the ride back to his place. Just held my hand in his, fingers laced, the anticipation revving me up like a race car.

He urged me through the back door leading into his workshop, guiding me with a firm hand on my back through the darkness and into his apartment. We walked up the stairs, still not speaking even while I was screaming in my head, the tension so thick it could prop me up if I fell forward. When I glanced down over my shoulder in the shadowed staircase, all I saw were two glowing golden eyes locked on me as he shouldered out of his jacket.

I almost tripped, but caught myself on the wall. He didn't reach out to me. Just kept coming, removing his jacket. At the top of the stairs, I turned around to face him, stepping backward toward his bedroom as he dropped his jacket and loosened his tie. I kicked off my shoes, but kept moving because the hungry look in his eyes had my heart triple-beating in alarm. I'd become accustomed to Mateo's gentle touch, swoony kisses, melting looks. But this . . . I wasn't sure I was ready for this. So I kept backing up, keeping my eyes on him, preparing myself . . . if that was possible.

He whipped off his tie with a sharp snap in the air. I jumped, the aggressive sound zinging along my skin, heat rushing between my legs. I wobbled, but kept backing up into his bedroom. He dropped the tie in the middle of the room before unbuttoning his starched black shirt and whipping it open with force. He let it fall to his bedroom floor. His perfectly sculpted chest covered in lovely olive skin distracted me for a minute. I didn't realize he'd corralled me to his bed until my knees hit the edge. But still, he hadn't touched me, his focus too intent on stripping.

Who was I to stop him? I stood there, mute and panting, watching the show. And hot damn, what a show. By the time he shoved off his pants and boxer briefs, I couldn't breathe. Just stood there, staring at his long, thick, and erect dick as he wrapped one of those large hands around the base and gave it a heavy stroke.

"Take off your dress," he commanded, eyes glimmering gold. And I do mean commanded, his voice thick with dark promises and immense pleasure. And Alpha. Yeah. He was here with me. I wasn't even sure if Mateo was present at all.

A flicker of both panic and intense arousal at the memory of us in that haunted house, his rough but sure handling of me, made me even wetter between my thighs. The moonlight coming through the window shone on half of his face. His nostrils flared again as he opened his mouth and inhaled a deep breath.

"I can smell how bad you want me." He tilted his head in a way I'd never seen him do before, his gaze dropping to my chest. **"Take it off. Now."**

Not hesitating, I unzipped it on the side, then let it slide off my shoulders and pool on the floor. Those golden eyes watched everything, saw everything, devoured me with a primal stare.

"Your bra." His voice, God, it was so fucking deep and rough I could feel it scrape against my exposed skin, brushing so hard I wobbled at the intensity. He was too much—too hot, too hard, too rough. Too hypnotic in the way he stood there, feet planted apart, his big, chiseled frame blocking me against the bed, his hand stroking his dick in a slow, measured rhythm, showing me the fierce body that would be covering me soon.

Obeying quickly, I undid the clasp behind me and let it fall, my nipples hardening to tight points beneath his feral gaze. Trembling, I went to push off my panties, but he shook his head.

"No." Another long stroke of his cock. **"Leave those on."** Then he was coming for me.

I stood there, arms at my sides, not quite knowing what to do. I mean, come on, I'd had sex before. With quite a few guys. But I felt like a lost little virgin standing there in front of Mateo. I wanted him so badly I was adrift. Thankfully, he had very particular plans, and I was completely content following orders.

His hands gripped my hips as he nuzzled into my hair, his teeth scraping the side of my neck. A flick of tongue, then he was whispering in my ear. **"I'm gonna give you what I promised in your bedroom that night. Make you come on my tongue."** He bit my earlobe till it stung and another wave of wetness pooled in my panties. **"Then I'm gonna need to fuck you from** behind, baby. The first time. I need you submissive. Do you understand?"

I nodded, gripping his muscular forearms, clawing into him. He didn't seem to notice. Or care.

"I need you bareback. Nothing between us. Skin to skin. It's not a want. It's a *need*." The gravel-deep rumble in his chest that accompanied that statement made me shiver. "But I'm clean. Do you get me?"

Another jerky nod. "I'm on the pill." And I was clean. I hadn't slept with anyone in a while, and I'd had a checkup between then and now.

It was definitely Alpha talking to me. This was crazy. Mateo feared letting him take control, but somehow he had anyway. Whether it was with Mateo's permission or not, Alpha was driving the bus. And I wasn't afraid at all. In fact, I was so fucking turned on I was more afraid I'd come the second he touched his rough fingers between my legs and embarrass myself.

He twisted me around in a quick move so fast, I fell forward onto the bed, catching myself with both hands. When I went to stand, he put a firm hand against my upper back between my shoulder blades.

"No." He pressed me harder until I fell onto my elbows. "I need you just like that." His palm pressed harder down the middle of my spine. "Arch for me." His hand slid farther down to mold over my right cheek. "Give me that ass." I did, arching my back. He trailed a finger along the outer seam of my lace panties, then edged the fabric inward a few inches. His palm smoothed over the exposed skin, disappeared altogether, then smacked down hard with an echoing slap off the bedroom walls.

I flinched on a gasp, but he soothed the sting with circles of his hot palm before his fingers trailed from the top of my crack over the lace and slid down to my throbbing clit. He rubbed torturous circles till not only was my ass pressing up high in the air for him, begging for more, but so was my mouth. "Please. *Please.*"

He dropped to his knees and opened his mouth over my panties, sucking me hard.

I jerked forward and screamed in shock, but he had his strong hands wrapped around the front of my thighs, high up near my hips. His rumbling groan vibrated against my clit as he licked and sucked me through the thin fabric.

"**Soaking wet for me**," he growled, nuzzling with his lips and nose. "**Yes, baby. Make that sound again. Let me hear you.**"

That's when I realized I was moaning porn-star loud, but I really didn't care. I fell forward, my cheek to the bed, giving him whatever he wanted. What I wanted. Then he snapped one side of my panties, dragging them down the other leg, his hot tongue sliding through my bare folds before he stroked a finger inside me. I thought I'd lose my goddamn mind.

"*Oh God.*"

"**Mmm, such a sweet pussy**," he hummed against my clit before two fingers pumped inside me, three long strokes, then they were gone and his tongue was on me again, lashing. "**I knew you'd respond to me like this.**" His lips tightened over my nub, pulling with a suction that made my vision haze. "**Open your legs wider.**"

I did. Arching my back even more so he could make it feel just right, so he could do whatever the hell he wanted, I whimpered, "Make me come. *Please.* I need to so bad."

He opened his mouth wider, his hot tongue working my clit while he sucked and groaned like a dying man. I split apart, screaming and trying to claw my way up his mattress. But that wasn't happening. He chuckled, holding my thighs while he kept lapping at me, just slower, letting me come down and ride it out, but not get away.

Even after a dizzying orgasm where I lay there panting, I wasn't satisfied. My inner walls clenched, wanting what he hadn't given me yet. That tease of his fingers for a few strokes wasn't nearly enough. I needed him inside me. Not just to fulfill the maddening lust vibrating under my skin, but to feel this man intimately bound to me. To be as close as two people could be.

His hands and mouth left me, but I stayed bent over the bed, ass up, right where I was. He lifted me by the hips till my knees were under me on the mattress. Then he leaned over me from behind, planting his hands on either side of my head, his chest brushing my back, his dick pressed into the cleft of my ass, whispering in my ear as he ground against me, "**You know what drives me fucking crazy?**"

Trying to catch my breath, my heart hammering, I asked, "What?"

"**That I've wanted you for so goddamn long. Just like this.**" One hand swept my hair off my neck, where he clutched it in his fist, dipping his mouth to my skin. "**That he kept us from you for so fucking long.**" A suckling kiss on the slope of my inner shoulder. "**Just look at you.**" A nibbling bite. "**The smell of you,**" he ground out, rubbing his hard dick along my wet seam. "**I've craved you too long, baby. It's gonna be rough.**"

I didn't bother telling him I would've freaked the hell out if Alpha had come at me like this in the beginning. Probably filed a restraining order and cast a dozen protection spells. Maybe thrown in a voodoo doll just to be sure. Because the electric aggression vibrating off him right now rattled me to my bones. My flesh was primed for the pounding he promised, but my spirit was scared shitless. And elated at the same time. The wolf caging me in, sniffing and nipping at my skin with little stings, telling me in harsh terms the intensity of his need for me, was truthfully a dangerous creature.

He said he needed me submissive. This, I understood. I remember from my late-night reading that a werewolf wanted his mate to surrender. His mate. His *mate?* Was that what this was? I had no idea. The only thing I did know was this felt so real. And right.

"I submit, Mateo," I whispered, some hair falling across my face.

He went still, that big paw of a hand caressing the loose strands away from my eyes. With a gentle but tight tug, his fist in my hair, he forced my gaze to his where he leaned on my left.

Holy fuck!

His eyes—bright, fiery gold—burned into me. Lit from within, his expression matched the fierce charge humming off his skin. He leaned close, his lips touching mine. *"Alpha."*

His correction vibrated through my body, telling me what was happening here. Mateo didn't need my submission. Just his wolf. I reached back and brushed my hand up his face till I cupped his jaw.

"Alpha," I whispered, arching my back that much more for him. "I'm yours."

Those burning eyes slid closed on a groan at the same time he shifted behind me, his cock crowning my entrance before he pushed inside me with a deep thrust. I sucked in a sharp breath at the sudden invasion, the thickness of him stretching me. With my face angled to the side, he bent to me and bit my bottom lip, then sucked it into his mouth before crushing his mouth against mine for a brief, hard, mind-spinning minute.

Breaking the kiss, he pressed his forehead to mine, eyes closed. **"Yes, baby."** Golden slits narrowed on me. **"You're mine."** He nipped my bottom lip, then licked the sting away. **"Now let me take care of you."**

Straightening off my back, his hands wrapped my hips, fingers curling into my flesh, then he was dragging in and out of me with a fierceness I'd never felt before. I clutched the covers on the bed, but there was really no holding on. A stream of curses spilled from his mouth as he pumped into me with a slick slap, the front of his thighs hitting the backs of mine in a pounding rhythm.

"Fuck, baby, fuck," he groaned, slowing his tempo for a few rounds before grinding against my ass, then hammering fast and hard again.

I reached back, finding one muscled thigh, and raked my nails over him. I needed to touch him, feel his skin. He must've known, because then he pulled out, rolled me over, and crawled up my body between my legs, sliding inside me with a slow glide. So achingly slow, his mouth hovering over mine, his wolf-bright eyes staring into my very soul. Digging deep. Making silent promises. Promises that yes, he'd be fierce and hard, but he'd be gentle too. That he'd kill or die for me if he had to. That he'd guard me, protect me. That he'd never hurt or leave me. That he was mine as surely as I was his.

"Yes, Evie," he whispered, pumping into me nice and slow now, gentle and deep. The tenor of his voice had shifted, Mateo returning to me. "Give it all to me," he demanded. "I want all of you."

Planting one foot hard on the mattress and wrapping my other leg high on his hip, I ground up into him, meeting his steady rhythm, spiking my pleasure into the stratosphere.

"That's my girl," he whispered, stroking me, his expression tightening, his eyes slanting into a pained look. "Fuck me hard, baby."

So I did, rocking my hips up to match his steady rhythm, relishing the thick pumping of his cock. He grabbed my ass with one hand, holding his weight off me with the other, using both as leverage to thrust into me with senseless need. It was at this literal climactic moment that I understood how much he meant to me, that I loved him. That beautiful yet frightening realization swept through me, crashing with violent force, telling me I was lost to any other but him. That he was indeed my mate. My soul mate, my best friend. My deepest love.

I cried out, arching my neck, the familiar build rolling in like the tide.

On a growl, he flipped us, with me falling to his chest. A hand wrapped around my hair, tugging me closer so he could whisper in my ear. "Ride me, Evie. Take me like I took you. Show me how much you want me."

If he only knew. I pushed up with my palms on his broad chest, his chiseled abdomen rolling to pump up inside me. I rocked faster, grinding my clit down just right, his gaze on my tits bouncing with each pound down. Then they were locked on mine, brown but rimmed in gold. Mateo and Alpha as one, watching me fuck him the way I wanted. Watching me fall apart for them both.

"Yes," he hissed, leaning up and sucking a nipple into his mouth. "It's yours, Evie." Then he burrowed his mouth into my neck, kissing and licking wildly. "I'm yours."

I'd never been bashful about sex, usually losing myself in the moment. But this was entirely different. I felt like I owned this moment, driving us both toward that blissful end. I lifted up and pounded back down, over and over. When he gripped my waist to steady me higher so he could thrust up, his mouth on my breast, sucking, teeth grazing my nipple, I was done. Done!

"Mateo!" I screamed, coming hard and clenching my nails into his chest.

He gripped me tight at the waist and rolled while my orgasm still rippled and stroked hard and fast. He kissed me hard, swallowing my little moans of pleasure. On a groan, he bit my lip, pumped two more times, then held himself deep, his dick throbbing inside me. His fiery eyes faded, darkened to cool brown, as he let my lip slide from his mouth, his lips ticking up into a knowing smile. He knew he had me. And I had him.

"Mateo." Emotion welled up in my chest. Sex had never been like this for me. Ever. It had been a release, a simple pleasure, a good time. But it never had been soul-stirring and heart-bonding. I could hardly look at him with the overwhelming emotion pouring through me on a euphoric rush. It was too much.

He kept himself inside me, those familiar dark eyes roving my cheeks, chin, forehead, mouth, then back to my eyes. "Are you okay?"

I laughed, refusing to cry, because what could I say. *No!* I'm not okay. I was an emotional wreck, but I was also home. Right where

I belonged. How could it be both? So I told him the truth, hopeful he felt half of what I felt. "I'm more fantastic than I've ever been."

Slowly, he dipped his head, sweeping his lips gently, sliding his tongue along the seam, coaxing me to open, asking to come inside. It was so insane, considering what we just did, but it was also so tender and sweet. So Mateo.

"You are fantastic," he said. "So incredible it scrambled my brain. I can't think straight."

I pressed my index finger into the cleft in his chin. "Only your brain was affected?"

His loopy smile dimmed, sobered. His expression shifted to sad hopefulness. A strange combination, but one I understood. "And my heart, Evie."

Combing my fingers in his hair, I pulled him down, licking my tongue alongside his. His cock twitched inside me, already stirring to hardness again. I hummed approval and broke the kiss. "So soon?"

He shrugged, smiling against my lips. "I'm a werewolf."

As if that explained everything. Then I recalled the mention of Lycans and their insatiability. Somehow, I was sure I'd be perfectly fine with that.

"Maybe a snack," he said between light kisses. "You're going to need your strength for tonight."

"We're not done then?" I asked playfully.

"Not even close." He grinned, staring at my lips, before brushing his own against mine. "Are you hungry?"

"Mm-hmm. I didn't have time to eat at the party."

"What do you want?"

We spoke through constant kissing, both of us unable to part just yet.

Then I grinned. "I want your meat pie."

Mateo fell to the side, laughing into the pillow. I joined him, both of us pretty giddy and high off post-amazing-sex endorphins. He turned his face toward me, our heads on the same pillow.

"You like my meat pie, do you?"

"I *love* your meat pie."

Just like I love you.

I couldn't say it yet, even if it was true. Mateo, and Alpha, wanted me intensely. That was certain, but whether that translated into what I already felt, I wasn't sure. It was scary and wonderful and beautiful to think he might feel the same way. I just wasn't ready to take that risk that he might not.

Mateo must've sensed my change in mood. He trailed his fingers from my temple down along my hairline and tucked a loose strand behind my ear.

"I'll give you whatever you want." His thumb skimmed over the slope of my cheekbone. "Anything you want of mine." And then his pad swept farther down to caress my kiss-swollen lips. "Just tell me and it's yours."

Our gazes locked, vulnerability sliding between us like a secret. I wanted his heart, his love. But I was too afraid to ask for it, even though I was almost positive that's what he was offering.

"Let's start with your award-winning meat pie," I whispered, giving him a little smile.

His expression softened. I imagined it mirrored my own—one of hope and adoration and desire. "That's a good place to start."

CHAPTER 31

~MATEO~

You're welcome.

I basked in the awesome feeling of watching a rosy-cheeked, smiley Evie finish off the breakfast I made for her.

Like I said, you're welcome.

I cooked her breakfast.

She ain't smiling like that because of a damn omelet.

I found some strange satisfaction in taking care of her. I loved feeding her.

Well, I love eating her. So we're even.

Picking up her empty plate, I walked over and set it in the sink while she drank down her orange juice.

Gotta keep our girl healthy. Full of energy. Round ten starts tonight.

No argument here.

Thank *Christ*. It's a fucking miracle.

Of course, we hadn't gone nine rounds last night, but it was close. We were both pretty damn tired with so little sleep, but somehow that didn't dampen our spirits this morning.

"I never did thank you for last night."

"You're quite welcome." I couldn't help grinning.

She laughed, a pretty blush flushing her cheeks. "Well, not that, though that deserves more than a little thank-you."

Damn straight, baby.

"What I meant was back at the party. I mean, coming and being all"—she lifted her shoulders on a heavy exhale—"amazing."

"I told you. I'll always be there for you."

She swallowed hard, standing from the table. "Well, I appreciate it. Derek was being a dick as always."

"Yeah. I heard him."

She scrunched up her brow. "You did?"

I ground my teeth together. "Werewolf hearing." And if that prick ever put his hands on her again, I was going to break his arm. It had taken more than a little restraint not to flatten him at the party.

Remember our Top Five Kill List? Derek the Douchebag is at number one.

Evie gave me a tight nod before her somber expression slid into a smile. "That reminds me. I have something to show you."

She ran over to the coffee table and picked up her little black purse from last night. Pulling out her cell phone, she eyed me and bit her lip, then kept flipping through some things on her phone.

Holding a deep breath in her chest before nervously blowing it out, she shifted from foot to foot. "Okay. It's not a really big deal, but it's a start."

Then she flipped her phone around that was open to the Webtoon's app she'd shown me for digital comics a lot of indies used.

Staring at the screen for a split second, I snatched the phone from her and clicked on the icon of a redheaded figure I recognized. Sure enough, it popped open to *Witches in the City, Episode One*. There were three episodes published, the first with 724 likes, the others trailing close behind it.

"Evie! You did it!"

She giggled and covered her mouth, a girlish sound I'd never heard her make before. A Christmas-morning-giddy kind of sound.

I flipped through the screens quickly, not reading, just soaking in the artistry of her illustrations, the creative layout and color schemes she chose. Amazing, all of it.

"Damn, girl." Reaching over, I pulled her into my arms and squeezed her tight. "I'm so proud of you." I pressed a kiss to her crown, inhaling a deep whiff of the delicious smell of her. I was so far gone.

Wrapping her arms around my waist, she nuzzled her mouth against my neck. "I just posted last week, the first three episodes. I haven't done much promotion or anything yet. And I'm working on getting them in print issues. I really want them in print for the comic book readers like myself. Bam even said he'd be glad to sell them consignment from his shop."

"That's so incredible." I rocked her in my arms. "Seriously."

She pulled back to look up at me. "I owe this to you."

"No, you don't. You always had this in you. I just gave you a nudge."

"It was such a necessary nudge though, Mateo."

The smile she gave me was worth dying for. She had no idea what she did to me. And after last night, I knew I couldn't hold my feelings in for long.

"Come on. Walk me out?"

"Of course."

She was back in her dress and heels, but with my hoodie over it, which hit her at the hem of the dress. She looked ridiculous, but she didn't care. Neither did I. I only cared that she was warm. The weather had dropped overnight, bringing in a brisk cold front.

You kidding me? She looks delicious. She should only wear our clothes from here on out.

Taking her hand, we went down the stairs. I flipped on the lights in the workshop, the few windows not helping with the overcast sky.

"Oh my God." Evie pulled away from me and walked toward my workshop table and the life-size sculpture standing in front of it. "Mateo," she whispered.

I met her next to my latest work, watching her expression of shock and wonder and happy surprise. "It's me," she finally said.

"It is." Inspired entirely by her, I hated to give it away now that it held a piece of my heart along the molded steel.

"But . . ." She shook her head, reaching out and touching the wavy hair cascading down the sculpture's face that was a mirror of her own in galvanized steel. "Your client didn't commission a statue of me."

"Actually, Sandra left me a lot of creative license."

"She looks like a witch. Kind of."

"Well, considering my muse." I shrugged a shoulder. She did indeed look like a witch in her billowy dress, hooded cloak, and the look in her eyes as if she held a secret. As if she held magic.

She was quiet for a minute before asking, "What were Sandra's requirements for the commission exactly?" After trailing a finger down the outstretched arm of the figure, she then circled the sculpture.

"Exactly?"

She swiveled her attention to me. I knew it by heart, so I told her, realizing I was admitting a lot, possibly risking a lot. But hell, I was bursting with it.

"She asked for a beautiful woman in a flowing gown and a hooded cloak. A woman who embodied hope, strength, and"—I swallowed hard—"love."

Evie's eyes misted and blinked quickly. I eased closer, slipping my hands up to cup her face, thumbs brushing those lovely slanted cheekbones.

"So you can see," I whispered, walking her backward till she bumped my worktable, "there was nothing else for me to do. No one else who would fit the bill."

Her heartbeat sped like a rabbit in a snare. I trailed one hand down her neck to wrap the base of her throat, my thumb resting on her pulse-point.

"You could've made someone up. Some beauty from your imagination."

I smiled, sliding my lips against hers. "Why bother? When I know a woman, now intimately, who I can't get out of my head. Who haunts me all day, every night. Who makes me feel—" I pressed my forehead to hers. "Fuck, Evie, the things you make me feel."

Her hands fisted in my T-shirt on my chest. "What do I make you feel?"

Gripping her waist, I lifted her onto the table and pushed my body between her legs. She opened wider, so I pulled her to the edge, wedging myself as close as I could, the skirt of her dress hiking high.

"You make me feel strong." I grazed my nose up the side of her neck, inhaling her heavenly scent. "And hopeful." I nipped my way up her jaw to her mouth, my heart about to pound right through my rib cage, knowing I was going to confess it. I kept hold of her eyes, refusing to be a coward, accepting whatever response I saw there. "And love, Evie."

Her mouth fell open, her expression full of something sweet, then she blinked rapidly. "Mateo . . ."

"Don't say anything." I kissed her hard, prying her lips open and stroking inside with hot intent.

Her moaning response was all I needed right now. That she was with me where this was going. Skating my palms up her bare thighs under her dress, my thumbs brushed against her pelvis, finding skin, not lace. Then I remembered I'd snapped her panties. Or actually, Alpha had.

Fuckin' right I did. She doesn't need panties anymore. I'm just gonna rip them all off anyway.

I would've argued that Evie wasn't only there for his pleasure, but at the moment, all I could think of was hers. She'd be too sore to take me right now after last night, but that didn't mean I couldn't give *her* pleasure. With a concerted effort, I pushed him out of my head and focused on Evie.

Her sweet tongue stroking against mine, the mewling sounds she made as I brushed the pad of my thumb down her slit, already slick and wet for me. Her fingers clawed into my hair, raking my scalp. I clamped one hand on her thigh to keep her in place and found her swollen clit with my thumb, spreading her wetness in a lapping circle.

"Mateo." It was a breathy protest at the same time she was clawing me closer.

"Don't worry." Skating to her neck, I licked a line down to the hollow of her throat. "I just want to make you come." A slide of my tongue. "Need to hear you come, baby."

Her moans grew louder, my fingers got wetter, then her scent hit me like a sledgehammer.

"*Christ*," I ground out.

With a hand right below her throat, I pushed her back to the table—thankful that I cleaned my station daily—and jerked the skirt of her dress up to her waist. Scooping her ass into both hands, I lifted her off the table, leaned over, and feasted on her wet slit.

The breakfast of champions.

Go away.

Just enjoying the ride now that we're finally on the same page.

Out.

Sweetest fucking pussy in the whole fucking world.

Out!

With a mental push, I shoved him. Then it was just Evie and me. I circled her clit, then flattened my tongue and licked through her folds. She squirmed, trying to get closer, trying to get away. But I was having none of it. I wanted her screams. I wanted my name on her lips. I wanted her shaking from an orgasm on my workshop table.

Something about her in this space where I worked, where I created and molded steel into something beautiful, made me fucking crazy to have her spread for me here. Panting for me. Some day in the near future, I was going to make love to her right here. Right now, I just needed to watch her come apart, hear her moans bouncing off the walls. Her pretty cheeks were flushed pink, her bright green gaze slanted down at me while I ate her thoroughly. I paused, lifting my head, to take her in.

"Whuh? No, Mateo. Don't you dare stop."

She wasn't smiling. She was desperate. I reached up and slid two of my fingers into her mouth, pumping twice to get them good and wet. She clamped her lips down and moaned, tonguing my fingers.

"There you go," I murmured, my pulse pounding hard at the sight of her like this.

I went back to work, licking from her clit down to her entrance, thrusting twice with my tongue before I switched and pressed two fingers inside her.

"Yes, Mateo. *Please.*" Her hips lifted off the table, pumping up against me. "Harder."

I groaned and stroked harder like she wanted, my knuckles hitting the sensitive flesh with each thrust. Then I clamped my lips over her tight nub and slightly curled my fingers up, finding that perfect spot.

"Mateo!"

That was a big one.

No way could I keep him out. Damn, he was right. She came hard that time. I licked and kissed her pussy, avoiding her sensitive clit, till she drifted down from the climax.

"Mmm." I couldn't help but let my appreciation slide out as I stared down at her, all pink and pretty from my attentions. "Shit." I shook my head and hissed in a breath, then dragged her skirt down to hide it from my sight.

Taking her hands, I hauled her up where she fell limp against my chest.

"Okay," she said, out of breath. "I'm going back to bed."

I laughed, pressing a kiss to her beautiful mouth. "You could hang with me today."

She looked so sad. "Dammit, I wish I could. But I really want to meet with Jules about that book."

"The book from Ruben? You got it?"

She hit herself on the head. "I totally forgot to tell you."

I'm sure my grin looked like the devil. "I'm glad you were so preoccupied that you forgot. Means I'm doing something right."

She clasped her hands behind my neck and said with such sincerity my heart thudded hard, "You're doing everything right."

You're welcome! Again. **Give me some credit over here.**

"Good to know." I helped her down. "So you and Jules are working on it today?"

"Yeah. I need to focus on the counter-spell for you. The next full moon is just a few days away." She quirked her brow. "It's funny that you don't seem agitated anymore. I mean with the need to shift like you did before."

I cleared my throat. "Yeah. It is, I guess."

"What do you mean you guess?"

Yeah, I might've just admitted that I loved her in a roundabout way, but I wasn't going to tell her that Alpha was dead set on her as our *one and only*. She was the only reason he wasn't still trying to claw out of my skin and make me feel like a paranoid schizophrenic on a daily basis. She was literally keeping the beast at bay.

"So . . ." Time to change the subject. "I guess that's a good enough reason not to spend the day with me. Since you'll be thinking of me anyway. Right?"

She shook her head. "I'm always thinking about you."

"You are?" Her admission shot a jolt of adrenaline through my veins.

"You know I am."

"Well, now I do."

"I'll be over tonight to pay you back for this." She glanced back at my worktable while doing a whole body shiver. My hard dick pushing at my zipper twitched a happy response.

I grinned, molding my hands over her perfect ass. "Pack a bag tonight."

"You want me to sleep over?"

I want you to never leave.

"Yeah. Dinner and a movie."

"More meat pie?"

"Nah. I can cook other things."

She pressed her body delectably against mine. "But I like your meat pie."

Yeah, you do.

"God, Evie. Stop it." I bit her bottom lip. "I only have so much control."

She laughed and pushed out of my arms, heading for the door that led across the courtyard and through the gallery. "Is seven good?"

"Perfect. You want me to drop you off at home?"

"No, I'm good. It's a short walk."

"In that?" High heels and my hoodie that not-quite-covered the hem of her cocktail dress.

"Doesn't bother me."

Crossing my arms, I stared at her disheveled outfit. "I was afraid you wouldn't want to do the walk of shame all the way down Magazine Street."

She tossed her head back with bubbly laughter. Again, that sound squeezed my heart tight. I could get used to that sound.

She opened the door to the courtyard and pulled up the neck of my hoodie, inhaling deep, taking in the smell of me with a little moan, giving me those eyes that made my dick swell even more.

"This isn't a walk of shame, Mateo. It's a walk of pride."

"That's it." I jogged over and took her hand, lacing our fingers together, then walked ahead of her.

"Where are we going?" she asked, smiling so bright my heart stuttered.

"I'm walking you home, and we're stopping for espresso at French Truck Coffee."

"We had coffee upstairs, Mateo." We passed through the courtyard and into the gallery. "Are you just finding excuses to be with me longer?"

"Of course I am," I admitted, tugging her closer to my side, catching sight of Missy opening up the register. "Hi, Missy."

"Hi, Missy," said Evie with a friendly wave, her face glowing with joy.

Damn, I loved her.

Missy blinked, a little confused, then gave a half-hearted wave. "Hi?"

Then we were out the door as Evie waved over my shoulder with her free hand. "Bye, Missy."

The walk was short and quiet since we did nothing but smile and gaze at each other. She had it as bad as me, but I was perfectly content to wait for her to say the words. It was shining in her eyes as clear as the blue sky above us.

Not surprisingly, no one glanced twice at Evie's strange attire when we entered the coffee shop. Actually, there were one or two others tucked into booths who might be having similar morning-afters. Though I highly doubt theirs was as fantastic as our night together.

Once we settled at the same table we had last time, we both sipped our espresso, just looking at each other. It was borderline ridiculous how besotted we probably looked.

She set her cup down, leaning her cheek into her palm, elbow on the table. "Thank you for *next time*."

Licking my lips, savoring the taste of strong coffee and the sweetness of her, I replied in a low rumble, "No. Thank you."

Her cheeks flushed pink, making me want to haul her across the table and kiss the hell out of her. I grabbed her hand across the table and brought her knuckles to my mouth, needing to taste her skin again. I was so greedy for her, I couldn't help it.

"You know—?"

"Mateo," came a familiar feminine voice. "What a nice surprise."

Sandra stepped up to our table with her coffee in a to-go cup.

"Sandra." I stood and gave her a quick one-armed hug. As usual, she was made-up and dressed to perfection. I caught Evie tugging the opening of my hoodie closed around her breasts.

"Sit down," she insisted sweetly. "I didn't mean to disturb you." I did as she looked over at Evie, smiling brighter. "So good to see you again too. I feel like I'm having déjà vu."

"Me too," said Evie with a little laugh. "Would you like to join us?"

"No, thank you. I have a hair appointment nearby and was just stopping in."

Her smile remained bright and heavy on Evie, then she raised her eyebrows at me, obviously figuring out this was more than casual. I'd known Sandra a long time, and I'd never been serious about a woman. But you'd have to be blind or stupid not to see what was going on between me and Evie.

"I certainly wouldn't want to disturb two young lovebirds like you," she said, admitting she knew exactly what this was.

I couldn't do anything but enjoy the rapid blush that flushed all the way down Evie's neck, her eyes twinkling with mischief. Finally, I looked back at Sandra.

"You're welcome to join us." Then I shot Evie a wink. "Even if we're behaving like two lovebirds."

Sandra gave a little throaty laugh. "Not today, thank you. But I meant to ask if you'd finished my commission."

"He did," chimed in Evie enthusiastically. "And it's absolutely beautiful."

"Is it? I can't wait to see it." Her attention swiveled from Evie to me. "I'm home this afternoon if you wouldn't mind bringing it over. I've been dying to get it set up in the garden."

I thought a minute, realizing I'd be going crazy with nothing but Evie on my mind today. Might as well prep and package the sculpture for delivery, give me something to do.

"Sure. What time?"

She glanced at her watch. "I'll text you later after my errands in the city if you don't mind."

"Not at all."

"I better be going then. Don't want to be late for the salon."

I stood and gave her a hug and cheek-kiss goodbye.

She held on to my arm and gave me a friendly squeeze. "It's good to see you relaxed, Mateo. So happy."

"Thank you," I said with a nod. "Never been happier."

She gave me another squeeze. "I'll be in touch later." Then she was gone.

As I settled back in my chair, staring at the beautiful, disheveled woman with sex-mussed hair across the table, I realized how unbelievably true that was. I'd never been happier.

CHAPTER 32

~EVIE~

"So what does the whole of these symbols mean? I need it reduced down to a word, Jules."

We'd been poring over the symbols that we'd seen on Mateo's skin the night we tried to break the hex, soaking up the information in the book Ruben had gotten for us, and discovered this was a live spell, which had to be handled differently than a hex. We knew that, but the book gave us a hint on what we needed. A counter-spell worked similarly to a hex in that you had to know its base purpose to channel its opposite in magic. As a hex-breaker, I would still be the strongest of the six of us to spin the counter-spell and unravel this hold it had on Mateo. But we needed that key element for me to channel its counterpart and split it wide open.

Jules stared down at the book open in her lap. "Honestly, what I see are symbols of birth and death and eternity. What can that be reduced to?"

"Life, like the circle of life," said Violet, sitting on the living room floor with Fred nestled in her lap. He was wearing a purple tie with little white dragons.

"The opposite of life is death." I popped three peanut M&Ms in my mouth. "I can't channel death," I said while chewing.

"No," agreed Clara, cross-legged on the couch next to me. "The bridge symbol isn't a part of life. I think, altogether, it encompasses power. The power over all these things. Birth, the giving of life. Murder, taking away life. Eternity to go on forever. It's about power, isn't it?"

Jules nodded, listening with her head in the book, flipping to the back where it gave instructions on how to interpret and use witch sign. I opened my phone to the pic of Mateo that Jules had taken and sent to all of us to study.

I flinched every time at the look of pure rage on his face as he lunged for me. Shivering at the memory of it, my stomach twisted at what he might've done if Jules hadn't stopped him. Not just because he might've hurt me, but because I knew he'd never forgive himself if he had.

"You're forgetting the fourth symbol," I said, zooming in on the pic of the symbol that only appeared once over his left pectoral. The other witch signs had been repeated, but there had only been one skeleton key symbol. "The key."

"What door is this witch trying to open?" asked Violet. "Jules, read the definition again."

Jules flipped back through the book and read aloud. "The key opens a doorway and can only be used in conjunction with other witch sign in a complex spell. The door is constructed by the witch. At the time a live spell activates, the key will bring the endgame to fruition."

"Hell, it's just a bunch of fucking nonsense. I need a break." Violet stood, cradling Fred in her arms. "Going to make some sandwiches for lunch if y'all want." Then left.

Jules heaved a sigh. "She's right. I wish Marigold Lord didn't speak in riddles. So we know this is a live spell that was put on Mateo. And there may be some sort of key that activates and completes the spell? That's all I can get from it."

"But what's this witch's endgame?" I asked, pissed off and frustrated.

Clara reached over and put her hand on my arm, giving me a gentle dose of patience with her magic. "This is frustrating, but we'll figure it out."

"Well, we've got three days till the next full moon, so not much time."

The full moon was when the elements of magic were strongest. It was also the time of transformation, and since the main symptom of Mateo's hex or spell, or whatever, still prevented him from transforming, we were sure this would be the best time to try the counter-spell.

"I think Clara's right. This spell seems to revolve around control and power."

"What's the opposite of that?" I asked, still sounding a little disgusted, even though Clara's magic was doing its job and calming me.

"You need to commune with your magic, Evie." Jules gave me a look Mom had given me a hundred times with the same motherly inflection in her voice. "It's intuitive. And this is your gift, not ours. You know how to do this better than any of us. Dig deep, and you'll find the answer."

The fact that Mateo's well-being fell on my shoulders gave me a panic attack. I wanted to help him more than anything. I needed to.

"Come on." Clara gave my arm a squeeze and hauled me off the couch. "Let's go eat lunch, then you can help me stock the new shipment for Maybelle's."

Heaving a sigh, I followed her, even though something dark kept niggling at the back of my mind.

~MATEO~

Winding up the gravel drive between a line of solid oak trees, their trunks thick, limbs hanging down, I recognized where Sandra got her inspiration for her oil paintings. Even now with the sun beginning to set, the orange rays brushed along the trees like in her paintings, Spanish moss swayed in a gentle breeze. This place was beautiful. Peaceful.

Her plantation home reared up as the drive circled around to the front. In Greek Colonial style, it was a mansion set in a lush green setting. Sandra walked out the front door to one of the Greek columns and waved, smiling brightly. She wore a red-orange dress, the long, flowy skirt catching the fading light.

I pulled up and rolled down the passenger window. "Good afternoon. I have something for you."

She laughed. "Hi, sweetheart." Her eyes darted to the tarp-covered sculpture that was tied down in the back of my truck, excitement lighting up her face. "I can't wait to see it." She clasped her hands together.

"I hope you're happy with it. But where are we going to put it? I'd like to back my truck up as far as I can go."

"Oh, of course." She leaned one forearm on the window ledge of the passenger door and pointed with the other. "Just back up between the azalea bushes. You won't be able to go too far back because of the water fountain, but I have the perfect spot in my garden not far away." She turned her bright smile on me. "I often paint in my garden, so she will keep me company." Her gaze flicked to the back of the truck again.

"Sounds perfect. Let me get this backed up then."

Swiveling around, I reversed between the azalea bushes along the side of the house that opened up to what appeared to be an extensive garden. I hopped out of the truck and quickly pulled down the ramp that I used for deliveries. Though she couldn't see it yet, the sculpture was bungee-corded to a large dolly and laid flat in the bed of the truck under the tarp. I pulled the sculpture out, keeping the tarp over it for a big reveal, hoping Sandra would be satisfied with the work.

"Oh my goodness, Mateo. It's huge. Can you manage moving it by yourself?"

"It's not as heavy as it looks."

That was a lie. It was crazy heavy with the amount of steel used to render her sculpture. But I was a werewolf and capable of lifting ten times what a human male could.

She didn't seem to realize that and walked slowly ahead of me into the garden. "It's not too far. This way."

We passed the water fountain, which definitely caught my eye. The sculpture in white stone at the center was the Greek gorgon Medusa, her snake hair writhing, her bare breasts jutting up proudly, her body transformed to a snake tail from the waist down. What was most surprising was that she held the head of a Greek man in one hand, and the water trickled from the base of his severed throat as though it were blood. Her beautiful face expressed triumph. Strangely, it looked like the famous sculpture of Perseus holding the head of Medusa, except it was the other way around.

"Weird," I muttered to myself. Sandra was eccentric like all artists, but it was really odd.

A low, deep, primal growl rumbled in my gut, the kind that raised the hair on my own arms, even though I was the one to make it.

"Right through here," said Sandra, already disappearing around a wall of shrub.

Settle down, I told him. But he didn't answer. Still, I could feel him crouching, as if to attack.

Maneuvering around the trickling fountain, I followed her into an open square of topiaries and shrubs shaped like mythological creatures. I caught sight of a dragon and a fawn before I focused forward. There was an empty stone slab at the center of the square.

Sandra stood just beyond the slab and gestured. "Right in the center. I can't wait to see it."

I'd grown accustomed to Sandra's excitability over the years. She often raved about my works when she'd stop by the gallery. But today, she practically radiated with glee. It was almost off-putting.

"Which way do you want her to face? Toward the entrance, I assume?"

"Yes. That sounds perfect."

She remained quiet while I maneuvered the dolly around, then pulled the sculpture from off the dolly's flat shovel at the base. I hauled it to the side, then started the work of unlatching the bungee cords.

"I really hope you're happy with it."

"I *know* I will be," she gushed.

"If not, I'll have to sculpt the replacement right here to avoid another big haul."

She laughed, moving closer as I pulled off the last bungee cord. Part of me wished she wouldn't like it so I could take it back home with me. I hadn't realized how attached I'd be to this re-creation of Evie.

"You ready?"

"Ready!" She clapped her hands together.

With a whoosh, I jerked the tarp off the top and revealed what her money had paid for.

She gasped, her hands going to her mouth. "*Mateo,*" she whispered on a throaty gasp that made my skin prickle for some reason.

"You like it?" I backed away, hands in my jeans pockets, and watched her circle the sculpture.

She laughed in a way that made my hackles rise. "I knew you would make her."

"Sorry?"

"The girl you were with in the coffee shop." Her gaze flicked to mine before she stepped closer, running her fingers along the sculptured Evie's hair.

"Evie."

"I knew you loved her when I saw you together." She studied the sculpture more closely, trailing her hand down the out-stretched arm. Then she leaned over and pressed her mouth to the billowing sleeve. "I can feel the magic you used to make her." Then she whispered so low only my werewolf hearing could pick it up. "So perfect, my darling. Though it did ruin my original plans."

"Excuse me?"

Alpha growled so fiercely it rippled out of my mouth and filled the square in the garden. Sandra didn't even flinch. Actually, she smiled. What the fuck was going on?

Kill her. Or run. *Now.*

I stood frozen for a millisecond too long. Sandra levitated backward off the slab in a blink and shouted, *"Lantul lui!"*

I recognized the Romanian tongue but not the words. It didn't matter. I felt it immediately. Invisible chains locked my feet in place. I roared at the same time she called out another enchant-ment. I didn't hear what she said because my mind, my mouth, and my wolf were all bellowing and snarling at the same time.

A circle rimmed with ethereal orange fire wreathed me inside with the sculpture. Sandra waved a hand, and the dolly flew out over the shrubs and out of sight, thudding with a clang.

"You're the fucking witch?" It came out as a question and deafening exclamation at the same time. "How?" I shook my head. I'd never sensed magic on her. Ever. I'd known her for years. Fucking *years* and hadn't known.

"My darling Mateo, I let you see only what I wanted you to see."

She walked in her bare feet, feet that I noticed now seemed entirely too youthful for a woman of middle age. Her hair lifted in the breeze, her gauzy skirt billowing in a supernatural wind.

"You're old, aren't you?"

She laughed. "Quite. Far past expectancy, actually. You're just a wee babe to me."

For the first time, she let another accent slip from her Americanized tongue, an English one.

"What do you want?"

She stood in front of me outside her witch's circle, a sinister look crossing her beautiful face. "I've had plans for you for a long time, darling. When we first met, I thought how perfect you were, so moral."

She frowned, her lip lifting with disgust. An ugly expression I'd never seen her make. She'd been a good actress.

"What are you talking about?"

"Influencer. If I'd thought I could break your moral code with my magic as an Influencer, I would've tried. But I knew that wouldn't bring me the success I wanted. So I'd have to corrupt you with a darker curse."

I couldn't believe what I was fucking hearing. "I thought you were a genuine artist with the means to build our community. My friend!"

"I was. I am. I have the means to do many things. But after I realized my natural magic wouldn't work on you, I knew you were meant for something more complex."

Complex. The spell.

"What does this spell do? How can you benefit from caging my wolf?"

Meanwhile, Alpha was snarling and snapping in my head, ready to draw blood, rip her throat out.

"One thing you made me realize"—she lifted her hand in the air, palm flat, and glanced over her shoulder before returning her attention back to me—"is that my goal required a special hex in order to achieve it."

The ice in her voice, the glacial fire in her eyes, and the superior tone she used all told me I never knew this woman at all. This woman who I'd thought was my friend, who'd helped me build my business, who'd shown me kindness over the years wasn't my friend at all. A dark witch with unbelievable power. With my body completely immobile in her casting circle, I was in serious fucking trouble.

"What do you want?" I ground out.

"Everything, my darling. And you're going to give it to me."

Something small zipped from the air and slapped into her open palm. She flashed me my own phone in her hands. She'd summoned it telekinetically from the seat of my truck.

"Fucking hell." To be able to move things telekinetically out of eyesight meant she was far more powerful than the average witch. "What does the spell do?" I asked while she tapped on my phone.

"Tell me, Mateo. What does your wolf need more than anything in the world?"

Blood.

I didn't open my mouth, my heart rate skyrocketing as she tapped on my phone, a text message she seemed to be typing with her thumbs. She finished and lifted her eyes, now glowing blue in the semidarkness.

"To kill. Your primal nature requires blood above everything else," she answered her own question, grinning. "And your needs perfectly fit mine."

"*What* are you planning to do?"

"Immortality comes at a high price, darling. Blood magic requires a special kind of sacrifice to consent to such a request." Her voice vibrated with magic, an intangible darkness rippling in the air. "And a very moral werewolf killing the woman he loves is the *perfect* sacrifice." She grinned with evil intent, punching the air out of my lungs.

"*No.*" I was panting now, chest heaving. Influencer.

"Oh yes." Her hair floated around her, billowing in a magical wind of her making. "I can't achieve immortality entirely, though I've managed to outwit death so far. I know this kind of sacrifice will gain me another century or two." She shrugged. "It did last time."

I wrestled with what she was implying, that I'd kill Evie for her sacrifice, bile rising in my throat. "I'll never hurt her. Never. You picked the wrong werewolf."

She tossed her head back and laughed like the demon she truly was.

"Oh yes, you will. I thought your wolf would have killed her by now the way you two have been spending so much time together. But when I saw you in the coffee shop, I realized your wolf needs a magical push."

She walked the circle a little ways, glancing down at the phone in her hand.

"I've ensnared you with all manner of blood spells. And your wolf. He's been caged for *far* too long."

She raised her free hand not holding the phone, then drummed her fingers in the air. A witch sign made of gold appeared above her fingers, floating in a perfect circle. It was a key.

"As soon as I activate the spell, your wolf will need to tear someone's throat out. I've made sure of it with my spell. There's *nothing* that will keep him from the taste of blood."

Yesssss.

The malevolent response from Alpha sent a shiver through my body. Sandra smiled, her eerie eyes now glowing red, shimmering with menace in the dark.

"Go to fucking hell."

"Not yet." She grinned again, looking down at the phone. "First, we need a blood sacrifice." She tapped my phone, then I heard the *whoosh* of a text leaving the type box. "And I'll bet that text gets her running to her lover's side."

The rush of fear and fury rocketed through my blood. I yelled and strained against her invisible chains. Sandra laughed again and flicked her finger, locking all sound inside the witch's circle. All I could hear as she walked back toward the house was my own anguished cries.

CHAPTER 33

~EVIE~

"This new amethyst is beautiful." I layered the chunks of purple crystallized rock onto the display plate Clara had set out on our front table.

"It is, isn't it? I also ordered some larger pieces of amber. Our customers snatch those up."

I sipped the tea I'd made that Beryl had given me. We were completely out of tea, so I went ahead and used it. Probably not what Beryl intended, but after last night's events, I needed a pick-me-up.

"What does amber do again?" Tons of people, including year-round tourists, came into the shop for some metaphysical help of some sort.

"Draws out negative energy, then heals the body and mind."

"Or you could just go to a witch healer," I offered, stroking Z's head where he lay by the cash register.

"True." Clara assembled her pretty display just right. "But how many witch healers are available for the thousands in pain?"

Funny how Clara could talk about the wounded spirits of the world as easily as she could talk about baking a cake.

My phone buzzed in my back pocket. Pulling it out, my heart leaped and did a somersault at Mateo's name.

"I know who that's from," said Clara, giving me a wry smile.

Without answering, I tapped the message open.

Mateo: Hey. I delivered my sculpture today, and you're not going to believe what I found out here. I know who cast the spell. Come meet me!

Me: No way! How? I thought you were at Sandra's house?

The little dots started moving before a message popped up.

Mateo: I am! Sandra knows who it is, but she's afraid to tell me everything. She wants to, but she seems scared. I thought you could help me talk her through this. Please come meet me.

I stared at the message. Talk her through this? It just felt off. Why wouldn't he just tell me over the phone? How did Sandra know anything? Before I could respond, another message popped up.

Mateo: If you're busy, that's fine. But I'm going to stay and talk to Sandra awhile. She's really scared and needs a good friend right now to comfort her. I may not be home till late. I just thought you would want to hear it yourself.

Well, hell. Now I *had* to go. I remembered the way Sandra had looked at Mateo in the coffee shop. Yeah, they were friends, but I wasn't stupid. She might have a crush on my man, and my green-eyed monster reared her ugly head. I wasn't going to hang here while he stayed and *comforted* her about whatever she was afraid of. Besides, she knew who the witch was who cast the spell?

"Clara, I need to go." I walked behind the counter and pulled out my backpack. "Mateo says the woman he delivered his commission to today knows who cast the spell on him."

"What?" Clara frowned at me, and I'm sure I was looking at her the same way. "Who is she?"

"A good friend of his. She actually is the whole reason he has that nice gallery."

Clara walked to the shop door, flipped the lock, and turned the door sign to closed. "I'm going with you."

"Awesome. Thanks." I brushed Z's head as I passed. He let out a strange meow. "Be back in a bit, Z."

Then we were off. I typed back to let Mateo know I was on my way, so he sent me the address. The trek outside the city was actually a nice drive, making our way from all the concrete to lush green.

Clara regaled me with the antics of our boisterous cousins after we left the cocktail party. Since Mateo and I had left a wake of tension behind us, Travis had decided to start a conga line. But only after Drew had led a round of shots where he poured them telekinetically down the throats of the eager witches at the bar.

"Let me guess. They were all stunning and a bit lusty," I said, following my GMap directions off the main road.

"This is Drew we're talking about. Of course they were. He could catch the eye of old, dried-up spinsters."

"That doesn't sound very exciting, though," I said. "Pouring shots telekinetically?"

"Oh, well, Drew had one stipulation to the participants. If even a drop spilled, he'd lick it off them."

I smiled. "That's my Drew. What was Cole doing? Scowling and rolling his eyes?"

"Yeah. But that always turns on the hard-to-get witches. They were doing their damnedest to get his attention too."

"Too bad the guys had to head back so soon." A warm tingle swirled in my chest, a buzzing that called to my magic. It was the tea. I wondered if maybe I shouldn't have drank it today since Beryl told me to wait till the right time. I felt focused. Strong.

Clara stared out the window as we passed through a rural area, very few houses around. "They were put out that, number one, you hadn't told them you were, quote, shacking up with a werewolf. And two, you hadn't introduced him."

"Please. They just wanted to try to intimidate him with their overprotective big brother vibes."

"Maybe. But poor Travis actually pouted."

"For what? Five minutes?"

"Ten," Clara said. "Then he formed the conga line and was all better."

I shook my head. "That's Travis for you. He just wants all the attention." I laughed, amused at Travis's antics, but the car went quiet all of a sudden. I glanced at Clara, her expression sobering quickly. "Hey. Are you okay?"

She was gripping the door handle, her knuckles white, and her face as somber as the grave.

"Hey, are you okay?" She stared out the front, her posture going rigid. "Clara?"

"Something's wrong."

We turned off the main road onto a tree-lined drive, then rolled to a stop in front of the house. Mateo's truck was backed up off to the left where he must've parked to offload the sculpture. The house was dark, but there were tiki torches lighting a garden path.

"Evie. Something evil is here."

"Text Jules."

Clara punched in a quick text while I parked and got out of the car. "*Wait*," she hissed, jumping out, too, and meeting me at the front. "We should wait."

"Is Jules coming?"

A buzz. Clara looked at her phone. "She's on her way. With Ruben."

I had a fleeting wonder why she'd bring Ruben, but then I couldn't think at all beyond the mind-bending compulsion to follow the path that led off into the garden.

"It's too quiet, Clara."

"I know." She glanced around nervously, fear marking her eyes. Something I never saw on Clara. "We should wait."

There was no sound at all, then suddenly a blood-curdling scream and a beast's roar came from the direction of the torches. Unable to hold still, I took off.

"Evie!" Clara ran right behind me. "Don't go!"

"It's Mateo!"

That was all the explanation I could get out, because there was no doubt in my mind that the roar came from the man I loved. He was in pain. Agony. I heard Clara's pounding feet behind me as I zipped past a fountain and followed the path, winding around some tall shrubs into an open square where I stopped on a gasp.

Inside a witch's circle of fire, which I'd never seen before, was Mateo on his knees. Like he was glued there. And yes, he was screaming, despair and fear shining in his eyes, glassy with tears, but there was no sound. None at all. I was confused. And horrified.

It took me only two seconds to take all this in before I summoned my magic, ready to punch a hole into the circle to get to him, when two devastating things happened at the same time. One was the distinct thud of something heavy hitting Clara and watching her body fall to the ground right beside me. The second was a strong telekinetic shove that pushed me through the fire and into the circle. I fell onto my stomach, sliding across the stone slab to Mateo.

My gaze flitted to the sculpture he'd made in my image, the silver steel glinting bright by the magical fire.

"My God, Evie." He hauled me to him and pressed me close. "I'm so sorry. So sorry."

A burst of magic sparked the air. I jumped in his arms, watching as Clara shot a bolt of her magic at Sandra. *Sandra*, glowing with a red-orange aura, her eyes glittering like a demon's. What the hell was going on?

I wondered what Clara's magic could do to someone with darkness wrapped around her like a cloak, but before I could find out, a large object in my periphery flew through the dark.

"Clara!" I screamed.

She glanced at me a split second before she turned, but too late. An empty stone planter knocked her on the side of the head. She fell limp to the ground. I screamed, hoping and praying she was just unconscious.

"Isn't that sweet?" came the sinister witch's voice. I tried to wrap my head around the fact that she'd been the one all along, but she spoke again and knocked me out of my dazed confusion. "What a fond farewell."

Sandra stood on the outside of the ethereal fire, flicking the fingers of one hand in the air, turning the witch sign floating above her palm.

"The key," I murmured.

"Yes," she hissed with venom, "the key."

"What does it do?" I was stalling for time, trying to figure out what to do, hoping Jules and Ruben got here fast. But it had taken us thirty minutes to get here by car.

"You're going to find out. Don't worry your pretty little head. Mateo will show you."

Then she flung her arm back and forward like she was throwing a baseball, muttering a charm in some other language. The fiery witch sign sped through the air like an arrow straight through my body into Mateo. He fell onto his back with an agonized groan, the etchings of witch sign shining on his skin like it did that night in Bayou Sauvage.

"Mateo." I crawled to him, but he shoved me away so hard I slid across the slab into the base of the sculpture.

Sandra continued to mutter some enchantment, the witch fire licking up now with bloodred flames, casting Mateo in an eerie glow. He stood to his full height, no longer chained to one place, his chest heaving so hard, his eyes glowing brighter than the sun.

He shook his head, his voice dropping to a guttural range as he said, "I'm so sorry, Evie." He tore his shirt from his chest with claws.

Fuck! Yes, black claws had extended from his hands that were elongating and bulging. So were his arms, his chest puffing out, growing, bones snapping as they re-formed into his other self. "Remember," he said, his voice almost inhuman, "I love you."

Then his head flung back with a terrifying sound that was part howl and part groan. A beast in pain. I couldn't even think straight, watching his skin, his body, burst out of his clothes. His jeans ripped as his limbs grew and shifted into the werewolf he was beneath the man. My nightmare came to life right in front of me, his face contorting, lengthening into a canine-like snout, jaws too wide and fangs too sharp to be of anything natural on this earth. He fell to all fours, and still, he was so huge, so giant.

The wicked laughter echoing outside this hellish circle dragged my attention to her. Sandra.

"Why?" I asked.

"You'll see." She grinned like a bad child with a secret.

I glanced at Clara, still out cold on the ground. "A blood spell," I whispered more to myself.

"Yes, dear one. The best I've ever created. This is by far my finest work of art."

I climbed to my feet, moving slowly, so slowly, behind the sculpture, watching Mateo who was heaving and breathing hard, his giant head lowered to the ground, saliva dripping from his open jaws to the concrete in a splat.

"You're an Influencer, aren't you?" That's the only way she'd gone undetected, hiding her magic with her own magic, a kind of glamour some like her kind were able to use.

"Indeed. A very old and experienced one. Though I need something from you to live longer."

"You need blood for a blood spell," I said like a total idiot.

"Yes, I do."

My God, my sisters. I needed them. *Clara, please be okay.* Tears pricked, but I blinked them away.

"What exactly is supposed to happen here?" I breathed in a hushed whisper.

"I've let the wolf loose, dear Evie. And he's so, so, so hungry for blood. He's been caged quite a long time. And you're going to provide the perfect meal."

"He'd never hurt me." I knew it in my bones.

"Maybe not. So I'll help him along with a little *influence.*"

I'd gripped the arm of the sculpture, then noticed that my hands didn't look like my own. I pulled some of my hair in front of my face to see that it was blonde.

"No." Bile rose up my throat when I realized her intentions. I couldn't believe it. She was going to trick Mateo. With his senses rocketing into orbit and wanting blood, he'd see me—looking like Sandra—as the enemy. I watched him, still on all fours, snarling low, heaving deep gulps of air.

I was to be the blood sacrifice.

Mateo would die once he discovered what he'd done. He wouldn't survive having killed me. My magic. I needed to seek my magic. While I was petrified, my mind was still clear and focused.

The tea. My small bit of psychic ability that all witches had must've prompted me to drink that tea.

Focus. I stared at the witch sign overlaying Mateo's skin, blazing with an eerie glow.

Mateo's, or rather Alpha's, gaze shot to mine, the fiercest look I'd ever seen twisting his face into a feral snarl. He rose up onto his hind legs, easily over eight feet tall.

"It's me, Alpha. Evie. You know me."

Thankfully, my voice still sounded like my own. But it obviously wasn't enough. His deadly focus on me, he lunged, scrambling around the statue to snatch at my arm. I screamed and punched a jolt of magic out, knocking him into the invisible wall of the witch circle. He shook his head, snapping at me again, a trickle of blood dropping to the white stone floor. He started circling around the statue. I moved in the opposite direction, trying not to panic with only two options here.

I could keep battering him up against the impenetrable wall Sandra had erected, which could very well kill him before it even knocked him unconscious. Or I could let him kill me.

There's a third option, hex-breaker, whispered a soft voice. A tingle in my veins and a gust of wind. My magic. She was speaking to me, filling my blood with promise and power.

Mateo pounced again. I rolled away, but his claws scraped the side of my ribs. I screamed and shoved him with a telekinetic push again, bouncing him against the barrier.

Hex-breaker.

Yes. I was a hex-breaker.

My gifts extended to twisting spells. When we were little girls, Violet and I liked the same boy in school, Tommy Hartford.

Right in the middle of Social Studies, Violet cast a chicken pox charm on me so that I broke out into bright red hives. Without a thought, I changed the direction of the spell and slapped it back onto Violet. As well as Mandy Parker and Carrie Henagan who happened to be hovered around Violet's desk at the time. I hadn't broken the spell, but changed it.

This wasn't a chicken pox charm. I didn't think I could twist a blood spell. But I was going to die trying.

When Mateo lunged this time, he leaped straight over me, clawing at my back. I screamed and punched a giant bolt of magic at him, throwing him with such force I heard his leg snap.

"You bitch!" screamed Sandra. "What have you done?" She paced on the other side.

Mateo whimpered, my magic radiating off my body, humming along my skin in a way I knew meant I was running out of energy.

"Mateo," I whispered, swiping away the tear that sprang from my eye and crawling across the slab.

He stayed on his side, whimpering, his chest heaving. Sandra was muttering again, charging up her spell, the pressure inside the ring compressing on my chest and my head. Mateo snarled, lifting the front half of his body onto his muscle-clad arms. As Sandra kept ramping it up, the witch sign on his body glowed white, seeming to burn into his skin. He howled in pain. The symbols swirled in my mind, that inner voice tapping on my shoulder.

So I closed my eyes and let go and listened. Blocking out my fear and my will to control what I couldn't, I watched the signs twist and turn in my head, spinning till they made no sense, till I saw nothing, but felt its meaning. Felt everything.

"It's not power." I opened my eyes, petrified of the look in Mateo's golden gaze locked on me as he crouched onto all fours, huge and imposing, stalking closer.

"It's hate," I whispered. "Hatred fuels her. Fuels the spell."

As if to agree, Mateo growled, bearing his razor-sharp fangs.

"*Viens á moi, mon amour,*" I whispered.

His pointed ears pricked at the sound of my voice, still seeing me in the guise of Sandra.

He did. He came to me, a monster predator stalking toward me, just like in my nightmare. I stayed on the ground and let him crawl up my body, hovering over me with terrifying menace and bloodlust in his eyes.

"*Attendez*, love." My voice trembled, but magic swirled around me, cocooning me with the rightness of what I needed to do. "Not yet. Don't kill me yet."

I pressed both my palms to my chest, pooling images of love in my mind: Clara making the speech on Thanksgiving, Jules putting her arm around my shoulders outside the Roosevelt, Violet laughing with pure joy in the living room, and Mateo. Mateo opening his truck door for me, dancing with me at the Cauldron, cooking breakfast, tucking my hair behind my ear and staring at me like I was the only woman in the world, rescuing me from the party, and loving me . . . loving me with his body, his hands, his words.

Balling it all inside my chest, I stared into his eyes and put my palms to his chest, covered in coarse hair and heaving in great gulps of air. "*Arrêtez.*"

A blinding flash of electric green light burst from my body and swept outward, guttering the red flames of the witch's circle.

Sandra screamed. I glanced at my hands still pressed to Mateo's chest, recognizing them as my own. The pressure was gone, but the witch's circle remained intact. My hands shook, my body going limp with the last drain of magic. They fell to my sides, and I stared up at what could still be the death of me.

My love.

Mateo's eyes narrowed, still golden, full of the wolf. Alpha. His jaws opened, a growl rumbling from somewhere deep and dark inside him. So I used the one power I had left in me.

"It's me, Alpha. *Your* Evie." A tear streaked out one eye and dropped into my hair.

His pupils dilated, focusing, watching the trek of another tear slipping free. Trembling, I reached up my hand toward his face, so slowly. He watched, his growl rumbling louder.

"Remember last night," I whispered. "Remember this." Fingers shaking, I pressed lightly to his giant jaw. "I'm yours, remember?" A jagged sob shook my chest. "Please remember."

His huge head dipped lower, then tilted toward the hand I'd put on his jaw. I let it fall, but he snapped out and clamped his jaws on my wrist—ever, ever so gently. Then he let it go and licked my wrist, my palm, my fingers, large, hot tongue lapping at my hand, his growl fading to a hound's whimper. Then he nuzzled his snout into my hair, licking my neck. Before I knew what was happening, he'd wrapped a clawed hand around my waist and lifted me into a half-sitting position, my back crossing his lap, my head on his chest.

"No! How!" screeched Sandra, throwing what Grandma Maybelle would call a conniption fit. "How did you do it, you bitch! He needs blood. All werewolves must have it after so long!"

She was railing now and slapped down the witch's circle, a wreath of smoke sifting into the night air. She started to cross the circle, but before she took two steps, someone else spoke from our right.

"The beast doesn't need to kill, no matter how long he's caged." Jules stood just outside the smoking circle, her hands haloed green with magic, her feet planted apart, and her eyes glowing with witch's power and a sister's revenge. Ruben stood right behind her. "Not when he's found his mate. And as you can see, he's found her."

Sandra's horrified gaze snapped to me and Mateo, then Jules let loose the full power of the Enforcer.

"Wow," I whispered.

I'd seen her suck the powers of those who'd broken our laws before. It was usually a rather uneventful, quiet moment. A flare of her magic, a snap, and it was gone. But the blaze of Jules's power bursting into Sandra, who was bloated with blood magic, was thunderous. Her scream was cut off into nothing after two seconds, her body punched with the full force of a Siphon's power. A deafening silence followed, smoke billowing around Sandra.

When it cleared, in the beautiful, powerful witch's place was a withered, bent hag, her gray hair limp and greasy. She trembled, staring at her wrinkly hands, whimpering at the loss of magic. For I knew that Jules had taken away every ounce from her. Her beauty that had been taken from the sacrifice of innocents had vanished, leaving behind a husk of a woman.

Ruben stepped forward next to Jules. Sandra's shrunken face and beady eyes snapped up. "Don't come near me, devil." Her voice had also lost its sweet melody, replaced with a craggy, croaking sound.

"Look who's calling who the devil," said Ruben in his even, controlled timbre. "Better run, witch. Or should I say, human? If we ever see you again, you'll not survive."

She screeched and limped away toward the woods behind her garden.

"I doubt she lives long anyway," said Jules. "Not without her magic."

I exhaled a breath of relief. Then Jules looked at me and ran across the stone slab. Mateo snapped his jaws with a feral growl at her, still holding me against his gargantuan chest. Ruben rushed over to Clara, who was still unconscious.

"Easy," said Jules, holding up her hands in surrender. "Easy, Mateo. It's just me."

He wasn't having it, growling deeper. I eased up out of his hold, petting him on his jaw, his shoulder. Yes, I was petting my boyfriend. He clutched my waist with one clawed hand, not letting me get far.

"Give us a minute," I said over my shoulder.

"Eveleen," she said in Mom's voice. "I need to see that you're okay."

"I'm unhurt. But he'll need medical attention. Let's get the hell out of here."

After a few seconds, she gave me a tight nod. "I'll call Beryl." She stood. "Ruben, is Clara okay?"

"She's fine. A bump on the head." He hauled her up into his arms. "I'll put her in Evie's SUV."

"I won't be far," she said, following Ruben.

I stared back up at my werewolf, whose gaze hadn't left mine except to snap and snarl at Jules. Even Alpha looked at me with the same longing Mateo did.

"Alpha," I cooed, stroking him near his ear. His eyes slid half-closed on a groan I recognized. "I need you to let Mateo come back." He chuffed at me, nuzzling against my hand. "We need to heal your leg, Alpha." He blinked. Heavy, staring. "We can't have sex till we heal that leg." A protesting growl rolled out. He leaned down and licked my neck again. "Let Mateo come back, baby." I clasped his bulging, muscular neck. "Please."

He started to shrink the second I said please, morphing back into a familiar frame. I held his head close as his body shifted, the coarse hair vanishing, the beast fading to the lean-muscled body of my man. When he was finally himself, panting into my ear, he pulled back, gazing down at me sprawled across his lap.

He cupped my face and pressed his forehead to mine, releasing a shiver and a shaky breath. "Evie."

I laughed, tears spilling as I sat up and wrapped my arms around him, burying my head in his neck. "Mateo." I kissed his scruffy cheek, my heart pounding like mad. "I love you. So much. I love you."

Pulling back so he could see me, he smirked, those warm brown eyes absorbing every line of my face. His mouth tipped up on one side. "I know."

What? Not what I expected, then I—

"Oh my God, Mateo. Did you just quote *Star Wars* to me?"

He grinned, no fangs showing at all. But the devilish wolf flared in his eyes anyway. "I sure did."

I tossed my head back, laughing at how insanely I loved this man. He chuckled, then I noticed a drop of blood at the corner of his mouth.

"Oh, baby, I hurt you." I sat up onto my knees and wiped it away.

He caught my wrist. "Thank you."

"For what?"

"For saving me. I had no idea—" He swallowed hard, his Adam's apple bobbing. "I didn't know she was a—"

"Stop." I pressed a quick kiss to his mouth. "None of us did. I'm just glad I realized how to break her spell."

He frowned, glancing over as Ruben walked back into the clearing. "How did you do it?"

"Easy," I answered, thinking about my mom. "I remembered I was stronger than her."

Ruben was there, leaning down. "Come on, man. We've got to get you to the car."

I winced at the sight of Mateo's obviously broken leg. I mean, it wasn't like a bone sticking out of his leg or anything, but there was a definite fracture below one kneecap. Werewolves healed fast, but Beryl could help set it with magic so it healed perfectly.

"Do you need help?" Jules walked into the square but then quickly whipped back around. "Whoa, boy."

I snickered. Mateo was completely naked.

"I'll wait in the car!" she called over her shoulder with a wave.

"Good," mumbled Ruben, scowling down at the ground as he helped Mateo walk using one leg.

I scurried under his other arm and held on to his waist, beaming up at him.

He winced a little but smiled down at me as we hobbled along. "Sorry to ruin our plans tonight."

"Not a problem. We've got a million more nights."

"A million?"

"Yep. Wait a minute. How old are you?"

"One hundred and twenty-three."

I sighed with relief, calculating. "We've got over one hundred thousand, to be more precise."

He raked my face with those penetrating brown eyes, shaking his head softly. "That won't be nearly enough."

"Mateo." My voice choked a little. I squeezed him around the waist, a lump forming in my throat.

He brushed a kiss to my forehead. "I love you."

Beaming from ear to ear, I lifted up and kissed his perfect mouth. "I know."

EPILOGUE

One year and one month later...

~MATEO~

I GRINNED LIKE A MADMAN, WATCHING EVIE BOUNCE ON HER TOES and slip on her exhibitor tag.

"It's real," she said.

"Yep. It's real." I grabbed her hand and marched forward to where I'd left Missy while Evie was checking in. "Now let's go see your booth."

"My booth," she said on a breath. "We're going to see my booth. *My* booth."

"That's where we're going."

"Holy shit, Mateo," she hissed, clawing one hand into my arm. She pointed at a guy with a long line, signing comics. She practically squealed, "That's Todd McFarlane."

"Don't know who that is, baby."

She scoffed with a giant roll of her pretty eyes. "Well, do you know *The Amazing Spiderman? Spawn? Venom?*" She stopped walking. "Oh my God. What am I doing? I don't belong here."

I turned and gripped her by the shoulders, leaning my face down to hers, nose to nose. "Yes, you do."

"Yes, I do," she repeated, wide blinking eyes.

"That's my girl." I pressed a kiss to her lips, linked our hands, then tugged her toward the table where Missy was finishing with the stand-up banner.

"Mateo!" Evie squealed.

Missy jumped and spun around, clutching her chest. "*Geez.*" She let out a big breath. "You almost scared me to death." Missy looked from Evie to the banner. "Did I do something wrong? Oh no. Don't tell me something's wrong!"

Evie stumbled forward and wrapped Missy in a hug. "It's perfect. So perfect."

I was really enjoying the role of supportive boyfriend.

Then Evie spun and leaped on me, wrapping her legs around my waist. I stumbled back, but caught my balance while she peppered kisses all over my face.

"You're the bestest boyfriend in the whole wide world."

"I'd like to argue, but I'm enjoying your enthusiastic gratitude," I admitted, grinning.

She grinned back for about thirty seconds, staring at me with the best goofy look I'd ever seen. Then she dropped her legs, glancing over my shoulder at people milling around the Wizard World Comic-Con. The banner was a giant blow-up of her main character with the title *Witches in the City* and her name in the edgy script she used in her comics.

"Thank you, Missy." I gave her a nod. "I appreciate all your help."

"Here's your tag." She fished it out of a box and handed it over. "You guys have a great day." Missy waved and headed toward the exit of the convention center.

I watched Evie's face as I put on my tag, her lips reading it silently, her sweet face lighting up.

"You're my assistant?" Her voice broke with emotion, eyebrows turning down like a puppy dog.

"I am." Then I spun her to get behind the table. "Let's get you in the right spot. People are really starting to come in now."

"Well, I'm just happy to be here," she said, taking her seat with a stack of her very own bright and shiny comics next to her. "I mean, I don't expect to actually meet too many people—"

"Omigod! You're Evie Savoie!" Two girls, one with short spiky blonde hair next to another with a faux-hawk, scurried up. She was holding her own copy of the first issue of *Witches in the City*. More like clutching it lovingly to her breast. "Could I, I mean, would you mind signing this for me?"

Evie grinned. "Of course. I'd love to!" She looked around the table, scrambling, pushing aside the postcards that featured a hooded figure in shadow, his wolf walking beside him, and the script *Mr. Wolfman, Coming Soon*.

"Here, Ms. Savoie." I handed her the black fine-tip Sharpie.

"Thank you." She beamed another smile that hit me in the gut.

Oh, fuck yeah. We're getting the best blow job of our lives tonight.

Probably, I admitted.

Even after the spell had been broken, Alpha hadn't left me. For some reason, I wasn't really surprised. And for some insanely freakish reason, it didn't really bother me. I'd become used to him, and with Evie at my side, he behaved. Most of the time.

The girls in front of her table both gushed over the issues they'd read, which was all of them, begging for news when the next one was coming out.

"You can follow her newsletter," I chimed in, handing them a business card with all of Evie's social media listed.

"Wow!" squealed the spiky-haired girl. "Thank you so much."

That earned me another beautiful smile from my beautiful girl. After another ten minutes, the girls asked for a selfie. I offered my services to get a good shot with her next to the banner, because that's the kind of boyfriend I was. Then her first fangirling moment was over. Evie looked up to the roof. "I can't believe it. I have fans."

"You know you have fans. As of last night, you're up to forty thousand likes on your Webtoon's episodes, and your print issues are selling very well. Bam can't keep them in stock."

Bam. That fucker. Love seeing him piss his pants every time we stroll in to deliver her new issue every week.

Yep. Me too.

We are so in sync.

"Oh, this looks cool," said a girl in a Jedi cosplay costume, looking identical to Rey from *Star Wars.*

"Your costume is amazing," said Evie, her jaw dropping open.

"Thanks. Love your T-shirt."

Evie blushed. She'd asked me at least ten times if her T-shirt was too naughty for Comic-Con. I had to remind her she was the one who told me it was the place where 'freaks and geeks unite.' That had been the deciding factor to wear the one with Deadpool licking a lollipop with a speech bubble saying *Practice makes perfect.*

"Are you the creator of this comic?"

"I am," she admitted brightly.

I watched her in her element, engaging with her new fan, completely relaxed and unbelievably happy, smiling and laughing with such joy it stopped my breath. This woman. So amazing. And she was mine.

Ours.

After a while, Rey bought the first three issues, then drifted off to another table with much longer lines, and the day went on. Fans who followed her on the Webtoon app and bought her comics in the city at Bam's filtered in throughout the day as well as brand-new fans. When I brought her back a lunch of shrimp po'boys and fries, because she didn't want to leave her table for a second, I found a guy standing across from her, his brow pursed in concentration and listening to Evie talk. She was being animated with her hands, so I knew she was excited about whatever she was saying.

When I took a seat beside her, she turned to me, her eyes wide and expressive with excitement. Her pulse tripped so fast, I put a hand on her knee under the table to try to ease her.

"Mateo, this is Hugh Morton. He works with The Holloman Agency."

"Nice to meet you." I shook his hand.

"Are you her agent?" he asked.

I shook my head. "Her boyfriend."

"Oh." He smiled brighter. "Well, she's going to need an agent. I represent quite a few comic book artists you may know." He gestured to a guy across the way who'd had long lines all day. "I'd be happy to send you some references, then maybe we can discuss what I can offer in more detail."

"Thank you so much. I mean, I'm a little floored here," she admitted on a nervous laugh.

"Well, I'll tell you. You're doing great on your own. That's how I spotted you. I've been following some comic book fandoms, and I kept seeing mentions of *Witches in the City*. Then I saw you on the list for Wizard World. Anyway, I'll be heading to the next stop for the con in Houston, then heading back to LA, but I'd really like to talk further." He handed over his business card.

"Thank you so much." She took the card and stared at it, biting her bottom lip.

"I understand if you want to remain indie. A lot of artists are very successful on their own in today's publishing climate." He tapped the card she held in her hand. "But if you want to pitch to the big dogs, I'd like to work with you."

She stared at him, wide-eyed. "I love the big dogs."

Fucking right, you do. *Really* big.

"Well, then. Think it over and give me a call next week?" He gave me a nod. "Nice to meet you." Then he returned to the table where his client was working his long-ass line.

Spinning in her seat, she shook her head, completely lost. Speechless. Grabbing her hand, I then dragged her down the corridor and around a section curtained off for breaks for exhibitors. Thankfully, no one was there. I pulled her close to the window with a wide view of the traffic stacking up on Canal Street near the Hilton that overlooked the Mississippi River.

"You see?" Cupping her pretty face in my hands, I pressed a soft kiss to her lips. "You did it."

"I can't believe it. I had a little help."

"Nah. Just a little nudge."

"A little big one."

Tasting her lips, I whispered, "I'd like to nudge you with another big one."

She had one hand in my hair, fisting and pulling my head down so she could reach. "I really, really want another big one."

She dove in, sweeping her tongue against mine in that aggressive way that got me hard as fuck. Scooping her up by the ass, I pressed her back against the window and indulged in her mouth. Those lips. That sweet, sweet smile.

I groaned, grinding into her. "When is this over?"

"Not for four more hours," she breathed, biting my lip and rubbing her jeans-clad pussy against me.

I glanced into the alcove, seeing a few doors leading who knows where. Surely, one was a closet. Wait, what the hell was I thinking? We'd left all her stock, the tablet with the credit card reader on the table, and a pouch of cash just sitting underneath the table. I swear, she made me lose my mind.

Breaking a kiss we shouldn't be having in semipublic anyway, I stared at her. The sun was high over the skyscrapers, shining straight through the halo of wispy hairs around her face that had loosened from her ponytail.

"We should get back," I whispered without much conviction.

"No. We should go find a closet."

Damn if she wasn't thinking too much like me. I laughed.

"Someone could steal all your stuff."

"I don't care." She grinned, shaking her head, her ponytail swinging in the sunlight.

I brushed the backs of my knuckles along her cheek. "You're so beautiful, Evie."

She moaned with a pout. "Now I really, *really* want to find a closet."

I set her on her feet. "No, baby. Your fans are waiting."

Her electric smile lit up her face. "I've got fans." Again, that matter-of-fact tenor like she was trying to convince herself.

"You do. Lots of them."

"And I've got a fine-as-hell boyfriend who's my assistant for the day."

"I'm actually your assistant for life."

"Gah." She blew out a breath. "You've gotta stop saying things like that. You're just the awesomest ever."

"Well . . ." I laced my fingers through hers, walking us back to the table. "Let's get your awesome ass back to your table, then I can take your awesome ass home."

"And have your wicked way with my awesome ass?" She waggled her eyebrows.

"Got that fuckin' right."

Couldn't have said it better, brother.

Author's Note

I sincerely hope you enjoyed book one in Stay a Spell. I have to thank my niece Jessen Judice for the many plot parties over margaritas, for feeding me inspiration, and for her constant encouragement in creating this world.

Thank you to my beta readers of this book—Naima Simone, Christina Gwin, and Cherie Lord. And also to my husband for letting me pick his brain on all things comic books. Who knew your addiction would come in handy, babe?

And finally, a little appreciation goes to the original Zombie Cat, the stray we tried to nurse back to health. You were only with us a few months, but we hope you're at rest and having fun chasing mice in kitty heaven. You'll be remembered in the lives of the Savoie sisters.

About the Author

JULIETTE CROSS is a multi-published author of paranormal and fantasy romance and the co-host of the podcast *Smart Women Read Romance*. She is a native of Louisiana, living in the heart of Cajun land with her husband, four kids, her dogs, Kona and Jeaux, and kitty, Betty. When she isn't working on her next project, she enjoys binge-watching her favorite shows with her husband and a glass (or two) of red wine.